PE

THE NEW YORK STORIES

JOHN O'HARA (1905–1970) was one of the most prominent American writers of the twentieth century. Championed by Ernest Hemingway, F. Scott Fitzgerald, and Dorothy Parker, he wrote seventeen novels, including *Appointment in Samarra*, his first; *BUtterfield 8*, which was made into a film starring Elizabeth Taylor; *Pal Joey*, which was adapted into a Broadway musical as well as a film starring Frank Sinatra; and *Ten North Frederick,* which won the National Book Award. He has had more stories published in *The New Yorker* than anyone else in the history of the magazine. Born in Pottsville, Pennsylvania, he lived for many years in New York and in Princeton, New Jersey, where he died.

STEVEN GOLDLEAF is a professor of English literature at Pace University in lower Manhattan and the author of *John O'Hara: A Study of the Short Fiction.*

E. L. DOCTOROW (1931–2015) wrote twelve novels, including *Andrew's Brain, Homer & Langley, The March, City of God, The Waterworks, Welcome to Hard Times, The Book of Daniel, Ragtime, Loon Lake, Lives of the Poets, World's Fair,* and *Billy Bathgate.* Among his honors are the National Book Award, three National Book Critics Circle awards, two PEN/Faulkner awards, the American Academy of Arts and Letters' William Dean Howells Medal and Gold Medal for Fiction, the presidentially conferred National Humanities Medal, and the PEN/Saul Bellow Award for Achievement in American Fiction, given to an author whose "scale of achievement over a sustained career [places] him in the highest rank of American literature."

JOHN O'HARA

The New York Stories

Edited with an Introduction by STEVEN GOLDLEAF

Foreword by E. L. DOCTOROW

PENGUIN BOOKS

PENGUIN BOOKS
Published by the Penguin Group
Penguin Group (USA) Inc., 375 Hudson Street,
New York, New York 10014, USA

USA | Canada | UK | Ireland | Australia | New Zealand | India | South Africa | China
Penguin Books Ltd, Registered Offices: 80 Strand, London WC2R 0RL, England
For more information about the Penguin Group visit penguin.com

First published in Penguin Books 2013

E. L. Doctorow's foreword appeared in *Selected Short Stories* by John O'Hara (Vintage Books, London). Published by arrangement with The Random House Group Limited, London.

These stories appeared in the following books by John O'Hara: "Frankie," "Pleasure," "The Public Career of Mr. Seymour Harrisburg," and "Sportmanship" in *The Doctor's Son* (Harcourt, Brace, 1935); "Good-bye, Herman" and "Portistan on the Portis" in *Files on Parade* (Harcourt, Brace, 1939); "Bread Alone" in *Pipe Night* (Duell, Sloan and Pearce, 1945); "Ellie" and "A Phase of Life" in *Hellbox* (Random House, 1947); "We're Friends Again" in *Sermons and Soda-water* (Random House, 1960); "Call Me, Call Me," "First Day in Town," and "It's Mental Work" in *Assembly* (Random House, 1961); "The Nothing Machine," "The Sun-Dodgers," "The Women of Madison Avenue," and "Your Fah Neefah Neeface" in *The Cape Cod Lighter* (Random House, 1962); "Agatha" and "John Barton Rosedale, Actor's Actor" in *The Hat on the Bed* (Random House, 1963); "The Brain" and "Can I Stay Here?" in *The Horse Knows the Way* (Random House, 1964); "The Assistant," "Late, Late Show," "The Portly Gentleman," "The Tackle," and "The Weakling" in *Waiting for Winter* (Random House, 1966); "The Private People" in *And Other Stories* (Random House, 1968); "At the Cothurnos Club," "Encounter: 1943," "Family Evening," and "Memorial Fund" in *The Time Element* (Random House, 1972); and "Harrington and Whitehill" in *Good Samaritan* (Random House, 1974). Some of these selections were originally published in *Brooklyn Daily Eagle, Esquire, The New Yorker, The Saturday Evening Post*, and *Sports Illustrated*.

LIBRARY OF CONGRESS CATALOGING-IN-PUBLICATION DATA
O'Hara, John, 1905–1970.
[Short stories. Selections]
The New York stories / John O'Hara ; edited with an introduction by Steven Goldleaf ;
foreword by E. L. Doctorow.
pages ; cm.—(Penguin classics)
Includes bibliographical references.
ISBN 978-0-14-310709-5
I. Goldleaf, Steven. II. O'Hara, John, 1905–1970. Agatha. III. Title.
PS3529.H29N49 2013
813'. 52—dc23   2013013890

Printed in the United States of America

Contents

THE NEW YORK STORIES

Foreword

John O'Hara and the Short Story

John O'Hara was a newspaperman before he turned to fiction
and the seeming ease with which he wrote his stories and novels must have come of that facility given to reporters who write
against a deadline. His output was prodigious, some seventeen
novels and hundreds of stories. In many instances his prose
has a reportorial tone. The presumptive reality in an O'Hara
first sentence is almost insolent. He is a writer who has made
it his business to know things and likes to tell you what he
knows.

O'Hara published his stories mostly in *The New Yorker*
magazine so they are usually characterized as *New Yorker* stories, as if that were a subspecies of the form. In fact few of the
pieces here dwell in that upper-middle-class suburban milieu
that is popularly thought to define such fiction. It is more
accurate to say that O'Hara practices the classic form of the
modern short story developed by Joyce and perfected by
Hemingway: The entry point is close in time to the denoue-
ment, the setting is circumscribed, and the piece ideally yields
some sort of revelation or what Joyce called an *epiphany*.
Writers today have mostly abandoned this tight form—
contemporary stories are more likely to have greater extension
and to cover expanses of time and space that recall the pre-
modernist tale of the nineteenth century.

That O'Hara was an aggrieved writer who lived a tempestu-
ous life is attested by the number of biographers he has had—
four at last count. Born in 1905, he grew up, an Irish Catholic
kid, in the WASP town of Pottsville, Pennsylvania, where the
caste system that only tolerated an O'Hara was to haunt him

the rest of his life. He had hoped to go to Yale but the family's impoverishment after his father's death made that impossible. He never did attend college, turning instead to whatever jobs he could find as long as they weren't in Pottsville. He had learned reporting there on the local paper and migrated eventually to New York, where he worked for various papers and magazines, including the *Herald Tribune* and the *Morning Telegraph* and *Time*. But from his teenage years O'Hara had been a drinker, and he was by his maturity a formidable alcoholic. This condition magnified an abrasive and truculent nature, presumably bred of his sense of himself as an irredeemable outsider. His life was an emotional shambles until he turned to the writing of fiction, and with his first novel, *Appointment in Samarra*, a book that was widely praised and that launched him on his productive life, he found his true calling. Even so, whatever recognition he would receive in his long writing career, it would never be enough for him. His rage and resentment focused on the literary establishment's lack of regard for his achievement. He married three times, always up, and would settle in those communities, Quogue, Long Island, Princeton, New Jersey, that were an emblem of social success. But O'Hara aspired to a status that is ever beyond the reach of one so obsessed. There is a story about him that when, in 1964, he received the prestigious Award of Merit from the American Academy of Arts and Letters, he stood before that assembly, speaking bitterly of the critical vilification he had all his life until that moment endured, and broke down, weeping.

None of this would matter to us as his readers if, at the same time, John O'Hara's lifelong grievance had not provided him with a rigorous schooling in the class structures of American life. His sensitivity to class in America is the engine that drives his writing, his empowerment, and the issue that dominates his best stories. His authorial voice—almost always omniscient—can be reflective, ironic, compassionate, or amused, but no character he speaks of is without a manifestation of class. Distinctions are made between townies and summer people, between those who wear the little golden pig of Harvard's Porcellian Club and those who cannot dream of it, between the bank trustee and the bank manager, the Hollywood wise guy and the westerner, between the aged and the young, between white and black, Protestant and Jew. But if he sometimes veers close to stereotype, he will surprise you with the complexity of a piece. The young man of family may be arrogant, snobbish, or simply stupidly complacent. The black butler in service to a house for a lifetime may be outspoken to the point of rudeness. The man of pedigree may be begging for a job. The snappish wealthy woman may be in mourning for her dead son.

O'Hara has a wide reportorial range; he is comfortable with characters at every level of society. Barkeepers, showgirls, wealthy widows, family doctors, cops, lovesick boys, night-clubbing drunks, federal officials, small-town school board members—his coverage is worthy of a Balzac. He knows that a description of physical appearance is incidental to effective characterization. His people are made from their positions in life, their relationship to one another, their clothes, their values, but above all from the way they talk. O'Hara's remarkable ear for American speech serves him time and again for his render-ings. Thus, an elevator operator will say he "use'n't" to stop at a certain floor. A secretary boarding a bus says to a flirtatious bus driver: "I have a good notion to report you. The nerve." A uni-versity club man speaking to an outsider says: "I don't know why fellows like you—you never would have made it in a thou-sand years . . . but I've said exactly the wrong thing, haven't I?" A chorus girl named Reba Gold is displeased with her married lover, Seymour Harrisburg, who is importuning her: "Take your hands off me," she says. "I and you are all washed up."*

The copyright notices indicate that some of the stories here were first published between 1933 and 1947. In those years, having barely emerged from the disastrous social experiment of Prohibition, America suffered the Great Depression and

---

* From the story "The Public Career of Mr Seymour Harrisburg," one of two or three in the collection that show O'Hara was not without prejudices of his own. He was of the same generation as Hemingway and T. S. Eliot, that found anti-Semitic expression useful in their work. In this case the authorial tone is one of derisive amusement.

then went to war. None of these monumental events are given direct mention. We know of World War II only as a woman mourns her son, or someone speaks of gas rationing, or a young naval officer dreams of the civilian life he will lead someday. One can wonder about this—how a writer who is as much of a photographic portraitist as O'Hara could so constrict his focus: no rum runners here, no Okies fleeing the dust storms, no workers on strike, no soup lines, no soldiers leaping from their landing craft or storming the redoubts of Iwo Jima.

Criticizing a writer for what he has not written is something that may be useful during the writer's lifetime, as questions about what literature should do, should be, are argued and reargued, and writers can come to define themselves or find realization as perhaps they would not were there no critical clashing of swords. But when the writer is no longer alive, such criticism may only be useful as a means of identifying the nature of his achievement. As readers, we take what we can get.

Perhaps it is relevant to note that O'Hara worshipped Ernest Hemingway and clearly understood the key to that master's short fiction: When composing a story, withhold the essential information—do not mention whatever it is that causes the characters to act as they do. O'Hara understood how such restraint is a means of fictive power, and he works this way in the gems of this collection. Read "A Phase of Life": A man and woman in an apartment talk idly of a past in show business that was clearly a better time in their lives. When the doorbell rings the man picks up a poker from the fireplace and goes to the door. But the arrivals turn out to be people he knows. He serves them drinks. He brings out a projector and shows them a movie.

Everyone except the man retires to the bedrooms and when a while later the guests emerge, they pay up and leave. The larger social condition underlying the story is left for the reader to infer.

And wasn't it Anton Chekhov who advised a young writer not to describe the moon shining but to show in a fragment of glass a glint of moonlight?

                                                    E. L. DOCTOROW

story set in New York City. The large number of very brief stories published by The ... late 1920s and early
1930s would alone present too much material for inclusion

Introduction

Dozens of John O'Hara's most powerful stories are set in New
York City, where he lived from the age of twenty-three, on and
off, throughout his long career. Born and raised in Pottsville,
Pennsylvania, a small city he called Gibbsville in his fiction,
O'Hara lived intermittently in Hollywood as well. Those two
locales have already been presented in the collections *Gibbsville,
PA* (1992) and *John O'Hara's Hollywood* (2007), both edited by
the late Matthew J. Bruccoli, leaving New York City as a major
locale not represented by a geographical volume. A fourth setting of O'Hara's stories is a general "suburbia," usually the suburbs of New York, many of which could have been presented
here if not for the abundance of strong stories set in the confines
of the city itself, and perhaps a fifth geographical setting would
be "Miscellaneous": O'Hara set one of his finest stories in Washington, D.C., but only one, as far as I can tell, and one story is set
in rural Ohio, and one other in Cambridge, Massachusetts, and
so on. But these three locations—New York City, Hollywood,
and "Gibbsville"—constitute the bulk of his stories' settings.
Presenting them in geographical collections gives readers a concentrated sense of what O'Hara felt made each place special.

O'Hara's short fiction falls into two discrete temporal
groups: the stories dating from before 1950, when, because of a
falling-out, O'Hara stopped writing for *The New Yorker,* and
those dating from after 1960 (O'Hara eschewed the short story
entirely in the 1950s). The pre-1950 group has already been
extensively represented in collections, some chosen by O'Hara
and then, after his death in 1970, others chosen by various editors. For example, *The Selected Stories of John O'Hara,*

published in 2003, draws exclusively from stories written
before 1949. The present volume, unlike *Gibbsville, PA* or *John
O'Hara's Hollywood,* does not seek to include every O'Hara
story set in New York City: The large number of very brief stories published by *The New Yorker* in the late 1920s and early
1930s would alone present too much material for inclusion
here, and are of varying quality and historical interest. *The
New York Stories* includes many more of the later, less frequently reprinted stories, as well as the strongest of O'Hara's
early New York stories.

O'Hara's stories could, of course, easily be arranged by subject matter or theme instead of geography. While it might seem
that O'Hara's stories about show business, for example, would
naturally be set in Hollywood, some excellent show-business
stories, such as "John Barton Rosedale, Actor's Actor" and
"The Portly Gentleman," are set on Broadway. In fact one of
O'Hara's finest examinations of show business, "Arnold Stone,"
is even set mostly in Gibbsville (oddly it is omitted from the
inclusive 854-page volume *Gibbsville, PA*). O'Hara's keen interest in business, as differentiated from show business, might
appear to belong to New York City, but again some of his
strongest stories about the intricacies of business, such as "The
Hardware Man" and "Yostie," are set, seemingly incongru-
ously, in the "third-class city," as he called it, of Gibbsville. For
the most part, however, O'Hara's stories about business, about
tycoons and their private clubs, or about working-class people
and their struggles and pleasures, are set in New York City.

In the early twentieth century, New York City was the world
capital of literature, and the ambitious young O'Hara aimed
to succeed there as a writer before he ever left Pottsville, sub-
mitting items to New York columnists from his hometown
until his physical arrival in the spring of 1928, when he worked
for a variety of newspapers, magazines, and press agencies as
well as freelancing his accounts of sporting events, celebrity
interviews, and "casuals," a term covering all types of short
pieces, including supposedly overheard conversations, which
may or may not have been fictional, but which did get his foot

in the door of *The New Yorker*, a brand-new slick magazine that ended up publishing most of his later short fiction. His earliest work for *The New Yorker* was journalistic—punchy, demotic, and fact-based—but O'Hara's aim was to write fiction, an aim he consistently realized after publishing his first novel, *Appointment in Samarra*, in 1934.

In the six years between 1928 and 1934, the young O'Hara hustled a living by writing what the market demanded, and he was busily acquainting himself with the widest variety imaginable of New Yorkers with interesting stories to tell. What he learned was that people are rarely what they seem, and that they often turned expectations on their heads to anyone willing to listen and to relate their stories to the public. He became a skilled listener, and a sensitive renderer of New Yorkers' voices—of what they had to say, what they were omitting, and how they expressed themselves. As he grew more settled as a novelist, screenwriter, and playwright (the turning point of his career was the success of the musical *Pal Joey* in 1940), he widened his social circle but retained the lesson he had learned as a young journalist: Every simple surface truth has a complicated and very rarely wholesome past, a principle he applied to the bankers, CEOs, and Broadway stars as well as to the bartenders, car-washers, and waitresses he continued to write about. His stories warn readers not to understand his characters too quickly—their motives will always be mixed, their emotions always mutable, their voices always revealing.

In a few of his early stories, O'Hara characterized people through techniques such as dialect, which is perhaps less amusing and less lucid today than it was in the 1930s. (One of these, "I Never Seen Anything Like It," omitted here, is narrated in wall-to-wall Brooklynese, and today practically requires a translator.) He gradually abandoned such glitzy quirks in favor of more subtle ways of developing character, and of playing with readers' expectations. With so varied a city as his subject, he worked at elevating his characters above clichés and stereotypes, and challenging his readers to abandon any easy assumptions they might have held based on superficial signifiers of social class.

In selecting the stories for this volume, I have been struck by the number of high-quality New York stories that take the form of dialogues between married couples. O'Hara's curiosity, always keen, was piqued particularly by the mystery of what went on between couples behind closed doors, especially bedroom doors. He was criticized for this by a generation of critics, but his curiosity ranged wider, and his prurient interests are so mild by current standards that it is the critics whose comments seem badly dated, not O'Hara's work, which seems insightful, psychologically and thematically. In a letter to a couple O'Hara knew well, written as they were divorcing, he observed, "No outsider knows what is between a husband and a wife," concluding that he pretended to know least of all: "But I know nothing. I know nothing." In his fiction, however, O'Hara explored what he guessed, what he believed, what seemed possible, what private actions might be deduced from public ones.

In this volume, such stories include "Late, Late Show" and "The Private People," both exploring complicated marital relationships using very different techniques. The scope of "Late, Late Show" is very narrow; the story takes the form of a single conversation between husband and wife as they watch a late-night movie on TV. Issues from their past emerge over the course of the conversation, which closes with the husband cutting it off as he realizes how near they are drawing to a topic he has long ago sworn secrecy on, even from his wife, who seems to accept this limit to their intimacy. In "The Private People," O'Hara makes his reader into a fly on the wall of another New York couple's apartment, though the scope of this story is much wider, stretching literally from coast to coast and taking in months and years of the couple's evolving relationship. The husband is a successful and famous actor who retires at an early age on Manhattan's Upper East Side with his wife, who is far less happy than he is with the relocation—so unhappy that she takes to heavy drinking, then decides to separate from her husband and move back to Hollywood, where she continues making an alcoholic spectacle of herself. Her estranged husband flies out to California, where

he rescues her from the clutches of the quack running a perni-
cious rest-home/detox-center, and they repair their broken marriage, settling once again in Manhattan with vastly reduced
expectations of happiness. In the story's final lines, O'Hara
writes that the wife requires a night light in order to sleep, but
reassures his reader, "Oh, it is not a very bright light," a typically elliptical ending.

O'Hara's endings increasingly intrigue and sometimes puzzle readers, often seeming to confirm the story's theme, and at
other times introducing a twist in the final moments that
changes that theme, as in the show-business story "The Portly
Gentleman." The titular character, a somewhat crude entertainer, finds his career suddenly thriving, then finds himself
escorting a socially refined woman, to whom he proposes marriage. Though his outlandish proposal is rebuffed, the two
characters seem to reach an empathetic understanding at the
story's conclusion. One of O'Hara's gifts, which shines more or
less directly in different stories, is to make plausible the improb-
able connections and sympathies between his characters.

O'Hara makes equally plausible the ways in which relationships suddenly deteriorate. "The Portly Gentleman" and "John
Barton Rosedale, Actor's Actor," a pair of New York stories
that combine show-business and marital relationships, turn
with startling ferocity when everyday conversations between
the title characters and, respectively, an agent and a producer
turn suddenly ugly. O'Hara's gradual introduction of tension
into the quotidian conversations prepares the reader for the
ugliness even as it shocks the reader when the volcanic action
erupts. O'Hara teaches us to pay attention to the most casual
exchanges between his characters, who are often perilously close
to professing deep affection for each other or to voicing their
fiercest animosity. The most succinct example of this sudden
switching of moods might be in the suburban story "The
Golden," not included here. O'Hara describes two dogs playing
for a long time, until the observing protagonist "saw that they
had reached the nipping stage. Then one dog's fang touched
another dog's nerve, and in an instant both animals were making the horrible gurgling sound that meant a fight." With O'Hara,

this process between people is more nuanced but no less shocking in its suddenness.

The longer stories, which are generally the later stories (the
date of first publication appears in parentheses at the end of
each story), frequently take a reminiscent tone, and delve further back into the earlier years of the characters' lives. This is
particularly so with the novella included here, "We're Friends
Again," which traces the course of the marriage of Charles
Ellis and Nancy Preswell through the perspective of Ellis's closest friend, O'Hara's alter-ego narrator, James Malloy. As the
title indicates, their friendship goes through peaks of affection
and valleys of deep animosity. Like many of O'Hara's later stories, "We're Friends Again" is longer not only because it contains more narrative material, but also because O'Hara's 1960s
style became increasingly discursive. The novella opens with a
mini-essay on the subject of men's clubs, particularly on a summer's weekend evening, and in the course of telling the story,
Malloy holds forth on several subjects that do not advance the
plot very much but that add to an understanding of his character. Malloy pauses in his narration to pass judgment on clubs,
Lord Byron's character, loneliness, the cachet of extra-long telephone extensions, the difference between New York society
and Boston society, and several other topics. He also pins the
story's plot upon an appreciation, doubtless hazy to today's
readers, of 1930s politics, particularly the positive and negative
nuances of the patrician class's response to the byzantine policies of Franklin Delano Roosevelt over the course of the decade. Similarly knotty are the love lives of O'Hara's characters:
Malloy is involved with an actress (named, presciently, Julianna
Moore), who is engaged to a stage designer, and his friend
Charley is seeing a married woman whose husband gets killed
in the course of the story, while Charley is also secretly in love
with a cousin of his, married to a multimillionaire, who eventually marries a WAVE ensign, while the multimillionaire's
ex-wife is carrying on an affair with a Boston socialite, whom
Malloy meets by chance in a theater and ends up working with
on an espionage unit during World War II. The multiplicity of
characters is sufficient for a much longer work than a novella,

but "We're Friends Again" succeeds despite the crowded cast in two ways: The passages of reminiscence are among O'Hara's finest, philosophizing on subjects O'Hara cares deeply about, and Malloy's career as a writer is examined at length here, providing a window on O'Hara as a writer. One fictional story is discussed extensively, as Malloy explains and listens to a reader's interpretation of his work, and also discusses his work habits: Like O'Hara's, his workday typically ended at dawn and, also like O'Hara's, Malloy's stories often begin when he overhears casual conversations between strangers. Malloy is among O'Hara's most hard-boiled narrators. In the novel *Hope of Heaven* (1939), for example, Malloy is a hard-hearted Hollywood scriptwriter, caught up in a tale of theft, false identity, and finally gunplay—it's easy to understand how Edmund Wilson included O'Hara in his 1941 review of hard-boiled writers, "The Boys in the Back Room." But in "We're Friends Again," Malloy's sentimental side prevails: When his friend accuses him of being "the lonesomest son-of-a-bitch I know," Malloy's response is not to laugh, or to grunt in agreement, or to take a swing at his accuser, but to break down in tears: "I bowed my head and wept. 'You shouldn't have said that,' I said. 'I wish you'd go.'"

The three-novella collection that "We're Friends Again" first appeared in, *Sermons and Sodawater*—a title taken from Byron's poem *Don Juan*—marked a crucial point in O'Hara's short fiction. The tone in "We're Friends Again" is distinctly more bookish and reflective—O'Hara quotes not only Byron but also Shakespeare, Milton, and Walter Scott—and reintroduces his recurring narrator, James Malloy, whose voice here is both reminiscent and moralizing, neither of which typified O'Hara's short fiction before 1960. From then on, when O'Hara wished to reminisce or moralize, he would do so in Malloy's voice; when he preferred his reader to infer the moral of his story, he would do so without Malloy. In the 1950s, when O'Hara eschewed the short story entirely, he was busy thinking about different ways to structure stories, and about how to employ the full array of techniques at his disposal, so that when he started up again with *Sermons and Sodawater*, he was prepared to begin the most productive and varied short-story writing of his career.

Which is not to diminish his pre-1960 stories, only to note that in complexity and craft they were comparatively hit-or-miss. "Bread Alone," to take one example from the 1930s, is one of his hits: As in so many of his finest stories during the Depression, such as "Pleasure" and "Sportmanship," O'Hara empathized with the working poor but never patronized their struggles. In "Bread Alone" he introduces a black workingman (an extremely rare protagonist for a white middle-class writer from the political center) with a practical dilemma: He wants to hide from his wife the fact that he wagered some money in an office pool, but he won a pair of baseball tickets, and he would like to take his young son, from whom he feels disconnected, to the ballgame. As the story develops, O'Hara's reader sympathizes with this character, coming to understand the delicate problems faced by black people in a white society and, in the story's final epiphany, the rich feelings between the two estranged males. In the tight constraints of a very short story, O'Hara both moves and educates his white audience to appreciate a side of American society that few of them would have had any prior access to.

The earlier, shorter stories usually lack the sweeping scope of his later stories, but nearly all O'Hara's stories share an elliptical quality that is one of their trademarks, eventually becoming an identifying trait of the prototypical *New Yorker* story, which O'Hara is largely responsible for inventing. The majority of the stories collected here were originally published in *The New Yorker*, whose legendary founding editor, Harold Ross, supposedly declared he would never purchase another O'Hara story he couldn't understand. But Ross was also aware that decoding the subtle events in an O'Hara story and deciding on their significance was a great pleasure for O'Hara's fans, so he and his successors continued purchasing them.

There is a quirk of arrangement in this volume that is worth discussing briefly: In his final five collections, from 1962 to 1969, O'Hara presented the stories as they are presented here, in alphabetical order by title, as if to suggest that the quality of the stories could be neither improved nor diminished by any artful arrangement. (The order in which stories in a collection are presented is typically discussed by authors and editors at astonishing length and with surprising passion, such as you might expect among the floral arrangers at a royal wedding, but O'Hara was foreclosing that discussion entirely, by authorial fiat: "This is it," he was saying in effect. "The stories themselves can choose their own order.") He was inordinately proud of the quality of his work, and I believe this alphabetical arrangement was one of the ways he expressed his pride in the consistently high level of his writing. At the same time, he tempered his pride with a reluctance to overexplain, or even to explain: He never, as far I can tell, discussed with anyone his thinking behind arranging his stories alphabetically. It wasn't until I read his third or fourth collection of alphabetically arranged stories that I even became aware of what O'Hara was doing, and what he might have been trying to communicate by it.

O'Hara's assertion of the absolute equality of all his stories, if that is what he was asserting, is one I'd quibble with—he wrote many masterpieces in the genre, but there are a few New York stories that continue to puzzle me: "The Sun-Dodgers" and "The Brain" and "A Phase of Life" are even more elusive than O'Hara's typically elusive gems. "The Sun-Dodgers" devotes a paragraph to a minor character who, the narrator promises, will reappear at a crucial point later in the story, "when he is needed." But the minor character becomes instead a noncharacter—he does not reappear. The problem in "The Brain" seems even less like an authorial oversight, because O'Hara tells the story of the titular "Brain," a New York businessman who is asked to resign, and O'Hara tells it twice. On the first go-around, his titular character is interrupted by a troubleshooter reporting directly to their boss, who, after being admitted by the Brain's secretary, a Miss Hathaway, discusses the possible reassignment of the Brain to Montana, finally telling him that he has the same chance of being fired as anyone in the company except their boss. O'Hara then switches to a more removed narrator who tells a similar story, except in the second version the troubleshooter is not admitted by the secretary, whose name is now Miss Hawthorne, and the state in question is not Montana but Colorado, and the "Brain" is unambiguously instructed to clear his desk out immediately. Since O'Hara could not possibly have gotten so many small details wrong, the likeliest explanation is that he was conveying something about how different versions of an event can change the event's essence, but if so, this is one of the few times O'Hara's point in telling a story gets muffled in the telling. "A Phase of Life" is clearer, though still a little hazier than usual: a relatively early story, it may typify O'Hara's early elliptical stories. Some unsavory characters get together for an evening of sex for pay, though the precise nature of the sex, and the pay, and the characters for that matter, never becomes explicit. This may be another of those stories that, as O'Hara said of his *New Yorker* stories in a 1936 letter, "I almost include a plea to the editors that if they can understand them, please to let me in on the secret."

In his best stories, O'Hara is a master of pacing and of action, of knowing when to paint a scene in fine detail and when to summarize. There is a moment in "John Barton Rosedale, Actor's Actor" that is amazing in its understated pace: The title character, having made an ego-satisfying but self-destructive career decision, reviews his suits hanging in his closet, and considers the hanging and rehanging of them—a duller subject can hardly be imagined. But in writing lively sentences on such a dull subject, O'Hara is not only showcasing his virtuosity but also suspending his narrative to build anticipation for the blowout marital fight that results from his character's cogitation. When that quarrel comes, his reader has been both entertained and prepared for it, though without knowing fully why and how. O'Hara excelled in the dual roles of entertainer and educator: He enlightened readers seeking amusement, and he amused readers seeking enlightenment, and at times he did so, as his tombstone claims, better than any other writer of the mid-twentieth century.

STEVEN GOLDLEAF

Suggestions for Further Reading

There hasn't been much scholarship on John O'Hara, for largely incomprehensible reasons other than personal antipathy or a prejudice against clear English prose that doesn't require much parsing, but there has been some, starting with the most inclusive and judicious biography, Matthew J. Bruccoli's *The O'Hara Concern* (New York: Random House, 1975). Bruccoli also compiled a detailed bibliography of O'Hara's publications, *John O'Hara: A Checklist* (New York: Random House, 1972), which contains a speech O'Hara gave late in his career. Of the other biographies, Finis Farr's *O'Hara* (Boston: Little, Brown, 1973) has the dubious advantage of being the first written, as well as the only one written by an acquaintance of O'Hara's. Frank MacShane's *The Life of John O'Hara* (New York: Dutton, 1980) is perfectly serviceable if slightly less inclusive than Bruccoli's. Geoffrey Wolff's *The Art of Burning Bridges* (New York: Knopf, 2003) is not quite a biography of O'Hara, and not completely satisfactory as an extended literary essay or as an autobiographical essay, either. It is a strange book.

Of the shorter criticism, Phillip Eppard collected some essays in his *Critical Essays on John O'Hara* (New York: G. K. Hall, 1994), which seems more insightful and various than some previous pamphlet-length attempts at criticism by such authors as Russell E. Carson, Sheldon Norman Grebstein, Robert Emmet Long, and Charles C. Walcutt, who have studied mainly O'Hara's novels. My own *John O'Hara: A Study of the Short Fiction* (New York: Twayne, 1999) contains a number of essays on O'Hara's stories, which Eppard didn't include (or couldn't have included), and also a long essay on the stories in which I attempt to chart O'Hara's story-writing career, more or less systematically.

Although copies of the *John O'Hara Journal*, published from 1979 to 1983, are all but impossible to come by, there is a website—oharasociety.blogspot.com—sponsored by the John O'Hara Society, a small group of non-academic O'Hara fans who meet on the Internet (and occasionally in New York City, Princeton, or Philadelphia) to discuss the man, his books, his career, and related matters. Those interested in reading O'Hara's short nonfiction (he wrote columns in various newspapers and magazines from time to time) can find them collected in *Sweet and Sour* (New York: Random House, 1954) and *My Turn* (New York: Random House, 1966), while his critical work on writers and writing has been collected by Bruccoli in *An Artist Is His Own Fault* (Carbondale: Southern Illinois University Press, 1977). Like the prefaces to the short story collections, these collections contain O'Hara's literary views at their most acerbic, and the *Selected Letters of John O'Hara* (New York: Random House, 1978), edited also by Bruccoli, contains insights into the composition and themes of many of O'Hara's stories.

But mostly, for the dedicated reader of the short fiction, there are the stories themselves. O'Hara published more than four hundred of them; reading them all is a satisfying goal for any O'Hara completionist.

A Note on the Text

The stories in this collection have been taken from the periodicals in which they first appeared (mostly *The New Yorker*) and the hardcover collections they typically appeared in shortly afterward. I have also used some paperback editions and collections published after O'Hara's death to see how certain textual discrepancies have been resolved.

The difficulty in editing O'Hara is that he declared his independence from convention in rendering colloquial American English, particularly in dialogue and in the dialect he used heavily at the beginning of his career. For example, in the story "First Day in Town," when he has a show-business outsider speak of "Eli Kazan," referring to the famous director, a scrupulous proofreader might simply flag this as a misspelling of "Elia," or it might be O'Hara's deliberate attempt to show how this outsider had mistaken "Elia" for the more common "Eli," or how this character clipped the "a" in his pronunciation of "Elia." Because O'Hara enjoyed playing phonetic tricks to indicate his speaker's eccentricities, it is never safe to assume that a seeming error was due to O'Hara's negligence, and so it remains rendered here as "Eli Kazan." When some editor tried correcting O'Hara's usage, in a story not included here, of the 1960s slang term "Cloud 90," saying that the dictionary did not recognize it, O'Hara dismissed him, saying, "Dictionary people consult me, not I them." O'Hara famously relied on his ear to guide him in rendering spoken English, though I question his infallibility. Anyone who listens closely to English being spoken will commit an error now and then, and I have corrected the

occasional obvious error but have mostly left O'Hara's idiosyncrasies as they appeared in his published works.

In the story "Bread Alone," the protagonist, a black New
Yorker during the Depression, speaks of his "sets" at Yankee
Stadium. Is this a dialectal rendering intended to show how
this character would have pronounced "seats," or a typo that
O'Hara (and his various editors) did not catch? I was inclined
to retain "sets"—it appears this way in the original *New
Yorker* story and the reprinted version in *Pipe Night*—but I
found that in *The Collected Stories of John O'Hara*, published
in 1984, and in *Selected Stories of John O'Hara*, published in
2003, it is spelled "seats." So there is precedent both ways;
which way is the error? Never having heard the word pronounced by any New Yorker, of any race or background, as
"sets," I've decided to follow recent editorial precedent.

Another example of ambiguity: In the story "Good-bye, Herman," the title character's last name is "Wasservogel," which
the protagonist's wife mispronounces slightly as "Wasserfogel." (The authentic Germanic "v" has a good deal of "f" in its
sound.) The protagonist himself, who grew up with Wasservogel, is shown to pronounce it properly, and his rendering is
spelled correctly. But toward the end of the story, the wife's
pronunciation seems to change, and in her speech, the name is
now spelled with a "v." Some editors have changed the spelling of "Wasservogel" in her dialogue as the story progresses;
because I think it's interesting that this pronunciation change
could reflect a subtle sign of some change in her attitude, I
leave it in.

In all cases I have simply tried to do right by O'Hara, and to
make changes only where I think he would have concurred.
But even in trying to respect his wishes, there are some tricky
points. In one early, and wonderful, O'Hara morality tale, the
ambiguous moral is expressed in a single word that happens to
be the story's title: "sportsmanship." Except that isn't exactly
the word O'Hara uses, either in the title or in the climax of the
tale—not in *The New Yorker* or in any of the several hard-
bound, softbound, or collected reprints. In those, O'Hara has
(intentionally or carelessly?) omitted the middle "s," and the

word appears as "sportmanship" throughout. This story is one in which O'Hara is still employing freely the use of dialect (his characters say things like "I think I smell sumpn" and "How long id take you?"), so it is possible that in omitting the "s" he is indicating some obscure local pronunciation, but if he is, as with "sets," it is a pronunciation that no New Yorker I've known has ever employed, nor any dictionary, either. On the off chance that O'Hara is purposefully omitting a letter, and with no precedent for anyone having previously treated "sportmanship" as a typo, I have let it stand, if only as a token of respect for his stylistic idiosyncrasies and innovations.

Elsewhere, O'Hara's idiosyncratic spellings mostly prevail ("cheque," "theatre," "glamor," etc.), except where they are internally inconsistent—O'Hara uses "gray" and "grey" interchangeably and without any pattern I can find, so I've standardized the spelling in the American style. He consistently omits the comma in the phrase "No, thanks," which would change the meaning from a polite negation to a rude assertion, but I have let that stand, too, in deference to his consistent usage.

STEVEN GOLDLEAF

AGATHA

Both dogs had been out. She could tell by the languid way they greeted her and by the fact that Jimmy, the elevator operator, had taken his twenty-five-cent piece off the hall table. Or was it Jimmy? Yes, Jimmy was on mornings this week; Ray was on afternoons and evenings. Jimmy liked dogs, Ray did not. The day was off to a better start when Jimmy took the dogs for their morning walk; it was nicer to start the day with the thought that Jimmy, who liked dogs, had exercised them, and not Ray, who made no attempt to conceal his distaste for the chore. Ray was paid a quarter, just the same as Jimmy, for taking the dogs down to the corner, but Mrs. Child had very good reason to believe that that was *all* he did—take them to the corner, and hurry right back without letting them stop at the curb.

"Good morning, boys," she said, addressing the dogs. They shook their tails without getting up. "Oh, you're such spoiled boys, you two. You won't even rise when a lady enters the room. Muggsy, don't you *know* that a gentleman *always* stands up when a lady comes in? You *do* know it, too, and you're not a very good example to your adopted brother, are you? How can I expect Percy to have good manners if you don't show him how? Percy, don't you pay a bit of attention to Muggsy and his bad manners." The dogs raised their heads at the sound of their names, but when she finished speaking they slowly put their heads back on their paws. "Oh, you're hopeless, the two of you. Really hopeless. I don't see why I put up with two such uncouth rascals."

She proceeded to the kitchen door and pushed it open. "Good morning, Mary," she said.

"Good morning, Mrs. Child," said the maid. "I heard you running your tub. Will you have toast this morning?"

"Just one slice, please. Maybe two slices, but bring me my coffee first, will you?"

"Yes ma'am."

"I didn't see any mail. Was there any?"

"Got it here on the tray. Which'll you have? Marmalade, or the blackberry jam?"

"Mary, you're not cooperating at all. You know perfectly well if you mention marmalade or jam, I'll *have* marmalade or jam, and I'm trying not to."

"Oh, if I don't mention it you'll ask for it."

"I'm such a weak, spineless creature. All right, you mean old Mary Moran, you. You know me much too well. I'll have the blackberry jam. Were there any packages?"

"None so far, but United Parcel don't usually get here before noontime. That's the way it works out. Some neighborhoods they only deliver in the afternoon, some in the morning. I guess they have a system."

"And speaking of other neighborhoods, when am I going to be able to lure you away from Mrs. Brown?"

"Oh—I don't know about that, Mrs. Child," said Mary Moran. "Will you have your first cup standing up?"

"No, I'll wait. I'll be in the livingroom," said Mrs. Child.

Mary Moran would have been expensive, and there really wasn't enough work to keep her busy, but Mrs. Child knew that Mary's other employer, Mrs. Brown, had been trying to persuade her to give up Mrs. Child and work full-time for her. It did no harm, every once in a while, to remind Mary that she had a full-time job waiting for her with Mrs. Child—and subtly to remind Mary that she had been with Mrs. Child a good two years longer than she had been with Mrs. Brown. There were a lot of things Mary could not do, but in what she could do, or would do, she was flawless. Mrs. Child did not need Mary Moran at all, when you came right down to it. The building provided maid service of a-lick-and-a-promise sort, and you could have all your meals sent up and served by the room-service waiters. But Mary Moran was acquainted with

AGATHA 3

every article of clothing that Mrs. Child possessed; she was a superb laundress of things like lingerie; a quick and careful presser; very handy with needle and thread. She could put together a light meal of soup and salad, and she could do tiny sandwiches and a cheese dip for a small cocktail group. But she would not serve luncheon or pass a tray among cocktail guests; not that she was ever there at cocktail time, but as a matter of principle she had made it one of her rules that serving was not to be expected of her. She was not very good about taking telephone messages, either; it had taken Mrs. Child two years to discover that Mary was ashamed of her handwriting and spelling. Nevertheless she would have been an excellent personal maid, and Agatha Child never gave up hoping that she could lure—lure was the word—Mary away from the Browns, whoever *they* were beyond the fact that they had a small apartment on Seventy-ninth Street and were away a good deal of the time. It would have been worth the money to have Mary Moran on a full-time basis, not only for the work she did, but because her coming to work full-time would have been an expression of the approval that Agatha Child suspected that Mary withheld.

"We haven't talked about that for quite some time," said Agatha Child.

Mary Moran had just brought in the breakfast tray. "What's that, Mrs. Child?"

"About your coming to work for me full-time."

Mary Moran smiled. "Well, it suits me, the way it is," she said.

"You'd make just as much money. And don't you find it a nuisance, to finish up here and then have to take the bus to Seventy-ninth Street?"

"I usually walk. I enjoy the walk. I get a breath of fresh air."

"Do you know what I think? I think you have a gentleman friend that you have lunch with. You almost never have lunch here."

"Well, there may be some truth to that. We have a bite to eat. It's on the way."

"Oh, my guess was right? How fascinating. Tell me about him."

"No, I don't think I'll do that."

"Of course not. It's none of my business, and I don't want to appear inquisitive. But of course I'm dying of curiosity. You've been with me eight years and this is really the first time we ever got on that subject."

"Well, you made a good guess for your first try."

"Is he Catholic?"

"No ma'am."

"You'd rather not say any more."

"Rather not. It's him and I."

"Yes. Well, I won't badger you any more. I just want to say that I hope he appreciates you, and if you ever feel the need to talk to someone about it—about him."

"Thank you, ma'am."

"Remember, I've been married three times."

"I know that, yes."

"And I'm a lot older than you. Probably fifteen years."

"Not quite. I'll be forty-one."

"Well, almost fifteen years. How did you know my age? Did you see it on my passport?"

"No ma'am. Your scrapbook, where you have that newspaper cutting of when you eloped and all. The big green scrapbook."

"Oh, yes. That's a dead giveaway, isn't it? Well, what difference does it make? Anybody can find out my age if they want to take the trouble. All they have to do is go to the Public Library, and there it is in big headlines, seventeen-year-old heiress and all that tommyrot. Never lived it down. But that's where I can be of help to you, Mary, in case you ever *need* any help."

"They'd never put *me* in the headlines, whatever I did."

"You can be thankful for that," said Agatha Child.

"Will you want me to—changing the subject—will I send the black suit to the dry cleaner's, or do you want to give it another wear?"

"I guess it could stand a cleaning. Whatever you think," said Agatha Child.

"I had a look at it this morning. It's about ready to go."

The day's mail was fattened up by the usual bills and appeals. She put a rubber band around the unopened bills, for forwarding to Mr. Jentzen, who would scrutinize them, make out the appropriate cheques, and send her the cheques for signature. She saw Mr. Jentzen just once a year, at income tax time, when he would deliver his little lecture on her finances, show her where to sign the returns, and have one glass of sherry with her. On these occasions Mr. Jentzen could almost make her feel that he was paying for the sherry and for everything else. Bald, conscientious Mr. Jentzen, who looked like a dark-haired version of the farmer in Grant Wood's "American Gothic," and who in some respects knew her better than any husband or lover she had ever had, but who politely declined her suggestion that he call her Agatha. "Not even if I call you Eric? It's such a nice name, Eric." And so unlike Mr. Jentzen, she did not add. She could have gone right ahead and called him Eric; she was, after all, at least five years older than he, but she knew that he was afraid of even so slight an intimacy because he was the kind of man who would be afraid to get entangled with a woman who had had three husbands and an undetermined number of gentlemen friends.

It occurred to her now, as she doubled the rubber band about the bills, that her life was full of small defeats at the hands of people who rightfully should have obeyed her automatically. Mary Moran, Eric Jentzen, and Ray the bellboy were three she could name offhand who refused to yield to her wishes. With Ray the bellboy it was a case of attitude rather than outright disobedience; he did what she asked, but so churlishly that his obedience became an act of defiance. Mary Moran, crafty little Irishwoman that she was, was practically an illiterate but she was adroit enough to avoid a showdown on the question of giving up the Browns. And Eric Jentzen used his sexual timidity to keep from losing the arrogated privilege of lecturing her on her extravagances. (It was quite possible that Mr. Jentzen got some sort of mild kick out of that safe intimacy.)

The dogs were now sitting up. "One little piece of toast is all you're going to get," she said. "No, Percy, you must wait till your older stepbrother has his. See there, Muggsy? If you'd taught him better manners he wouldn't be so grabby. One piece is all you're going to get, so don't bother to look at me that way. Down, boys. I said down. *Down*, God damn it! Percy, you scratched me, you son of a bitch. You could cause me all sorts of trouble, explaining a scratch like that. *If* there was anybody I had to explain to." She lit a cigarette and blew smoke in the dogs' muzzles. "Now stay down, and don't interrupt me while I see whose sucker list I'm on today."

Two of the appeals were for theatrical previews at twenty-five dollars a crack. By an amusing coincidence both contained similarly worded personal touches. "Do try to come" was written across the top of the announcements; one was signed with initials, identifiable by going down the list of patronesses; the other was signed "Mary," and didn't mean a damned thing. Mary. What a crust a woman had, to sign just Mary and expect people to know who Mary was. Agatha Child went through the list and discovered three Marys behind the married names and one Mary who was a Miss. "I'll tell you what you can do, Mary dear. You can invite me to dinner and the benefit and shell out fifty dollars for me and some likely gentleman, and I *will* do-try-to-come." She dropped the announcements in the wastebasket. She immediately retrieved them and went over one of the lists again. Yes, there it was: Mrs. W. B. Harris, the wife of her second husband. What a comedown that would be for Wally, if he should ever learn that she had seen that name, which once she bore, and it had failed to register. True, she had always given the name the full treatment: Wallace Boyd Harris. True, too, there were so many Harrises. One too many, or two too many, if it came to that, which was how she happened to become Agatha Child. For the second time she dropped the announcements in the wastebasket, but at least they had given her some amusement. Wally Harris, afraid of his own shadow—more accurately, afraid of the shadow of her first husband. Well, it hadn't been a mere shadow; more like a London peasouper that lasted four years. Four dark, miserable years that she could recall in every detail and had succeeded in suspending from her active memory, by sandwiching the whole period in between her first marriage and her third, so that it was worthless even as a wasted segment of her time on earth to cry over. He was an intimate man, Wally, wanting to know everything about everything she did, until there was nothing left to learn except all the things she felt and could not tell him, that no one can tell anyone unless she is asked the right questions, at the right moment, in the right tone of voice, and for the right reason which is love. Finally he had learned just about every fact of her marriage to her first husband and had accidentally discovered a few facts about the man who was to be her third. All that time that he had consumed in pumping her about Johnny Johns, in contemning Johnny Johns, in emulating Johnny Johns—a little of that time, only a little, Wally could more profitably have devoted to the maneuverings of his friend Stanley Child. When the blow fell and there was that tiresome scene that Wally had insisted upon ("I want you to hear everything I say to Stanley"), the thought kept running through her mind that Wally hated Johnny much more than he did Stanley. Despite the fact that she had been having her affair with Stanley right under his nose, Wally managed to bring up Johnny Johns, whom she had not seen or heard from in five years. "I thought you were all through with that kind of thing when you got rid of that Johns fellow," said Wally.

"I was—to marry you," she said. "Johnny could have been very unpleasant about *you*, don't forget."

"That lightweight," said Wally, unmistakably implying that Johnny was incapable of sustained indignation. Two years later Wally married the present Mrs. Harris, the lady of the patroness list, and immediately started having lunch with Stanley again. By Wally's lights it was all right to resume the friendship with Stanley Child as soon as he remarried, but not before. The friendship in its second phase was stronger than it had ever been, and it did not include the wives. "Wally and I are going over to play Pine Valley . . . Wally got me an invitation to Thomasville. Will you be all right?" At first she was not all right, at all; it was not her idea of fun to sit in a New York apartment while the two big boys, her husband and her ex, went off to play. She was not worried about what they would say about her; Stanley Child was simply not the kind of man who would discuss his wife with another man on any terms, and insensitive though he may have been about many things, Wally Harris would know better than to mention Agatha except when it was unavoidable. No, it was not the fear of their talking about her that annoyed her; it was her growing conviction that she could be the wife of two men and yet remain completely outside their lives, one after the other and the two together. In olden days they might well have fought a duel over her; in the fifth decade of the twentieth century they played golf together and tacitly denied her existence.

It was a dismal record for a girl who had only wanted to be liked, who had only tried to be pleasant to people. She loved Johnny Johns now, today, so many years later, but she had not even believed at the time that she was marrying Johnny for love. He was a screwy boy who would come charging into Canoe Place late Saturday nights, arriving alone and always leaving with some other boy's girl. Nothing vicious about him; he made no phony promises, and he nursed no hard feelings against the girls who refused to ditch the boys they had come with. To such steadfast types he would say, "Okay, but you don't know what you're missing," and it was as close as he ever came to the surliness of some of the other wolf types. At this point in her reminiscing she smiled.

Canoe Place, a Saturday night after a dance at the Meadow Club. He came and sat down beside her—actually in back of her—pulling up a chair from the next table. "Aggie Todd, I've a bone to pick with you. I hear you said I wasn't a wolf."

"You heard I said you *weren't* a wolf? Were not? Why is that a bone to pick with me?"

"You trying to ruin my reputation?"

"You're getting me all confused," she said.

"Did you or did you not say I was not a wolf?"

"I said you were not," she said.

"That's what I heard. What right have you got to go around saying nice things about me?"

"Huh?"

"The first thing you know, all the mothers and fathers will start approving of me. Then where will I be?"

She was young, and not very quick. "Oh, now I get it," she said. "You glory in a bad reputation, is that it?"

"I sure as hell don't want to turn into a Henny Ramsdell."

"You won't, never fear." This was fun because Henny Ramsdell at that very moment was seated on her left.

"Or a Bucky Clayton." Bucky Clayton was sitting across the table, looking at them and straining an ear to hear what they were saying. "Take a gander at Bucky, trying to read our lips."

"I know," she said.

"Why did you rush to my defense, Aggie?"

"Because I think—well I *don't* think you're a *wolf*."

"Well, one of these days maybe I'll say something nice about you." He was a little more serious, and started to rise.

"Why not now?"

"All right," he said. Then, "No, I guess not. I don't want to turn your head."

"Ah, come on, turn my head, Johnny."

"You really want me to?"

"Yes."

"All right, but you asked for it, Aggie. I think you're the only girl in this whole damn bunch that I give a hoot in hell about."

"Is that true?" she said.

"It's true."

"Scout's honor?"

"Now don't push it. Yes, scout's honor. Come on, let's dance. Mr. Ramsdell, boy, I'm taking your girl away."

"The hell you are," said Henny Ramsdell.

"The hell I'm not," said Johnny. "Come on, Aggie, while you have the chance."

A week later they eloped, and during the next four years all the predictable mishaps of their kind of marriage came to pass. There was, in addition, a handicap that the pessimists had not counted on and the optimists had not foreseen: she was too young for companionship with most of the young wives in her set, and as a wife she was no longer compatible

with the unmarried girls who were her contemporaries. It
came down to a problem of often not knowing whom to have
lunch with, and Johnny, working downtown, was impatiently
lacking in an understanding of the problem. "You would never
think," she said to Wallace Harris, "that a thing like that
would make so much difference, but it does."

Wallace Harris was a bachelor, a few years older than Johnny.
"Do you mean to say you're lonely?"

"That's *just* what I'm saying."

"Why don't you have a child?"

"We did. I never saw it."

"Sorry."

She had not been very bright about Wallace Harris. She had
had no curiosity about him, and when she drifted into an
affair with him she was all but shocked to discover that he had
always been promiscuous, that women by the dozen had succumbed, if that was the word, to his availability. It was difficult to believe him as he told her the number and kinds of
women who had slept with him, but she could not wholly
doubt him since she was now one of that list herself. What
made it difficult to believe him was her unthinking acceptance
of the notion that roués had fun, and inevitably were gay; but
for Wally there seemed to have been no fun, only a succession
of women who used him as much as he used them. As for gaiety, one of his outstanding characteristics was a total lack of
it. In this respect, however, she came to understand his success
with women: he was so lacking in gaiety that a woman would
automatically credit him with discretion and reliability. But
poor Wally was essentially nothing more than a well-scrubbed
male, who never needed a haircut or a manicure, and would
have been far happier without women if the men he liked had
been able to do without them too. He would never have been
clinically curious about her life with Stanley Child as he had
been about Johnny Johns; without asking, he would guess that
Stanley's demands on a woman were much like his own—and
he would have been right. He understood Stanley, but Johnny
Johns was a lightweight . . .

Agatha Child heard herself say, "What? What?"

Mary Moran was standing in the doorway, with the jacket of the black suit over her arm and holding up the skirt. "I didn't mean to startle you, ma'am."

"Oh—I was off somewhere," said Agatha Child. "What is it, Mary?"

"Well, I was wondering if maybe there's a little hole in the skirt we should have rewoven."

"A hole in it? Let me see."

"Right here, ma'am, just back of the knee. You musta caught it on something."

"Yes. I wonder if it'd be worth it. Reweaving is awfully expensive."

"Now if it was a country suit, you wouldn't care so much. But you don't want to go around with a hole in your skirt in the city."

"I forget how much they charged the last time I had something rewoven. I paid four hundred dollars for that suit, when was it, three years ago?"

"You had this three years, that's right. It's a beautiful suit, no doubt about that. I think it's worth getting it rewoven."

"It's too bad you can't wear my clothes. I'd give it to you, then I'd have an excuse to buy myself a new one."

"No, I could never get into this. I was always too big an eater."

"You *could* have a nice figure, if you'd take off about fifteen pounds. You really ought to be ashamed of yourself, Mary. That's all since you've come to work for me."

"Aach, and if they don't like me this way it's too late for me to change."

"Too late? Nonsense. Forty-one. If I gave you a course at Elizabeth Arden, would you go through with it?"

"Me at Elizabeth Arden's? Huh."

"Well, any place."

"Thanks just the same. I got the determination, if I want to starve off the fifteen pounds, but I'd only put it back on again."

"Do as you please," said Agatha Child.

"And what about the suit, ma'am?"

"Have it rewoven, of course. And tell them not to take so long. The last time I think they took over a month."

"That was a big cigarette burn, in your gray."

"You don't have to make excuses for them, Mary. Just tell them what I said."

Mary Moran left, saying no more. If she had stayed longer, said any more, Agatha Child would have fired her. The woman had snubbed her twice within the hour, less than an hour, actually. Agatha, at the thought of time, glanced at the little gold and enamel clock at her side. It was twelve-twenty-two, according to the clock—which obviously had stopped during the night. She reached for the clock to wind it, but it had *not* stopped; the winder took only one full turn. She held the clock to her ear, and it was steadily ticking away. Was it possible that she had been sitting here for an hour and ten minutes? Had she fallen asleep after her coffee and cigarette? She looked for her cigarette. It was not in the ash tray, and yet she remembered having a cigarette, blowing the smoke at the dogs.

Casually, so that Mary Moran would not come in and catch her in the act of looking for the cigarette butt, she bent over to the right and then to the left of her chair. The cigarette was on neither side. She leaned forward, and there it was, having burnt itself out and formed a small crater in the carpet. She *had* been asleep, and once again she had gone to sleep with a cigarette burning, just as she had done while wearing the gray suit, which Mary Moran knew about, and one other time that the maid did not know about, all within a space of six or eight weeks.

She picked up the cigarette butt and put it in the ash tray. Then she dipped a napkin in the glass of icewater and tried to rub the blackened crater in the carpet so that the burn would not show. This was only partially successful. The crater remained, and some of the piling was permanently blackened.

It was no time to panic; it was a time to face facts, to look at things calmly. She would begin by admitting that this was the fourth, not only the third, time that a cigarette had given her some kind of trouble recently. The third time, fortunately, was in a taxicab. The fourth time—a week ago—was here in the apartment, when she went to the bathroom and found a merry little fire in the tin wastebasket. She extinguished that fire easily by putting the basket under the bathtub tap and letting the water run. The contents of the basket she flushed down the toilet; the scorched basket itself presented a bit of a problem, which she solved by wrapping it in newspapers and taking it down to Madison Avenue and dropping it in the city basket. Mary Moran noticed that the bathroom basket was missing. *She* noticed everything. "I got tired of it," Agatha Child told her. "I threw it out with the trash last night."

"It was kind of pretty," said Mary Moran.

"Cheap," said Agatha Child. "I saw a nicer one at Hammacher's."

"Oh, one of them with the mirrors all around it?" said Mary. "Mrs. Brown has two of them."

"Yes. The other basket was here when I took this apartment, and I don't know why I kept it so long. But yesterday I decided I couldn't look at it one more day."

It was the kind of explanation that would satisfy Mary Moran, with her unspoken but unmistakable opinion of Agatha Child as a frivolous woman. The same opinion had made credible the explanation for the burn in the gray suit. "I'm almost sure that it was some awful woman at the cocktail party I went to yesterday. She carried a long cigarette holder, and I noticed her waving it around."

Explanations were imperative. Agatha Child had heard of some woman who had been asked to leave some apartment-hotel because she was a fire hazard, falling asleep and setting fire to her bedclothes. It would not do, it would not do at all, to let Mary Moran know that Agatha Child had had any such experiences.

Agatha Child rose and sauntered to the livingroom door, listened, heard Mary Moran humming a tune, which she did when she was busy. Now quickly Agatha Child got a bottle of ink and a fountain pen and went back to her chair. She carefully poured ink on the crater in the carpet, watched it soak in, then sharp and loud she exclaimed, "God damn it! Oh, God damn it."

Mary Moran appeared in the doorway. "Something the matter?"

"Look at the mess I've made. Trying to fill my pen."

"They can get that out."

"I wonder. I know they can get the stain out, but look how deep this is. One of those places where the dogs have chewed the carpet. Boys, you really do try my patience sometimes. Oh, well this was my fault, no use trying to blame the dogs."

Brilliant. Inspired. At the moment of pouring the ink she had not even thought of the dogs and their, or Muggsy's, habit of digging holes in the carpet. It was the kind of inspiration she would not have had if she had not refused to panic. Face facts, look at things calmly.

"Will I phone the rug man?" said Mary Moran.

"Yes, will you, before you leave? And I won't be here this afternoon, Mary. I've just decided to blow myself to a new suit."

"Another black, ma'am?"

"Anything but. This is something for spring," said Agatha Child. "Do you think I'm mad, Mary? I *am* a little mad, aren't I?"

(1963)

THE ASSISTANT

The alarm clock went off, and she did not remember setting it. It was a small clock, brass-plated, with a dial that was less than two inches in diameter, and the noise-making apparatus of it was annoying but not powerful enough to be commanding. Without stirring from her pillow she looked at it and said the first defiant thing that came into her head—and let it ring itself down. Then, before closing her eyes again, she looked to see what time it was. It was half past five.

She closed her eyes and dozed off into an enjoyable half-sleep, rather delicious it was because it was stolen sleep. Half past five itself meant nothing to her, but half past six might mean something. Half past six, or more likely, seven o'clock. Seven o'clock. What was there that she had to do, where was there that she had to be, at seven o'clock that would cause her to set her alarm clock for half past five? Seven o'clock was the time, all right. It would take her at least an hour to dress, and another half hour to get anywhere. She was to meet someone at seven o'clock, or at seven o'clock someone was coming here to her apartment. The big question was not so much where as who.

Now she reached out and with the skill of a blind person she took a cigarette out of a china box, and with somewhat less confidence she groped around the night table until her fingers found a lighter. With her eyes still closed, to protect her eyes from the glare—sometimes that first flame lighting that first cigarette could be as blinding as the bomb on Nagasaki—she brought the lighter to the end of the cigarette and took in that first shallow drag. Now, to all intents and purposes, she had come awake, or as a friend of hers was fond of saying, had

rejoined the human race. George Waller. As he took his first
drink of the day, he would nearly always say that he was
rejoining the human race. He had got it out of a book somewhere. She wished it was as easy to remember whom she had a
date with as it was to remember George Waller—or to forget
George Waller, for that matter.

Less tentatively she took a fuller drag on her cigarette and
sat on the edge of the bed, scratching little itches with her free
hand and rubbing the area of the right clavicle. It was a little
too soon to know how she was going to feel when she got to
her feet, but so far the day was not as bad as some had been
lately. Bravely, she stood up and went to the kitchen and put
the water on to boil. By the time she finished her first visit to
the bathroom the water would be ready for the instant coffee.
Certain things she did methodically, no matter what might be
said about her life in general. She was not, for instance, going
to rack her brain with her seven o'clock problem until she had
had some coffee.

It was not necessary.

On the kitchen table, under a pepper-mill to keep it from
being blown away, was a note: "Seven P.M. Jimmy R." It was
in her handwriting, and now it all came back to her. She
poured the hot water over the two teaspoonfuls of coffee powder, stirred it, put in a lump of sugar, took a sip, lit another
cigarette, and slowly drank the strong hot brew. Jimmy
Rhodes, who had brought her home last night, was coming for
a drink at seven o'clock, and her entire future could depend on
what happened then.

In all the years she had been in show business, all the parties
she had gone to, the meals and drinks she had had at the old
Romanoff's, the new Romanoff's, at 21 and Elmer's, the Copa
and the Chez in Chicago, the This and the That in cities all
over the country, the Savoy and the 400 in London, Maxim's
and the Boeuf in Paris—she had never met Jimmy Rhodes
until last night. He had said exactly the same thing. "You
know, Maggie, we should of met before this. I been hearing
about you since—well, I go back to when you were singing
with the old Jack Hillyer band."

"For *get* it," she said. "My God, you know my exact age."

"Within a year or two, most likely. Where you living now? Here, or on the Coast?"

"Oh, here," she said.

"Yeah, I guess the Coast is through," he said.

"Not for TV," she said.

"No, I guess not for TV, but who cares about TV?"

"I do. I go out there every so often to do a guest shot," she said.

"Well, I don't watch it much. What about Vegas?"

"They don't pay anything," she said.

"You know, I heard that, too," he said. "I heard some of those people supposed to be getting like twenty-five gees, I hear it's closer to two or three."

"If that, in a lot of cases," she said. "There's nothing there for me."

"Well, you don't have to work anyway, do you?"

"No, I don't have to. Unless I want to eat. Whose gag is it? I formed a bad habit when I was young. Eating."

"Come on, I thought you—"

"That's what everybody thinks," she said. "Do you think I'd take some of the jobs I take if I still had all that glue?"

"Well, it was over a million bucks, wasn't it?"

"It was nowhere near that," she said. "The papers called it a million-dollar settlement, but what it actually was was twenty-five thousand dollars a year. It'd take me forty years to get a million. So now you know. And I had lawyers to pay."

"Didn't you make Robinson pay the lawyers?"

"That was part of the settlement, yes. But it didn't end there. In other words, the money my lawyers got from the Robinsons didn't entitle me to a free ride for the rest of my life."

"What was the inside on that story, Maggie?"

"The inside? There wasn't any inside, unless you want me to tell you what Robinson was like in the hay, and there you'd be wasting your time, because I wouldn't tell you. Not because I want to protect him. He didn't care what people thought about him, but I just as soon forget about it. And I more or less have. That was a long time ago, and I've had to work for a living. I met worse than Robbie since then."

"Did he beat you?"

"Sure he beat me. That was all proved in court."

"And that caused you to lose the child?"

"Yes. The Robinsons' own doctor had to admit that," she said. "You got me talking about things I stopped talking about seventy-five years ago. Why?"

"Well, I always wanted to meet you. I was in the army when your case came to trial, but I followed it in the papers."

"I didn't know you were ever in the army," she said.

"The army, and then the air force. I was in air force public relations, mostly."

"Well, that figures," she said. "What were you?"

"I came out a major."

"No, I meant what did you do?"

"Oh—a little of this and a little of that. Public relations. I handled the war correspondents from the big papers and press associations. Fellows I knew in civilian life. And some of the big political brass."

"What did you do? Get girls for them?"

"Well, yes, I introduced them to a few girls. How did you happen to pick that out?"

"I didn't pick it out, exactly. You were kind of famous for that, weren't you?"

"At one time, maybe. But I don't have to do that any more."

"Now you're a big shot. Well, I know that, too. I mean, I see your name in the papers. Jimmy Rhodes, Rhodes Associates and all that jazz."

"Why do you want to put me on, Maggie? If I did a little pimping twenty years ago, are you gonna hold it against me now? You ought to come and have a look at my office. I have forty-two people working for me. Six Harvard graduates. Two Vassar girls. A Bryn Mawr girl. I got a half a dozen of my people that are in the Social Register. I got the daughter of a United States senator and I just took on a retired major general of the air force. I got offices in London, Paris, and Madrid."

"My, you're so important I'm surprised you'd even talk to me," she said.

"Well, there were some things I wanted and I never got," he said. "You were one of them."

"Maybe you should have tried a little harder. I was as they say available."

"Not always, and I had a wife a good deal of the time. Two kids. A daughter just graduated from Wellesley last June, and my son's a junior at Princeton."

"You said you had a wife. Past tense. What happened there?"

"Well, she's married again. Married a fellow he's now the managing editor of a paper out West. He was one of the guys I got a girl for in London, and then he came home and moved in on my wife. They were cheating on me for four or five years before I ever got wise to it."

"And all that time you were behaving like a model husband."

"No, I couldn't say that. But when they had me up before that Senate committee, that was when my wife and her boy friend hit me with the divorce suit, and I didn't stand a chance. She got the children, and a bundle of dough. I was practically fighting for my life with those senators. I very nearly went to the cooler. And one night during the hearings I dropped in the Statler and you were there."

"I remember that date. Ted Straeter's band. A two weeks' booking and they held me over another week."

"It was before you married Robinson. He had a table at ringside. I stood. I didn't have a table. And you sang 'More Than You Know,' which I'd never heard you sing before. And 'So in Love.' Those are two I remember. They were giving it to me but *good* in the Senate Office Building, and on top of that my wife's lawyer had got in touch with my lawyer. I had about seventy-five Scotches and I said to myself, this was the night to move in on Maggie Muldoon. So I said to the maître d', a friend of mine from the old days, how about fixing it up for me? He shook his head. 'Not a prayer, Jimmy,' he said. He pointed to Robinson. 'Een like Fleen,' he said. And he was right."

"Yes, I married Robbie two weeks later," she said.

"I know you did. That was as close as I ever came to meeting you."

"Well, where would we be now if you had?" she said.

"Sixteen years. Seventeen years," he said. "You lasted two years with Robinson, and then you married another fellow. How long did that last?"

"Four."

"What was his name again?" he said.

"Dick Hemmendinger. Guitar player. Ladies' man. Junkie. Crossword puzzle expert. And financial wizard—with my money. He died of pneumonia."

"Or froze to death? You ought to know, but didn't I read about him freezing to death?"

"Yes, you could have. They found him in an alleyway in Toronto, Canada. But it was pneumonia. Nobody ever knew what he was doing in Canada. I hadn't heard from him in over a year, and I have to admit I hoped he was gone for good. Well, he was. He was very pretty when I first met him. Kind of on the order of Eddy Duchin. That kind of looks. *And* a good guitar player. But a bum, in spades."

"What did you, marry him on the rebound?"

"Oh, I don't know. He was with Hillyer when I first started out with the bands, but I was Hillyer's girl then. My God, I thought Jack Hillyer was all a girl could ask for. I would of no more thought of cheating on Hillyer, and he was paying me two hundred a week, except weeks when the horses weren't running so good. Most people used to complain about one-nighters, but I didn't. I liked the one-nighters. That meant I got paid. But when we got booked into a hotel or a club date, then Jack'd make a contact with the local bookmakers and I could never be sure if I was going to get paid that week. So a couple times I had to borrow money from the sidemen, like Dick Hemmendinger. For coffee and cakes. Lipstick. The hairdresser. I remember one night in Boston, I showed up with my hair all straggly and no makeup on and Hillyer took a look at me and blew his lid. 'That's what you get,' I said. After that he never held out the whole two hundred, but when he broke up the band he was still in me for over a thousand. And the price

of one abortion. But imagine having a kid by that louse, what
he probably would have been like. Anyway, that was how I
first got to know Dick, and then he wrote me a very sympathetic letter when I was in court with Robbie. I saw Jack Hillyer about two weeks ago, standing at the corner of Fifty-second
and Broadway. Over there near the Local 802 offices. You
know, he was just standing there on the curbstone, not with
anybody, and he looked about seventy-five years old. I could
still recognize him, but he was old. He even had a cane. I went
up and said hello to him. I said, 'Do you remember me, Jack?'
And he looked at me, but I'm positive he's blind in one eye.
'Yes, hello there,' he said. But he didn't know me. 'It's the Muldoon,' I said, and he said, 'The Muldoon, oh, yes. The Muldoon.' Then when he said it a couple times he remembered me.
I asked him what he was doing and he said he was around
looking for musicians. He said he was starting up a new band.
The big name bands were coming back, he said, and he'd been
talking to—then he named off a half a dozen musicians, and
at least half of them were dead. He said he was going out with
an integrated band and he was getting Fletcher Henderson to
do most of his arrangements. Well, how long is it since Fletch
passed on? Is it ten years? It's at least five. He looked just
awful, Hillyer. Clean, but an old polo coat and a Tyrolean hat
with a feather in it. This man I'd been to bed with a hundred
times or more, and there he was all wrapped up in an old polo
coat that was too big for him. So was his hat. His hat was too
big for him, it sort of rested on his ears. And his chin kind of
kept moving up and down, even when he wasn't talking. You
know, I was brought up a Catholic and thought I got over all
that a long time ago, but standing there talking to Jack Hillyer, this man I used to quiver when he touched me, I suddenly
after all these years got a guilty conscience. Sin. I committed
sin with this old man. I didn't, you know. I mean, I slept with
him all those times, but then he was young and built like a life-
guard. Shoulders, and no waistline. I never thought of sin in
those days. But here he looked like he could of been my own
father, and that made me feel like I ought to tell the whole
thing in confession. His neck. The back of his neck so thin and

weak-looking. I didn't mind the lies he was telling. He was always a liar. In fact, that was all that was left of the original Jack, the lies. I don't know how to explain it, how he made me feel sinful. Anyway, I said to him I remembered I owed him twenty dollars from the old days, and I was glad I ran into him. He took the twenty dollars and looked at it, and I knew it would have killed him to part with it, but he said, 'Well, if you're sure you can spare it, and I said yes, and he stuffed it in his coat pocket. Then something went through his mind and it slowly dawned on him that he actually had twenty dollars on him, and he said how would I like to go to Charlie's and have a drink, but I said I had to run. And he began to remember me. I mean, you could see that something was telling him that he used to sleep with me and he said we ought to get together. In the voice of an old man, with his chin moving up and down. And I said to call me, I was in the phone book, which I'm not, and it wouldn't of made any difference because he'd already forgotten my name. So I said goodbye and left him standing there. I saw him put his hand in his pocket and feel the money, but he just kept standing there."

"Jack Hillyer," said Jimmy Rhodes.

She took a long sip of her drink.

"You thinking about Hillyer?" he said.

"I'm thinking about you. There's something you told me and it isn't quite kosher."

"No? What's that? What did I say?"

"Some things I remember and some things I don't, especially before and after I had seventy-five drinks. But I know this much, Mr. Jimmy Rhodes Associates. You're some kind of a liar."

"I'm a habitual liar," he said.

"You are? So am I. That is, I'll tell one to get out of something any time. Mind you, I don't like to be a liar, but in this rat-race that I been in for the past seventy-five years, I never knew anybody that wasn't a liar. Sooner or later, you catch them. But I caught you right away. You said you read about my divorce while you were in the army, but the war was over when I got my divorce. I didn't even marry Robbie till after the war, and if you think back a minute, you just proved it. But your touching little story about being in Washington when I was working at the Statler. That was a couple years after the war. I ought to know when I got married. You see this rock? Six carats. Robbie gave it to me the week we got married, and it's just about the last thing I got left of his presents. But if you wanted to take the trouble to look inside, if you had a magnifying glass, you'd find the date. April the fifth, 1948. So that makes you a liar."

"Well, it wasn't much of a lie. I got a little mixed up, that's all."

"Perfectly all right," she said. "I knew there was something wrong about your stories, because I made a record of 'So in Love,' and I had Robbie at the studio with me. It was the first time he ever saw a recording date, and that had to be at least a couple years after the war."

"Don't tell me you're still in love with Robinson," he said.

"Well, maybe I am. You know, I get these moments when I think back over some fellow. Sometimes it's Robbie. Sometimes it'll be Jack Hillyer. Dick Hemmendinger. George Waller."

"There's George Waller over there in front of the fireplace."

"I know. I came with him. We're nothing now, but we did a little swinging a few years ago. Now I just call him up when I want somebody to take me to a party and I don't have an escort. George went fag a couple years ago."

"That's what I was wondering," he said.

"But every damn one of them—and I didn't give you the whole box-score—they all meant something to me at the time. You take like Hillyer, Jack Hillyer. I was a young kid singing with a band and I was naturally stuck on Hillyer. But if I didn't get stuck on Hillyer, I was the only girl traveling with fifteen musicians and every one of them more or less on the make. I knew one girl—well, never mind. She was with a bigger band than Hillyer's, and she went through them all. But lucky for me I liked Hillyer, and the guys working for him didn't try very hard. Then I went into a couple of shows, and radio, and I married Robbie. He was a dumb cluck, but he had all that glue. And I want to tell *you*, any time I hear anybody talking about the rich people and the way they live, they can ask me, because Robbie's family were really loaded. And I had close to four years of that. They didn't like me, but I was their son's wife, so I got the full treatment. My own personal maid, my own personal car with a chauffeur. I could go to the best restaurants in town and I didn't even have to sign the tab. They put the tips on. Twenty percent for the waiter, ten percent for the captain. I didn't even have to sign my initials. Of course when you have to level and be the man's wife, just you and him, that's the payoff. You're just the same as if you were married to a thirty-five-dollar-a-week guy like my father was, back in Hazleton, PA. Not that Robbie was so bad. But after Hillyer he was kind of a nothing and he knew it, and that's why he began using me for a punching-bag. Some day I knew I'd have to go back to work, and I didn't want him to ruin my looks, so one day I just walked out and didn't come back. There was no objections by his family, and they sent me all my jewelry and clothes. They kept the Cessna. I had a little Cessna I learned to fly, and I logged over two hundred hours in it, but it belonged to some corporation of Mr. Robinson's. It was the only real fun I had all the time I was married to Robbie, was flying that airplane. That, and getting gassed. My grandfather was a lush, and my old man was a strict temperance man, but I take after my grandfather. He used to hold up a glass of whiskey in front of him and smile at it and say, 'My assistant.' He always called it his assistant. So do I, but people don't know what I'm talking about. They think I'm saying my 'assistance,' but they're wrong. I consider it my assis-tant. I don't know what I'd do without my assistant."

"Would you care for another assistant?" said Rhodes.

"You don't call this an assistant, what's in my glass now. Sure."

She opened her purse and looked at herself in the mirror. Her makeup did not need refreshing, and Jimmy Rhodes had been sitting quite close to her for a good half hour. So long as she held up her chin it did not double up, and all things considered—as she looked around at the other women at the party—she did not have to apologize for her appearance. She had been a star, she had been the wife of the heir to a fairly famous fortune, and in the world in which she lived and even beyond it she did not need an introduction. Everyone knew who she was. Jimmy Rhodes certainly knew who she was; he had been having a ball. It was too bad that there was not more to him. He was masculine enough, with a clear and practically unwrinkled complexion. About half of his front hair was gone, but he had all his teeth and obviously he had used them on many good steaks. He was probably twenty-five pounds overweight. His dinner jacket was not what Robbie would have worn—the lapels too narrow, and touches of satin piping at the pockets and on the sleeve. His shoes were funny; patent leather with tassels. And his shirt was frilled down the middle. The rims of his glasses were just a little thicker than they had to be and the lenses were larger than most. There was thought behind everything he had on, and behind the thought no taste. She had learned, in four years, to look at men's attire as Robbie's father or the Robinson butler would look at it, and Jimmy Rhodes was all wrong. Instinctively all wrong. With a great deal of care, all wrong. By the way he had pulled down the jacket when he got up to get her highball, she knew he thought he was all right. He had six Harvard graduates working for him, and nobody to tell him anything.

"Your assistant," he said, handing her the glass.

"Don't you drink?" she said.

"Never after dinner," he said. "I got no taste for it. The same way with smoking. I quit smoking right after I got outa the service. I like to be in good physical condition."

"What for?"

He laughed. "Well, I'm not a weight-lifter. But I can pick up say about a hundred and thirty pounds."

"Close," she said. "I'm a hundred and thirty-two."

"I judged you to be somewhere in there."

"Do you play the field, or do you go steady?" she said.

"Oh, the field. No more wedding bells for me."

"How do you get away with it?" she said.

"How do I get away with it? Well, for a while I used to tell them I was carrying the torch for Grace Kelly. I never even met Grace Kelly, but I owe her a debt of gratitude."

"Send her a planeload of Texas millionaires."

"They don't gamble," he said.

"They don't?"

"They spend it, some of them, but not foolishly, like you and I would. A Texan'll buy a cream-colored Rolls-Royce for $30,000, but don't forget he has the Rolls after he spent that money."

"Who'd want a cream-colored Rolls?"

"Me. I happen to have one downstairs. Wuddia say we take a ride in it? As soon as you're finished with your assistant. Don't hurry."

"Where is this ride going to take us?"

"Well, I have an apartment over on Park."

"Not far enough."

"All right, where is your apartment?"

"That's too far. Much too far," she said.

"Like how far?" he said.

"A lot farther than you're gonna get," she said.

"Do you wanta bet?"

"Not on a sure thing. I'm not a Texan. I don't mind betting but not on a sure thing."

"Why? Don't you like me?"

"The funny thing is, I do," she said.

"What's funny about it? A lot of dames like me."

"Well, I like you," she said.

"Then what's funny about it?"

"It's kind of hard to put into words," she said.

"You're a good talker. You know how to express yourself. Go ahead."

"Well, I like you, but you could never mean anything to me."

"Why not?"

"You don't give out enough. A man has to give out, and you don't. Didn't any other girl ever tell you that?"

"They not only didn't tell me that, but I never even heard about this giving out. You mean like an extrovert?"

"That's a word I never knew the definition of. Try something else."

"Well, a guy that's always giving out, I guess. I give out, but I always keep something in reserve."

"That's what I mean. You keep more in reserve than you give out."

"I guess that's true."

"See, that's where we differ. I give out. With a song, I always gave out. I couldn't belt one like The Merm, but in my own style I always gave out like I was never gonna sing another number the rest of my life. They used to tell me to modulate, but I couldn't modulate. My agents and the a. and r. men at the record companies used to pick numbers for me that I had to modulate, but I gave out anyway. It worked out pretty good on some recordings. Look what Peggy Lee did with 'Lover.' A sickly kind of a waltz that she took and just whaled the hell out of it into an exciting number. Peggy and Ella. This new kid, Eydie Gorme, she might make it. Although she isn't getting to be a kid any more. One more assistant and then I think I'll cut out of here."

"Have it with me, at my apartment."

"Now don't start to be a bore, Jimmy. If you want to take me home, all right. But if you got any ideas about tonight, forget it. I had about seventy-five drinks tonight, and if Richard Burton came knocking on my door I'd send him away. I don't take anybody to my apartment when I made the load. There's two things I don't do. I don't smoke in bed, and I don't take strange guys to my apartment when I get saturated. Those are my only two rules, for my own protection. If you would of come over and introduced yourself to me earlier, it might be a different story. But I got a little bell inside of me that says, 'Maggie, no strange men tonight.'"

"In other words, if I would of come over when you only had thirty-seven and a half drinks? That's half of seventy-five," he said.

"Maybe. But the little bell rang about two hours ago."

"How about if I catch you early tomorrow?"

"How early?"

"We have a couple drinks and go some place for dinner," he said.

"All right. Why not? You call for me at seven o'clock."

He had a cream-colored Rolls. She remembered that, but not much from then on. She got up from the kitchen table and made herself another cup of instant coffee. It was bringing her around. She lit another cigarette and sat down again and as she sipped the coffee she began making plans. Take a shower, and that would bring her to and she could have a vodka after her shower. She would wear her little black dress that actually did more for her figure than the new one with the deep décolletage. She had no idea where he would be taking her in the course of the evening, but she was determined to give him an altogether different impression from the one she had given him last night. The black dress would help there. She would space out her drinks, and if they saw any society people she would be sure to introduce him to them. Society people liked it when she spoke to them, even if they never invited her to their houses. She would show him that she knew how to order a meal—those little questions to the headwaiter, like "Is this hothouse asparagus, or fresh?" She would let him see any number of little things that she had picked up from the Robinsons' butler during those four years. She would come home sober and early, and if everything went as she planned, she soon would have nothing to worry about the rest of her life.

It was bad luck to sing before breakfast, but two coffees were all the breakfast she was going to have, and she hummed a tune as she rinsed out the cup and saucer. She went back to the bathroom and put on a rubber cap and took a shower. She toweled herself, put on her bra and panty-girdle and dressing-gown, and now she had earned her vodka.

The living room was still dark. She switched on the ceiling lights and went to the portable bar. And then she saw him seated in one of the highback chairs. "How the hell did *you* get here?" she said. But even before she finished the question she knew she would never get an answer from him. He was in an attitude of sleep, an unattractive attitude. His mouth was open, and so were his eyes. The poor slob, in his frilly shirt and tasseled shoes. For all she knew, or would ever know, he had died while waiting for her to call him to her room. The worst was his eyes, seen through those thick lenses.

She had her vodka, her assistant, and went to the telephone in her bedroom. The logical person to call was her lawyer, and she did not have to look up his number. She knew it by heart.

(1965)

AT THE COTHURNOS CLUB

Although the Cothurnos Club was founded by actors a limited number of writers and painters are taken in from time to time, and that is how I chance to be a member. It is the pleasantest of places; in the reading- and writing-rooms pin-drop quiet prevails, while in the bar and billiard room and dining room there is very little likelihood of a man's feeling lonesome. Especially is this true of the dining room, where most of the members eat at a large round table. After I had been honored by admission to the club I took to lunching there nearly every day and that was how I happened to notice Mr. Childress. He always ate alone at a small table against the wall. He never seemed to speak to anyone, for surely the nod that he gave the men at the round table could not be taken as a greeting. A few days ago I asked Clem Kirby, who put me up for the club, to tell me about the reclusive Mr. Childress. "Has he been a member long?" I said.

"Oh, yes," said Kirby. "About thirty years, I should say."

"But was he always like that? I don't see why a man like that joins a club, he's so anti-social."

Kirby smiled. "Maybe it's hard to believe, but up till about ten or twelve years ago George Childress was just the opposite of what you see today. Full of beans. Witty. Here every day, down in the bar, drinking with the boys, and so on."

"What does he do?" I asked.

"He paints, or did. He was what's commonly called a fashionable portrait painter, and he made a lot of money, and while I don't think anyone could call George stingy, he took care of his money. He hasn't done anything in recent years. That's probably why you've never heard of him."

"Vaguely I have," I said.

"He married Hope Westmore," said Kirby.

"Oh, of course," I said. "That's where I've heard of him. Hope Westmore's husband. She was one of my all-time favorite actresses. So that's George Childress. Are they still married?"

"Married, yes," said Kirby. "But of course—" Clem did not finish his sentence. His eyes turned sad. "I'll tell you about George.

"He wasn't exactly a practical joker, but he was something of the sort, especially with, well, someone like you, a new member. He'd find out all he could about you, and then before being introduced to you he'd discuss your work, whatever it was, in your hearing, and I may say the opinions he'd come out with would be devastating. He did it, of course, to get a rise out of new members. A cruel trick. What you younger fellows nowadays call a rib. He had several little tricks like that. He also invented another one, with a new twist.

"He would join a group of fellows in the bar, all old members except one. Everybody was on to the trick but the new member. George would be introduced and he'd be his most charming, affable self. Then slowly he would get the conversation around to the theater and he would say, 'What was the name of that actress a few years back. Terribly good actress. Beautiful. But drank herself out of every job she had?' And he'd pretend to rack his brains, trying to recall the name. The fellows who were in on the trick would also pretend to search their memories, and of course what would happen would be that the new member, trying to be helpful, would volunteer a name. Now George's point was that he never got the same answer twice, or did very seldom.

"Well, I see you know what happened. You're right. One day we were down in the bar and there was a new member, a young fellow, and when George couldn't remember the actress's name the young fellow popped up with a name, and of course the name was Hope Westmore."

"Good Lord," I said. "What happened?"

"Well," said Clem Kirby, "there was a stillness that I thought would never end. You've seen for yourself, George is a powerfully built man and I've never seen anyone exercise such self-control. But he took a deep breath and said, 'You see, gentlemen, I never get the same answer twice,' and then he excused himself. As far as I know that's the last time George has been in the bar."

"What about Hope Westmore. Was it true?" I said.

Kirby looked at me long and steadily. "I don't see that that makes the slightest difference," he said.

(1972)

THE BRAIN

A certain type of man gets a certain type of headachey look about him long before his headaches become more or less chronic. In the case of Robert Ammond, vice-president of Ammond & Stepworth, publishers of technical books for the electrical and mechanical engineering professions, the look preceded the incidence of migraine headaches by about fifteen years. In his late twenties Robert Ammond began wearing glasses full-time, but already he had a fixed, intense, squinty look in the triangle between the tip of his nose and the extremities of his eyebrows. He seemed to be concentrating all the time, especially during those moments when it could be presumed that there was no call for concentration. Gazing out a train window, standing on the first tee while the foursome ahead of him got under way, sitting in the company box at the Yankee Stadium while one team was taking the field and the other getting ready to go to bat, Robert Ammond gave every appearance of having his mind on one of the hard problems in an A. & S. textbook. The truth was that Robert had had a liberal arts education and was in the advertising department of A. & S., and he could not have solved a problem in high school physics, although he had passed physics with a little to spare. Nevertheless people gave Robert credit for concentrative powers. He remembered every card that had been played during a hand of bridge, and his post-mortems were exhaustive. He was very good at reciting the complete casts of old movies. No one challenged his memory for baseball statistics. "I wouldn't take your money," he would say when someone offered to bet him on who had the record for the most putouts in World

Series play. Such demonstrations of a head for figures and a powerful memory were of course supported by the concentrative look, and there was hardly any doubt that Robert deserved the routine promotions that were given him in the A. & S. organization. "Fellow's smart as a whip," they said. "*His* name didn't have to be Ammond," the only possible inference being that Robert's younger brother George was in the organization only because his grandfather was its founder. George was in the production department, with the title of vice-president, but the work was done by a plant superintendent and a couple of foremen. George was a good-time Charley who was always put in charge of the A. & S. exhibits at the engineering conventions and acted as host in the A. & S. suite down the hall. He had early symptoms of emphysema at the age of thirty, but he could stay up all night with the best of them. His untimely death at age thirty-eight left Robert the only direct descendant of the founder still in the organization, and while ownership and control of the company had passed on to the vast Wycherly Enterprises, Robert apparently was set for life, at $30,000 per annum and bonuses. Wycherly Enterprises did not sign that kind of contract, but Robert Ammond and his friends were far from worried. Robert, as well as his friends, took the position that a contract carried with it certain disadvantages for a man who could reasonably count on twenty good years ahead of him. The electrical and mechanical field was wide open, and family pride would not tie him down if for instance a Wycherly competitor should decide to organize a new publishing house. The Ammond name was one of the oldest in the trade, and Robert had no contractual obligations to prevent his going on the board of a brand-new outfit.

To that extent Robert Ammond did begin to concentrate. That is to say, he began to give a great deal of thought to the possibility of a new publishing firm. Wycherly (which was headed by a man named Dennis Brady, from Chicago) had put all its own men in the top jobs at A. & S., which was to be expected, but at the end of two years Robert Ammond had not been put on the new A. & S. board, which was definitely not expected. During those two years Robert had been bereft—temporarily, he believed—of his vice-presidential title and he had been functioning with the title of advertising manager. He continued to use—and to use up, as he put it—his old stationery, which proclaimed him "Vice-President in Charge of Advertising," but only in personal correspondence with friends in the advertising business and in such trivial communications as letters to his alumni weekly. He had about a thousand sheets of the old stationery still to be used up when he was visited one afternoon by a fellow called Spencer, who was known as Mr. Brady's troubleshooter.

Spencer did not customarily make appointments, nor did he for his visit to Robert Ammond. He opened the door of Robert's private office—unannounced by Miss Hathaway—and poked his head in and said, "May I come in?" He was wearing his perpetual grin.

"Why, hello, Spencer. Yes, come right in," said Robert.

"Thank you," said Spencer. He sat down without shaking hands or taking any other notice of the fact that this was his first visit to Robert's office. "Minor matter, and not important enough to put in an inter-office memo. But Mr. Brady is a stickler for form in some things."

"Oh, really?"

"Yes. In as big an organization as Wycherly, the uh, the uh, precise position of one man vis-à-vis the other members of the organization has to be stated and maintained. Do you know how it works in the federal government, for instance?"

"You mean where they give a man a classification number, and that determines whether he rates a Chevy or a Buick?"

"Exactly. Who gets pictures on the wall, who gets a leather easy chair and so on. I see you're familiar with that. Good. That makes it easier for me, and *you* won't misunderstand."

"Let's have it, if it's something I've done."

Spencer took a deep breath, and put his fingertips together. "I only want to call your attention to the fact that since the reorganization, you have not yet been made a vice-president. I stress that *not yet*, thereby not ruling out the possibility that you'll get your old title back. However, for the present, Ammond, you're not actually a vice-president in the Wycherly organization."

"No one knows that better than I do, Spencer."

"I'm sure of it. And yet I have here in my pocket, let's see, here it is. This is from the Princeton Alumni magazine. It seems to be a letter you wrote, fairly recently, and it gives your title as Vice-President in Charge of Advertising."

Ammond laughed. "I can explain that easily enough."

"Before you do, I also have a Xerox copy of a letter you wrote to a man in one of the big advertising agencies. It's a personal letter, nothing about Wycherly Enterprises or Ammond & Stepworth. Nevertheless, it was written on old stationery that has your name and your old title."

"A small economy on my part. I never use that letterhead in business correspondence."

"I know you don't. Before coming in here I took a sampling of your recent files."

"Boy, you are thorough."

"You bet I am. That's my job." For just a brief moment the perpetual smile all but vanished. "This may seem picayune to you, Ammond, but what's actually happened here is not so damned lintpicking at all. By that I mean, the Wycherly organization is very, very big, as you well know. And getting bigger all the time. And unless we have well-defined policies concerning certain things, we're going to have inefficiency and confusion. You don't know it, but you have an opposite number in a smelting operation we own in Montana. Personnel might decide to have you and him switch jobs. We do that all the time, and it often works out very well. Not always, but by the time we're ready to move, we've studied the various factors pretty carefully."

"I hope you're not going to ask me to transfer to Montana, because I might have a little to say about that."

"The point is, if the Montana man came here and discovered that he was being swapped for a Wycherly vice-president, he might get off to a very bad start. Do you see why this isn't lintpicking? The Montana man would want a promotion to vice-president before we were ready to give it to him."

"Uh-huh. And the vice-president wouldn't want to be downgraded," said Ammond.

"Well, in actual practice we don't do much of that. We buy up the rest of a man's contract, if he has one, or we turn him loose. A downgraded man is a sorehead, and he's no good to anybody, least of all himself. If a man is to be downgraded, that is, if a man reaches a stage where we have to lift him out of his job, we want to be as fair as we can. We'd much rather fire a man than demote him. He can put himself in the executive market and maybe even better himself. Some men, of course we may come across a special situation where a man ought to take a long leave of absence. We have a talk with him. Personnel. Psychiatrist. Medical man. Marriage counselor. We may talk to his wife. We're not all that inhuman, you know. We have fifteen men right now, men in grades above the one you're in, who are on temporary leave of absence, trying to straighten out one problem or another. And of course we're always helping men to place themselves with other organizations. And always on the lookout for good men who want to leave other organizations. We steal, just like the rest of them. Well, I have to be in Chicago in two hours from now. Glad to've had the chance to talk to you."

"I'll see that those letterheads are destroyed."

"I wish all my chores were as easy as this one. Tonight I'm having dinner with four United States senators."

"In Chicago?"

"No, no. In Washington. I'll only be with Mr. Brady a half an hour."

"I feel strangely honored to take up so much of your time. Four U.S. senators. I'd like to meet Mr. Brady sometime."

"So would the senators, face to face across the table in the Caucus Room. My chore is to try to persuade them that that would serve no useful purpose, and I'm licked before I start, especially in a presidential year. They want Mr. Brady, and they're going to get Mr. Brady, and he'll be completely cooperative. But I have to make it a little hard for them. Not telling you any secrets. It'll be in all the papers the day after tomorrow."

"Are you thinking of firing me, Mr. Spencer?" said Robert.

"The only man not facing that possibility is Mr. Brady himself. How's that for an equivocal answer? So long, Ammond."

One of the most difficult tasks Robert ever had was to give Miss Hathaway the order to destroy the remaining stock of old letterheads, and she was sympathetic. She was always on his side, always saw his side of every question, and she had become indispensable. If she had been just a little less plain, perhaps just a little less devoted to her mother, she could have been, might have been, more to him than merely his secretary. For things at home were going through one of those periods of strain that can develop in any marriage. Yolanda Ammond, with both children away at boarding-school, had more time on her hands, but she could not find the time to do things she wanted to do because she was not sure what she wanted to do. She had become, for example, a lingerer: she was the last to leave ladies' luncheons because she had no place else to go. She engaged in long conversations with the people in the markets and in the shops, and she despised them because they were always having to excuse themselves to go wait on another customer. Yolanda was a retired pretty girl. Twenty years earlier she had been the prettiest girl in all The Oranges, or anyway a strong contender for the title. She had retained much of her girlhood prettiness, but no one retains it all, and in some cases, like Yolanda's, the prettiness of girlhood is anomalous in a woman of forty. A hostile acquaintance described Yolanda as an overgrown midget, which some women in their circle of friends took as an oblique reference to Yolanda's intellect. She was *not* a brain, and some of Robert's admirers thought it unfair to make any comparison between her mind and his. The extremely fair among their friends, who were aware of the imperfect state of relations between Yolanda and Robert, said it was a pity that Yolanda had no resources to fall back on, but Robert had always been so far ahead of her mentally that he had never taken the trouble or had the patience to develop that side of her, such as it was. You had only to look at the two of them together—Yolanda with her empty, pretty face, and Robert deep in thought—to see that this marriage had been headed for trouble from the start. Yolanda was no good at bridge, just as bad at canasta, and a pigeon at gin rummy. It took her three months to read *Peyton Place*, and after all that work she confessed her disappointment in it. She said she did not know whether it was well written or not, but the stuff in it was no worse than some of the things she knew about friends of hers, if they wanted to be truthful about it.

Sympathy was not entirely on Robert's side. Not only was it felt that he could have tried a little harder to interest Yolanda in the things of the mind, but he had not always been fully appreciative of the job she did in running the household and bringing up the children. Robert took an awful lot for granted, and he did not seem to realize what a lot of work went into having a neat, attractive home and kids who were a credit to their parents. A man like Robert Ammond, prominent in the publishing business, thinking up new ideas and dealing with those scientists, could probably be darn hard to live with. And one thing you had to say for Yolanda: although she was still pretty and had a nice figure, she did not play around. Two cocktails was her limit, and if any of the boys got the least bit out of line, Yolanda knew how to put a stop to it, and did so. Robert, on the other hand, was not *all* intellectual. Edna Watlinger had accidentally opened the coat closet one night at a party at Peggy Stuart's and found Peggy and Robert in a very compromising position, to say the least. And there were other little stories here and there that would not have amounted to much if they had been about anyone else, but they certainly proved that Robert Ammond was not perfect. Not that Robert had ever gotten involved in a big thing with any other girl, but he certainly was not perfect.

Other marriages had weathered worse storms than this, and as far as their friends knew, the Ammonds' difficulties had not reached any crisis. Nothing that could be called dramatic. It was what might be called a familiar American situation, in which the wife found herself with not enough to do, and the husband was so intent on business that he did not find the time to rectify matters before they got worse. This belief, this diagnosis, as it were, was so strongly held by the Ammonds' friends that no one could believe the real news about Robert. But it was true. Robert Ammond, surely one of the brightest men around, had been fired.

As it happened, Stan Musgrove was the only man among the Ammonds' friends who was in a position to get close to the story. Stan was in Research at an advertising agency, and he had never had any direct business contact with Robert Ammond. But when a thing like this happened to a friend of yours, you wanted to know more about it. Robert would only say that he had been fired and ask to change the subject, but it was plain to see that that mind was turning the subject over and over, and his friends were sure he would come up with something pretty good. Meanwhile, however, his friends had to have *some* information, and Stan inquired around until a perfectly credible story had been pieced together. It was incredible, but Stan insisted that his best contacts would vouch for its authenticity.

According to Stan's version, Robert had had some unimportant tangle with Dennis Brady's chief troubleshooter, a man named Spencer. It started over nothing, as those things will. The Wycherly crowd had asked Robert to do some kind of survey of some mining properties that Wycherly owned in Colorado. It was not to be a scientific, or engineering survey, but a study of executive personnel. Robert protested that it was not his kind of work, but Spencer tried to persuade him that that was the way they often did things in the Wycherly organization. The outsider with the fresh point of view. But when Spencer mentioned that Robert would probably have to spend two or three months in Colorado, Robert turned down the whole thing, flat. Spencer was quite disappointed, because he had to go back to Dennis Brady and report failure. Robert, being no fool, perceived that this could mean a loss of face for Spencer, and that Spencer, who was a sort of high-powered errand boy, would bide his time and at the right moment, no matter how long it might take, would give Dennis Brady a bad report on Robert. Any man with a responsible job is bound to make some mistakes. John J. McGraw never fined a ballplayer for a fielding error; McGraw's theory was that the man was in there trying, and it was the same way in business. You did occasionally come up with a real blooper.

Well, according to Stan Musgrove, Robert had the thing all

figured out, as he would with that analytical mind of his, and so he quietly and carefully and methodically went about the business of interesting various individuals in an idea he had. The idea was simply to start a new publishing house, just as his grandfather had done. He lined up some pretty good men, men who were not too old to be set in their ways and not so young that later, when they went to the money men, they would be turned down for their youth and lack of experience. Bolger Brothers, who had about the same kind of setup as Wycherly Enterprises, were a natural for the financing of the new publishing firm, and one of the fellows Robert had lined up had a very good in at Bolgers'. Some family connection. But the fellow must have spoken too soon, and certainly without Robert's authorization, because the leak could almost positively be traced to Bolger Brothers. And that cooked it.

Apparently Spencer flew to New York one morning in time to be sitting in Robert's private office when Robert arrived for work. Robert's secretary tipped off Robert that Spencer was waiting for him. Her name was Hawthorne. Miss Hawthorne. Had been with Robert for fifteen years, and she was one of those really loyal secretaries that every executive dreams about. In any case, Robert went in and found Spencer sitting at his desk and actually reading his mail. The argument started right away, and it could be easily overheard. They made no effort to keep their voices down.

"What the hell do you think you're doing?" Robert said.

"I'm reading the company mail," said Spencer. "What's it to you?"

"It's this to me, if you don't get the hell out of here, I'll resign."

"You have resigned," said Spencer. "All you have to do is put your signature at the bottom of this letter." And Spencer handed him a letter of resignation, all written out, with all the details about its being his understanding that the resignation was to take effect as of above date, that same day, and that he agreed to accept one year's salary as final payment and in return for his discontinuing his efforts to organize a publishing company in direct competition with the firm of Ammond & Stepworth.

"I won't sign this," said Robert. "That's more like a confession than a resignation."

"Then you'll take what you get, which is the absolute minimum," said Spencer. "You're fired, as of nine-thirty-five this date. The inkstand belongs to you, and those family photographs. The rest is ours, so beat it."

And that was Stan Musgrove's version, not necessarily accurate in every small detail, but all from pretty reliable sources. Miss Hawthorne, Robert's secretary, stayed on at Ammond & Stepworth because she had this mother she supported, and anyway Robert would not need a secretary until he made up his mind about what he wants to do next. Yolanda has been taking a course in typing, and at least that gives her something to occupy her time. Their friends say they are not really so terribly badly off, except for Robert and his migraine headaches. He ought to take it easy for a while.

                                                                    (1964)

BREAD ALONE

It was the eighth inning, and the Yankees had what the sports-writers call a comfortable lead. It was comfortable for them, all right. Unless a miracle happened, they had the ball game locked up and put away. They would not be coming to bat again, and Mr. Hart didn't like that any more than he was liking his thoughts, the thoughts he had been thinking ever since the fifth inning, when the Yanks had made their five runs. From the fifth inning on, Mr. Hart had been troubled with his conscience.

Mr. Hart was a car-washer, and what colored help at the Elbee Garage got paid was not much. It had to house, feed, and clothe all the Harts, which meant Mr. Hart himself; his wife, Lolly Hart; his son, Booker Hart; and his three daughters, Carrie, Linda, and the infant, Brenda Hart. The day before, Mr. Ginsburg, the bookkeeper who ran the shop pool, had come to him and said, "Well, Willie, you win the sawbuck."

"Yes sir, Mr. Ginsburg, I sure do. I was watchin' them news-papers all week," said Mr. Hart. He dried his hands with the chamois and extended the right.

"One, two, three, four, five, six, seven, eight, nine, anduh tenner. Ten bucks, Willie," said Mr. Ginsburg. "Well, what are you gonna do with all that dough? I'll bet you don't tell your wife about it."

"Well, I don't know, Mr. Ginsburg. She don't follow the scores, so she don't know I win. I don't know what to do," said Mr. Hart. "But say, ain't I suppose to give you your cut? I understand it right, I oughta buy you a drink or a cigar or something."

"That's the custom, Willie, but thinking it over, you weren't winners all year."

"No sir, that's right," said Mr. Hart.

"So I tell you, if you win another pool, you buy me *two* drinks or *two* cigars. Are you going in this week's pool?"

"Sure am. It don't seem fair, though. Ain't much of the season left and maybe I won't win again. Sure you don't want a drink or a cigar or something?"

"That's all right, Willie," said Mr. Ginsburg.

On the way home, Mr. Hart was a troubled man. That money belonged in the sugar bowl. A lot could come out of that money: a steak, stockings, a lot of stuff. But a man was entitled to a little pleasure in this life, the only life he ever had. Mr. Hart had not been to a ball game since about fifteen or twenty years ago, and the dime with which he bought his ticket in the pool every week was his own money, carfare money. He made it up by getting rides home, or pretty near home, when a truck-driver or private chauffeur friend was going Harlem-ward; and if he got a free ride, or two free rides, to somewhere near home every week, then he certainly was entitled to use the dime for the pool. And this was the first time he had won. Then there was the other matter of who won it for him: the Yankees. He had had the Yankees and the Browns in the pool, the first time all season he had picked the Yanks, and it was they who made the runs that had made him the winner of the ten dollars. If it wasn't for those Yankees, he wouldn't have won. He owed it to them to go and buy tickets and show his gratitude. By the time he got home his mind was made up. He had the next afternoon off, and, by God, he was going to see the Yankees play.

There was, of course, only one person to take; that was Booker, the strange boy of thirteen who was Mr. Hart's only son. Booker was a quiet boy, good in school, and took after his mother, who was quite a little lighter complected than Mr. Hart. And so that night after supper he simply announced, "Tomorrow me and Booker's going over to see the New York Yankees play. A friend of mine happened to give me a choice pair of seats, so me and Booker's taking in the game." There

had been a lot of talk, and naturally Booker was the most surprised of all—so surprised that Mr. Hart was not sure his son
was even pleased. Booker was a very hard one to understand.
Fortunately, Lolly believed right away that someone had really
given Mr. Hart the tickets to the game; he had handed over his
pay as usual, nothing missing, and that made her believe his
story.

But that did not keep Mr. Hart from having an increasingly
bad time from the fifth inning on. And Booker didn't help him
to forget. Booker leaned forward and he followed the game all
right but never said anything much. He seemed to know the
game and to recognize the players, but never *talked*. He got up
and yelled in the fifth inning when the Yanks were making
their runs, but so did everybody else. Mr. Hart wished the
game was over.

DiMaggio came to bat. Ball one. Strike one, called. Ball
two. Mr. Hart wasn't watching with his heart in it. He had his
eyes on DiMaggio, but it was the crack of the bat that made
Mr. Hart realize that DiMaggio had taken a poke at one, and
the ball was in the air, high in the air. Everybody around Mr.
Hart stood up and tried to watch the ball. Mr. Hart stood up
too. Booker sort of got up off the seat, watching the ball but
not standing up. The ball hung in the air and then began to
drop. Mr. Hart was judging it and could tell it was going to hit
about four rows behind him. Then it did hit, falling the last
few yards as though it had been thrown down from the sky,
and smacko! it hit the seats four rows behind the Harts,
bounced high but sort of crooked, and dropped again to the
row directly behind Mr. Hart and Booker.

There was a scramble of men and kids, men hitting kids and
kids darting and shoving men out of the way, trying to get the
ball. Mr. Hart drew away, not wanting any trouble, and then
he remembered Booker. He turned to look at Booker, and
Booker was sitting hunched up, holding his arms so's to protect his head and face.

"Where the hell's the ball? Where's the ball?" Men and kids
were yelling and cursing, pushing and kicking each other, but
nobody could find the ball. Two boys began to fight because

one accused the other of pushing him when he almost had his hand on the ball. The fuss lasted until the end of the inning. Mr. Hart was nervous. He didn't want any trouble, so he concentrated on the game again. Booker had the right idea. He was concentrating on the game. They both concentrated like hell. All they could hear was a mystified murmur among the men and kids. "Well, somebody must of got the god-damn thing." In two minutes the Yanks retired the side and the ball game was over.

"Let's wait till the crowd gets started going, Pop," said Booker.

"O.K.," said Mr. Hart. He was in no hurry to get home, with the things he had on his mind and how sore Lolly would be. He'd give her what was left of the ten bucks, but she'd be sore anyhow. He lit a cigarette and let it hang on his lip. He didn't feel so good sitting there with his elbow on his knee, his chin on his fist.

"Hey, Pop," said Booker.

"Huh?"

"Here," said Booker.

"What?" said Mr. Hart. He looked at his son. His son reached inside his shirt, looked back of him, and then from the inside of the shirt he brought out the ball. "Present for you," said Booker.

Mr. Hart looked down at it. "Lemme see that!" he said. He did not reach for it. Booker handed it to him.

"Go ahead, take it. It's a present for you," said Booker.

Suddenly Mr. Hart threw back his head and laughed. "I'll be god-damn holy son of a bitch. You got it? The ball?"

"Sure. It's for you," said Booker.

Mr. Hart threw back his head again and slapped his knees. "I'll be damn—boy, some Booker!" He put his arm around his son's shoulders and hugged him. "Boy, some Booker, huh? You givin' it to me? Some Booker!"

(1939)

CALL ME, CALL ME

Her short steps, that had always called attention to her small stature, now served to conceal the fact that her walk was slower. Now, finally, there was nothing left of the youth that had lasted so long, so well into her middle age. Her hat was small and black, a cut-down modified turban that made only the difference between being hatted and hatless but called no attention to the wearer, did not with spirit of defiance or gaiety proclaim the wearer to be Joan Hamford. Her Persian lamb, a good one bought in prosperous days, was now a serviceable, sensible garment that kept her warm and nothing more. She wore shoes that she called—echoing her mother's designation—"ties." They were very comfortable and they gave her good support.

The greeting by the doorman was precisely accorded. No "Good morning," but "You'll have a taxi, Miss Hamford?" If she wanted a taxi, he was there to get her a taxi; that was one of the things he was paid for; but he could expect no tip now and she gave him little enough at Christmas. She was one of the permanent guests of the hotel, those whom he classified as salary people because he was paid a salary for providing certain services. Salary people. Bread-and-butter people. Not tip people, not big-gravy, expense-account people. Salary people. Budget people. Instant-coffee-and-half-a-pint-of-cream-from-the-delicatessen people. Five-dollars-in-an-envelope-with-his-name-on-it-at-Christmas people. The hotel was coming down in another year, and the hotel that was going up in its place would have no room for salary people. Only expense-account people.

"Taxi? Yes, please, Roy. Or I'd make just as good time walking, wouldn't I?"

"I don't know, Miss Hamford. I don't know where you're going."

"It is a little far," said Joan Hamford. "Yes, a taxi. *There's one!*"

She always did that. She always spotted a taxi, so that it would seem that she had really found it herself, unaided, and really owed him nothing. He was wise to that one. He was wise to all her little tricks and dodges, her ways of saving quarters, her half pints of cream from the delicatessen. She must be on her way to a manager's office today. Most days she would not take a taxi. "Such a nice day, I think a stroll," she would say, and then stroll exactly one block to the bus stop. But today it was a taxi, because she didn't want to be worn out when she applied for a job. Yes, today was a job day; she was wearing her diamond earrings and her pearls, which were usually kept in the hotel safe.

"Six-thirty Fifth Avenue, will you tell him, please, Roy?"

"Six-thirty Fifth," he said to the taxi driver. She could have given the address herself, but this was a cheap way of queening it. He closed the door behind her and stepped back to the curb.

"Number Six Hundred and Thirty, Avenue Five," said the driver, starting the meter. "Well, you got anything to read, lady, because the traffic on Madison and Fifth, I can't promise you nothing speed-wise. You wanta try Park, we'll make better time going down Park, but I won't guarantee you going west."

"How long will it take us if we go down Fifth?"

"Fifth? You wanta go down Fifth? I give you an honest estimate of between twenty and twenty-five minutes. Them buses, you know. You ever go to the circus and take notice to the elephants, the one holds on to the-one-in-front-of-him's tail with his trunk. That's the way the buses operate. Never no less than four together at the one time, and what they do to congest up the traffic! You see they could straighten that out in two hours if they just handed out a bunch of summonses, but then the union would pull the men off the buses and the merchants would holler to the powers-that-be, City Hall. I'm getting out of this city . . . We'll try Fifth . . . It's Miss Joan Hamford, isn't it?"

"Why, yes. How nice of you."

"Oh, I rode you before. You remember when you used to live over near the River? Four-what-is-it? Four-fifty East Fifty-second?"

"Oh, heavens, that long ago?"

"Yeah, I had one of them big Paramounts, twice the size of this little crate. You don't remember Louis?"

"Louis?"

"Me. Louis Jaffee. I used to ride you four-five times a week regular, your apartment to the Henry Miller on Forty-third, east of Broadway. Fifteen-and-five in those days, but you were good for a buck every night. Well, I'm still hacking, but you been in movies and TV and now I guess you're on your way to make another big deal for TV."

"No, as a matter of fact, a play. On Broadway. I'm afraid I can't tell you just what play, but it isn't television. Still a secret, you know."

"Oh, sure. Then you was out in Hollywood all that time I remember."

"Yes, and I did a few plays in London."

"That I didn't know about. I just remember you rode out the bonnom of the depression in Hollywood. The bonnom of the depression for me, but not for you. You must of made a killing out there. What does it feel like to see some of them pictures now, on TV? You don't get any royalties on them pictures, do you?"

"No."

"Now they all go in for percentages I understand. Be nice to have a percentage of some of them oldies. Is Charles J. Hall still alive?"

"No, poor Charles passed on several years ago."

"You always heard how he was suppose to be a terrific boozer, but I seen him the other night on TV. You were his wife, where you were trying to urge him to give up the Navy and head up this big shipbuilding company."

"*Glory in Blue.*"

"*Glory in Blue,* that's the one. How old was Charles J. Hall when you made that picture, do you remember?"

"How old? I should think Charles was in his early forties then."

"Christ! He'd be in his seventies."

"Yes, he would."

"I'm over the sixty mark myself, but I can't picture Charles J. Hall in his seventies."

"Well, he never quite reached them, poor dear."

"Booze, was it?"

"Oh, I don't like to say that."

"There's a lot worse you could say about some of those jerks they got out there now. Male *and* female. What they need out there is another Fatty Arbuckle case, only the trouble is the public is got so used to scandal."

"Yes, I suppose so."

"You know I was just thinking, I wonder how I missed it when Charles J. Hall passed away. Was it during the summer? I go away in the summer and I don't see a paper for two weeks."

"Yes, I think it was."

"They would have had something in."

"They didn't have very much, not as much as he deserved, considering what a really big star he was."

"But there was a long time when he wasn't in anything. That's when I understood he was hitting the booze so bad. Where was he living during that time?"

"In Hollywood. He stayed right there."

"Wouldn't take anything but big parts, I guess. That's where you were smart, Miss Hamford."

"How do you mean?"

"Well, they forgot all about Charles J. Hall. Like my daughter didn't know who the hell he was last week. But she'd know you. She'd know you right away, because from TV, when you were that lady doctor two years ago, that serial."

"Unfortunately only lasted twenty-six weeks."

"I don't care. Your face is still familiar to the new generation. I don't know what any actress fools around with Broadway for."

"Some of us love the theater."

"Sure, there's that, but I'm speaking as a member of the public. You could be in *My Fair Lady* and there wouldn't be as many people see you as if you went in one big spectacular. When I see my daughter tomorrow night, when she comes for supper, I'm gunna tell her I rode Joan Hamford. And right away she's gunna say 'Doctor McAllister? Doctor Virginia McAllister?' So they took it off after twenty-six weeks, but just think of how many million people saw you *before* they took it off. Up there in the millions. The so-called Broadway theater, that's gettin' to be for amateurs and those that, let's face it, can't get a job in TV."

"Oh, you mustn't say that."

"Well, I'm only telling you what the public thinks, basing it on my own conclusions. Here you are, Six-three-oh. Eighty-five on the clock."

"Here, Louis. I want you to have this."

"The five?"

"For old times' sake."

"Well, thanks. Thanks a lot, Miss Hamford. The best to you, but TV is where you ought to be."

She hoarded her strength during the walk to the elevator, and she smiled brightly at the receptionist in the office of Ralph Sanderson–Otto B. Kolber. "Mr. Sanderson is expecting you, Miss Hamford. Go right in."

"Good morning, Ralph," said Joan Hamford.

Sanderson rose. "Good morning, Joan. Nice of you to come down at this hour, but unfortunately it was the only absolutely only time I had. You know anything about this play?"

"Only what I've read about it."

"Well, then you probably don't know anything about the part."

"No, not really. I read the book, the novel, but I understand that's been changed."

"Oh, hell, the novel. We only kept the boy and his uncle, from the novel."

"The boy's aunt? She's not in the play? Then what is there for me, Ralph? Or would you rather have me read the play instead of you telling me?"

"No, I'd just as soon tell you. Do you remember the school-teacher?"

"The schoolteacher? Let me think. There *was* a school-teacher in one of the early chapters, but I don't think she had a name."

"In the novel she didn't. But she has in the play."

"You really must have changed the novel. How does the part develop?"

"Well, frankly it doesn't. We only keep the teacher for one scene in the first act."

"Oh, well, Ralph, you didn't bring me down here for that. That isn't like you. Good heavens, even if I'd never done any-thing else, I was Dr. Virginia McAllister to God knows how many million people, and I got twenty-two-fifty for that."

"Three years ago, Joan, and you haven't had much to do since. That's why I thought of you for the teacher. I'd rather give it to you than someone I don't know. I'll pay three-fifty."

"What for? You can't bill me over the others, the part isn't big enough to do that."

"I couldn't anyway. The boy gets top billing, and Michael Ware is co-star. Tom Ruffo in *Illinois Sonata with* Michael Ware. But I admit you'd lead the list of featured players."

"You know how these things are, Ralph. Not a manager in town but will know I'm working for three-fifty."

"But working, and I'll take care of you publicity-wise. The theater doesn't pay movie or TV salaries, you know that."

"I understand Jackie Gleason got six thousand."

"He may have got more, but Virginia McAllister wasn't Ralph Kramden. I wish you'd think about this, Joan. It's not physically very demanding. You don't have to stand around or do any acrobatics."

"Or act, either, I suppose. No, I'm afraid not, Ralph, and I really think you were rather naughty to bring me down here."

"Joan, this is a fine play and with this boy Ruffo we're going to run ten months, and maybe a lot longer. For you it would be like a vacation with pay, and you'd be back in the theater. Stop being a stubborn bitch, and think back to times when I paid you sixty dollars a week for more work."

"In that respect you haven't changed, Ralph."

"Four hundred."

"Take-home that's still only a little over three hundred. No, I'm going right on being a stubborn bitch."

"I'll give you four hundred, and I'll release you any time after the first six months that you find a better part."

"Can you write me into the second and third acts?"

"Impossible. The locale changes, and anyway, I know the author wouldn't do it. And frankly I wouldn't ask him to. No more tinkering with this play till we open in Boston."

"Well—still friends, Ralph. You tried."

"Yes, I certainly tried."

She reached out her hand. "Give me five dollars for the taxi."

"Joan, are you that broke?"

"No, I'm not broke, but that's what it cost me to come here."

Sanderson pulled a bill from a money-clip. "If it cost you five to get here it'll cost you another five to get home. Here's a sawbuck."

"I only wanted five, but of course I'll take the ten. In the old days you would have spent more than that on taking me to lunch."

"Considering where we usually ended up after lunch, the price wasn't high."

"I guess that's a compliment."

"You know, you have delusions of Laurette Taylor in *Menagerie*. All you senior girls have that."

"Senior girls. That sounds so Camp Fire-y."

"You're going to be sore as hell when you see who gets this part. I don't know who it'll be, but I'm going to pick somebody you hate."

"Good. Don't pick anybody I like, because I'll hate her if the play runs."

"And yourself."

"Oh—well, I hate myself already. Do you think I like going back to that hotel, feeling sure you have a hit, *hoping* you have a hit, and stuck with my own stubborn pride? But you know I can't take this job, Ralph."

"Yes, I guess I do."

"You wouldn't stretch a point and take me to lunch, would you?"

"No, I can't, Joan."

"Then—will you give me a kiss?"

"Any time." He came around from behind his desk and put his arms around her.

"On the lips," she said.

He bent down, she stood on tiptoe, and his mouth pressed on hers. "Thank you, dear," she said. "Call me, call me."

"I hope so," he said, as she went out.

(1961)

CAN I STAY HERE?

The famous actress went to the window and gazed down at the snow-covered Park. The morning radio had said there would be snow, and there it was, an inch of it settled on trees and ground, and making her warm apartment so comfortable and secure. She would not have to go out all day. John Blackwell's twenty-one-year-old daughter was coming for lunch, and would probably stay an hour and a half; then there would be nothing to do until Alfredo Pastorelli's cocktail party, and the weather had provided an excuse for ducking that. As for dinner at Maude Long's, any minute now there would be a telephone call from Maude. Any minute—and this was the minute.

"Mrs. Long on the phone, ma'am," said the maid.

"I'll take it in here, Irene."

"Yes ma'am," said the maid.

"Hello, Maudie. I'll bet I know what you're calling about."

"Oh, Terry, have you taken a look outside? I just don't think it's fair to ask George and Marian to go out in weather like this. I could send my car for them, but that'd mean O'Brien wouldn't get home till after midnight. And he's been so good lately."

"So you've called off the party. Don't fret about it, Maudie," said Theresa Livingston.

"You sure you don't mind? I mean, if you'd like to come to me for dinner, just the two of us. We could play canasta. Or gin."

"Maudie, wouldn't you just rather have a nice warm bath and dinner on a tray? That's what I plan to do, unless you're dying for company."

"Well, if you're sure you don't mind," said Maude Long.

"Not one single bit. This is the kind of day that makes me appreciate a nice warm apartment. Oh, the times I'd wake up on days like this and wish I could stay indoors. But would have to get up and play a matinee at the Nixon. That's in Pittsburgh, or was."

"Yes, it's nice to just putter, isn't it?" said Maude Long. "What are you going to wear?"

"Today?"

"Yes: I always like to know what you're wearing. What do *you* wear when you're just staying home doing nothing?"

"Well, today I'll be wearing my black net. That sounds dressy, but I'm having a guest for lunch. A young girl that I've never met, but her father was an old beau of mine and she's coming to see me."

"That could be amusing. Could be a bore, too."

"I can get rid of her, and don't think I won't if she turns out to be a bore."

"Trust you, Terry, well, let's one of us call the other in a day or so, and I'm sorry about dinner."

Having committed herself to her black net, Terry Livingston reconsidered. In fairness to John Blackwell she could not give his daughter the impression that his actress girl friend had turned into a frump. Not that the black net was frumpish, but it *was* black net, and something brighter would be more considerate of John, and especially on a day like this. "I'm not going to keep this on, Irene. What have I got that's brighter?"

"Your blue silk knit, ma'am. With that you can start breaking in those blue pumps."

"I wonder what jewelry. This young lady that's coming for lunch, I've never seen her, but her father was one of my biggest admirers, back in the Spanish-American War days."

"Aw, now ma'am."

"Well, it wasn't World War Two. I can tell you," said Theresa Livingston. "And not too long after World War One."

"Try her with one good piece," said Irene. "I always like your diamond pin with the squiggly gold around it."

"With the blue silk knit, do you think?"

"If you wear it over to the one side, casual."

"All right. You've solved the problem. And I suppose I ought to start breaking in those pumps."

"They've been just sitting there ever since you bought them, and the old ones are pretty scuffed," said Irene. "Will you be offering her a cocktail, the young lady?"

"Oh, she's old enough for that. Yes. Let's put out some gin and vodka. They drink a lot of vodka, the young people."

"And I'll send down for a waiter at one o'clock."

"A little earlier. Have him here to take our order at one sharp."

"I won't promise he'll be here. That's their busiest time, but I'll try. In case you may want to get rid of her, what?"

"The usual signal," said Theresa Livingston. "At two fifteen I'll ask you if you've seen my cigarette holder. You pretend to look for it. You find it and bring it in and remind me that I have to change for my appointment."

"Where is the appointment supposed to be?"

"Three o'clock, downtown in my lawyer's office."

"Just so I make sure," said Irene. "I made a botch of it the last time Mrs. Long was here."

"Oh, well, with Mrs. Long it didn't matter. I wonder if I ought to have some little present for Miss Blackwell. Her father was very generous to me. Some little spur-of-the-moment gift that I won't miss."

"You have any number of cigarette lighters that you don't hardly ever use."

"Have I got any silver ones? A gold one would be a little too much, but a silver one might be nice."

"You've one or two silver, and a couple in snakeskin."

"The snakeskin. Fill one of the snakeskin and put a flint in it if it needs it. I'll have it in my hand. A spontaneous gesture that I'm sure she'll appreciate, just before she's leaving. 'I want you to take this. A little memento of our first meeting.' "

"I'll pick out a nice one. Snakeskin or lizard, either one."

"And you'll see about the drinks? Tomato juice, in case she asks for a Bloody Mary. Now what else? We'll have the table in the center of the room. I'll take the chair with my back to the light. At this hour of the day it doesn't make a great deal of difference, but she's young and she might as well get the glare. You listen to what I order and be sure the waiter puts my melon or whatever on that side of the table."

"Yes ma'am."

"When she gets here I'll be in my bedroom. They'll announce her from downstairs and I'll wait in my bedroom. You let her in. She'll naturally turn right, I imagine, and you tell her I'll be right with her. I don't like that picture of President Eisenhower where it is. Let's take it off the piano and put it more where she can see it. I don't suppose she'd recognize Moss Hart, so we'll leave that there. Dwight Wiman? No, she wouldn't know who he was. She might recognize Noel Coward's picture, so we won't disturb that. That's a wonderful picture of Gary Cooper and I. I must remember to have that enlarged. Gary. Dolores Del Rio. A writer, his name I forget. Fay Wray. That's Cedric Gibbons. He was married to Dolores Del Rio. Frances Goldwyn. Mrs. Samuel. Dear Bill Powell and Carole Lombard. There we all are, my first year in Hollywood. My second, actually, but I have no pictures of the first time. That was a Sunday luncheon party at Malibu. Look at Gary, isn't he darling? He wasn't a bit interested in me, actually. That was when he and the little Mexican girl, Lupe Velez, they were quite a thing at that time. You know, I haven't really looked at that picture in ages. Certainly dates me, doesn't it? And this one. Do you know who that is? I must have told you."

"I never remember his name."

"That's H. G. *Wells*. One of our *great* writers. Not one of ours in the American sense. But British. I think he was out there visiting Charley Chaplin or somebody. They all went to Hollywood sometime or other. Never mind. I made a lot of money in pictures, and people heard of me that never would have if I'd confined myself to the theater. Well, this isn't getting into my blue knit."

"You have over a half an hour," said the maid.

They went to the bedroom. Irene laid out the blue dress, and produced three cigarette lighters. "You don't want to give her the one with the watch in it," said Irene. "I took notice, the watch is from Cartier's."

"No, I'll take this little thing. I think it must be lizard. Quite gay, don't you think? And doesn't go at all badly with my dress. I haven't the faintest idea who gave me this one."

"Just so it wasn't the young lady's father."

"Oh, no. Not John Blackwell. Downstairs, in the safe, that's where I keep his presents. Or at least I've had most of them reset, but he never gave me any cigarette lighters. He's president of the United States Casualty and Indemnity Company, and his father was, before him. One of those firms that you don't hear much about, but I wish I had their money. Baltimore. Did you ever hear of a horse called One No Trump? A *famous* horse. I'm not sure he didn't win the Kentucky Derby. This girl's father owned him. I'll tell you another little secret to add to your collection. For when you write your memoirs. Mr. Blackwell, John, always wanted to name a horse after me, but of course he was married and I was too, at the time, and we were both being *very* discreet. I just wonder how much this girl today knows about me. Anyway, John knew he couldn't actually call a horse by my name, but he had a very promising filly that he thought would win the Kentucky Derby. Only one filly ever won the Derby, you know. A horse with the unfortunate name of Regret. So John wanted to name this filly after me, but instead of giving it my name, he gave it my initials. He called it Till Later. T.L. That was our secret. *One* of them, I might add. Oh, dear, I think of all the little lies we told to protect other people. Including this girl that's coming today. *There.* How do I look?"

"Let me just smooth the skirt down over the hips," said Irene. "It has a tendency to crawl up. I wonder if I ought to put on another slip?"

"You'll be sitting down most of the time. It's not very noticeable. Here's your pin," said Irene.

"Right about here, do you think?"

"Yes. Maybe about an inch lower."

"Here?" said Theresa Livingston.

"Just right."

"There. Now we're ready for Miss Evelyn Blackwell."

"She ought to be here in another five minutes."

"I hope she's prompt."

"She will be, if she knows what's good for her," said Irene.

"Well, if she's anything like her father. He had the best manners of any man I ever knew." Theresa Livingston lit a cigarette, had a couple of looks at herself in the full-length triplicate
mirrors. She was alone now; Irene was in the kitchen. Being
alone was not bad. Ever since she had rated her own dressing-
room—and that was a good many years—Theresa had always
insisted upon being alone for the last five minutes before going
on for a performance. It gave her time to compose herself, to
gather her strength, to be sick if she had to be, to slosh her
mouth out with a sip of champagne which she did not swal-
low, to get ready for the stage manager's summons, to go out
there and kill the sons of bitches with her charm and beauty
and talent. Perceptive of Irene to have realized that this was
just such a time, if only for an audience of one young girl. Too
perceptive. All that prattle had deceived Theresa herself without for one minute deceiving Irene.

She wanted to remain standing so as not to give the blue silk
knit chance to crawl up, but after ten minutes she was weary.
The buzzer sounded, and Theresa heard Irene going to the hall
door. It was the waiter with the menus. Loyally Irene was
annoyed by the young girl's lateness. "Why don't you just order
for the both of you?" said Irene. "Or do you want me to?"

"I'm not terribly hungry," said Theresa. "You order, Irene."

"Yes. Well, the eggs Florentine. Start with the melon. The eggs
Florentine. You won't want a salad, so we won't give *her* one.
And finish up with the lemon sherbet. Light, but enough. And
you'll want your Sanka. Coffee for her. How does that sound
to you?"

"Perfect. And it'll take a half an hour before it gets here. She
certainly ought to be here by then."

"If she isn't, I'm not going to let her come up."

"Oh, well, traffic. She'll have *some* good reason."

"What's wrong with the telephone? She could of let us

know," said Irene. "I'll give him the order and *you're* gonna have a glass of champagne."

"All right," said Theresa.

"We'll give her till ha' past one on the dot," said Irene.

It was ten minutes short of one-thirty when the girl arrived. "She's here," said Irene. "But you'll have to judge for yourself the condition she's in."

"You mean she's tight?" said Theresa.

"She's something, I don't know what."

"What is she like? Is she attractive?"

"Well, you don't see much of the face. You know, the hair hides the most of it."

"What makes you think she's tight?"

"'Hi,' she said. 'Hi. Is Miss Livingston at home? I'm expected. Expec-ted.' I said yes, she was expected. Didn't they call up from downstairs? 'Oh, that's right,' she said. 'Oh, there's Ike,' she said. 'Isn't he cute?' Ike. Cute."

"Oh, dear. Well, let's get it over with," said Theresa. "Tell her I'll be right out."

"I'll tell her you're on the long distance," said Irene.

"It might be a good idea to stay with her. Keep an eye on her so she doesn't start helping herself to the vodka. Is she that type?"

"I wouldn't put it past her," said Irene. "I wouldn't put anything past this one. And remember, you're supposed to be going downtown and see your lawyer."

"Yes, we won't need the cigarette holder bit."

Theresa Livingston allowed a few minutes to pass, then made her brisk entrance, and saw immediately that Irene had not exaggerated. The girl stood up and behind her lazy grin was all manner of trouble. Theresa Livingston gave her the society dowager bit. "How do you do, my dear. Have you told Irene what you'd like to drink?"

"She didn't ask me, but I'll have a vodka martini. I might as well stick with it."

"Irene, will you, please?" said Theresa Livingston. "Nothing for me. I've ordered lunch for both of us. Save time that way, you know. The food is good here, but the service can be a little slow."

"I know."

"Oh, you've stopped here?"

"No, we always stay at the Vanderbilt, but I was with some friends in the What-You-Call-It-Room, downstairs."

"I see," said Theresa.

"I guess I was a little late, but I got here as soon as I could."

"Well, let's not talk about that," said Theresa. "Why don't you sit there and I'll sit here. I was so pleased to hear from your father. I hadn't realized he had a daughter your age. Did you come out, and all the rest of those things?"

"Oh, two years ago. The whole bit."

"And from your father's note I gather you've given up school. Are you serious about wanting to be an actress?"

Irene served the cocktail, and the girl drank some of it. "I don't know. I guess I am. I want to do something, and as soon as I mentioned the theater, Daddy said he knew you. I guess if you were a friend of Daddy's you know how he operates. If I said I wanted to be in the Peace Corps he'd fix it with President Johnson, or at least try."

"Well, I don't know about that, but your father was a very good friend of mine when we were younger. Not that I've seen him in—oh, dear, before you were born."

"Oh, I know that. It's been Mrs. Castleton ever since I can remember."

"What's been Mrs. Castleton?"

"Daddy's girl friend."

"But your father and mother are still married, aren't they?"

"Of course. Mummy's not giving up all that loot, and why should she? Could I have another one of these? I'll get it, don't you bother."

"Well, yes. You may have to finish it at the table."

"Do you want to bet?" The girl took her glass to the portable bar. "First Mummy said they'd stay married till after I came out, although why that's important even in Baltimore. But then I came out, and nothing more was heard about a divorce. If Aunt Dorothy wanted him to get a divorce he'd get it, but being Dorothy Castleton is still a little bit better socially than being Dorothy Blackwell. And they're all old."

"Yes, we are."

"I didn't mean that personally, Miss Livingston."

"I don't know how else you could mean it, considering that I'm the same age as your father and mother. I don't know about Mrs. Castleton, of course."

"Same age. All in their late fifties or early sixties, I guess. Anyway, not exactly the *jeunesse dorée*."

"No. Well, Baltimore doesn't seem to be very different from any place else, does it? And meanwhile, your father asked me to have a talk with you about the theater. Which I'm very glad to do. But *you*. *You* don't seem to have any burning, overwhelming desire to become an actress."

"I couldn't care less, frankly. It's Daddy that as soon as I mentioned the theater—"

"How did you happen to mention it, though?"

"How did I happen to mention it? Well, I guess I said I wanted to do *something*, but when it came down to what I could do, we exhausted all the possibilities except riding in horse shows and modeling."

"So naturally you thought of going on the stage."

"No, I didn't. That was Daddy's idea. This whole thing was his idea. I think he just wanted to name-drop that he knew you. I have no delusions about being an actress, for Christ's sake."

Irene went to the door to admit the waiter with the rolling table.

"You would have lost your bet," said the girl. "I won't have to finish my drink at the table."

"Well, then, it isn't a question of my using my influence to get you into the American Academy or anything like that," said Theresa. "I must say I'm relieved. I certainly wouldn't want to deprive a girl of a chance that really cared about the theater."

"Forget it. I'm sorry I wasted your time, but it wasn't all my fault. Daddy's a powerhouse, and when he gets an idea he keeps after you till you give in."

"Shall we sit down? Why don't you sit there, and I'll sit here," said Theresa.

They took their places at the table, but the girl obviously had no intention of touching her melon. "Would you rather

have something else?" said Theresa. "Tomato juice, or something like that? We wouldn't have to send downstairs for it."

"No thanks."

"We're having eggs Benedict," said Theresa.

"Eggs Florentine, ma'am," said Irene.

"Don't worry about me," said the girl.

"Have you had any breakfast, other than a vodka martini?"
said Theresa. "Why don't you have a cup of coffee?"

"Where's the bathroom?" said the girl.

"Will you show her the bathroom, Irene?"

"Yes, ma'am."

"Just tell me where it is, don't come with me," said the girl.

"Through that door, which leads to the bedroom. And the
bathroom you can find," said Theresa.

"The eggs Florentine," said the girl. "Eggs anything." She left
the room quickly.

"I hope she makes it," said Irene.

"Yes," said Theresa. "I think you'd better move this table
out in the hall. Leave the coffee. I'll have some myself, now,
and you might make some fresh, Irene."

"You're not gonna eat any lunch?"

"No."

"Nine dollars, right down the drain."

"I know, but I'm not hungry, so don't force me."

Theresa had two cups of coffee and several cigarettes. "I
think I ought to go in and see how she is," she said.

"You want me to?" said Irene.

"No, I will," said Theresa.

She went to the bedroom, and the girl was lying on the bed,
clad in her slip, staring at the ceiling. "Do you want anything,
Evelyn?"

"Yes," said the girl.

"What?"

"Can I stay here a while?"

"Child, you can stay here as long as you like," said Theresa
Livingston.

ELLIE

Although my sister and I were born in Texas, we have lived most of our lives in the North, from the time our father and mother were killed in a railroad accident, about twenty-five years ago. We were brought up by an aunt and uncle who lived in Westchester. I was eleven and Caroline was seven when Father and Mother died, and I never went back to Texas except briefly, on business. Our aunt and uncle sent me to camp in New Hampshire in the summer, and I went to boarding school when I was fourteen. Caroline, however, did go back to Texas several times and kept up a few friendships there. She was always lavishly entertained, and, naturally, when her Texan friends came to New York, she did her best to show them the town. This was simple enough; it usually involved one big evening of dinner at "21," the theatre, and supper at Larue's. Caroline lives her own life and I live mine, in apartments in different parts of town. Her job is in the midtown district, and I work downtown. For a sister and brother who are quite fond of each other, we are together infrequently, and it is unusual for her even to ask me in for a cocktail when she has some Texans to entertain.

When she telephoned me that Ham and Ellie Glendon were in town, I had to ask who they were. "He's a lawyer in Dallas, and they've never been to New York before," said Caroline. "They're about my age, a year or two younger, but they were awfully nice to me the last two or three times I was down there."

"Uh-huh," I said, waiting.

"She's very pretty and quiet. He's—well—more Texan. He

likes to get tight, and I thought—well—you know more places than I do. They'll want to go to '21,' but that won't be all. I mean he will . . . You're *not* being very helpful."

I laughed. "I get it. Colonel Glendon wants to raise a little hell. O.K. Does he carry a gun?"

"Probably," said Caroline. "They all do."

"Well, tell him to check the gun and I'll take you around. What did you have in mind?"

"Nothing in particular, but I just know he'll want to go someplace where I don't know the proprietor. Night-club kind of place. And it's my treat. You don't have to spend any money. I just want you to sort of steer us around. Black tie. My place at seven."

Ham Glendon was a rather large man with red hair and a red face, the kind that does not tan. In Caroline's hall, I saw one of those cream-colored hats with a half-inch band and I heard his voice, soft and for the moment not unpleasant but likely to become tiresome. He was wearing a double-breasted dinner coat and new patent-leather shoes and diamond-and-onyx studs. He called me Jim right off the bat, when he introduced me to his wife. She was something.

She was standing when I entered, Caroline having gone to the kitchen. As I shook hands with her, I was surprised that I so quickly had to change my first impression of her height. She was not nearly as tall as I'd thought when I came into the room. She held her head back, but the top of it did not reach my chin. "I'm happy to know you," she said, and turned and sat down. Her figure was beautiful, and Neiman-Marcus had done their best by it—or probably had been delighted to clothe it, as much of it as was clothed. When she was turning to sit down, I caught her taking a quick look at me; she was trying to see what effect she had had on me, and when she found out, she dropped her eyes and reached for a cigarette.

We went to "21" and to "Oklahoma!," which Caroline and I had seen three times. At dinner, Ham and Caroline did most of the talking, about Texas friends whom I barely remembered or did not know. Ham would ask Ellie to fill in details on some of

the people, and that was about all of her contribution to the
conversation. I contributed even less, but I knew I wasn't bored
and I was sure Ellie wasn't, because every once in a while she
would look at me and smile. I remembered that Caroline had
said she was quiet, and she didn't seem to expect much talk
from me or to want to converse with me herself. In fact, she
seemed to be quite happy just knowing that she had had an
effect on me. At the restaurant and at the theatre other men
looked at her too, and their admiration was something she
breathed in.

When we came out of the theatre, Caroline suggested going
back to "21" for a drink while we decided where we wanted to
go. I wanted to go someplace where we could dance; there
were some things I wanted to say to Ellie. But when we got to
"21" Ham fixed that. "Jim, I raickon from here on we're in
your hands." He laughed and I laughed.

"A pleasure," I said. "What kind of a place did you have in
mind?"

"Well, more or less leave that up to you, Jim," said Ham.

"No, be frank, Ham," said Caroline. "My ne'er-do-well
brother knows them all."

"Yes," I said.

"Well, *Harlem* is one place. We heard a lot about that Dorchester Ballroom."

"Oh, sure," I said, and thought of the way we were dressed.
"You'll see some of the best dancing up there you'll ever see in
your life. Of course, the smaller places don't begin to open up
for quite a while, and if we wanted to go to one of them, I
think we ought to change our clothes."

"Tell you the truth, Jim, we more or less had our hearts set
on the Dorchester. You asked me to be *frank*."

"By all means," I said. I had the waiter bring a telephone to
the table, and I called the manager of the Dorchester, a white
man, whom I had known for many years. I was very careful to
emphasize that I was with my *sister* and *some friends from
Texas*. Max, my manager friend, was not obtuse and he promised he would save a box for us.

More than that, when we arrived at the Dorchester, he was waiting for us on the curb, and I was grateful, for there was a long queue of Negro boys and girls at the box office. Max took over and led us past the box office, and when we were inside, we were accompanied by Al Spode, the old-time Negro heavyweight who was head bouncer at the Dorchester, another old friend of mine.

They usually don't serve hard liquor at the Dorchester, but Max put a couple of coke bottles filled with bourbon on the table, and I thanked him and he went on about his business.

Ham turned out to like jazz and Caroline is a minor authority, so they were entertained by the two good bands. Our box, which was on the level of the dance floor and quite near the bandstand, was conveniently situated for me, or so I thought; the noise of the bands and the dancers would cover up the questions I was going to ask Ellie once we got settled. For the time being, we watched the superb dancing and drank our drinks. It was that way until one band finished a set. The dancers stood where they had stopped, waiting for the other band to start, and when it did, and the noise began again, I spoke to Ellie: "You know, if I'd had my way, we'd be where we could be dancing without being conspicuous, which we certainly are now." And she knew I meant the way we were dressed.

"Would we?" She half sneered and raised her eyes and let them indicate the dancers.

"Maybe Ham and Caroline will get bored soon and we can go someplace else. I don't think you're having too good a time."

"Oh, don't mind me."

"But I want you to have a good time. Do you like to dance? Because if you do, there are a few places where there's tea dancing. Now, for instance, if you were going to be free Saturday afternoon." I came down heavy on "free," so she would be sure I meant her, alone, without Ham.

"Saturday I was planning to have lunch with an old school friend I went to Randolph-Macon with." She paused and shifted in her seat. "But who ever heard of two girls just sitting around all afternoon in New York City? I imagine we'll have said all we have to say to each other by three, and after that I'll

just saunter down Park Avenue in the direction of the Vanderbilt, and if I happened to meet somebody . . ."

"That's exactly the vicinity I was going to be in," I said.
"Walking up Park Avenue around three."

I poured her a drink and one for myself, and I had that
moment of peace when you know everything is settled and
nothing much has been said. For all I know, Ham had been
conversing in like manner with Caroline. Presently the set ended
and the bands were changing again. The dancers slowed down,
then stopped while the outgoing musicians left the bandstand
and the incoming group took their places.

A boy and girl whom I had been half observing came over to
the railing near our table. The girl leaned against the railing, her
back toward us. The boy, who was very black, was facing in our
direction. They had the confidence of artistry; they were surely
the best dancers in the ballroom, and it may be that I myself
showed applause by my facial expression. It doesn't much matter.

"Ham," said Ellie.

"Yes, honey," said Ham.

"Ham, that niggah's *lookin'* at me," said Ellie.

I looked at her and at her husband. "Now, wait a minute," I
said.

"Which one, honey?" said Ham.

"Oh, God," said my sister, appealing to me.

I rose. "Up! Up, everybody! Come on!" I put a bill on the
table and took Ellie's wrist. "We're getting out of here now,
this minute."

"Not before I—" said Ham.

"Listen, you silly son of a bitch," I said. I pulled Ellie along
with me, counting on Caroline to grab hold of Ham, which
she did. We got out fast and stepped right into a taxi.

The ride downtown through the Park was a silent one until
we were among the buildings south of Fifty-ninth Street. "Jim,"
said Ham, "you hadn't oughta called me a son of a bitch."

"I know," I said. "I'm sorry."

"Well, that's all right, then, if you apologize." He grinned.
"Now wuddia say we all go over to the El Morocco club?"

"I don't think so," I said.

"*It's* all right, Jim," said Ham. "All's forgiven. I take into consideration you been living with Yankees too long."

"That may be," I said.

They dropped Caroline and then me. I went to bed with my mind made up that that was the last I'd ever see of Missy Ellie, but when Saturday came, I got out my car and at three o'clock I was cruising along lower Park Avenue, excited as a kid. But when I saw her, actually saw her, walking down Park, keeping her date with me, I grew old and cautious, and I drove away from her and trouble, her kind of trouble.

(1946)

"I just mentioned the first name of an actor that came into

ENCOUNTER: 1943

Allen was standing near the curb, waiting with the other people to cross Forty-sixth. He was glad he wore his muffler and
he wished he knew where his gloves were. The last cheating
taxi whizzed past and the cops' whistles blew and Allen was
ready to move when he got the little punch in the ribs. It wasn't
a hard punch, feeling it, but it must have started as a pretty
hard punch to feel as much of it as he did through his overcoat, and without looking he knew who it was all right.

"Hey," she said, and he looked down and around, and it was
Mildred all right. She was grinning.

"Hyuh," he said.

"Didn't they get you yet?" she said.

"Didn't who?" he asked, then, "Oh. No, I'm too smart for
them."

"Yeah, I'll bet," she said. Somebody bumped her. "Which
way you going, I'll walk along with you."

"Just uptown," he said. "I'm not headed anywhere in particular."

"Well! Then we could go some place and have a beer or
something. I'd like to *talk* to you."

They were walking slowly uptown. "What about?"

"What about?" she said. "Anything. Mutual acquaintances.
Or maybe you do' wanna sit and talk and have a drink with me."

"I do' wanna sit and have a *fight* with you," he said.

"Why do we *have* to fight? We don't have to fight if you
control your temper and so forth. Let's go down the street to
Eddie Spellman's."

"All right," he said. They turned at Forty-seventh.

"Now *don't* do me any *favors*," she said. "If you rather not go, say so now but don't act disagreeable when we get there."

"They'll think I'm Victor Mature," he said.

"Yeah? *They* will, but *I* won't. Oh, you mean *polite*. Victor Mature isn't polite. He's a blabber-mouth."

"I jist mentioned the first name of an actor that came into my head," he said.

"Well pick one that's polite if that's what you mean. Herbert Marshall. Ronnie Colman. But don't pick Victor Mature if you're picking a person for their politeness. My God! Victor Mature polite! Anybody as dumb as you I'm surprised you had the sense enough to wear an overcoat if you're that dumb. You'd be more typical if you came out in a bathing suit."

"All right," he said. They turned in at Spellman's and went straight back to a booth. A bald-headed Irishman came to them before they had sat down.

"Well, here's a couple of strangers for you," he said.

"Hello, Eddie," they said.

"But don't go start getting ideas," said Mildred.

"Now I wasn't getting no ideas, Mrs. Allen. I only made the statement that it was a pleasure to see a couple of old customers."

"That's all right, Eddie," said Allen. To her: "A rye?"

"No," she said. "Why do I have to have a rye? Because it's cheaper? I think I'll have a Ballantine's and soda and with some lemon peel in it."

"I'll have a rye," said Allen.

"Right," said Eddie, and went away.

"That Mick will have us in bed by five o'clock," said Mildred.

"You never liked him," said Allen.

"He never liked me, so why should I like *him*?"

"You're crazy. Eddie likes everybody," said Allen.

"All right, he likes everybody, then I don't want to be everybody and be liked by Mr. Spellman."

"Well, only—you suggested going here," said Allen.

"Because I assure you only because I ran into you. I assure you I didn't give him or his lousy joint a thought since the last time we were here together two years ago, and I never would of given it another thought for another two years if it wasn't that I ran into you."

"How are conditions at the 21 and the El Morocco?" said Allen.

"If that was intended for sarcasm it just shows how wrong you are. I was at Elmer's twice last week if you want some information."

"Who said anything about Elmer's?"

"See? That's how much you and your sarcasm. Elmer's is what they call the El Morocco."

"Don't get me wrong. I believe you go to them places. Once in a while I read the papers."

"When somebody leaves them on a subway train," she said.

"When somebody leaves them on a table at the Automat," he said. A waiter, not Eddie, served their drinks. They drank. She drank about half of hers and looked at him, at his face, his hair, his tie, both shoulders.

"Did I ever sleep with you? I can't believe it," she said.

"No, it was two other fellows," he said. "Or twenty."

"I'll hit you right across the mouth with this bag, you talk like that to me. You started it, you with that little bum off the streets from Harrisburg."

"All right, I apologize. Only I don't know what you expect me to do. Sit here and take it while you look at me like I was a ghost and then come out with 'Did I ever sleep with you?'"

"I shouldn't allow myself to even get mad at you."

"Then why do you?"

"Oh, it isn't because I'm still in love with you. Don't think that, for God's sake. I *don't* even get mad at you. I get mad at myself. My God, seventeen years old . . . Say, I *voted*."

"Yeah? Who for?"

"None of your business. I don't have to tell who I voted for. I didn't tell—anybody else. A lot of people asked me to vote for certain people because they knew it was my first vote and they all said to get started right, then when 1944 came along I'd know which way."

"I get it," he said.

"You get what?"

"It's easy. The gang I see your name in the paper with, they were all for Dewey."

"Very clever, aren't you? Well, I'm not admitting anything, see? Oh, what about you?"

"Who did I vote for? Al Smith. That's the last person I voted for."

"I didn't mean that. I mean, where are you in the draft?"

"Where do *you* think?" he said, sipping his drink.

"I don't *know*. You could put your mother down for a dependent, and are you all right again?"

"Go on," he said.

"That's right," she said. "I guess you're over age too."

"I'm surprised I didn't see you in some Waac uniform or something."

"Is that a crack?"

"No. You mean a corny crack about wacky? Give me credit for better than that."

"Well, I never can tell with you," she said. "Do you think I have time for another drink?"

He laughed. "How should I know?"

"My date," she said. "Oh, that's right, I didn't tell you what time I had the date for." She looked at the bar clock. "No, I guess not. I'm going to a cocktail party but I have to meet somebody before I go."

"You're right up there, aren't you?" he said.

"What do you mean?"

"Cocktail parties. Elmer's. All that big stuff."

"Well, why not?"

"Sure. Why not? You're young, and you're a dish."

"You think so, Harry?"

"I still got eyes," he said.

"Well, thanks for the compliment," she said. "I apologize for what I said when we came in. About rye being cheap. You were always all right with money when we had it. It wasn't money that was your trouble—*our* trouble."

"Thanks, kid," he said. "I guess you better blow now or you'll be late."

"Don't you want me to stay for another? We aren't fighting now."

"No, but maybe in two minutes we would be," he said.

"Maybe you're right," she said. She stood up. "Well, I guess I better say goodbye. I'd like to see you sometime, Harry."

"Why?"

"Didn't we get along all right just now? We had a little scrap but we ended up all right. Here—" She reached in her purse and tore the back off a pack of matches. "That's where I live. Give me a call."

"All right," he said.

"Don't forget," she said. "G'bye." She smiled and left.

From his corner of the booth Allen called out to Eddie, who came back and stood at the table. "Yes, Harry," he said.

"Could you let me have a quart?"

Eddie rubbed his hand over his smooth bald head. "I don't know, Harry. That tab is gettin' pretty big and you oughtn'ta be drinking so's it is." He turned his head, looked in the direction in which the girl had gone, then he looked at his diamond ring. "All right, Harry. I'll wrap it for you."

(1972)

FAMILY EVENING

"Mother," said Rosie, "who's the fourth for dinner tonight? Are you planning some neat surprise for me, like Gregory Peck? Fat chance, end parentheses."

"It just so happens that Gregory Peck backed out at the last minute," said Mrs. James. "No, we're having Bob Martin, a friend of ours from home."

" 'From home,' " said Rosie. "Mother, isn't this home? This is where we live, isn't it? I was born in New York City. What about Mr. Martin?"

"He's what you used to call one of the B.D.s."

"*I* used to call the B.D.s? I never even heard the expression. It rings no bell here."

"Well, I remember it, and so does your father," said Mrs. James.

"Then lift me out of this suspense. What does it mean?"

"Oh, a few years ago when we were all spending the weekend at Aunt Ada's we overheard you and Kenny and the rest of you talking about B.D.s." Mrs. James waited. "You were referring to me, and your father, and Aunt Ada, and Uncle Archie, and people of our age."

"Oh, yes! The *Better Deads*. I must have been at the Brearley then," said Rosie.

"Yes, and it made me cry," said Mrs. James. "I was only thirty-five or thirty-six then. Only. I don't suppose thirty-five seems like the prime of life to you even now."

"A girl in my class quit college to marry a man thirty-*four*. That brings thirty-five much closer to me. I'm capable of marrying a man thirty-five. What's to stop me? You, of course, but I mean theoretically. What about Mr. Martin? Is he attractive?"

"He used to be. I haven't seen him for years."

"Well, I like that. Every Christmas vacation you make me spend one evening at home with you and Father, then you go and invite some total stranger. I call *that* consistent."

"We don't *make* you spend an evening at home. We ask you to because we want to see something of you, and Bob Martin is not a total stranger. He was an usher at our wedding and he's somebody we've known all our lives. He called up this afternoon and it's the only time we could see him. He wanted to take us to 21."

"Three good parties I passed up to be with the bosom of my family. If he's remotely presentable can't we all go to Larry's later?"

"Larry Who?"

"Larue's," said Rosie.

"Let's see how it works out," said Mrs. James.

"Maybe you're right," said Rosie. "A little caution now."

Martin turned up in evening clothes and when Libby James chided him he made the old joke about dressing for dinner in the tropics. It was neither old nor a joke to Rosie, but she noticed he wore pumps, of which she definitely approved. He was heavy but not yet fat, so that his regular features were not altogether lost in cheek and chin.

"Martinis okay for you, Robert?" said Rosie's father.

"They better be. It's what I've had a string of," said Martin. "Why don't you pour Rosie's in the cup I gave her and she can catch up with me?"

"Oh, a tragedy, Bob," said Libby James. "Your cup was lost in the fire. We had a fire when we were living on Fifty-first Street. Luckily most of our things were in storage, but the cup Bob gave you when you were born, Rosie, that was one of the things we lost. I was convinced the firemen stole it, but Norman said I was crazy. I still think I was right. Firemen are honest, they look honest, but with the thousands of them in New York City there must be one or two."

"Well, I'll give Rosie another one when she has her first

baby," said Martin. "Or will you settle for a cocktail shaker now, Rosie?"

"I'll settle for a cocktail shaker," said Rosie.

"Why, Rosie!" said her mother.

"Well, Mr. Martin suggested it, and I haven't got a cocktail shaker."

"You'll have one tomorrow afternoon," said Martin.

"No such thing, Bob Martin," said Mrs. James.

"There'll be no more discussion. This young lady needs a cocktail shaker, and it's Christmastime, and that's what middle-aged friends are for. E.R.J. I *know* somebody, so I can have it engraved right away."

"I don't use the 'E,'" said Rosie. "Too much confusion."

"Okay. R.J.," said Martin.

"Let's have dinner," said Libby. "We're letting the servants off early."

"I'll take mine in with me," said Martin.

"We all will," said Norman James.

Throughout dinner Rosie could see that Martin thoroughly approved of her and of her mother. She was less sure that she approved of him. He told the story of the time he broke his leg while skiing at the country club, and of the time Libby's father forbade her going out with him because he kept her up so late, and of the time they drove seventy miles to a dance that was not to take place until the following evening. Libby James remembered almost all of it in the same detail as Martin's. Norman James smoked a good deal and kept his champagne glass empty and full, supplying a name or a date when he was called upon, or admitting total ignorance of an entire episode. Once or twice Mr. Martin began stories with the statement that Rosie would like this item, if she wanted to know what kind of person her mother was at *her* age. The martinis and the wine, in addition to the string of martinis he had had before his arrival, had no apparent effect on Mr. Martin. This was not quite the case with Rosie's mother and father. Rosie herself did not like to drink much.

"Wanta come in here, Robert?" said Norman James.

"Why sure, if you do," said Martin.

"I do. I do indeed," said Norman James. Rosie and her mother went to Rosie's room.

"Well," said Rosie, "I'm getting a bird's-eye view of an old romance."

"How do you mean, dear?" said her mother. "Bob Martin? And I?" She laughed.

"Stop giggling. You've been giggling all through dinner. I'll bet it wasn't Father that asked him here."

"As a *matter* of *fact*, it *was*," said Libby James.

"Well then, he was just being polite."

"Oh, stop. I was thinking I might put on my new evening dress and you could put on yours, and we could step out. Not if you're going to be disagreeable, though."

"Well, if you think I'd wear my new evening dress for this occasion, pardon me. I'm in favor of lights and music, especially if Mr. Martin wants to pay for it, but I'll wear the pink I got last summer."

"Wear what you please, my dear. Could you do something about my hair? Does it look all right?"

"Mother, Mr. Martin hasn't said anything about going out. Besides, he probably has a late date."

"You're such a child. I know he hasn't said anything, but what if he hasn't? I'll merely suggest it to your father, and if Bob Martin has a late date I'll take great pleasure in watching him wriggle out of it." She studied herself in the mirror, at first arrogantly, chin up; but then that disappeared. She looked at the mirror's reflection of Rosie's face. "How do I really look?" she said.

"You look fine," said Rosie.

"No, I don't," said her mother. She turned away from the mirror. "Do me a favor, Rosie. *You* suggest it."

"Me! . . . All right, if you stop feeling sorry for yourself all of a sudden. You and the rest of the B.D.s."

Her mother smiled. "*Dear* Rosie. It hurt, but it worked." She got up and followed Rosie down the hall, humming "Do It Again," a danceable number of 1922.

(1972)

FIRST DAY IN TOWN

At twenty-five past one Nick Orlando, alone, got out of a taxi, punched the doorman playfully in the ribs, and entered the restaurant. In the foyer there was a crowd, mostly women, who wanted to sit downstairs but who, as matinee time got nearer, were about to decide to go upstairs. Nick Orlando firmly pushed his way forward among these women. At his touch they would turn angrily and say, "I *beg* yaw podden— *oh, Nick Orlando!* It's Nick Orlando!"

The captain of waiters raised his hand high. He had not immediately seen Nick Orlando, whose height only flatteringly could be called average, but the repetition of the Orlando name reached the captain. "I have your table, Mr. Orlando," he said. Then, when Nick Orlando had pushed his way to the rope, the captain whispered, "I don't have a table, but maybe you see somebody." Nick Orlando, who had not said a word since getting out of the taxi, squeezed the captain's arm. He nodded; he saw somebody.

He made his way to a banquette where two women were seated side by side; the one a girl of twenty or so, with a scarf knotted about her neck; the other a woman in her late thirties, who had a ballpoint pen in her right hand and was writing something in a stenographer's dictation tablet. Nick Orlando, heading for this table, picked up a chair without asking permission of a threesome at an island table. He set the chair down so that he faced the two women on the banquette. The girl squinted. "Go away. You're lousing up my interview," she said, laughing.

"Oh, say, this is a treat," said the interviewer. "Nick Orlando. You know where I met you? At Harry Browning's."

"Who is Harry Browning?" said Nick Orlando.

"Get him! Pretending you don't know who Harry Browning is," said the girl. "Five years ago you *didn't* know who Harry Browning is, you'd be telling the truth then, you big faker. When did you get *in*, you dog?"

"What's the interview for?" said Nick Orlando.

"My syndicate. My name is Camilla Strong."

"Your syndicate? I bet it ain't the syndicate I got friends in. Syndicate. A syndicate is a man that knows the price of everything and the value of nothing. Who said that, Camilla?"

"Oscar Wilde."

"You *know*, hey? Wud you, go to college, Camilla?"

"I sure did," said Camilla Strong.

"This jerk just stard reading books three years ago, and now the whole field of literature is all his. All his. Nobody ever read anything before him, hey, jerk?"

"Where did you two know each other? Is this a thing with you two?" said Camilla Strong. "Should I have known about this?"

"Her? This tramp?"

"Don't make it too emphatic, jerk, or otherwise she'll think we did have a thing," said the girl. "No, we didn't have a thing, but not for want of him trying."

"That's where everybody makes a mistake with this tramp, is trying. Nobody has to try with this one."

"Oh, I wish I could write this the way it really comes out," said Camilla. "If they'd ever print it."

"Go ahead write it," said Nick Orlando. "You're not gonna destroy any illusions. You seen her that night on the Paar show."

"Aah, shut up with the Paar show," said the girl. "Why'd you have to remind her of that? We been here since one o'clock and not a word about the Paar show till *you* crashed the party."

"Two nominations for Tonys, and one Academy Award, and what are you famous for?" said Nick Orlando.

"You know what really happened, Camilla, was I never drink. I don't have any tolerance for it. And this jerk made me take two drinks before I was to go on. Two, and one is all I need to get looping. Write that in your article. The inside story of Mary Coolidge getting cut off the air. I think he did it on purpose, too."

"What else? I told you I did it on purpose. You were getting too big for your britches. Your *head* was getting too big for your britches."

"You know, Nick, I really hate you. I hate you with a cold, consuming, venomous hatred."

"I know you do, but I can't get you to admit it."

"You kids, do you talk this way all the time?" said Camilla.

"When we're talking. Sometimes we aren't on conversational terms," said Nick Orlando.

"I wish that was now," said Mary Coolidge. "How did you know I was here?"

"Stop with the kidding. Camilla knows I was with you till an hour ago," said Nick Orlando.

"Oh, now you said too much, Nick," said Camilla. "Unfortunately I've been with Mary since ten o'clock this morning."

"She said you were here since one o'clock," said Nick Orlando.

"Interviewing. But all morning I was with her picking out the dresses for the new play. If you're going to ruin a girl's reputation you've got to do better than that, Nick. What about *you*, by the way? I know you're in town for the opening of *Mad River*."

"You seen it yet?"

"No, I missed two screenings, but I hear you're only great in it. If I call Irving Rudson maybe we could set up an interview. Are you booked pretty solid?"

"Irving don't know I'm in town. I come in a day early."

"To louse up my interview," said Mary Coolidge. "And you succeeded, so go away."

"Oh, he didn't louse it up, Mary. I can have sort of fun with this. It'll read better than just an ordinary interview."

"I don't give ordinary interviews," said Mary Coolidge.

"Ooh, I think this one is burning," said Nick Orlando. "I don't know if it's me or you she's sore at."

"Mary isn't sore at anybody. Where are you staying?"

"Sixteen Twenty-four Pitkin Avenue."

"That's Brooklyn. You're from The Bronx."

"Kidding. I got an uncle living on Pitkin Avenue. I'm at the Sherry. You set it up with Irving."

"And I'll come along and louse it up," said Mary Coolidge.

Camilla Strong pressed the button of her ballpoint, and closed the notebook. "I don't know what your act is, you two. I can't fathom whether you're a thing or not a thing. Come on, level with Camilla before I go."

"I'm mad for him, but religion keeps us apart," said Mary Coolidge.

"Religion? You're both Italian extraction, aren't you?"

"Yeah, but I want to be a nun and he wants to be a priest. So religion keeps us apart," said Mary Coolidge.

"This is a very fast little girl, Nicky," said Camilla.

"Talking, but not running," said Nick Orlando. "She can outtalk anybody but I never heard of her outrunning anybody. Never."

"I kind of think she outran you," said Camilla Strong. "But I'll find that out when I interview you. 'Bye now, kids." She left.

Nick Orlando moved to the vacated seat. "That'll be the day. When that broad interviews me."

"You son of a bitch. I had her in the palm of my hand till you came along. I'm doing the sweetness-and-light bit. The new Mary Coolidge. You know what's in that notebook? All about how I want to do Joan of Arc, for God's sake."

"They all want to do Joan of Arc."

"They all do do Joan of Arc, but I'm right for it. I'd hit them with a Joan of Arc that they could smell burning flesh."

"I'd pay to see that. Where did you go last night?"

"None of your God damn business."

"I heard Harry Browning was giving a party. I damn near went," said Nick Orlando.

"Who is Harry Browning?"

"That's *my* line. When did you get my wire?"

"I got your wire Sunday, in plenty of time if I'd of wanted to have a date with you, but I don't. You're a Hollywood hambo."

"Oh, that again. If you were prettier and more photogenic there wouldn't be any knocks on Hollywood."

"You got it mixed up. I said *you* were a Hollywood *hambo*."

"Is that worse than a Broadway hambo?"

"Infinitely. A Hollywood hambo is chicken, sells out for security. At least a Broadway hambo fights for parts, parts he wants. But you Hollywood hamboes take anything the studio says."

"Not me. I don't have to, it's in my contract."

"*Mad River.* I hear you play a cowboy. You a cowboy?"

"So you're right for Joan of Arc. What the hell are we talking in circles? Why won't you have a date with me? And don't give me that Hollywood hambo answer."

"I could ask you, why do you keep pestering after me? From the first time I ever met you you thought all you had to do was ask, and I'd give you a date. That *paisana* stuff."

"Answer the question. Why didn't you? Why don't you now?"

"Because nobody gets a date with me that I don't want to go out with. You tell me I'm not pretty. All right, then why do you want a date with me? You know why? Because from the first I'd never go out with you and it's no different now with you a star and me a star. You know what the trouble is? You're jealous of me, and if you get me in bed with you you think you don't have to be jealous any more. The kind of a fellow you are, I go to bed with you and it doesn't make any difference if I'm a better actor than you. You can go around and tell everybody you slept with Mary Coolidge. I know bellboys that slept with famous actresses, but does that make them a better actor? You want to get in bed with me, Nick, I'll be proud to—when you're a good enough actor so I can brag about sleeping with you. But not before. So give up. You know who I get phone calls from? From Paris and London and all over? A really big star. Not like you or I, but a *big* star. And you know why I won't have a date with him? Because as an actor he stinks. And you know what his trouble is? He's jealous of me. He's like you. Last season he came to see me every night for a week and two matinees, torturing himself. 'If I could be as good as that little bitch up there, that homely little bitch.' So he wants to take it out in going to bed with me. Like you."

"What the hell is acting?"

"Right! It's a phoney business, but you don't have to be a phoney *in* it. If you're gonna be an actor, don't be a phoney actor. If you're gonna be in a phoney business that's all the more reason why you shouldn't be a phoney in it."

"You're a phoney."

"No. If I was a dishwasher I'd want to be a good one. You know what I'm gonna give this waiter for a tip? Ten dollars. Because he's a good waiter. That waiter over there, I give him ten percent if it comes to forty-eight cents. I count out the three pennies."

"They pool their tips, so what's the difference?"

"Because this waiter I hand him the ten bucks and say thank-you, and the other waiter I just put the money on the dish and say nothing. That's the difference, and they both know the difference. My applause. Don't tell me applause doesn't mean anything to you?"

"You want to know something? I get a hand in *Mad River*. I got two scenes in there where I get a hand."

"How many takes?"

"What?"

"How many takes before you got the scenes right?"

"Ah, nuts," said Nick Orlando. He got up and pushed his way through the matinee-bound crowd. *"Nick! Nick! It's Nick Orlando! Could I have your autograph please? On this menu? On this package?"* He did not stop until he reached the curb.

"Get me a hack, quick," he said to the doorman.

"Right away," said the doorman. He stood in the street, a few feet from the curb, waving for a taxi. "I hear very good reports on *Mad River*," he said.

"Yeah, I'm spreading them all over," said Nick Orlando.

The doorman laughed. "Well, I'll say this for you, Nick. You didn't change. You're just the same. Some of them go out there . . ." He shook his head.

2

At the next restaurant Nick Orlando was not so well known. He was recognized by the doorman and by the hatcheck boys, but this was not a theatrical crowd, and Nick Orlando could not count on a headwaiter to fake a reservation. "Good afternoon, Mr. Nick Orlando," said one of the proprietors. "You meeting someone?"

"Well, sort of," said Nick Orlando. "I have a sort of a half date."

"Well, if they're here I can tell you. Who is your party?"

The first name that came to Nick Orlando's mind was Harry Browning's. "Sort of looking for Harry Browning."

"Mr. Harry Browning is here, lunching with the eminent playwright Mr. Asa Unger. You know Asa, I'm sure. I'll take you right to them myself. Just follow me, sir."

The proprietor led Nick Orlando to a remote table, in a section usually referred to as left field. Nick Orlando hated every step of the way, which took him farther from the choicest tables, and his only consolation was that Harry Browning, a steady customer, and Asa Unger, a writer of hits, had done no better. Browning and Unger were sitting with their backs to the wall and could see everything that was going on, including Nick Orlando's approach. They both showed some surprise when it became unmistakable that Nick Orlando was joining them.

"Nick-ee, Nicky boy!" said Harry Browning.

"Your party," said the proprietor, leaving them. Nick Orlando did not speak until the proprietor was out of earshot and unable to guess that he had not been expected.

Harry Browning held out both hands and closed them over Nick Orlando's hand. "You know Asa, Asa Unger."

"Sure. Hi, Asa," said Nick Orlando.

"Hello, Nick. Long time."

"Long time is right."

"Cohasset, four years ago," said Asa Unger.

"That's right, you played Spike in *Dangerous Illusion*. Right?" said Harry Browning. "Nicky, why don't you stir up a little enthusiasm for a picture buy? Asa don't need the money, but I'd like to see *Illusion* a picture. I *always* said it was a natural for any studio that had the right man for Spike. Well, you're it, Nicky, and they'll listen to you now. They *gotta* listen to you now. *Mad River*—a blockbuster. I was talking to Irving Rudson before, and he read me the *Time* and *Newsweek* notices over the phone. You see them yet, Nicky?"

"No."

"Irving read them to me over the phone. They echo what the trade reviews said. Nicky, what did they bring *River* in for, do you happen to know?"

"Two million four was the last figure I heard."

"It'll do seven and a half. It'll do eight. You eat yet or you meeting someone?"

"I ate before, but I'll have a cup of coffee with you," said Nick Orlando.

"Listen, fellows, I got a train to catch," said Asa Unger.

"Asa opened in Philly the night before last," said Harry Browning.

"I know," said Nick Orlando, lying. "How'd it go, Asa?"

"Don't read the Philadelphia notices," said Asa Unger. "I'm getting into another line of work."

"They weren't that bad, Asa. Honestly they weren't. You read them over again and the *Bulletin* fellow, he only said what we were saying all along. I'll be over tonight on the six o'clock train. See you, Asa."

"Hang in there, boy," said Nick Orlando.

"Thanks," said Asa Unger. He left.

"Take his seat, Nicky. Sit here," said Harry Browning. "Asa got a real dog for himself this time. They murdered him in Philly. Sheer murder. He didn't want to show his face in the theater. You know, a sensitive guy like Asa. He wrote a kind of an open letter to the cast, that he wanted to put up on the bulletin board, but I persuaded him. I said id be a mistake. But he's taking it to heart, Asa. Nicky, get the studio to offer him forty thousand for *Illusion*, and I'll let it go for fifty."

"They don't want it for five. They don't want it for free."

"I don't know, Nicky. You may be making a mistake," said Harry Browning. "He may have other properties later on, something you like. This guy's an in-and-outer, and maybe the next one could be very big. Take *Illusion* for fifty now, and I promise you first refusal on his next hit. That's a firm promise."

"I can't do it. *Illusion* stinks."

"All right, well I tried. Now what's with you? Got in when, yesterday? I had a big bash and I looked for you, but I guess you had something lined up."

"Something, yeah," said Nick Orlando.

"There's a lot around. I don't know where it all comes from, but suddenly there's seventy-five new faces. It happens that way every year. Suddenly you look around and while you been busy the new stuff's been catching up on you. At my party there was four or five I never saw before."

"You been busy?"

"As busy as an agent at option-time—and who else should that happen to? Yeah, I been busy. A little thing called Mary Coolidge that I don't doubt for a minute that you know her, but who would ever figure me going for her? Talent and all that, but a mutt. A homely mutt. And egotistical? That's all right if she was doing the intellectual bit with Asa. But I'm not Asa. I like a dumb, pretty broad that looks good without any clothes on and never knew from Ibsen. Nevertheless, I found myself calling her up two-three times a day and couldn't wait, *couldn't wait* till I got her in the kip. And it's nothin' there, believe me. Oh, you know, it's all right, but can you explain to me what I want to bother with her for, when you know yourself, Nicky, like you see that broad just getting up over there? The tan suit? I get a call from her about every two-three months, notwithstanding although she was kept by two millionaires and married one of them." The handsome girl in the tan suit turned and waved to Harry Browning, just a tiny little wave with her fingers to which he responded in kind, an exchange which passed unnoticed by others in the restaurant. "The Ivy League type with her is the husband. I can have that any time I want to, but the last six months I been concentrating on Mary Coolidge."

"Does Coolidge go for you?"

"I gotta be truthful with you there. In three words, I don't know. Here's the situation, Nicky, and you figure it out. This egotistical, homely little mutt, she got two pet names for me. Not dearie or sweetheart. She calls me rascal and scoundrel. Hello, Rascal. Hello, Scoundrel. She says I'm the only pure, unmitigated scoundrel she ever knew. Well, I get called all kinds of names and epithets, but who is she to call me anything? Five years ago she was lucky to get a walk-on in that play of Asa's, *Mainliner*. About the junkies. What was *I* doing five years ago? Well, I had my elder son graduating from Deerfield and I give him a T-Bird for graduation. I had a little piece of property, six acres in Mount Kisco. I had twelve people on my payroll in New York, and I was spending more money in this place alone than Mary Coolidge could earn in two years. Then. She's big now, I grant you. Money-wise and billing-wise, she's big. But I saw bigger ones come and go before she knew if rascal was spelt with a *k*. She's what I call a ten-dollar thinker."

"Yeah? How, Harry?"

"Well, I tell you. She'll give a waiter a ten-dollar tip for a meal that only runs her three or four dollars. Or else she'll give the waiter thirty-five cents, depending on if she likes the waiter."

"I get it, yeah."

"No, I didn't finish. The point is, she has a ten-dollar psychology. Ten dollars is still a lot of money to her. The big gesture. That's the difference between her and some of the dames I used to know. A lousy sawbuck? I used to go out with dames that gave a sawbuck to the woman in the little girls' room. This one, this Mary Coolidge, she'd be good for a quarter, a half a dollar at the most. You know, I wish I'd of known somebody like Anna Held. *There* was no ten-dollar psychology. Or even Bernhardt. Bernhardt was slow with a dollar, but you know what she used to do on tour? She got twenty-five

hundred dollars a night, and every night before she'd go on, it
had to be all there in gold. In gold. Before she'd go on. Ten dollars for a tip. Big deal. Nicky boy, where can I take you? You
want to use my car and shofer for the afternoon?"

"What are you riding in these days?"

"The same. I got the Rolls. You know me, Nicky. I gotta
hear that clock ticking. Very soothing. You sure you don't
want to help Asa? I gotta go over to Philly tonight, and I wish
I had something to tell him on the positive side."

"Well, I know the studio is looking for something."

"You're my boy, Nicky. Offer forty and we'll take fifty, and
then you can burn the God damn play. Asa will come up with
something one of these days, and he listens to me."

"You're a scoundrel, Harry."

"I know. And a rascal. Thank God I don't have to listen to
that tonight. Gettin' weary, Nick. If you want to make a move
in that direction, she's all yours."

"Why would I?"

"Well, we did a lot of talking about her. That's what I call
buyer-interest. We wouldn't of done that much talking if you
didn't show some buyer-interest, Nicky. Hey?"

"A little. I know her, but I never thought of her that way."

"Well, as far as I'm concerned, I've had it. You take it from
the top, boy."

"Maybe I'll do that, once around," said Nick Orlando.

3

"Take me over to 414 East Fifty-second. I'm sure you know
the way," said Nick Orlando.

"I been there a couple times," said Harry Browning's chauffeur.

"How long did Harry have this rig?"

"This is our fourth year for it."

"You buy it new?"

"Imported it brand new. Mr. Browning has a corporation."

"Oh, yeah. That gag."

"The garage we use, there's eight other Rolls and there's only the one owned private. The government'll slap down one of these days, but we'll still have a good car. We only got less than seventy thousand miles on this."

"Just driving around New York City?"

"Oh, no. I go to Boston for when the boss has a play opening there. Like tomorrow I go to Philly."

"Why doesn't Harry go with you?"

"He gets car-sick on a long ride. Over twenty miles he goes by train or flies. And like some of the clients have the use of the car as a favor. Where you're going now the young lady had me and the car for a week in Boston and a week in Philly, a year ago, during tryouts."

"She a good tipper?"

The chauffeur shrugged his shoulders. "I get a good salary."

"In other words, she's a stiff?"

"I don't want to talk about a client."

"Come on, give. What the hell?"

"Well, you don't have to tell *her* this, but if you're gonna ride around in a Rolls, you don't have to give out with a lot of communist propaganda. I'm not ashamed to wear a uniform. A uniform goes with the job. She wouldn't insult a subway guard, but he has to wear more of a uniform than I do. If it wasn't for the cap you wouldn't know this *was* a uniform. And the cap ain't so bad. It's just a cap that matches the suit. I wear this suit to Mass on Sunday, with a regular hat."

"What's the most tip she ever gave you?"

"Oh, I don't want to talk about that."

"For a week in Boston? Ten bucks?"

"On the nose."

"And in Philly?"

"In Philly, nothing. I give her an argument in Philly. I told her, I said she had to wear costumes in her line of work, and I wear a uniform in mine, and I didn't see no difference. I don't, either. I'm not a downtrodden servant. I'd just as soon punch you in the nose if I had cause to. Or anybody. But I bet you she wouldn't punch Mr. George Abbott in the nose, or Eli Kazan. Would you punch Spyros Skouras in the nose?"

"I'd think twice about it."

"Well, there you are. Any of those people I'd punch them in the nose if I was driven to it. I'm not show business, see? Oh, where you're going, she don't like me. I seen her for a phoney right away." The back of his neck had begun to redden. *"And you can tell her, go ahead!"*

"What made you so sore all of a sudden?"

"That's the way she affects me. As soon as I begin thinking about her I boil up."

"She's your boss's girl friend."

"Oh, he knows how I feel about her. It's impossible to keep a thing like that from Harry Browning. He's too smart. In some ways. In other ways—but he's learning about this one."

"You think he is, eh?"

"I know he is. Nine years with a man, I can tell when he's getting fed up sometimes before he knows it himself. You're from The Bronx, aren't you? What parish are you in?"

"I used to go to St. Nicholas of Tollentine."

"Yeah? Our Lady of Mercy, not very far away. The same section."

"Our Lady of Mercy, sure. We used to call it Old Lady Murphy."

"This creature you're on your way to, she attended O.L.M., but you wouldn't know it today, to hear the propaganda. Her and the boss have arguments, and there's a man that made a couple million dollars at least. Maybe he don't have it all, but he made it. And *she* tells *him* about the economic system. Why, a day that he don't net a thousand dollars he considers it a waste. He told me that, himself. A funny man. He'll spend forty dollars for lunch any time it'll net him five thousand. That's what he says to me. I could listen to him by the hour. Orlando. Did you've a cousin living on Marion Avenue worked for Con Edison?"

"No, Orlando isn't my real name. I took the name Orlando because my own name was too long. Too many *c*'s in it."

"Pete Orlando. He lived on Marion Avenue near 196th Street. He had a job with the Consolidated Edison, and I used to bowl with him. You know what her name was before she took Coolidge?"

"Cuccinello. Mary Cuccinello. That had a lot of *c*'s in it too."

"Fred Allen would have been just as funny with the name Sullivan."

"Fred Allen? Oh, Fred Allen."

"Don't tell me you're forgetting the great Fred Allen."

"Oh, no, I used to listen to his program when I was a kid. That was on radio."

"Senator Claghorn and Mrs. Nussbaum? Don't you remember them? And the feud with Benny? Jack Benny? That was great entertainment. Who have they got like that today, I ask you? Well, maybe Bob Hope, if he was on oftener. But what do they consider funny nowadays? This young woman you're on your way to, accidentally on purpose saying something dirty."

"You think she did it on purpose?"

"Sure I do. I said to my wife, 'You watch her. Before the night's over she'll say something dirty,' and by God it wasn't two minutes later she come out with the remark and they cut her off the air. They ought to have some way to fine them when they do that, a good big fine, five thousand dollars, and they'd soon put a stop to it. If they knew there was a fine hanging over them, there wouldn't be them slips, so-called."

"How did you know she was going to say something?"

"Because I had enough experience with her, driving her here and Boston and Philly. I know her ways."

"What if I said I was in love with her?"

"Huh. Then I'd say God help you."

"Your boss has been stuck on her for a long time."

"Huh. You don't know the first thing about it. Harry I. Browning knows what he's doing, every minute of the time, whether it's a girl friend or a client or who it is. Well, here we are. I'll be parked along here somewhere."

"You don't have to wait."

"The boss said you could use the car all afternoon and

tonight, if you wanted to. I don't mind waiting. I'll be up talking to the other drivers up at River House, in case you don't
see me when you come out."

"I don't know when I'll be out."

"Well, you suit yourself about that, Mister. If you don't
want me to wait."

"I don't. Here. Thanks." Nick Orlando gave the driver a
ten-dollar bill.

4

"What made you so sure I'd let you in? What made you so sure
I'd even be here?" said Mary Coolidge.

"I wasn't sure, but I had a hunch you'd be here reading the
new play. I know that much about you," said Nick Orlando.

"Smart."

"What is the play? What kind of a part have you got?"

"You don't read the New York papers any more? You got to
that stage, hey?"

"I been on location in Idaho. You know where Idaho is?"

"Yeah. Lana Turner comes from Idaho."

"On location, living in a trailer. You weren't in pictures long
enough to spend much time on location."

"The name of the play is *A Pride of Lions*," she said, waving
a script. "Nobody in Idaho will ever see it because there's no
picture in it."

"Maybe that's a good reason for going back to Idaho. Who
wrote it?"

"You never heard of him. But you will. He's a young Paki-
stani, or he was. He hung himself two years ago at Cambridge
University, in England."

"Well, that way you're not gonna have any author-trouble at
rehearsal. Who's directing?"

"A brilliant, brilliant boy I discovered in an off-Broadway
theater last winter. A brilliant, brilliant, brilliant boy."

"Is he grateful, grateful, grateful?"

"Huh?"

"This brilliant, brilliant boy. You know what I like in a director is a director that will take direction, but they're pretty hard to find."

"This boy is creative."

"Oh, then him and you are rewriting the play."

"Wud you come here for, Nick? To rape me or just upset me?"

"I don't know, What do you want me to do?"

"Go back to Hollywood is what I want you to do. You know what I see when I look at you? A dead man. Dead. You started out with something and then you sold out for a Hollywood Cadillac."

"A Maserati. I got a special Maserati. Cadillacs are for Squaresville."

"Then you oughta have one, because you're cubic, man. That's square to the nth degree. Cubic."

"I read you, Maria. Loud and clear. What are you doing tonight?"

"Working, on this. We start rehearsals in two weeks."

"Don't *tell* me you're not up in your part. I thought you were a perfectionist."

"My part? You know how many lines I got in the first act? Four. The second act, ten. The third act, ten or eleven. The fourth act, two."

"What happened to the fifth act? Were you running over? Who has the speaking parts in this play?"

"This play is almost pure pantomime."

"Jevver see a picture, *The Thief*, with Ray Milland?"

"No, but I heard about it. Propaganda."

"No dialog, though."

"Don't mention it in the same breath."

"Then three or four years from now, after you finish your run in this play, you want to do Joan of Arc, you said."

"I don't know if we'll be finished with it in three years."

"We? You mean you and some writer are collaborating on a new one?"

"Not *some writer*. A. R. Lev."

"Who?"

"A. R. Lev, my director in *A Pride of Lions*."

"Oh, *that* A. R. Lev. I thought you were talking about A. R. Lev that works for J. P. Morgan and Company."

"What's with this dichotomy of yours all of a sudden? Ha' past one you were like a high school teen-ager that I wouldn't give a date. Now you sit here and all you are is destructive. What happened in the meanwhile?"

"I don't know. I guess I finally figured out what a real jerk you are."

"Then why are you sitting here in my apartment?"

"Yeah, but I'm not." He got up. "I just wanted to have the pleasure of telling you. So long, Cuccinello."

"*Nicky!* Don't leave me?"

(1961)

FRANKIE

Frankie had bustled into the shop one afternoon when things were quiet. The usual rush of men who get their late shaves around noon had passed, and there were no haircuts in the shop. Frankie walked in and said: "Who's the big shot here?" Dimello introduced himself, or rather said: "I am the propri'tor," and Frankie said he had noticed there were only four barbers but there were six chairs. "I'm a first-class barber," he said. "You gimme a job, straight commission? I'll work union or scab; do' make any difference."

"Do you drink?" Dimello asked.

"Wuddia got? . . . . Oh, you mean do I get drunk? Well, I get drunk, but I never missed a day in my life from hangover. You do' needa worry about that. You just gimme a job and you'll be happy. I'm first class."

Dimello took him on and Frankie proved an efficient barber. He never seemed to talk to people without their enjoying it. That, of course, was because he knew when not to start a conversation. He made a lot of money for the shop and he wasn't there two weeks before he had a couple of regulars. He also had had a date with Betty, the manicurist.

Betty always had made it a rule never to go out with any of the barbers because she disliked Italians, but she liked Frankie's teeth. Besides, he pestered her to death until she said she would go out with him. He didn't know any girls in New York, he said, and he was getting lonesome, going to the moving pictures by himself. Betty hadn't been out with a man less than ten years older than herself in God knows how long, and she couldn't ever remember having been out with a kid ten years younger than she was. So she said she would go to the pictures with him. "How naïve," she told Marline, her room-mate. "Isn't it naïve of me to be having a date with a kid twenty-five years old and going to the movies with him?"

Frankie came for her and he was something to impress Mar-line, all right, with a graceful powder-blue suit that buttoned once just below his chest, and a little white stone in his solid-blue tie, and a white shirt with a collar that had long starched points. He was a little short for Betty, but he had an air about him and nice manners. "I'm pleased to meet you, Miss Burns," he said to Marline. "I heard a lot about you at the shop." He showed his teeth. "And it was all flattering." Betty could see that Marline was impressed, all right. Maybe he was only a kid, but he was no mugg. Betty had a lone, favorite epigram which she now thought of: "Guys with gold in their pockets would be swell if they didn't have a lot of gold in their mouth too."

They went out and walked to Columbus Circle, at Frankie's suggestion. On the way over Frankie said: "Got any special idea where you want to put on the feed bag?"

"No, no place special."

"Oke. Because I was thinking about a Wop place I went to the other night where they got good wine. Me being a Wop I like good wine. Do you like wine? You're Irish, aren't you?"

"No, I'm half English and I have Spanish blood in me on my mother's side. But I like wine, all right." The fact of the matter was that Betty was no longer so entranced with the novelty of a tame movie. They went to a speakeasy and had a lot of wine, and they both got a little tight. Frankie suggested getting a couple of bottles of wine and going back to Betty's apartment, but Betty knew that probably Marline's friend would be there, so she said no. Frankie took her home and she wouldn't let him come up, not even for a little while.

For the next couple of days he was polite and that was all. One day he said: "How's Marline?"

"She's fine."

"Does she ever ask about little Frankie?"

"Not that I can recall. She's innarested in a very dear gentle-man friend."

"Oh. Oh-ho-ho." Frankie smiled. That night he called Marline, who had a date, but she mentioned the call to Betty. The next day at the shop Betty said: "Listen, little boy, it ain't any of my concern, but just as a friend, if I were you I would lay off calling Marline."

"She told you, eh?"

"We have no secrets from each other. She is my closest friend. And I just wanna advise you that Marline is innarested in a very dear gentleman friend. In fact she's ingaged to be married."

"So am I," said Frankie, and laughed. He walked away, a few steps, and then he went back and said: "Of course you ain't jealous by any chance, Betty?"

"Why, you little—!"

"I get it! I get it!" said Frankie.

After that he made Betty's life a hell. She would be at work on some old punk's nails or maybe trying to promote a date with one of the "Garden mob," but Frankie never would let her get to first base. He would interrupt her conversations and look at the man with a we're-both-men look of understanding, and the prospective date would smile at Frankie and begin to kid Betty, but it wouldn't be the kind of kidding that leads to dates. The man would say slightly insulting things and laugh and glance around at Frankie, who would laugh too. God knows how many dates Frankie spoiled for Betty.

And when the shop was empty he would stand there, leaning against his chair, smoking a cigarette. He would look over at Betty, and not say a word for a few minutes; then he would say, "Pull your dress down, sweetheart; this here is a dignified shop, eh, Mr. Dimello?" Dimello, who liked Frankie, and liked Betty, too, would smile and mumble something that didn't matter. Frankie was always making cracks, always tormenting her. But the time that she wanted to kill him was when she came home at four o'clock in the morning and found him there with Marline.

From then on he stopped making cracks, but worse than the cracks were the looks he would give her. Always smiles. Betty wanted to give up her job. She compromised by not living with

Marline any more. She got to hating the shop, which she once
had liked, and even when she was working on a man's hands
at some chair other than Frankie's, she wouldn't start a conversation, nor would she continue one that had been started.
Her tips dwindled.

This went on for six or seven weeks. Then one day two large
men with flat fat faces came in the shop. One of the barbers
snapped to attention and indicated his chair, but the man who
was in the lead didn't even take off his hat. He walked straight
to Frankie's chair and said: "Now no fuss, Jimmie. Finish the
man's shave, becuss it's going to be the last you'll do for about
ten years."

Frankie turned around and grinned. "Well, Murph, it took
yuz long enough. How's every little thing in Phillie?"

Frankie finished the man's shave and then took off his own
white coat. He went up to Dimello and whispered a few words,
and Dimello reached in his pocket and gave Frankie a couple
of twenties. Frankie shook hands with him and was just about
to leave. He remembered Betty. "How about a little goodbye
kiss, sweetheart?"

Betty looked dumb for a second, and then said: "Why not?"
Frankie kissed her.

"Always give the ladies a break," he said, and departed.

(1932)

GOOD-BYE, HERMAN

Miller was putting his key in the lock. He had two afternoon papers folded under one arm, and a package—two dress shirts which he had picked up at the laundry because he was going out that night. Just when the ridges of the key were fitting properly, the door was swung open and it was his wife. She was frowning. "Hello," he said.

She held up her finger. "Come in the bedroom," she said. She was distressed about something. Throwing his hat on a chair in the foyer, he followed her to the bedroom. She turned and faced him as he put down his bundle and began taking off his coat.

"What's up?" he said.

"There's a man in there. He came to see you. He's been here for an hour and he's driving me crazy."

"Who is he? What's it all about?"

"He's from Lancaster, and he said he was a friend of your father's."

"Well, has he been causing any trouble?"

"His name is Wasserfogel, or something like that."

"Oh, hell. I know. Herman Wasservogel. He was my father's barber. I knew he was coming. I just forgot to tell you."

"Oh, you did. Well, thanks for a lovely hour. Hereafter, when you're expecting somebody, I wish you'd let me know beforehand. I tried to reach you at the office. Where were you? I tried everywhere I could think of. You don't know what it is to suddenly have a perfectly strange man—"

"I'm sorry, darling. I just forgot. I'll go in."

He went to the living room, and there sat a little old man. In his lap was a small package, round which he had wrapped his hands. He was looking down at the package, and there was a faint smile on his face, which Miller knew to be the man's customary expression. His feet, in high, black shoes, were flat on the floor and parallel with each other, and Miller guessed that this was the way the little old man had been sitting ever since he first arrived.

"Herman, how are you? I'm sorry I'm late."

"Oh, that's all right. How are you, Paul?"

"Fine. You're looking fine, Herman. I got your letter and I forgot to tell Elsie. I guess you know each other by now," he said as Elsie came into the room and sat down. "My wife, Elsie, this is Herman Wasservogel, an old friend of mine."

"Pleased to meet you," said Herman.

Elsie lit a cigarette.

"How about a drink, Herman? A little schnapps? Glass of beer?"

"No thank you, Paul. I just came; I wanted to bring this here. I just thought maybe you would want it."

"I was sorry I didn't see you when I was home for the funeral, but you know how it is. It's such a big family, I never got around to the shop."

"Henry was in. I shaved him three times."

"Yes, Henry was there longer than I was. I was only there overnight. I had to come right back to New York after the funeral. Sure you won't have a beer?"

"No, I just wanted to bring this in to give to you." Herman stood up and handed the little package to Paul.

"Gee, thanks a lot, Herman."

"What's that? Mr. Wasserfogel wouldn't show it to me. It's all very mysterious." Elsie spoke without looking at Herman, not even when she mentioned his name.

"Oh, he probably thought I'd told you."

Herman stood while Paul undid the package, revealing a shaving mug. "This was my father's. Herman shaved him every day of his life, I guess."

"Well, not every day. The Daddy didn't start shaving till he was I guess eighteen years old, and he used to go away a lot. But I guess I shave him more than all the other barbers put together."

"Damn right you did. Dad always swore by you, Herman."

"Yes, I guess that's right," said Herman.

"See, Elsie?" said Paul, holding up the mug. He read the gold lettering: " 'J. D. Miller, M.D.' "

"Mm. Why do you get it? You're not the oldest boy. Henry's older than you," said Elsie.

Herman looked at her and then at Paul. He frowned a little. "Paul, will you give me a favor? I don't want Henry to know it that I gave you this mug. After the Daddy died, I said, 'which one will I give the mug to?' Henry was entitled to it, being the oldest and all. In a way he should have got it. But not saying anything against Henry—well, I don't know."

"Mr. Wasservogel liked you better than he did Henry, isn't that it, Mr. Wasservogel?" said Elsie.

"Oh, well," said Herman.

"Don't you worry, Herman, I'll keep quiet about it. I never see Henry anyway," said Paul.

"The brush I didn't bring. Doc needed a new one this long time, and I used to say to him, 'Doc, are you so poor yet you won't even buy a new shaving brush?' 'I am,' he'd say to me. 'Well,' I said, 'I'll give you one out of my own pocket for a gift.' 'You do,' he'd say, 'and I'll stop coming here. I'll go to the hotel.' Only joking, we were, Mrs. Miller. The Doc was always saying he'd stop coming and go to the hotel, but I knew better. He was always making out like my razors needed sharpening, or I ought to get new lights for my shop, or I was shaving him too close. Complain, complain, complain. Then around the first of last year I noticed how he'd come in, and all he'd say was, 'Hello, Herman. Once over, not too close,' and that's all he'd say. I knew he was a sick man. He knew it, too."

"Yes, you're right," said Paul. "When'd you get in, Herman?"

"Just today. I came by bus."

"When are you going back? I'd like to see some more of you before you go away. Elsie and I, we're going out tonight, but tomorrow night—"

"Not tomorrow night. Tomorrow night is Hazel's," said Elsie.

"Oh, I don't have to go to that," said Paul. "Where are you stopping, Herman?"

"Well, to tell you the truth, I ain't stopping. I'm going back to Lancaster this evening."

"Why, no! You can't. You just got here. You ought to stick around, see the sights. Come down to my office and I'll show you Wall Street."

"I guess I know enough about Wall Street; all I want to know. If it wasn't for Wall Street, I wouldn't be barbering. No. Thanks very much, Paul, but I got to get back. Got to open the shop in the morning. I only have this relief man for one day. Young Joe Meyers. He's a barber now."

"Well, what the hell? Keep him on for another day or two. I'll pay him. You've got to stick around. How long is it since you've been in New York?"

"Nineteen years last March I was here, when young Hermie went to France with the Army."

"Herman had a son. He was killed in the war."

"He'd be forty years old, a grown man," said Herman. "No. Thank you, Paul, but I think I better be going. I wanted to take a walk down to where the bus leaves from. I didn't get my walk in today yet, and that will give me the chance to see New York City."

"Oh, come on, Herman."

"Don't be so insistent, Paul. You can see Mr. Wasservogel wants to go back to Lancaster. I'll leave you alone for a few minutes. I've got to start dressing. But not too long, Paul. We've got to go all the way down to Ninth Street. Good-bye, Mr. Wasservogel. I hope we'll see you again sometime. And thank you for bringing Paul the cup. It was very sweet of you."

"Oh, that's all right, Mrs. Miller."

"Well, I really must go," said Elsie.

"I'll be in in a minute," said Paul. "Herman, you sure you won't change your mind?"

"No, Paul. Thank you, but I have the shop to think of. And you better go in and wash up, or you'll catch the dickens."

Paul tried a laugh. "Oh, Elsie isn't always like that. She's just fidgety today. You know how women get."

"Oh, sure, Paul. She's a nice girl. Very pretty-looking. Well."

"If you change your mind—"

"Nope."

"We're in the phone book."

"Nope."

"Well, just remember, if you *do* change your mind; and I really don't know how to thank you, Herman. You know I mean it, how much I appreciate this."

"Well, your Dad was always good to me. So were you, Paul. Only don't tell Henry."

"That's a promise, Herman. Good-bye, Herman. Good luck, and I hope I'll see you soon. I may get down to Lancaster this fall, and I'll surely look you up this time."

"Mm. Well, *auf Wiedersehen*, Paul."

"*Auf Wiedersehen*, Herman."

Paul watched Herman going the short distance to the elevator. He pushed the button, waited a few seconds until the elevator got there, and then he got in without looking back. "Good-bye, Herman," Paul called, but he was sure Herman did not hear him.

(1937)

HARRINGTON AND WHITEHILL

Mary Brown went to the door and opened it. "Hello, Jack," she said.

"Hello, Mary," he said. "How are you?"

"Very well, thank you," she said. "You know where to put your coat. Gretchen just got home a little while ago, so you're going to have to wait."

"I have all the time in the world," said Jack. He hung his coat and hat in the foyer closet.

"Would you like a drink?"

"Sure. What have you got?"

"What you see. Whiskey, and gin," she said.

"Shall I make a cocktail?"

"Not for me, thanks."

"Not for me, either," he said. He helped himself to a strong whiskey and water.

She was uncomfortable, ill at ease under his gaze.

"You don't have to entertain me, Mary. Do whatever you were doing."

"I was washing stockings, and Gretchen's in the tub," she said.

"You staying home tonight?"

"I'm going out later," she said. "There's a dance at the Squadron, but Billy won't be here till—I don't know—not before ten, I guess."

"You going to marry Billy?"

The question annoyed her. She held out her left hand.

"I didn't ask you if you were engaged to him. If you announced your engagement I'd probably hear about it."

"Then why don't you just wait till you do hear about it?"

"I don't think you want to marry him, but all the same I'll bet you do."

"Jack, why don't you keep your nose out of my affairs? I really don't like those kind of questions."

"It wasn't a question you disliked. It was my analysis of your innermost thoughts. I don't think you want to marry Billy, but I'd bet fifty dollars you're married to him within one year. Would you like to take that bet?"

"Suppose I won? Would you ever pay me?"

"If I happened to have fifty dollars I would. Yes, I'd pay you."

"I'm sorry I said that," she said.

"What the hell? I don't often have fifty dollars, and nobody knows it better than you do. Except Gretchen. And you're a Brown, and the Browns are all very money-conscious. So am I, of course. But you're money-conscious because you have it, and I am because I haven't."

"It *wasn't* a very nice thing to say," she said. "But you always make some remark that just infuriates me, and I say things I don't really mean."

"I do it on purpose," he said.

"Sometimes I think you do," she said.

"I do," he said.

"What pleasure do you get out of it?"

"Oh, come on, Mary. Isn't that obvious? You never fail to rise to the bait. Never."

"Well, I admit I'm not as clever as you are."

"Who said anything about clever? You're so used to having the same things said to you, and saying the same things yourself, that anything out of the ordinary throws you off."

"I'm not used to clever people. My friends aren't clever people."

"If you're talking about Billy, I'll agree with that. No one will ever accuse Billy Walton of being clever. He's safe there."

"He has a very *fine* mind."

"Maybe he has. *Mens sana in corpore sano*. A sound mind in a sound body, that's Billy Walton. You ought to have very healthy children. Although I'm only going on what I see. There may be all sorts of loathsome diseases in the Walton family history. The Browns, too, for that matter. But just from looking at the present generation, you and Billy, I'd say you had a pretty good chance of producing fine specimens. Reproducing, I should say. Because that's what you'll do. You'll reproduce. The offspring will bear some resemblances to you and some to Billy, but they'll be essentially the same. You perpetuate the line, without incurring the risk of bringing forth genuine idiots, as you would if you married your brother or a first cousin."

"When I was working with the Junior League I saw children that had mixed ancestry, and believe me some of those were far from perfect."

"I know," he said. "I've seen them too. It makes you realize what a big chance you're taking when you bring *any* children into the world."

"Therefore, why not pick someone you know something about?"

"Like Billy Walton," he said.

"Yes. He was the twelfth highest man in his class, and he rowed on the varsity crew for *three years*."

"I see what you mean, all right. It was a winning crew, too. I never rowed, myself. Not that I was big enough for the varsity, but I never went out for the jayvees or the hundred-and-fifty pounders. I know it's very good discipline and teaches you teamwork and all that, but I didn't have the real spirit. Besides, I heard that oarsmen all got boils on their asses. I had a boil on my ass once, and it's no fun. Did you ever have a boil on your ass, Mary?"

"Another of those remarks. But this time I know you said it on purpose."

"I always do. I told you," he said. "Did you ever have a boil there, Mary?"

"No."

"Where?"

"On my ass. You wanted to make me say it, so now I have."

"I'm glad you escaped that," he said. "Not only because of the pain, the discomfort. But for aesthetic reasons. A boil just doesn't belong on your ass. Or anywhere else on you. Or on Billy Walton either, except in line of duty for good old Yale."

"Harvard, and you know it," she said.

"Yes, I did know it. But the Yale varsity and the Harvard varsity, except for all those Saltonstalls on the Harvard crews, they're both just a continuation of Groton and St. Mark's. Hard to tell them apart."

"Billy didn't go to Groton *or* to St. Mark's," she said.

"*Why* didn't he? Maybe you ought to do a little digging on that, Mary. You might learn something before it's too late. Where *did* he go to school?"

"He went to Pomfret, where all his family went."

"Oh. Well, I guess you're safe. If there were family reasons for going to Pomfret, you'll have to make allowances."

"Is that supposed to get a rise out of me, too?"

"Nothing will, tonight," he said. "You're on your guard. Do you mind if I cadge another drink off you?"

"Gretchen pays half, it's not all mine," she said.

"Well, do you mind if I cadge another drink off you and Gretchen?"

"Go right ahead," she said.

"After all, you're first cousins. And I guess Billy Walton takes a drink here now and then. So, in a sense, you might say half of his drinks are practically mine, inasmuch as I'm the one that comes to see Gretchen. And Gretchen pays half the liquor bill. Do you follow me?"

"Oh, yes," she said.

"I wasn't sure. I had a little trouble with it myself."

"Don't make the next one so strong," she said.

"Oh, my present state of mind wasn't produced by the drink I just finished."

"I didn't think so," she said.

"You're so observant, Mary. Did it show, that I stopped off at Dan Moriarty's on the way here?"

"I could tell you'd stopped off somewhere."

"It's payday, and I wanted to reestablish credit. Today it was

Dan's turn. I'm all clear with Dan now, which means that Gretchen and I will dine at Giuliano's, on the cuff. The week after next, not next week, but the week after next, I shall reestablish credit at Giuliano's."

"How can you *live* that way?" she said.

"Huh. You might better ask, how could I live any other way? Were it not, were it not for the liberal policy of certain speakeasy proprietors, I would often go without food or drink. Not only what I charge to my account, but I can cash cheques. They don't bother to try and put the cheques through. They just hold them for a while, and tear them up when I come in with the cash. But don't you tell Gretchen."

"Don't you think she knows?"

"Not positively."

"You'll never be able to get married if you don't start saving *some* money."

"Wrong," he said. "If I were to save ten dollars a week—a very unlikely prospect—but say I saved ten dollars every week, in one year I'd have five hundred and twenty dollars. Right?"

"Yes."

"In *two* years, *two years*, I'd have one thousand and forty dollars. In *ten* years of this fantastic scheme, I'd have amassed the sum of five thousand, two hundred dollars. Fifty-two hundred bucks. Do you know what that is?"

"Well—"

"Don't bother to think about it. It's exactly, I happen to know, exactly the allowance Gretchen gets from her mother in one year. Not what she gets from both parents, but from one parent. Her father gives her the same amount plus birthday and Christmas presents."

"I know. But still—"

"Wait a minute, I haven't finished. Do you know how much I get paid?"

"Seventy-five dollars a week."

"Oh, she told you. Well, that's right. Seventy-five a week. I pay sixty dollars a month rent. That's one I have to pay. If I don't pay the rent, out I go. No place to rest my weary head. So I do pay my rent. Not right on the dot, but somewhere in the first two or maybe three weeks of every month. Sixty bucks, cash. And I pay a woman six dollars a week to clean up my apartment. She doesn't come in Sunday, and a damn good thing she doesn't, some Sundays. But that's twenty-four dollars a month. Sixty and twenty-four, eighty-four. More than a week's pay and so far I haven't even bought a pound of coffee. I make my own coffee and have a couple of doughnuts every morning, but so far we haven't come to that. I haven't paid the phone company yet. The rent, the maid, the phone company, and the laundry bill. You can't wear a shirt two days in New York City, not if you have a white-collar job. The light company. They'll turn off the light. Gas. No hot water for my coffee. The dry cleaners. When you have two suits and a Tuck, there's always one or the other at the dry cleaners'. And so far, no food, no coffee, and no cigarettes, not a damn thing to drink. I haven't even left my apartment."

"But people live on a lot less than that. When I was with the Junior League—"

"I know that, too. When you were with the Junior League you saw families getting by on twenty-five or thirty dollars a week. But did they want to? *I* don't want to. I can't get by on *three times* that much. I can't save four dollars a month, and live the way I have to. It's no use arguing that I could stop going to Dan Moriarty's and places like that. Why should I? To save fifty-two hundred dollars in ten years? Ten God damn miserable, joyless years? And be thirty-six years old at the end of it?"

"Well, I don't know," she said.

"Mary, your grandfather, or maybe it was your great-grandfather—"

"My grandfather, if you're going to say what I think you are."

"Opened a little store in Cleveland, Ohio, on probably a great deal less than fifty-two hundred bucks capital. And now your family are worth God knows how many millions. Well, your grandpa worked very hard, raised a large family, made a big pile of dough, and now I'm drinking his liquor. And whenever she's ready, I'm going to take his granddaughter out for dinner."

"Yes?"

"Well, why should I sweat and strain to save five thousand dollars when I can go out with Gretchen tonight and have a better time than old J. J. Brown ever had or ever gave anyone?"

"If a good time is all you want to get out of life," she said.

"I sure as hell don't want to have a bad time."

"But you are having a bad time. You worry about money, you can't marry Gretchen. You're not having a very good time, Jack."

"No?"

"No."

"Well, are you? Are you having a good time? Washing your stockings and waiting for a stuffed shirt to take you to a dance at Squadron A?"

"Of course I am," she said.

"And wondering if this is going to be the night Mr. Billy Walton will propose honorable marriage? And you can go back to Cleveland, Ohio, and get ready for the big wedding. Got yourself a real, genuine, old Knickerbocker family specimen."

"I think you're horrible! And I mean that," she said. "You're detestable."

"Sure. But you're all right. The one life you have to live, and what are you doing with it? Saving your virginity for him. You may be a peasant, but you're a virgin peasant."

"Horrible, horrible," she said, and began to cry as she left the room, her face covered with her hands.

He sat silent for a moment, took a sip of his drink, then got up and threw the glass in the fireplace. He was staring at it when Gretchen came in.

She went to him without a word, and they embraced.

"Sorry I'm late," she said.

"Why do you let them get away with it?"

"With what?"

"I'm sure everybody else goes home at five, but they don't seem to care how long they make you stay. God knows they don't pay you enough."

She smiled. "The last two weeks they didn't pay me at all," she said.

"The next thing will be when they try to get you to put money in the business."

"They've already asked me to," she said.

"Are you going to?"

"I don't know. I might. It wouldn't be a lot. Where are we going?"

"Giuliano's," he said. "Shall we go?"

"Could we wait a few minutes? Mother phoned and I wasn't here, and I think she may call back. I'd like to find out how Father is."

"Is he home from the hospital?"

"He got home yesterday, but they're keeping two trained nurses."

"He must be a lot better or they wouldn't have let him go home from the hospital."

"That's what I'm hoping," she said. "We can have a cocktail here. Will you mix me a Martini? And what are you having? No drink?"

"Don't pretend, Gretchen. You know I've had a lot to drink."

"I wasn't going to say anything. How did you happen to break the glass in the fireplace?"

"I was drinking a silent toast to Mary and Billy Walton."

"Oh, she told you? How can you worm those things out of her? She hasn't even told her family."

"She hasn't told me, either. I just guessed."

"She must have told you something," said Gretchen. "What did she tell you?"

"She told me I ought to start saving money."

"Well, I'm sure you had a good answer for that. She worries about you, you know. She really likes you."

"Am I supposed to jump for joy because Mary Brown likes me?"

"You could be more agreeable. Whenever you have any conversation with her you always manage to somehow hurt her feelings. You say things."

"Yes, damn near every conversation I have with anybody, I say things."

"Oh, don't start picking on me. It doesn't get you anywhere.

I know your ways. But Mary *isn't* used to having people make her feel like an absolute dumbbell. And she's not, either. She's very bright. But you're always so condescending with her, trying to trip her up on everything she says."

"How long are we going to have to wait for your mother's call?"

"Why? Are you in any particular hurry?"

"I don't want to go an hour without a drink."

"Well, have one. It's there. And I told you, I asked you to fix me a Martini. What's got into you tonight?"

He started the business of making her cocktail. "Money."

"Money?"

"The whole damn subject of money. Your cousin got me started on it, and before I knew it I was telling her all about my finances."

"Well, she understands."

"Understands? Who gives a damn whether she understands? I wasn't trying to make her understand anything. But it made *me* realize what a hell of a state my finances are in. I hadn't stopped to think about it lately."

"Then maybe it's time you did. You have a good job—"

"A good job—and I make less than you get for spending money. You have a job that's supposed to pay you twenty-five dollars a week, and when they don't pay you, you can laugh it off as a joke."

"It's not a joke, and I don't laugh it off. Neither do they. These two boys are trying to publish good things, not just mystery stories and trashy novels. But all the good authors are signed up by the big publishers. These boys are trying to keep their heads above water until they discover someone that hasn't been published before, and that's not easy, because the literary agents, if they find somebody good but without an established reputation, they take their discovery to one of the big publishers like Scribner's. Doubleday. I'm in favor of what we're doing, and I wish I could help."

"They'll give you your chance to help."

"Well, I'd rather put my money in that than in a lot of other things I could think of."

"Such as?"

"What other things? Well, museums, for instance. Grandfather put a lot of money into the Museum, and we're all expected to contribute once a year. But I'm not going to this year. I'm going to put my money into Whitehill and Grimes."

"The boys."

"Well, they're not boys any more. Both over thirty. But they're young in the publishing business. What I can give them, or lend them, is only a drop in the bucket, but they need all the help they can get. And I'd get much more satisfaction out of helping them than just writing a cheque to the Museum and then forgetting about it. Wouldn't you?"

"I'm not faced with any such dilemma."

"Oh, come on. Don't you agree with me? Isn't it better to do what you can to help develop new writers than—excuse me. I'm sure that's Mother's call." She went to the telephone.

"Hello . . . It's all right, Mary, I've got it . . . Mother? How are you, dear? . . . How did it go? . . . Oh, they did? . . . Well, how is he now? . . . Oh, dear. That's not very good, is it? . . . Oh, you poor dear . . . Who else is there with you? . . . That's good . . . What does Dr. Brady say? . . . Uh-huh. Uh-huh. Yes . . . Then I'll tell you what I'll do, Mother. I'll take the midnight . . . Well, I'll sit up in the day coach if I have to. But I think I ought to be there, knowing Dr. Brady. He isn't prone to exaggerate . . . I hope *you're* getting some rest, but I suppose you're not . . . Well, I'll take the midnight, and don't have anyone meet me. I'll get a taxi . . . I know, dear, and all we can do now is hope . . . Goodnight, Mother."

She hung up and sighed. She lit a cigarette. "Not so good. Not so damn good. He had a hemorrhage this afternoon and he's been in a coma ever since. Wonderful Dr. Brady, I adore that man. He said we'll know tonight, but I think he knows already. He's trying to spare Mother. Poor Daddy. Strange. Calling him Daddy. We stopped calling him Daddy when my brother was born. He didn't want his son calling him Daddy, so we all changed to Father. I hope he is in a coma, a real one. He couldn't stand to have people fuss over him."

"What can I do, darling?"

"Oh—sit with me. Put your arms around me, and if I cry, let me, a little. I don't think I'm going to, but yes I am." She began to weep quietly and he sat with her. "I want to see him once more," she said.

Mary Brown stood in the doorway, unseen by Gretchen and Jack, and she quickly vanished.

2

It is two years later. A Sunday at lunch time, the apartment of Jack and Gretchen on Park Avenue. Jack was reading the Sunday paper when the doorbell rang, and he went to admit Billy and Mary Walton. He kisses Mary on the cheek, shakes hands with Billy.

"Look at you two," said Jack. "You look as if you were all set to pose for the rotogravure." He inspects Bill Walton, who is attired in short black coat and striped trousers and has a bowler in his hand.

"I've always been meaning to get one of these outfits," said Jack.

"Adore them," said Mary. "They make any man look distinguished."

"Well, I'd put that to a severe test, but damn it, I'm going to order one tomorrow," said Jack. "You two been to church?"

"Not only to church, but you made a good guess," said Billy. "About the rotogravure."

"I was going to wait and tell Gretchen," said Mary.

"You've been posing for the roto section?" said Jack.

"For the *Herald Tribune*," said Mary. "It's linked up with some charity. Mr. and Mrs. Williamson Walton, and I think Borden's Milk."

"I don't think we *are* Borden's Milk, Mary. Didn't the man say that that had been a mistake? I know he did, as a matter of fact. He said we were Hellman's Mayonnaise. The Borden's Milk people have the Schermerhorn twins."

"Oh, I didn't hear that part of your conversation."

Gretchen came in. "Hello, my dears," she said. "Did you have your picture taken?"

"In front of St. Bartholomew's," said Mary.

"And I happen to be a member of St. Thomas's. *We* are," said Billy.

"Was it bad? Mary was dreading it," said Gretchen.

"It wasn't really so bad," said Mary.

"Except having people stop and stare at us. I felt like a model," said Billy.

"And you look like one—I mean that as a compliment. Do you want to see the baby, Mary?"

"Of course," said Mary.

"Billy, I won't subject you to that," said Gretchen.

"Oh, why I'd love to—"

"No, you stay and talk to Jack," said Gretchen. She and Mary left the room.

"You're a coward," said Jack. "I don't know how many times I've had to say goo-goo to your kid. And frankly, she isn't half as good-looking as my young man."

"That's a matter of opinion," said Billy. "What's new at Harrington, Whitehill and Grimes?"

"Can you keep a secret?"

"I think so," said Billy.

"I'm buying out Grimes. We're going to keep his name for a year, but only a year. Next year it'll be Harrington and Whitehill."

"Congratulations," said Billy.

"Thank you."

"Did you have to pay Grimes a lot of money?"

"Quite a lot. Or at least let's put it this way. It wasn't a very large sum, but it had to be cash. He wouldn't agree to any other terms. But it worked out all right. When he insisted on cash, that made it just that much easier to tell him that we weren't going to carry his name. And therefore, if we were not going to carry his name, he wasn't entitled to very much money for good will. He outsmarted himself."

"I think you probably *let* him outsmart himself," said Billy.

"Frankly, Jack, I have more and more respect for you as a business man. There was a time when I didn't think you had it in you, but I was good and wrong about that. I used to think you were one of those Greenwich Village Bohemian types, but I take it all back now."

"I thought I was, too."

"By the way, I spoke to Harry Judson. Your name comes up on the fifteenth, I think it is, and according to Harry you can start wearing the hatband as soon as you send them your cheque. In other words, you're in."

"Well, thank you for that, too, Billy. I wouldn't have made it without you."

"You're damn right you wouldn't. Because three years ago if your name had come up, and anyone asked me about you, I'd have said no. Shows how wrong you can be."

"No, three years ago you'd have been right. But three years ago I wouldn't have been up for any club."

"I suppose a lot of fellows go through that phase. I never did. I know it sounds stuffy, but I never felt that I had to rebel against my mother and father. I don't know of two finer people in the world. I liked Harvard and my friends there. I didn't like everybody in prep school, and I got into a few scrapes there, but nothing very serious. So I never went through that phase. As a matter of fact, the rebellious ones always struck me as a bunch of soreheads. I don't mean you necessarily, but yes, I do. You were sore at something."

"I was sore at everything."

"Well, you have the courage to admit it, and it takes courage. What were you sore at, if it's any of my business?"

"I was adopted. My father and mother both died in the flu epidemic in 1918, and my aunt and uncle adopted me."

"Were they nasty to you?"

"Not a bit. But I was sixteen years old when my parents died, and at that age you don't grow a new set of parents. They're not the same as your own father and mother, and no matter how much they did for me, and it was as much as they could afford, I resented it because I felt they were doing it out of a sense of duty."

"Well, if you don't mind my saying so, you sound as though you were already a bit of a sorehead when you were sixteen."

"Maybe I was. But let's not go into this too deeply or I may find out that I'm still a sorehead."

"No, I don't think you are any more. You've had a change of heart, and Gretchen's responsible for that. That's a girl I think the world of, and so does everybody else. Mary feels much closer to her than if she were her own sister. She's often said so to me."

"Well," said Jack. "How about a drink?"

"Can't. We have to go to Mother's this afternoon, and she just hates it when Father or I have a drink in the middle of the day. Her brother, my Uncle Phil Williamson, was a notorious rumpot. Died of it in his early thirties. I don't know if you've ever noticed, but when you've been to Mother's for lunch, you're offered one sherry. One sherry, and that's all."

"I've never been to your mother's for lunch."

"Yes you have, haven't you? Well, anyway, now you're forewarned. Don't ever go there with a hangover and expect the hair of the dog. My father wasn't very much of a drinker, either."

"Mine was. Periodic benders. And I guess that's why we never had very much money. But my uncle didn't drink at all, and he wasn't exactly rolling in wealth."

"Your father was a lawyer. Why do so many lawyers like the booze? I should think you'd have to have a pretty clear head to be a lawyer. But some of the hardest drinkers I know are lawyers, and yet it doesn't seem to affect their work. One of the most brilliant lawyers I know makes absolutely no bones about it. I'm not telling tales out of school. It's George Wingman, partner in Mortimer and Miller. I've seen him in his own office, put the bottle right up on the desk, and slug away at it. But when you know the tax laws as well as he does, you don't have to worry about where your next job is coming from."

"I know George Wingman," said Jack. "Some day you're going in his office and it won't be a bottle on the desk. It'll be a dame."

"So I've heard. A tail hound. That's something I never could see. I don't say I was a purity boy, but this thing of chasing one woman after another—I just don't see it. Do you?"

"I suppose I've done my share of it."

"Well, maybe in your Greenwich Village days. But George Wingman, for instance, he's married."

"Yes, I know his wife. She's from my home town, or one of my home towns."

"How does she put up with it? She must *know*."

"She knows, all right," said Jack.

"Oh. Meaning that what's sauce for the goose and so forth?"

"They seem to have some kind of an arrangement."

"What a way to live. What a way to live. Why be married if that's all it means? Whenever I hear of friends of mine considering getting a divorce—I think you can solve any problem except that one. Unfaithfulness. Infidelity. I'd never try to help out two friends of mine if I knew for sure that one of them had been unfaithful. I have helped one or two, when there were financial problems. And one guy that let his wife sit at home while he went to the hockey matches or the ball game. You know, sometimes just a word will do the trick. But not when—" he interrupted himself as Gretchen and Mary returned to the room "—you have that other problem."

"Problem? Problem? What other problem?" said Gretchen.

"Oh, we were discussing a legal problem," said Billy. He looked at Jack, rather proud of his half-truth and quick thinking.

"Oh, yes," said Gretchen. "Jack's been spending a lot of time with lawyers lately. Did you tell him, dear?"

"Yes, I did," said Jack.

"Everybody's in on this but me," said Mary.

"You tell her, Jack," said Gretchen.

"Simply that I've bought out Grimes."

"Grimes?" said Mary. "Oh, your partner, Grimes. Why, that's wonderful, isn't it?"

"We think so," said Gretchen. "Next year the firm will be known as Harrington and Whitehill, without the Grimes."

"Well, didn't you tell me that Grimes was more or less of a weak sister?" said Mary to Gretchen.

"She shouldn't have said that, if she did," said Jack. "He after all was one of the original founders of the firm."

"Well, heavens, I don't go around repeating everything Gretchen tells me."

"I'm sure you don't, Mary. But—"

"Wait, wait, wait, wait," said Gretchen. "*I* was the one that *originally* said Stanley Grimes was a weak sister. Long ago. When I was still working for Whitehill and Grimes. Stanley was a nice, ineffectual boy. He was supposed to be the one that would discover new authors, and Ray Whitehill would manage the business end. But Stanley would take the authors to lunch and make all sorts of promises, then Ray would have to repudiate the promises. If Stanley Grimes had had his way, the firm would have gone bankrupt. Five-hundred-dollar advances for little slim volumes by unknown poets. Nobody has to feel sorry for Stanley. When Jack decided to buy him out, Stanley suddenly developed a very keen sense of the value of money. He insisted on cash. Thirty-five thousand dollars cash."

"Wow!" said Billy.

"I should say so," said Gretchen.

"But we got rid of him," said Jack.

"And it was Jack, not Stanley, that discovered the only two authors on our list that have made money, so far. Jack discovered Julian Joplin and Serena Von Zetwitz."

"Hot stuff, that Von Zetwitz woman," said Billy. "Is that her real name?"

"Yes, why?" said Jack. "Doesn't it sound real?"

"It sounds real, but I'll bet she never goes back to that town in Iowa, not after that book."

"Nebraska," said Jack. "No, I guess she won't be going back there for a while. Anyway, she's living in Italy."

"What's she like, to meet, I mean?" said Mary.

"Rather plain," said Gretchen. "Soft-spoken."

"How old?"

"Early thirties. Maybe thirty-three or four," said Gretchen. "This was her third novel—"

"Fourth," said Jack.

"That's right. Three unpublished, and then she wrote *Harvest Time*. Jack read the manuscript of one of her earlier novels and encouraged her to try again. And guess where he discovered that manuscript? In a pile of manuscripts that Stanley Grimes had rejected but hadn't got around to returning. *Harvest Time* is entirely due to Jack. I'm very proud of my husband."

"Well, she didn't pull any punches," said Billy. "Some of it was pretty raw. Pretty raw."

"And I don't think it's a true picture," said Mary. "You can go to any small town in America and find *some* queer birds, but why doesn't she write about some of the decent people?"

"Wouldn't sell," said Billy.

"Oh, I don't know, Billy," said Jack. "*Laughing Boy* is selling. Edna Ferber has a new book out, and that's selling. Naturally we'd like to have Edna Ferber and Oliver LaFarge on our list, but we haven't got them. But we also want to publish new people, like Serena Von Zetwitz and Julian Joplin."

"And how exciting it is when they sell," said Gretchen. "A year ago nobody'd ever heard of either one of them, and today they're both famous."

"Well, they've all heard of the Von Zetwitz dame, all right," said Billy. "Especially in Boston. Did you plan that, Jack? Getting her book banned in Boston?"

"Naturally," said Jack.

"Oh, you did not," said Mary.

"Of course I didn't, but Billy likes to think I did," said Jack.

"I was only kidding. Can't you take a joke?" said Billy.

"Not very well, I guess. Not where our books are concerned."

"The one I'm dying to meet is Julian Joplin," said Gretchen.

"Oh, haven't you met him? I thought you met all your authors," said Mary.

"Most of them, but he hasn't been to New York."

"Not even when you published his book?" said Mary.

"Won't come," said Gretchen. "He won't budge out of Kentucky."

"He's one I'd be afraid to meet," said Mary.

"Why? I didn't read *his* book," said Billy. "Does he write like the Von Zetwitz dame?"

"Yes, and no," said Mary. "He describes worse things than she does, but you have to read it over again to make sure. Isn't that right, Gretchen?"

"Yes. He has such a complicated style that you *can* read and reread long passages in his books, and then it begins to dawn on you that he's been describing something perfectly awful."

"Like what?" said Billy.

"Well—it's sex, but not just ordinary sex. Jack, you explain," said Gretchen.

"Perversion."

"You mean like a couple of fairies?" said Billy.

"No. A man and a woman, but having an extremely unconventional affair. Read the book. Maybe you won't even notice it."

"I'll sure as hell notice it if Mary did."

"Well, I had to go back and reread it, to make sure. Even so I'm not altogether sure," said Mary. "Did you get it first time you reread it, Gretchen?"

"The scene in the churchyard? Yes, I think I did."

"You didn't have to ask Jack?"

"I did ask him, but I'd guessed right," said Gretchen.

"Well, you're a lot more sophisticated than Mary," said Billy.

"Don't ever say that about any woman, Billy, that she's less sophisticated than another woman," said Jack.

"I suppose I'm less sophisticated than Gretchen, but I'm getting there," said Mary. "You make me sound not quite bright, Billy, but I know a lot of things I don't necessarily talk about."

"Well, don't talk about them, because I think it's very unbecoming. Gretchen *is* more sophisticated than you are, but still she doesn't talk about such things the way some girls do nowadays. Have you got anyone else coming for lunch besides us?"

"Yes, are you getting hungry?" said Gretchen.

"A little, but no great hurry. I had breakfast at ha' past eight."

"What on earth for, on Sunday morning?" said Gretchen.

"I didn't say I got up at ha' past eight. I only said I had break-fast. We didn't actually get up till about an hour later. Mary got up early, but then she came back to bed."

"You might as well describe our whole morning," said Mary.

Billy was baffled, then realized the inferences that could be taken. "Oh," he said. "Well, we're married."

"Oh, hush up, Billy. You're only making it worse," said Mary.

"I'm not, but you are. To change the subject, who *is* coming for lunch. Or *are?*"

"You've never met them. Michael and Josephine Landers. Jack just hired him a few weeks ago, as a sort of general assis-tant in the editorial department. And she writes for *Harper's Bazaar*. She's had some light verse published in *The New Yorker*, you may have seen. He's written a novel that we're going to publish, but he needed a job and Jack hired him."

"He got the novel out of his system. Pretty terrible. But I think he's going to make a very good assistant. Anyway, we agreed to let him try it for a year," said Jack.

"And they needed the money. Michael spent over a year writing his novel, and they apparently had to live on her sal-ary, which wasn't much. Michael was really quite desperate for a job, and he's very grateful to Jack."

"Well, we don't have to go into that," said Jack. "We're not paying him much, but I think he has a hell of a future in the office. I just hope he doesn't decide to go back to writing novels. The one I read was really quite bad, and I think I know."

"You certainly do," said Gretchen. "There! There they are."

"What's their name again?" said Billy.

"Landers. Michael and Josephine Landers," said Gretchen.

Michael and Josephine Landers came in and were intro-duced. They were slightly younger than the others. Josephine was smartly dressed in a good but not new suit, Michael in Brooks clothes from tie to shoe, all new and stiffish. It could be guessed that his new outfit had coincided with his new job. She was smallish and pretty, with light brown hair and bright blue eyes. He was tallish and thin, under six foot, loose-limbed and not quite awkward in his movements and his manners, saved from awkwardness by an integral self-confidence that came near to being arrogance, but was not.

Immediately after the introductions Michael Landers addressed Billy Walton. "Didn't you row on the Harvard crew?"

"Yes, I did. How did you know?" said Billy. "Did you row in college?"

Michael looked quickly at Mary Walton, then back at Billy. "No—I just recognized your name."

"Were you at Harvard?"

"No, I went to Brown." He spoke with a finality that indicated his unwillingness to continue past the identification of Billy. But then he had a change of mind. "You don't remember me at all?"

"That's kind of putting me on the spot, but no, I'm afraid I don't."

"I don't mean that you'd recognize me, but doesn't my name mean anything to you? Michael Landers?"

"You've got to help me out," said Billy. The others were taking a keen interest in their conversation.

"All right," said Michael. "My father was the gardener on your family's place in Mount Kisco. Now do you remember?"

"Of course. Now I remember. But you have to admit, that was a long time ago," said Billy.

"How interesting," said Gretchen. "Your father worked for Mr. Walton's father?"

"For about twenty years," said Michael Landers. "Do you want to tell her, Walton?"

"I don't particularly want to, but I will, if you insist," said Billy. "Mr. Landers's father, David Landers, was the head gardener at our place in Mount Kisco. And when I was about thirteen or fourteen, at Pomfret at the time, there was a robbery at our house. A lot of my mother's jewelry was stolen, and the police were convinced it was an inside job. They questioned Mr. Landers's father."

"They didn't only question him. They arrested him."

"Yes, I guess they did actually place him under arrest, on

suspicion. But they released him. It was an inside job, but the guilty party was my mother's maid. She confessed, and they recovered all the jewelry. But Mr. Landers's father quit his job, although my father and mother wanted him to stay. Is that a fair statement of what happened?"

"Oh, very fair. You never knew what happened to my father, did you?"

"No. I was away at school, and about all I knew was that he quit his job, and he and his family, which would include you, left Mount Kisco."

"Under a cloud, would you say?" said Michael.

"Not as far as we were concerned. I know my father wanted him to stay."

"But didn't keep the police from arresting him."

"I don't know anything about that part of it."

"But that's the important part, as far as my father was concerned. And as far as *I'm* concerned. My father was incapable of stealing anything. He'd worked for your father and your grandfather, for twenty years. But they allowed the police to put him in jail."

"No necessity to bring my grandfather into it. My father couldn't have prevented the police from—"

"Your father, in Mount Kisco, could have prevented anything. If he hadn't suspected my father, they never would have arrested him." He turned to Gretchen. "I'm sorry, Mrs. Harrington, but you'll have to excuse us."

"Well, under the circumstances, I suppose there's nothing else to do," said Gretchen.

"Yes there is," said Billy. "You can excuse us. Mr. and Mrs. Landers can stay. We were going to have to leave early anyhow, to go to Mother's. So I really insist, Gretchen."

"I don't know," said Jack. "Why don't you all stay?"

"Ridiculous," said Mary Walton.

"No more ridiculous than reopening an old wound and then not trying to do something to heal it," said Jack.

"Sorry, Jack, but I didn't reopen it, and I don't think it can be healed. Mr. Landers could have postponed this little scene till some other time, but as soon as he heard my name . . . No, we'll leave, and you can get the rest of the story from Mr. Landers."

"I'll see you Tuesday, Gretchen," said Mary.

The Waltons left.

"There's no use trying to talk about something else," said Gretchen. "What happened to your father, Michael?"

"Do you know what gardeners are like, Mrs. Harrington?"

"In what way?" said Gretchen.

"They're generally very quiet men, really more interested in what they're doing than they are in people. Most of the time they're working with dirt, the soil. And all they produce is beauty, and often the most beautiful things don't last very long. A few days, maybe a few weeks. But it's worth it to them, to bring that beauty up out of the ground. My father knew every flower in the Waltons' garden, and every petal on every flower. He was up at five o'clock every morning, seven days a week most of the year, and in all kinds of weather. He was no more capable of stealing Mrs. Walton's diamonds and pearls than he could have taken one of her prize roses and crushed it in his fist. My father didn't even carry a watch. He had a watch. This one. It was given to him on his twenty-first birthday, but he never carried it. He only owned one necktie, to wear to church on Sunday. But as soon as he came home from church, right after Sunday dinner, he put on his work clothes and was back in the garden. He had two helpers, two Italians, but they wouldn't work on Sunday, and some things had to be done while the weather was right. He was paid twenty dollars a week and we got the cottage rent-free and all our fresh vegetables, that he grew, although one of the Italians did do most of the work in the truck garden. He wouldn't have known a diamond from a piece of cut glass.

"Well, that was the man that J. W. Walton suspected of stealing his wife's jewelry. Locking him up in jail, even just for one night, was the most heartless, most senseless, cruelest thing I ever knew of. He didn't understand it at the time, and the more he tried to understand it later, the worse he got. I mean—well, it affected his mind. He wasn't very bright anyway. He hardly ever read the newspaper. Seed catalogs and books on gardening were all he ever read. I'll tell you something else about my father. When they released him from jail, he was actually going back to work in the garden. He'd missed a whole day. It was my mother that stopped him. I was about seven years old, but I can remember coming home from school and my sister telling me that Pop had been arrested and was in jail. She and I and my younger brother cried all night, and the next day we stayed home from school. Then when my father got home we packed our suitcases and cardboard boxes and went and stayed with my uncle and aunt in New Rochelle.

"My father got a job in a greenhouse in New Rochelle, but two years later he got t.b., and the next year he died.

"Maybe no one else would call it murder, but I do."

3

The editorial and business offices were on the second and third stories of an old brick-and-plaster house in East 38th Street. Jack Harrington's private office was on the second story rear, and except for the furniture the room remained as it had always been, with an open fireplace, two long windows, residential wallpaper. Jack, in shirtsleeves, was at his desk, with his back to the window at an angle, so that he could look out by swiveling his chair. It was evening.

Michael Landers came in, likewise in shirtsleeves, and carrying some papers. "I finished it," he said.

"What's that?" said Jack.

"The Julian Joplin novel."

"And the answer is?"

"No," said Michael. "At least as far as I'm concerned."

"Well, that's pretty far, Michael. I haven't overruled you yet. What's the matter with it?'

"You haven't read any of it, at all?"

"No, you're the only one that's seen it. I *will* read it, of course, but you don't think we ought to publish it?"

"It's absolutely filthy, for one thing. It would never get through the mail. But it isn't worth fighting for. It's all shock.

Four-letter words, five-letter words, one shocking scene after another, and without a single redeeming feature. In other words, I don't see that it has any literary value, none whatso-ever."

"You liked his first novel."

"This one makes me doubt that it was written by the same man. In the other one he had scenes of depravity and degener-ation, but he was subtle about it. Artistic. Poetic. In this one he writes like a dirty little boy, putting down all the dirty thoughts he ever had. I may be wrong, but I'd be willing to bet that he wrote this one a long time ago, and now he wants to cash in on his reputation."

"That often happens, of course, but Julian Joplin, he didn't strike me as that kind of a guy. I don't think this *is* out of the trunk, but I guess we'll never know."

"It's not out of the trunk, it's out of the cesspool."

"You realize, of course, if we don't publish this, we lose Jop-lin. And he's one of the two authors that kept this firm going. He and Serena Von Zetwitz."

"You can't publish this, Jack. It'll be banned all over the country, and rightly. And it's not going to help the reputation of Harrington and Whitehill. Here, let me show you one page," said Michael. He laid the typescript on Jack's desk, and Jack read it in silence that lasted a full ten seconds. When he finished he looked up.

"Yeah," he said. "That could get us into a lot of trouble. Is there more like that?"

"As bad, and worse," said Michael. "And it isn't a question of cutting. I couldn't edit this, and I don't think you could either."

"Not if there's more like this," said Jack. "Horace Liveright and Alfred Knopf both think Joplin is great. I do too, for that matter. But Joplin isn't a guy you can reason with. He owes us first look at this book, and if we reject it, he's free to go where he pleases. That's the contract. Well, I'll read it tonight and let you know in the morning."

"Don't show it to Gretchen," said Michael.

"Oh? Why not? She's seen worse than this. You're still

pretty new in this business, Michael. This is bad because it was written by Julian Joplin, but I've seen worse and so has Gretchen."

"*Gretchen* has seen worse than this?"

"We got a manuscript two years ago, maybe three. A translation from the Portuguese, written by a Brazilian millionaire. Gertrude Gelsey, the literary agent, was handling it, and it finally came down to us after everybody else had had a look at it. The English title was something like *Forgive Us Our Sins*, and it was this millionaire's memoirs. It was like reading all the Havelock Ellis case histories, but all happening to one man. I asked Gelsey why the fellow would want to publish it under his own name, and she laughed. She said he wouldn't let it be published *unless* it was under his name. That was going to be his greatest thrill, to be famous as the most depraved man of our time. Yes, Gretchen read it."

"She must be awfully well balanced to read that kind of stuff and be as normal as she is."

"That's what well balanced means, doesn't it?" said Jack. "Anyway, I wouldn't dare reject Joplin's novel without letting her read it. You know where the money comes from in this firm. Everybody does."

"Yes, but I know who's doing most of the work, too," said Michael. "Are you going to buy out Ray Whitehill?"

"I could say that that's none of your business. But unfortunately Ray gets a few drinks in him and tells the whole Yale Club bar that I am."

"He wasn't in today," said Michael.

"I know. Why do you think I'm working this late? I'm not going to let Whitehill or anyone else wreck this business. The book business generally is taking an awful beating, just at the time we were beginning to get somewhere. But it'll come back. Statistics show that more people are finishing high school, and that means more people will be going to college. They won't all read books, but education is going to have a good effect on the book business. Things may not look so good now, but if we can survive this depression, we'll be all right. Meanwhile,

I'm working my ass off because I want to. We have to stay a while longer in this old firetrap, instead of having office space in the Graybar Building, but we're a young firm. We can put up with inconveniences. You don't happen to have forty thousand dollars on you, do you?"

"Not just now," said Michael. "Do you need forty thousand?"

"To buy out Whitehill. Grimes got thirty-five. The only thing that's going up in price these days is a partnership in this firm."

"I wish I had forty thousand dollars, and I'd buy in."

"I wish you had, too, Michael. You better get home to your wife. I'll see you in the morning," said Jack.

"Goodnight, Jack," said Michael, and left.

Jack telephoned home. "Speak to Mrs. Harrington, please. Dear? I'm stuck here. I'll send around to the delicatessen. I like liverwurst sandwiches. I used to like them when I *had* to like them. It's a delicatessen down on Lexington Avenue. We often patronize them. I promise, I'll phone them right away. Not before ten-thirty or eleven. Kiss him goodnight for me, and tell him I'll have a story for him *tomorrow* night. I'll be home when I get there, and I'll have a manuscript for you to read. You can read the first half while I read the second. Goo'bye." He hung up, got to his feet and stretched, then returned to his desk and telephoned the delicatessen. "Mr. Kleinhans? This is Mr. Harrington. Harrington and Whitehill? Very well thank you. Have you got one of your boys there that can bring me a liverwurst sandwich on rye bread? No mustard. Your liverwurst doesn't need mustard, that's right. A quart of coffee, sugar and cream separate. One quart. No, no thank you. No strudel. Tell the boy to ring the doorbell, on the right hand side of the door, and my office is on the second floor. All the way back. No, I won't let him in. The superintendent will let him in, but I'll be here in my office. And as soon you can, huh? Thank you, Mr. Kleinhans. Auf wiedersehen. Ja. Ja."

He looked at the work he had been doing, dismissed it for the moment and picked up the Joplin manuscript and went to an easy chair with the idea of putting in a few minutes on the novel. He thought he heard the front doorbell, frowned, but decided he must be wrong. Too soon for the liverwurst.

His door opened, and it was a cleaning-woman, with bucket, floor brush, and rags. "Oh, *you're* still here?"

"Still here."

"When can I do this room?"

"Maybe you'd better skip it tonight. I'll be here quite late."

"That's all right with me, if it's all right with you. You don't want me to just dust around a little?"

Now the doorbell could be heard distinctly.

"No thank you. Wasn't that the doorbell?"

"The super'll get it. That ain't my job, answering the door."

"I'm expecting some sandwiches from the delicatessen."

At that moment Mary Walton appeared in the doorway. The cleaning-woman looked at Mary, smartly dressed, and then at Jack. "Here's your sandwiches," said the woman, and went out.

"What did she call me?" said Mary. "A witch?"

"Not exactly," said Jack.

(1974)

IT'S MENTAL WORK

It was nearly half-past four and the last customer had been let out the side door. The barroom was dark except for the weak night light over the cash register. For early risers it was Tuesday morning, but here it was still Monday night. Rich Hickman, the bartender, had his street clothes on, very dapper, and seeming not at all tired as he came in the back room.

"You all through, Rich?" said Wigman, the owner.

"All through *here*," said Rich, with a smile.

"Yeah, you look as if you had some place to go," said Wigman. "One for the road, as they say?" Wigman pointed to the bottle of bourbon on the table.

"I don't know. Sure," said Rich. He looked at his wristwatch, a hexagonal shape with square hollow links of stainless steel. "You want company a little while?"

"Get yourself a glass and sit down," said Wigman. "I don't know whether I got a date or not. It all depends."

"Yeah, I know," said Rich, speaking while he fetched a shot glass from the bar. "Those all-depends dates. I give that up for a coupla years, but now I'm back playing the field. All depends, all depends. They give you that all-depends chowder, but it's still better than being tied down."

"I don't know," said Wigman. "I don't know which is better, to tell you the truth. I'm forty-four years of age and twice in my life I thought I was settled down. *Settled* down. But it got to be *tied* down, and I was too young for that. I still feel pretty young, but I know what I am. I'm forty-four going on forty-five, and if I'm gonna be ninety years old, I'm halfway there. Halfway to ninety. Cheers, Rich."

"Cheers," said Rich. They raised glasses and drank.

"What did we do tonight?" said Wigman.

"Around three and a quarter."

"Yeah, quiet. Well, a Monday," said Wigman.

"You don't even figure to break even on a Monday," said Rich.

"That reminds me. How is it you never owned a joint of your own?"

"Oh, I don't know. I got offered the chance to, to go partners with a guy in Fort Lauderdale, but I didn't. I didn't like the fellow. And I had a rich dame in Miami Beach used to give me the big talk, but for two years straight as soon as it was April she went back to New York, and I was still on the duckboards. I guess she didn't have the money. The cash, I mean. She had a forty-dollar-a-day room all season, and she had a coupla rings there that shoulda been good for fifteen, twenty thousand apiece. But I know for a fact she was a two-dollar bettor at the track. Her husband wouldn't let her have any cash."

"Were you in?"

"Oh, sure, I was in. I had the use of a big Chrysler and she give me like all my slacks and sport shirts she used to put on the tab at the hotel. They had a woman's shop there that carried men's shirts and slacks and a couple times special orders for an Italian silk suit, sports jackets. And you know, that husband never got wise, because it was a woman's shop. It all went on the tab at the hotel. But cash, no. She was a two-dollar bettor. Didn't cash ten bets all season, all long shots. Every race she had the long shot. That many long shots don't come in."

"That many favorites don't come in either," said Wigman.

"No. Not when I have them at least. So anyway, I stop going steady with her and ever since I been playing the field."

"How old are you, Rich?"

"How old am I? I'm thirty-seven. I'm not so much younger than you."

"You look it, though. I got too much weight on me."

"Well, you think about it and it's very seldom you see a bartender overweight. If he's just a working stiff. An owner that tends bar, he'll put on the weight. But just an ordinary bartender, he's on his feet, moving around. Like a cashier in a bank. A paying teller. How many of them do you see fat? I figured it out why. You're on your feet all day and the lard don't get a chance to grow on you. Furthermore, you don't think of a bartender as using up mental energy, but we do. You carry on these conversations with the customers, you got maybe twenty-thirty customers at one time, and they all say, 'Hey, Rich, will you do this again, please?' and you're supposed to know what every one of them wants. Then the cash register, the prices. And the guys that want the bottle on the bar, you gotta keep an eye on them. It's mental work, and that uses up energy. We're not very different than a paying teller. Except the respectability."

"And the wages, Rich. You get better wages."

"That we do."

"And you're not stuck in the one place all your life."

"No. Oh, I'm not complaining. How long would a teller in a bank last if they found out he was driving some broad's Chrysler and living it up in a forty-dollar-a-day room? I had a room over in Miami, a fleabag over there, but most of the time I was in Miami Beach."

"A good tan goes well with your white hair."

"Oh, I used to pass for ten years younger. This broad thought I was around twenty-six, twenty-seven. Gave her a little priority over the other broads. Priority? You know what I mean. Not priority."

"Superiority."

"That's it."

There was a metallic rap on the window. "I guess I got a date after all," said Wigman.

"I'll get it," said Rich, going to the door. "Howdy do?"

The woman said: "Hello. Is Ernie here?"

"Come on in," called Wigman. "That's Rich Hickman, my bartender. Come on in, June."

"Hello," said June to Rich, acknowledging the introduction.

"Nice to meet you," said Rich. "I'll be going."

"Stick around, don't go," said Wigman.

"I better go," said Rich, looking at his watch.

"Time you meeting your date?" said Wigman.

"Well, I don't know. She was gonna be here or give me a buzz."

"Well, stick around a while," said Wigman. "So she's a little late. They're always late. Hello, Junie."

"*I* wasn't so very late," said the woman. "I told you between four and five, so I'm early."

"What'll you drink?" said Wigman.

"Oh—I don't know," said June. She looked at the bottle on the table. "Not bourbon."

"Well, you can have anything you want, and if you want a mixed drink, this is the guy to do it for you. This guy is only the best. Take my word for it."

"You know what I think I'll have is a Rob Roy. I had a Scotch earlier."

"That's easy," said Rich.

"Live up to your reputation now, Rich. Give her the best Rob Roy she ever hung a lip over."

"What an expression!" said June. She lit a cigarette and Rich went to the barroom. "What happened to the other fellow you used to have?"

"He quit, and I got this fellow. This fellow's twice as good. No spillage. No getting out of hand with the customers. And pretty, too, isn't he?"

"He's almost too pretty. He dyes his hair. Is he queer?"

"If he is, I should be as queer. The women go big for this guy."

"Does he go big for them is the question," said June.

"I got an idea that it's mutual. How was your business tonight?"

"Off. Way off. They're talking about closing Monday nights entirely. I heard they're trying to make a deal with the unions. It may pick up though, towards the end of the week. They moan and groan every Monday, but as soon as it begins to pick up towards the end of the week, you don't hear any more about it."

"I know," said Wigman. "We were way off tonight."

"It starda rain out," said June. "I just got a few drops on me, getting out of the cab."

"I owe you for the cab," said Wigman. He took a bill out of

a money clip. She looked at the bill and then at Wigman. She shook her head.

"This five has an O behind it," she said.

"I don't need glasses," said Wigman.

"You want to give me fifty dollars?"

"Why are you acting surprised? It isn't the first time I gave you fifty dollars."

"You don't have to give me fifty dollars," she said. "I don't mind when business is good, but you said you were way off tonight."

"We were very good Saturday and Sunday."

"Ernie, you don't *have* to do this," she said.

"But I'd rather," he said. "Here's your Rob Roy. A good way to unload the cheap Scotch."

"I didn't use the cheap Scotch," said Rich. "That's as good as we have in the house."

"Well, that's all right, considering," said Wigman.

Hickman looked at the rain-streaked window. "Hey, you know it's starting to come down."

"You might as well wait here till it stops."

The fifty-dollar bill disappeared into June's purse and she sipped the cocktail, moving her eyes from right to left, left to right as she judged the taste. "Good," she said. "Just right."

"Thanks," said Rich.

"I told you, this guy is only the best," said Wigman. "You better stick around in case she wants another one."

"Well, if it's all right with all concerned," said Rich. "My friend should be along any minute, or phone."

"There's the bottle," said Wigman. "Help yourself. You know the combination."

"Do you mind if I ask you something?" said June.

"Go ahead," said Rich.

"Did you used to be in Miami Beach, driving a big kind of a Cadillac or one of those?"

"A Chrysler, yeah," said Rich.

"Last season. You know you almost knocked me down?"

"Me? I don't remember even coming close. Seriously, are you sure it was me? I don't remember no accident."

"You wouldn't remember me, but I remember you. Corner of Thirty-first and Lincoln. You were so busy talking to your lady friend you never even saw me. Or heard me. I really gave it to you, but it was all wasted. I think you were having a little fight with the lady friend. A blonde with those big sun glasses?"

"That could fit forty-five thousand dames in Miami Beach, but I guess it all adds up. I apologize."

"I knew I seen you some place before. That hair gives you away."

"Next question. Do I dye it? No, I don't. I stard getting gray hair when I was twenty-three years of age."

"I didn't ask you. That's none of my business."

"Well, then you're the exception because they all ask me," said Rich.

"That's funny, because I wasn't," she said. "It's too bad you don't have that big car tonight. You could ride Ernie and I home."

"What is this, the needle? You know damn well it was never my car or I wouldn't be tending bar for a living."

"Ernie, I thought you said this man never got out of hand with the customers."

"You're not a customer, and let's face it, you got the needle in there pretty deep. But enjoy yourself, the both of you," said Wigman.

"Yeah, how much do I have to take when I'm not getting paid for it?" said Rich. "You know what I mean? I got the apron off now, a first-class citizen after four A.M. What do *you* do, June? Are you a hatcheck chick?"

"What if I am?"

"Well, then, relax," said Rich. "You know what I mean? So you take it all night for a lousy buck, so do I. But here it is close on to five o'clock in the morning and we're people now. Not only you, but me. What'd somebody give you the big pitch tonight? Is that what's bugging you?"

"Nothing is bugging me, and nobody gave me any big pitch."

"Maybe that's what's bugging you, nobody give you the pitch. Did I strike oil there, June?"

"Easy does it there, Rich," said Wigman. "Don't get personal."

"You mean I shouldn't call her June? How's the cocktail, ma'am?"

"I must say you're a sarcastic son of a bitch," said Wigman. "I never realized that before."

"Oh, I hold it in when I got my apron on, but this is after hours, Ernie."

"*Ernie,* huh?" said Wigman.

"All right. *Mr. Wigman,* if that's the way you like it. But I coulda been Mr. Hickman in Fort Lauderdale, and then maybe you'da been one of my customers. Mr. Hickman and Mr. Wigman."

"You coulda been Mr. Hickman in Miami Beach if the broad had the cash, only her husband wouldn't let her get her hooks on any cash," said Wigman.

"Now who's sarcastic?" said Rich.

"I think you're making a fast load," said Wigman. "You only had three sitting here—"

"And one when I was mixing her drink, making four."

"Well, that's a half a pint in about fifteen minutes," said Wigman.

"Do you do everything fast?" said June.

"That depends on how you mean that. Some things I take it slow and easy."

"All right, Rich. Down, boy," said Wigman.

"The lady asked me a question. I thought she wanted to know. Some things I can take it slow and easy, whereas I know some women don't like it if you take it slow and easy. Speaking of shaking up a Dackery, for instance."

"Yeah. Sure. Well, I tell you, Rich," said Wigman. "I think you better take a slow and easy powder out of here while we're all still friends. I see you tomorrow night."

"Okay, Ernie. Okay. Goodnight, Ernie, and good night, June. Watch out for reckless drivers." He got up and went out the side door.

"The idea asking him does he do everything fast?" said Wigman. "You couldn't have but only the one meaning to a question like that."

"So?"

"You mean you go for that guy?"

"I don't go for anybody. I'm so sick of men. I wouldn't care if I never saw another man for the rest of my life, the way I feel now."

"Well, that won't last."

"But you're so *right* it won't last. I didn't say it would last. I was only telling you how I feel now, tonight."

"Well, you want to go home with me or don't you? Either way."

"Put me in a cab and I'll see you tomorrow night. Here," she said, and handed him the fifty-dollar bill.

"Forget it, forget it. It's only human nature. I'm kind of beat too, myself. Let me stash this bottle and I'll get you a cab."

They went out together and he hailed a cruising cab. "That's all I am, Ernie. I'm kind of beat, too. I'll see you tomorrow night, yeah?"

"Sure. Goodnight, kid."

"Kid. Thirty-six years old. Goodnight, Ernie."

Wigman hailed another cab, got in, had the driver stop for the morning papers, and proceeded to his hotel. During the night, his night, he had a heart attack and died. His body was found by the waiter who had a standing order to bring his breakfast at one o'clock in the afternoon. Ernie Wigman's lawyer, Sanford Conn, was out of town and could not be reached, and the place ran itself that night, as it always did when Ernie did not show up. But a policeman had been around, asking questions, and the news of Ernie's death was known to the bartenders and waiters and kitchen help, and to the regular customers. Rich Hickman took charge. "I'll close up," he told the others. They were agreeable; they did not want to have to account for the money in the till.

Rich got the last customer out a few minutes after four in the morning. In the back room was a cop named Edwards, the man on post whom Rich had asked to be there. "I just want you here when I tot up what's in the till," said Rich.

"I'm not suppose to do that," said Edwards.

"Well, do it anyway as a favor."

"Who to?"

"To Ernie. I think he has a kid somewhere, and Ernie was always all right with you guys. That I happen to know. I just want you to witness that I'm not stealing off a dead man."

"I won't sign anything."

"Who asked you to sign, Edwards? I'll count it up in front of you, and lock it up in the register and give you the key. Is there anything in the book against that?"

"Nothing in the book against it, but—well, what the hell? All right. But I don't take any responsibility."

"You don't take any responsibility, but this way no son of a bitch is going to say I robbed a dead man."

"You could of been robbing him all night long, that's the way I gotta look at it, Hickman."

"I couldn't of been robbing him much. All you gotta do is compare tonight with last Tuesday or any Tuesday. If I was robbing him all night long I didn't get rich on it."

"I guess that makes sense," said Edwards. "Go ahead and count it up."

The cop sat bored on a bar stool while Rich made his count. "Cash on hand, five hundred and twenty-eight dollars and eighty-seven cents. Okay?"

"That's what it looks like to me," said Edwards.

"You wouldn't do me a favor and initial this slip before I lock it up?"

"I guess I can do that," said Edwards. "There's somebody at the back door."

"Let him in, will you? No, you keep your eye on the money. I'll let him in. I hope it's his lawyer, a fellow named Conn."

"Conn is a good name for a lawyer," said Edwards.

Rich went to the back door, opened it, and admitted June. "Ernie here?" she said.

"No. Come on in," said Rich.

"What's with the cop?" said June.

"I'll tell you later."

"Trouble? I don't go for cops."

"Then wait here."

"I don't like this. Where's Ernie?"

"Ernie is dead."

"A stick-up?"

"Nothing like that. He had a heart attack. If you'll sit down I'll take care of the cop and then I'll tell you all about it."

Rich returned to Edwards, put the money in the cash register, and gave Edwards the key. "All right, Edwards?"

"I guess so."

"Thanks a lot."

"All right. See you." Edwards left, and Rich mixed a Rob Roy, put it on a tray and took it to the back room. In his other hand he carried a bottle of bourbon with a shot glass inverted and resting on the cap.

"Ernie had a heart attack at the hotel. They found him around one o'clock yesterday."

"That's when he usually had breakfast," she said. "Are they having a service for him?"

"I don't have any idea. He had a kid, didn't he?"

"He had two kids around eighteen and twenty years of age, but I don't know where they are or any of that. I guess they'll show up. He was divorced, that I know."

"I closed up tonight and I had the cop come in to see that I didn't steal anything out of the till. Do you know Ernie's lawyer?"

"Sanford Conn, his name is. He had a piece of the joint. I know him from him going out with Ernie and I a couple times."

"This joint could do a lot better, a *lot* better. Ernie was a nice guy, but I could of told him ways to save a little here and make a little there. You know Conn, eh?"

"That well. Been out with him and his wife, with Ernie. A young fellow about thirty-five. He's the lawyer for four or five joints like this, and I think he's in for a piece of all of them."

"Then he's a guy I could go to with a proposition?"

"If there was a buck in it, he'd listen . . . So Ernie cooled. You know I was almost with him last night."

"How do you mean, almost?"

"Almost is what I said, almost is what I mean. I didn't go home with him. He put me in a cab outside here. I wouldn't of liked that, waking up with a dead man."

"What stopped you from going home with him?"

"Didn't feel like it. I guess I got so burned up with you that I was sick and tired of men. Now I think of it, Ernie said he was tired, too. I wonder if he knew anything beforehand. He *said* he was *tired*."

"He often said he was tired. I used to say to him, not come right out with it, but he'd sit and put away a quart of bourbon and eat a steak and a whole meal and sometimes he was here for ten-twelve hours, eating and drinking and never get up and walk around. I said to him about a month ago, I said—well, I didn't say anything, if you want the straight of it. But I thought, this guy he never moves out of his chair, and all that booze and rich food. Ten-twelve hours he'd sit here. They get that way, some of them. I worked for guys that did the very same thing. And they kid themselves that they're working, just because they're sitting in their own joint. Work? What work? Why, one of the day men was stealing from him right in front of his very eyes, that's how much work he was doing."

"Stealing how?"

"Oh, there's ways of working with a waiter. There's plenty of ways you can steal. *You* steal a little, don't you? The concession don't get it all."

"Most of it. You know, I'd like to have the concession here."

"Yeah, but would Conn give it to you?"

"Maybe not Conn, but maybe a new owner would. Or a new partner."

"You mean like if I got to be partners with Conn?"

"You must of attended a mind-reading school," said June.

"Graduated," said Rich. "You wouldn't mind working for me? I got the impression last night you wouldn't spit in my eye."

"I wouldn't be working for you, exactly. I'd have the concession, so I'd be working for myself."

Rich thought a moment. "Usually the syndicate owns the concession, and they pay so much for it. You know that."

"I ought to know it after—I been in this business. But here they never had a checkroom. Ernie didn't want one."

"I know. But you were softening him up."

"It's a lot of money going to waste," said June. "I could do a hundred and fifty a week here."

"You could do two hundred, two and a quarter."

"So?"

"Well, that's what I think it's worth, not a hundred and fifty. So if you got it it wouldn't be on a basis of a hundred and fifty. Don't play games with me, June."

"I want to make a little for myself. It's not all clear profit. All right, so you're big-hearted and you give me a concession worth maybe two hundred a week. But first you gotta convince Sanford Conn, and who knows Sanford Conn? I do."

"Yeah, we were coming to that," said Rich.

"One word from me, either way."

"Honey, I'm with you. How much money you got, and how much can you raise?"

"Ha ha ha. Would I tell you? How much do *you* have, and how much can *you* raise?"

"This is serious. If you could get your hands on fi-thousand dollars, I think I could raise twenty-five. With thirty gees I could talk to Conn. Conn don't have to know you got the checkroom till him and I make a deal."

"You want me to put up five thousand dollars for the concession?"

"The way you say that I know you got it."

"Where is your end coming from?"

"What do you care, or what does Conn care, as long as I get it? I don't have that kind of money myself, but I can come pretty close to raising it."

"That dame that you almost killed me with in her car."

"Good for a little, but not much. She don't have any cash, only some jewelry."

"No heist. I don't want any part of a heist. Don't even talk about it. I got no record downtown and I want to keep it that way."

"If I had a record I couldn't work either. And I'm not talking about a heist. But her and a couple others I know, and a couple liquor salesmen. Plus your five, I could go to Conn with a proposition. This is a very good chance for the both of us, June. And me and you could save rent."

"Yeah, that was coming, too. You move in with me or I move in with you. Which?"

"You got an apartment, I'd move in with you. I only got a room way the hell up on West Eighty-fourth Street."

"Where do you think I live? In the Waldorf Towers? I got an apartment but it's only one room."

"By the month?"

"What else?"

"We could save money on a lease. Wuddia say?"

"I don't know. I'd have to think it over. How would I get rid of you if I didn't like you around?"

"How would you get rid of me? Start leaving your stuff on the floor, your hair curlers all over the can."

"I'm tidy."

"I noticed that, or I wouldn't broach the proposition."

"I take a bath twice a day, sometimes more," she said. She snickered.

"What?"

"This way I'd know for sure if you dyed your hair."

"You wanta know something, I touch it. It's near all gray, but I touch it."

"I like it."

"Thanks."

"Well, we didn't talk much about Ernie," she said.

"No, but we didn't say anything against him," said Rich.

"That's true. We didn't say anything against him. I guess he was that kind of a guy, Ernie. He checks out and you start forgetting him right away, but at least you don't say anything against him."

"Well, he done us a favor," said Rich.

"You mean you and I getting together? Yeah, if that's a favor. It's too soon to tell."

"I think we'll work out all right, June."

"Maybe we will. And if we don't—"

"You can start leaving hair curlers around."

She smiled. "Yes," she said. "If they all would of been that easy to get rid of."

"What are you, divorced?"

"Twice. What about you? Are you divorced?"

"No, I never got married. I came close a couple times, but something always happened, so I never had it legal. You know, I go south in the winter, and when the season's over I come north or I been to the coast a couple times, working."

"This'd be the first time you ever settled down? I mean with a place. I don't know, Rich."

"You worried about your five gees?"

"Wouldn't you be?"

"Don't worry about it. I like you. I knew that right away last night. I would of gone after you, Ernie or no Ernie."

"Yeah, and I wouldn't of run away from you. I didn't have anything permanent with Ernie."

There was a banging on the side door and Rich went to the door and peered out at two men. "I don't know these guys," he said. There was a roller shade on the door and similar shades on the windows of the back room. "We're closed," he shouted, and let the shade fall back in place. The banging was resumed.

"Maybe you better see what they want," said June.

"I think I heard one of them say Hickman," said Rich. "Will I take a chance?"

"Talk to them through the door," said June.

Rich opened the door a few inches, and immediately it was pushed against him and he was driven out of the way. "What's the idea?" said Rich.

"What's the idea? What's your idea?" said one of the men. Then he saw June at the table. "Hello, June."

"Hello, Sandy. It's all right, Rich. This is Sandy Conn."

"You're kinda rough, Mr. Conn," said Rich.

"Maybe, and you're kind of stupid. Close the door, Jack," Conn commanded his companion. Jack was obviously a hoodlum, a muscle man.

"I heard you were out of town," said Rich.

"You're Hickman, the bartender?" said Conn.

"Yes. I heard you were out of town and I decided to take care of everything till you got back."

"Yeah, yeah. All right, what's in the till?"

"Five hundred and twenty-eight dollars and some cents," said Rich. "In the register."

"A good thing it isn't in your pocket. Give me the key," said Conn, extending his hand.

"I don't have it. I gave it to Edwards, the cop on the beat."

"You what?"

"I can vouch for that," said June.

"You? I wouldn't ask you to vouch. You're in with this fellow now. Give me the key or do I get Jack here to take it away from you? Whichever one of you has the key, hand it over. I don't care which one Jack has to take it away from. Do you, Jack? You have any objection to wrestling with a woman?"

Jack laughed.

"I guess not," said Conn.

"Call the precinct, if you don't believe me," said Rich. "But if this goon gets any closer to me or her, I break this bottle over his head. Then I take care of you, Mr. Conn. You I could handle easily."

"I could almost handle you myself, Sandy," said June. "This man is telling the truth, you silly son of a bitch. He was protecting your interest."

"I ain't worried about the bottle, Mr. Conn," said Jack.

"I'm thinking," said Conn. "What'd you say the name of this cop was?"

"Edwards. He's a patrolman."

"You don't have to tell me. If he was a sergeant I'd know him." Conn went to the telephone booth and was gone about five minutes. "I guess I owe you an apology," he said, when he returned. "Edwards has the key." He turned to Jack. "Okay, Jack. Thanks."

"That's all?" said Jack.

"Come around the office tomorrow and I'll give you a check."

"You wouldn't have five or ten on you?" said Jack.

"Here," said Conn, handing him a bill. "Goodnight, Jack."

"Thanks, Mr. Conn. Goodnight all," said Jack, leaving.

Conn sat down, across the table from June. "Too bad about Ernie, but the amount of liquor he consumed. Where you from, Hickman?"

"Why?"

"Well, I liked the way you took charge tonight. I like a take-charge guy. Bill Dickey, you remember used to catch for the Yanks? A real take-charge guy. You ever owned a joint, or managed one?"

"No."

"I know you got no police record, but give me the names of some places where you worked before."

"Why?"

"Well, June here will tell you, I got an interest in five other saloons. I kind of specialize in cafés."

"That's what you specialize in?" said Rich.

"I got other clients, naturally, but I been building up a café-owner practice."

"I thought there for a minute you specialized in something else."

"Like what? Explain."

"Like hiring some goon to beat up a woman," said Rich.

Conn tapped his fingernails on the table and watched Rich in silence. "Don't start anything, Hickman," he said presently.

"Jack ought to be a long way off by this time," said Rich.

"You lay a hand on me and it goes on your record downtown."

"Then I better make it good, huh?" said Rich.

Conn pointed to June. "She don't work, either."

"I'd of been in great shape after Jack got through with me, too," said June.

"What'll we do with him, June?" said Rich.

"If it was me, I'd kill him."

"What'd be the best way?" said Rich.

"Knock him out and dump him in the river. You got a car," said June.

"I told you the car don't belong to me, June."

"Oh, yeah, that's right. You got any other suggestions?"

"They got a walk-in icebox back in the kitchen. We could leave him there."

"I know you're kidding, you two," said Conn. "I tell you—"

"Shut up," said Rich, and slapped him hard on both cheeks.

"I got a better idea." He got a hammer lock on Conn's left arm and forced him to his feet. He pushed him forward and kept pushing him through the cellar door, down the steps, and into a closet that was lined on both walls with wine bins and case goods. He closed the door and locked it.

"Will he suffocate?" said June.

"No. But I'll bet he has a headache by the time they find him. He can holler his head off and nobody'll hear him."

"How long'll he be there?"

"Oh, the day man comes on around ten o'clock. That gives him around five hours. In the dark. It's gonna seem longer."

"I hope," said June.

They went upstairs, and in the back room he said: "Well, have a good look at the joint. You won't be seeing it again."

"No," she said.

They went out the side door, and as they headed west she took his arm. "You," she said.

"That's right," he said. "Me."

(1960)

JOHN BARTON ROSEDALE, ACTORS' ACTOR

There is a lot of truculent style to John Barton Rosedale as he goes to his mailbox—never locked—and flips open the little brass door and slams it shut. He knows there will be nothing of importance in the box; he knows that the other actors, whom he has to pass on his way to the bank of mailboxes, know it too. Nevertheless he continues to make that defiant entrance every afternoon. He will not let those other actors keep him from observing this small ceremony. If he once gives in, if he once fails to *pretend* to pretend that he has good reason to expect to find some important communication in the box, he will be just like the rest of them.

He comes to the club every afternoon, timing his arrival so that the non-theatrical and semi-theatrical members will have gone back to their offices in Madison Avenue and Radio City. They know who he is. Even the younger ones, who may never have seen him on the stage, know who he is. Their connections with the theater, which justify their membership in the club, may be tenuous, but their interest in it, whether lifelong or recent, would almost make it mandatory that they know who John Barton Rosedale is, or was. His name is a mouthful and not liable to be forgotten; and if they really know, have taken the trouble to learn, a little about the theater, they associate his name with those of the venerable stars and the prominent managers and the deceased playwrights who were so busy and successful between 1910 and 1930. The young fellows look at him now, and not many of them stop to think that in, say,

1925 John Barton Rosedale was younger than they are today. "Don't ask me if I ever knew Clyde Fitch," he has been known to say. "And for Christ's sake, no! I didn't play with the divine Sarah." But he has also been known to say, to one of the Madison Avenue-Radio City boys, "Who did you say? Terence Rattigan? Is he one of the Abbey crowd? I knew Barry Fitzgerald. Real name Shields. But I never heard of Rattigan." In truth he has heard of Rattigan and of everyone else of any consequence in the New York and London theater; was, in fact, extremely critical of Lunt's performance in *O Mistress Mine*. But he will concede nothing to these smarties from the ad agencies and the television studios. If they want to talk theater with him, let them talk business first, and stop giving all the parts to Cedric Hardwicke and Nehemiah Persoff. "*I* can play a Chinese general," he says. "I'd be wasted, but I can play one if the money was right. If I can play an Irish priest, I can damn sure make up to play a Chinese general. But the money'd have to be right." These Madison Avenue-Radio City boys have never done a thing for him, and now that he has told off so many of them, they probably never will. But they know who he is. He is John Barton Rosedale, never a bad performance, never a really bad notice, an actors' actor. "And I'm not broke, either," he has said; a boast that is literally but only literally true.

After he pays his ceremonial visit to the mailboxes, he goes to the bar and orders a half-Scotch. He drinks it alone, and it is his only drink in the clubhouse. He declines invitations to join other actors at the bar, and when he has had his drink he says to the bartender, "My people here yet?"

"In the cardroom. Mr. Dowell, Mr. Ruber, and I just saw Mr. Hafey on his way up."

In a sudden hurry John Barton Rosedale will scribble his last name on the chit and be off to the cardroom. He does not like to be late, but he likes to be last, and he always is.

The others, his people, are in the cardroom, sitting near but not at the bridge table. "Hello, Rosey," they say.

"The ever punctual Rosedale," he says. "Always just under the wire. Shall we cut?"

They cut for partners and deal, the game begins, and they play until five o'clock. It is quiet, serious bridge. The players understand each other's game so well that instead of a lengthy post-mortem, it is only necessary for one player to say, "Harry's spade lead did it," and the others will nod, and they will use the time between hands to make brief exchanges of conversation that are cut short at the conclusion of the deal. The four men are not close friends. Their congeniality, such as it is, has been achieved as a result of weeding out players in the past who played badly or much too well, and who by temperament revealed characteristics that were unsuitable to the atmosphere toward which this table was headed. In the beginning it had been John Barton Rosedale and Harry Hafey. Judd Ruber and George Dowell joined the table after other players were left out because they were too argumentative, played too slowly, drank too much, did not bathe often enough, could not be counted on to appear every day, or—in one case—wanted to talk about his troubles with his wife. For six years now the table has been made up of the same four players, who meet every day except matinee days when one or more of the four are working. They all have been actors, but Rosedale and Hafey have remained actors while Dowell makes his living as a free-lance writer, and Ruber is a staff announcer at a radio station. In six years Hafey has been in four flops, and Rosedale has been in one play that ran seven months on Broadway and five weeks on the road. Consequently the rule concerning matinee days has seldom been invoked. It was agreed at the start that no substitute would be invited to sit in for an absent player.

The four men, though not deliberately avoiding each other, make no effort to continue their companionship away from the bridge table. Hafey and his wife live in a theatrical hotel in the West Forties; Dowell, a widower, lives at the club; Ruber, a homosexual, shares an apartment with a friend in West Fifty-eighth near Fifth Avenue; and Rosedale and his wife live in London Terrace. It is a question whether Hafey, who worked regularly for good salaries in the days before heavy taxes, or Ruber, who is highly paid at present, is the best fixed financially.

Hafey has an annuity; that much is known. He has one son a lieutenant colonel in the Air Force and another a dentist in Manhasset, Long Island, and both seem to be self-sufficient. Ruber wears a star sapphire ring and has a large collection of oversize cuff links, and he has at least twenty suits that he rotates, a Patek Philippe wristwatch, and a golden dollar-sign money clip which he displays when the day's bridge score is totted up. He is the youngest member of the foursome—fiftyish—and he was not even a featured player in the days before the income tax became confiscatory. George Dowell, who no longer receives royalty payments for a radio serial based upon his most successful comedy, writes little pieces for the magazine sections of the Sunday newspapers, and is believed to pick up fifty dollars here and there for one-liners he sells to television comedians. He has eighteen thousand dollars in compound interest accounts that he opened when his wife's estate was settled, and he is writing a book of reminiscences that eventually will appear as the autobiography of a quite well-known actress. She has already paid him more than five thousand dollars for his work, and she now wants to start it all over again, this time without the reticence that she imposed upon herself while her third husband was still alive. Dowell is confident that he will get at least another year's work out of it and that the book, in its new conception, will be a best-seller.

The four men avoid the topic of their personal finances. Hafey and Ruber, the well-heeled, may now and then exchange more or less general comments on the state of the stock market, but if the money talk continues overlong, they run the risk of another recital by John Barton Rosedale on the subject of his experiences with Goldman, Sachs and Aviation Corporation in the early Thirties. He can be very angry about having been a near-millionaire, and they have heard it all before. "Everything went," he says. "Everything. The house in Great Neck. My thirty-eight-foot cruiser. I had to resign from North Hempstead, and haven't been on a golf course since. I had to start all over again, just when I thought I'd never have to worry again about money. But luckily I was in my early thirties and in demand. I was absolutely smashed, financially, but do you know that for the next three years I was never out of work? And I went from a thousand a week to eighteen hundred in the *theater* before Hollywood beckoned. *They* started me at twenty-five hundred, and I got all the way up to five thousand before they decided I was too difficult. But I learned one lesson—stay out of the stock market, and don't put your money in express cruisers. It couldn't have happened to me at a better time. I suppose nothing would have stopped me from spending my money the way I did when I was in my twenties, but you can be damned sure I was more careful thereafter. You see, by that time I was old enough to get a little sense in me, and I said to Millicent, 'This time we're going to put it away.' No more cruisers and fancy cars—we had a big Lincoln convertible a block long. And no more houses in the suburbs. Or for that matter, apartments on Park Avenue. I know fellows, actors that weren't making half what I was making, and they loved to give that Park Avenue address. But after I was burnt the first time Millicent and I've *never* had an apartment bigger than four or five rooms. What would we do with one of those large apartments? Millicent does very little entertaining. Mostly the opera crowd for little informal suppers. Spaghetti and red wine, and Millicent loves to cook. I just sit back and relax while they all tell these fascinating stories about grand opera. You think there's bitchery in the theater? You ought to hear what goes on up at the Met. Stories about Jeritza, and Scotti, and all those people, and going back to Caruso and Tetrazzini. Millicent of course gave it all up when we got married, but she knows the racket inside and out, and they all like to come to our place for our little informal parties. Six, eight people at the most, so it doesn't get unwieldy. And it's quite something, you know, to see one of your big opera stars put on an apron and help with the dishes. They love Millicent. I, of course, I'm only that actor fellow that seduced Millicent away from grand opera and made her give up her own career. I didn't, but that's what they say, and they really don't hold it against me. On an opening night I get almost as many wires from Millicent's opera crowd as I do from show people. They're very loyal to Millicent. Confide in her, ask her advice. And all they really care about Rosedale is that I'm her husband and apparently made her happy. Oh, I take second billing there, all right, but I don't mind a bit. It does any actor a world of good to get around in other circles outside of our own profession. And these are talented people, don't forget. They're real artists. God knows they're lousy actors, that I can't deny. Once in a while I'll put on my white tie and tails and take Millicent to hear some newcomer that's been recommended to her, and as far as the singing is concerned, I take my cue from Millicent. If she says a soprano is good, then I know she's good. But while they're about it, learning all the various languages and vocalizing and all that, it beats me why they don't spend a few hundred dollars on a dramatic coach. I wouldn't want the job myself, but occasionally I've made a few suggestions. I don't know whether they ever took them or not. The last thing I'd ever want to do would be to try to teach anybody to act. Hell, I took fencing lessons for two years when I was starting out, and I'm sure they taught me how to move about. But I didn't believe then and I don't believe now that you can be taught how to act. The tricks, yes. But not what has to come from down here and up here. The old ticker and the old gray matter, that's the combination. Plus the dedication, the pride, the love of the whole stinking God damn racket, regardless of the cheap sons of bitches that run things today."

"You're absolutely right, Rosey," says Hafey.

"Where is there a man like Hoppy today?" says John Barton Rosedale.

"You don't mean the billiard player?" says Ruber.

"Arthur Hopkins," says George Dowell.

"Of course! I thought of Willie Hoppe because he came on a show I was announcing, oh, several years ago."

"Shall we cut? I didn't mean to get launched on that subject," says John Barton Rosedale. "How did I get started? We were talking about Wall Street, for Christ's sake. Well, it's lucky we got away from that. I have the nine of clubs. George, it looks like you and me start."

"And I believe it's my deal, with the diamond king," says Harry Hafey.

John Barton Rosedale is an honest sixty-seven now, and when five o'clock comes and the day's last rubber has been scored, he goes downstairs and has a cup of free tea and the free Lorna Doones and Hydroxes that are served with it. He is at home with a cup of tea; it has been a prop of his in three or four plays, and nowadays he gets a lift from the brew itself. He needs that lift; the bridge game could go on for many more hours and so long as he was playing he would not notice how tired he was getting. But at five o'clock or thereabouts he is ready to quit; his body and his brain are ready to quit. His long legs have been too long in a fixed, sitting position, and he has learned to get slowly to his feet, to move about slowly while Harry Hafey is totting up the day's score.

"I have this damned sacroiliac," says Judd Ruber, the youngest of the players. "I think it must have something to do with my weight. I ought to take off thirty pounds. But I can't resist starchy foods. As Alec Woollcott said, everything I like is either illegal, immoral, or fattening."

"I think G. K. Chesterton said it first," says George Dowell.

"Well, whoever said it, it applies to me," says Judd Ruber. "Rosey, how do you keep in such good shape? Do you do exercise?"

"Exercise? Yes. I stand up while I'm shaving. That's my exercise," says John Barton Rosedale. But he is pleased that no one has noticed that he has been hesitant about getting to his feet. "I don't believe my weight has varied five pounds since I was a young fellow in my twenties. This jacket and waistcoat—"

"I was about to ask you," says Ruber. "You had them made in England?"

"In London in 1930. English friend of mine sent me to Jason Driggs, just off Savile Row, and being flush at the time, I ordered four lounge suits, a dinner jacket, and a suit of tails. I've still got them all. This suit, the trousers have gone, but I rather like it with slacks."

"It's very country, the black and white check, but *you* can wear that and get away with it," says Ruber.

"Well, I don't know about that," says John Barton Rosedale.

"That is, I don't know whether I do get away with it or not, but I know damn well there isn't a better-made suit in the club, and I've always been whatever the opposite is to a slave of fashion. I wear what I think is right for me, not for Jack Paar, or Douglas Fairbanks Junior. I have that other Driggs suit that I wear with slacks. The plaid?"

"Doesn't have quite the same snap, the same dash as this one," says Ruber.

"Well, this is a check, and the other's a Glen plaid. But do you know what these suits would cost me to duplicate today?"

"I certainly do. Not less than two-fifty apiece at any halfway decent tailor's," says Ruber.

"Two seventy-five, the fellow I go to," says Rosedale "I can't see myself paying that much for a suit."

"Well, you could probably go to Brooks and get something off the rack and look well in it," says Ruber.

"Thank you, Judd. If the part called for it, that's what I'd do. Last year I read for a part, a university president. A good part. But I wouldn't work for the money they were paying, so we never did get together. However, for that part I most likely would have gone to Brooks, got one off the rack." They say their farewells and go their separate ways, John Barton Rosedale to his cup of tea and Lorna Doones.

He does not stay long. It is now the time that the Madison Avenue-Radio City types begin to drift in for cocktails. "Why do they want to come here?" he asks, when there is an actor friend to listen. "They have their own places. The Advertising Club is where they belong, not here. But no, they have to come here because they want to be part of show business. Show biz, I hear them call it. Show biz. But do they do anything for any of us?"

"Well, you know they do, Rosey, once in a while. Paul Ingles."

"Paul Ingles. Every time I ask that question I always get Paul Ingles for an answer. Now let me tell you about Paul Ingles. In the first place, Paul Ingles is a toady, a sycophant. He got a job on a radio serial, ten years ago, and he's the one brought these radio and television people into the club. They know he's on their side, so they always see to it that he gets a job. Where else could he? I recognized his voice the other day on a radio commercial. For dog food. That's Paul Ingles, and that's the man that's supposed to be the great example of how those people help us. Not that it makes any difference to me personally. I'm not *quite* reduced to doing dog food commercials or any other commercials. And I'd never be a toady for anyone. But you look around here any afternoon and you'll see half a dozen good actors that come here hoping one of those outsiders will give them a television job. It's enough to break your heart, seeing fellows like Earl Stafford hamming it up for one of these hucksters. 'I don't believe we've met,' he said to one of them the other day. 'I'm Earl Stafford, welcome to the club.' And buying drinks for them. They have expense accounts, but has Earl Stafford got an expense account? I happen to know that Earl is supported by a group of members that work in Hollywood. And how much longer will that last, with Hollywood the way it is now? Earl Stafford, this is. Not one of your Ed Minzers. Poor Ed was always one jump ahead of the sheriff, but Earl knew the time when he could practically command his own price. He was a *draw*. But now he feels he has to buy drinks for advertising hucksters, and what does it get him? Maybe you'd better not be seen talking to me. They know how *I* feel about them."

And they do know. They know who he is, and they know how he feels about them. They would be extremely obtuse not to know. In times past John Barton Rosedale, making use of his professional reputation and of the energy available to him in his thirties, could be enormously persuasive in club affairs. He led the demand for better food and more efficient operation of the telephone switchboard, and his electioneering defeated Earl Stafford for a fifth term as club president. John Barton Rosedale denied having anything personal against Earl Stafford, but he argued that Earl had been in office too long and would be fifty on his next birthday. High time, in other words, for Earl to make way for younger blood.

In times more recent, John Barton Rosedale has not been in the diningroom and he rarely receives telephone calls. But he has tried to interest his friends in a tightening of the eligibility rules that will keep out people like Norman Bahs. He had paid no attention when Norman Bahs's name appeared on the list of candidates for membership. Later he vaguely recalled having seen the name, the designation "theatrical manager," and the names of two actors as proposer and seconder. Six months passed, and Bahs's name now appeared among the list of the elected.

John Barton Rosedale was introduced to Bahs at the bar. He was a bright-eyed, tooth-flashing, fat little man in a blue serge suit, white shirt, and plain blue silk tie with a Windsor knot. "I've always wanted to meet John Barton Rosedale," said Bahs.

"Well, he's usually around here somewhere. I'll see if I can arrange it," said John Barton Rosedale.

Bahs laughed. "Say, you're quick, Mr. Rosedale. Somehow I always thought of you as—I don't know. More like the parts you play."

"This is one place where we let down our hair. Impossible to maintain one's dignity among these ruffians. Look at some of these scoundrels. Ed Minzer. Harry Hafey. A den of thieves if ever I saw one. Let me buy you a drink, Mr. Bahs."

"I'd consider it an honor and a pleasure," said Bahs.

"And well you might. What will you have?"

"Same thing. Bourbon on the rocks," said Bahs. "Do you mind if I ask, are you reading any plays for next season, Mr. Rosedale?"

"What a question to put to an actor. Of course I am. Why? Have you got one you'd like me to read?"

"Yes I have."

"Then why haven't you sent it to me?"

"I did, but I never got any answer."

"What was the play?" said John Barton Rosedale.

"It's a play called *Perihelion,* by an unknown. I guess you never got around to reading it."

"Tell me a little bit about it," said Rosedale. "Maybe it will refresh my memory. I have a stack of plays I've been meaning to send back to my agent."

"It's modern. Time, the present. This young fellow has come

back from the war. World War Two. Switches around from job to job and doesn't find anything to interest him. Then he meets this Japanese girl—"

"She was in one of those internment camps during the war. I remember that much of the play. I thought it was sent to me by mistake. Nothing in it for me. I have as much vanity as any middle-aged actor on Broadway, but I didn't see myself playing a twenty-five-year-old veteran. I'd have to stretch my imagination *and* my skin."

"Oh, you didn't read the second act?"

"As far as I know, there is no second act. No, when the curtain falls for the end of the first act, that's as far as I got. Don't tell me there's a fat juicy walk-on in Act Two for a man in my age bracket."

"Well—you don't know about the judge?"

"The judge? He's mentioned in the first act. That one?"

"Yes sir."

"Yes, I could see that coming. When you've read as many plays as I have you can spot a planted character immediately. Your judge is going to be very intolerant of the young Japanese girl. Am I right?"

"That's one way to put it."

"Is there any other way? Yes, I could see that coming. But why did you send *me* that play? Do you need backing?"

"The money is raised, Mr. Rosedale."

"Sometimes—too many times—a manager will send me a play and then put out an announcement that I'm reading it. That's in the hope of raising money."

"I don't operate that way, Mr. Rosedale. I have the backers for my next two plays."

"Have you indeed?"

"I wish you'd read the second act before you send it back."

"What for? I can guess what's going to happen. You admit that yourself."

"I said the judge is intolerant, yes. But there's a lot more to it than that. This play could do a lot of good for an actor like yourself, Mr. Rosedale."

"How?"

"Well, it's a strong dramatic role."

"That's a matter of opinion, too, isn't it? And you still don't answer my question. How would it do a lot of good for an actor like me, as you put it?"

"It just would. Any good part is good for an actor."

"That's a very sweeping statement, isn't it? But let's pass it for the moment," said John Barton Rosedale. "Roughly, what sort of money were you thinking of offering me?"

"Seven-fifty. I know it'd be no use trying to get you for less."

"You never said a truer word. Do you realize that what you're offering me is less than a hundred dollars a performance?"

"Well, I could go to eight."

"My dear fellow, you can go to *hell.* What do you *mean* by coming to this club and using your brand-new membership to chisel on actors' salaries? Is that why you joined? I'm going to find out who put you up, and have a little talk with them."

"I'm sorry you feel that way about it, Mr. Rosedale."

"I've never done this before, but I'm going to let it get around how much you offered *me,* and then everybody will have a pretty good idea what you're paying the poor slob that takes the part. You may have a hard time getting a three-hundred-dollar actor."

"No I won't," said Bahs. "But don't you start fouling up my business, Mr. Rosedale. Don't you *do* that. Maybe I'm not big yet, but I had as good actors as you in a couple my plays. Don't you start fouling *me* up."

"If you're threatening me, that's a chance I'm going to have to take."

"You're the one that threatened. You threatened me."

"Oh, you're tiresome, really you are, old boy," said John Barton Rosedale.

He went home that day—it was easily ten years ago—and was so unaffected by the encounter with Bahs that he neglected to give a report of it to Millicent. She was in the midst of preparing onion soup, which took a while the way she made it, and until eight o'clock he occupied himself with his wardrobe, rehanging his suits so that they would not get that closet look;

polishing his shoes, which he called boots; inspecting his shirts for signs of fraying. Millicent, in and out of the kitchen, had the radio tuned in on an FM symphony program. Both of them were looking forward to eight o'clock and dinner, and conversation was not necessary or even especially desirable, since she enjoyed her cooking to a musical accompaniment, and he liked fussing around with his clothes, every item of which was associated with starring roles in plays that had paid him well.

It was a little past eight when they sat down in the dining alcove, with the entire meal on the table and Millicent's candles the only light. The onion soup and scallopini were kept warm in glazed earthenware containers; the Rosedales owned sets of Limoges and Meissen china and an assortment of solid silver, and the only concession they made to modern living was in the use of paper napkins, and even that was elaborately justified by pointing to the work it saved Millicent and the avoidance of wear and tear on the good napery. They had a bottle of wine—the musical friends of Millicent always brought more wine than they drank, and tonight's bottle from the surplus was a Riesling that went well with the veal.

"Who did this come from?" said John Barton Rosedale.

"This was from Lenny Giordano. He brought three bottles that night and we didn't open a one. But this is the last, isn't it?"

"Yes. The last of the Riesling. We're getting low on wine. Maybe we ought to have another party soon."

"All right. I'm willing. I want to try out some new recipes. Eddie Petruccini found me an old Italian cookbook, in Milano last summer."

"Mee-*lann*-no! Fee-*renn*-zeh! Love to hear old Eddie pronounce those Italian names. Mee-*lah*-no! And he sure does love to eat."

"So do you. I just wish I could eat what you eat and stay thin."

"Baby, you're going to eat, so why torture yourself about it."

"I know, but to think that when I was twenty years old I only weighed a hundred and thirty. And five feet seven and a half."

"Well, you're still five-seven-and-a-half."

"It was Zumbach that made me eat. Eat, eat, eat, he used to tell me. You'll sing it off in one performance, he'd say. And sometimes I did. But you, you bastard, you let me go on eating. You should have stopped me."

"Don't blame it on me, baby. You were a food addict before I came along."

"I know, but you could have made me stop."

"Well, you were a nice bed-full. I'd had enough of scrawny dames, onstage and off. In bed and out. My mother, my sisters, my first wife, and Diana. All built like boys."

"Diana wasn't built like a boy."

"Pretty near. You ready for espresso? I want to take a look at a TV show. Jack Masters particularly asked me to watch a show he's on. It goes on at nine o'clock. Channel Two."

They cleared the table and left the dishes in the sink, and were seated comfortably with a bottle of grappa when the television program began. "I have no idea what Jack's doing," said John Barton Rosedale. "I don't even know when he comes on. But he particularly asked me to watch this show, so he must be good in it."

The first twenty minutes passed and Jack Masters had not yet made his appearance, but during the commercial interval John Barton Rosedale had little to say.

"What do you think of it so far?" said Millicent.

"Good," he said. "The sets are awful, and the lighting is something fierce. Did you notice those shadows in the hospital room? Somebody ought to be shot for that. But the play's all right—if they can keep it up. This is only the first act."

Halfway during the second twenty minutes Jack Masters came on the screen. He played the proprietor of a Mexican cantina.

"Good heavens," said Millicent. "Jack's as fat as I am."

"Sh-h-h."

At the end of the second act John Barton Rosedale refilled his glass. "Now I know why he wanted me to watch," he said.

"Yes. He's good," said Millicent.

"He's better than good, baby. This is the best he's ever been.

Jack Masters, Jake Moscowitz, playing a Mexican saloon-keeper. I wonder how much the Hollywood people watch these things? They pretend they don't, you know, but I hope for Jack's sake they're watching tonight. I wonder if Bogey ever watches these things?"

"Which Bogey? Humphrey?"

"Naturally. He has his own company now, and he used to be a friend of Jack's. The play isn't holding up very well, but they sure are getting a performance out of old Jack."

The play resumed, and they remained silent through the third act, to the very end. "Shall I turn it off?" said Millicent.

"Wait a second, I want to see the credits. This is what they call the crawl, or the crawler, I'm not sure which. Sometimes the names go slow, sometimes fast, depending on how much time they have left. There we are. Pedro Gomez, Jack Masters. Now let's see who directed it. That usually comes last on a movie. Here we are. Produced by—Norman Bahs. For Christ's sake. Directed by—Norman Bahs! No! I don't believe it."

"Who is that? I never heard of him."

"Oh, I'll tell you about him later. Now I have to call Jack and congratulate him." John Barton Rosedale telephoned the broadcasting company, asked for the studio, and learned that the play he had just seen was on tape. "I'll call him at his house," he said, and did so.

The line was busy.

"You were going to tell me about the director. I've forgotten his name already."

"Producer and director. His name is Norman Bahs. Over there in the light blue envelope on my desk is a play he wanted me to do. I just got finished telling him to go to hell."

"Oh, Rosey. Again?"

"What do you mean again? I only met him this afternoon."

"You know what I mean. Was it money again? What did he offer you?"

"He offered me seven-fifty. That's not even a hundred dollars a performance. Then he said he might go to eight, and I said he might go to hell, too. And don't you start on seven-fifty is better than nothing."

"It is, though. It's seven hundred and fifty dollars a week better than nothing. I know that much. What's better? Waiting a year for a thousand and then maybe working four or five weeks, or getting seven-fifty while we're waiting?"

"I'm not broke. We have enough to eat—even enough for you."

She had her glass in her hand. She looked at it, quickly raised it to her lips and drank, and got to her feet and went to the kitchen. He waited for her to turn on the FM radio, with one of her musical programs, but the only sounds that came out of the kitchen were the small noises of china on china, water running out of the sink, closet doors closing. Then the barely audible click of the light switch.

She walked through the livingroom. "Goodnight," she said, as she passed him. He could tell by the later sounds that she was preparing to sleep in the guest room, and then he heard the guest room door pulled to.

(1963)

LATE, LATE SHOW

Sherman Gallagher got up and turned off the TV. "I just wanted to see how he got out of it," he said.

"Our hero?" said his wife.

"Our hero? No, not our hero. Any time Ronald Colman was in a picture he was a sure bet to emerge triumphant, with not a hair out of place. Dashing, debonair. All the rest of it. Oh, they had him up a tree for a while. Sure. But somehow you always knew that dear old Ronnie would come through unscathed."

"Then I don't get it," said Mary Gallagher. "Who were you worried about?"

"I wasn't *worried* about *any*body," said Sherman Gallagher. "What I meant was, I wanted to see how Ralph P. Stimson was going to get out of it."

"Ralph P. Stimson? Which was he?" she said.

"You just saw his name. Do you mean to say you've forgotten already who Ralph P. Stimson was?"

"Was he the friend? No, he couldn't have been. He gave his life to save Ronald Colman. Come on, Sherry, tell me. Who was Ralph P. Stimson?"

"Only the man that was responsible for the screenplay. Screenplay by Ralph P. Stimson."

"I don't see why you cared about him," said Mary Gallagher. "You mean to say you sat there rooted to your chair, for almost two hours—do you *know* Ralph P. Stimson?"

"Of course I know him," said Gallagher.

"I've never heard you speak of him," she said.

"Oh, yes. A long time ago, you did. Twenty–twenty-five years ago. I guess it was more like thirty years ago."

"Where did you know him? Under what circumstances?"

"Well, as a matter of fact I used to have lunch with him almost every day for a while," said Gallagher.

"When you were with McClanahan and Souder, that must have been. Did he work there, this man?"

"He sure did," said Gallagher. "He was an absolute ball of fire. They took him on right after he got out of Harvard. I think actually he was related to Ted Souder in some way or other. Anyway, they found a spot for him as a junior copy-writer. Junior meant that he had to be satisfied with a hundred dollars a month, but I guess he must have had *some* money of his own, because the son of a bitch certainly wasn't living on any hundred-a-month scale. The rest of us usually had lunch at Childs. That was when they gave you all you could eat for something like eighty-five cents, but they were on some kind of a health-food kick. Do you remember that? They were pushing some vegetable diet or something."

"I do remember, yes," she said.

"And it almost broke them. But if you wanted to stuff your-self, you could. You could eat enough to do you all day, pro-vided you weren't carnivorous. If you were herbivorous, Childs was the place to go. A full meal for the price of a Clover Club."

"Oh, Clover Clubs! How long has it been since I've heard anyone order a Clover Club. They were quite wicked. Not as bad as a Martini, but much more deceptive. I'm going to have one the next time we go to a restaurant. Excuse me. You were saying?"

Her tangential remarks did not bother him. "He was known as Rafe Stimson, which is English, of course. I think he may have given himself that name. He was very English in a lot of ways. The Harvard fellows I knew all wore Brooks Brothers Sack Suit Number 1, and the white shirt, and quite a few of them wore black knit ties. But I never saw Stimson dressed that way. Double-breasted gray flannels. Homburg hats. Tab collars. Not the slightest trace of the Harvard Yard, sartorially speaking. A lot of us carried canes, but he carried a brolly. An umbrella. *And,* horror of horrors, he wore a moustache. Not a full-thickness Brigade-of-Guards moustache, but not one of your thin little lines of hair either. It was a proper moustache, and it did what he wanted it to. It made him look older. Consequently, it embarrassed Ted Souder to have Stimson a junior copywriter, and he was promoted out of the junior class."

"Oh, come now. Ted Souder wouldn't be embarrassed by a thing like that," said Mary Gallagher. "I know Ted Souder."

"Not ordinarily, he wouldn't have been. But Stimson was no ordinary guy. His walk, for instance. He walked very slowly. In the morning, or after lunch, he'd come in the office and walk as though he were pondering some weighty problem. Umbrella tapping the floor. Bowing to this one and that one. His entrances were always an event. 'Ralph P. Stimson is here! Everything is under control,' he seemed to be saying. The fact that he was getting a lousy twenty-five bucks a week didn't seem to make much difference to him. And it didn't. He knew he was good. That's really why Ted promoted him, of course. They gave Stimson the Madame Olga account. A headache that everybody else tried to duck, but he did the whole magazine campaign by himself, and the old bitch not only liked the campaign but more to the point, it sold perfume. So Stimson got his raise and his promotion. And then he promptly quit."

"He quit the agency?" said Mary Gallagher.

"I asked him why he was quitting and he said he'd always suspected that there wasn't really very much to the advertising business. He wanted to try something else."

"And he had money of his own," said Mary Gallagher.

"He had *some* money of his own. But he was far from rich. He had a ground-floor apartment on East Fifty-first Street. Two rooms and a garden. Probably seventy-five a month. He needed every cent he got. He used to go to 21 before it was 21, and he had a car. A Baby Renault touring car. His clothes, I suppose he could run up a bill at his tailor's. And he made all the deb parties and on Sunday he'd always be in a short black coat and striped trousers. Free lunch. Cocktail parties. Sunday night supper. In those days a young bachelor could get by on fifty a week if he played it right. But it took a certain amount of arrogance to give up that job."

"And courage, I suppose," said Mary Gallagher.

"Courage? Well, courage of a kind. More arrogance. And you can be sure he wasn't going to starve. Arrogant self-confidence is what he had. He quit his job and read the scripts of all the big hit plays for the previous five years. Then he sat himself down and wrote a play. I don't even remember the name of it. But he got it produced and it was sold to the movies for $10,000. And he was to get $250 a week to adapt it."

"I don't remember *any* of this."

"Probably because if I'd told you how easy it was for him, you'd have tried to coax me into writing a play."

"No doubt I would have," said Mary Gallagher.

"But he told the movie company that he'd be glad to work for them but not on his own play. He said it needed a fresh point of view, and he'd worked on it for five years, which was a God damn lie, and he'd rather work on something else. The play wasn't a hit, and they could have come back at him and said five years seemed a long time to spend on a play that folded in three or four weeks. But they wanted it for one of their stars. Nancy Carroll? Or Claudette Colbert. In any case, they had bought his play and a big star was going to be in the movie version. Therefore, he was the author of something that the studio was going to spend a lot of money on, and therefore he might come up again with another good idea. So they agreed to his terms, and he went out to Hollywood and learned everything he could about the movie business."

"Is he still there?" said Mary Gallagher.

"God no. He lasted there two or three years at the most. I've only seen his name on a couple of pictures. This one tonight and maybe two others. I suppose that being Stimson, he figured he'd mastered the art of the cinema just as he conquered the advertising business."

"Did he ever marry?"

"Oh, yes. Do you remember an actress called Mavis Ware?"

"Vaguely. Was he married to her?"

"Yes. She was never one of the top stars, but she was quite good. You see her on TV once in a while, in old movies."

"You do. I don't," said Mary Gallagher.

"Well, anybody that likes George Raft."

"I adore George Raft. Don't you say anything against George Raft as long as you can watch Elissa Landi, for heaven's sake. And who's that other one that—Priscilla Lane! Mavis Ware was something like them. Wholesome."

"Mavis Ware didn't happen to be wholesome. If you really knew anything about the stars of that era, you'd recall that Mavis Ware figured in one of the worst scandals that ever rocked the motion picture industry to its very foundations."

"She was still wholesome. What scandal was that?"

"A scandal that rocked the motion picture industry to its very foundations," he said.

"You said that. What was it?"

"That night at Ciro's when she danced naked to the waist."

"I don't remember that at all."

"Well, you see?"

"That wholesome, sparkling-eyed pieface danced naked to the waist, at Ciro's? With somebody, or alone? I never heard anything about that."

"It was never printed. Only hinted at."

"I don't recall that she had very much to offer in that department."

"Well, you're just about as wrong as you can be, I'll tell you."

"Only fair, nothing sensational," said Mary Gallagher.

"Hunh. What she had was real, not falsies. And she proved it."

"Did they kick her out of pictures?"

"They did not. They had to officially pretend it never happened."

"Is that why your friend Stimson left her?"

"You have the chronology all wrong," he said. "The thing at Ciro's happened long after she divorced him."

"Why would someone as smart as he was supposed to be marry a dumb little cluck like her?"

"Maybe because he got a preview of what they all saw the night at Ciro's." He laughed. "Not bad. A private preview."

"She'd have to do more than that to attract attention nowadays."

"Yes, but this was back in the Thirties, so don't call her wholesome."

"Well, I hope for his sake she wasn't. Not as wholesome as she looked. Was she married to someone when she put on this exhibition?"

"I don't know. I wasn't there."

"No, but you wish you had been," said Mary Gallagher.

"You're damn right I do."

"If we hadn't stopped going to the club dances, you could have seen the exact same thing last summer. The Brayton kid. Susan Brayton."

"Not on the dance floor. Sitting in somebody's car. And not Mavis Ware. The Brayton kid isn't even attractive."

"That's a matter of opinion," said Mary Gallagher. "Then what happened to Stimson?"

"Became a communist."

"A what? With that background, that history? Would they have him? I always thought they were—well, stuffy I guess is the word, when it came to people like that. He sounds like the last person they'd want around."

"He wasn't around very long. But he was active for a while."

"Then what?"

"I guess he became an expert on communism and decided to devote his talents to something else. I know he went to Paris and started up one of those little magazines. But it wasn't a very good time for starting up little magazines."

"Where are we now, time-wise?"

"Time-wise, about 1931."

"That's the year I met you, so you see you couldn't have said much about him when he was working for Ted Souder."

"I guess you're right," said Gallagher. "Let me check." He looked at the television program. "That picture was made in 1932. Or released in 1932. Could have been made before that. I seem to be all mixed up in *my* chronological order."

"You jumped me quickly enough when I was confused," said Mary Gallagher.

"We're supposed to remember things that happened a long time ago better than something that happened yesterday. At our age, that is. Everything I told you about Stimson was true, but from the time he quit the agency on, I'm going on hearsay. I never saw him again, except once. I saw him once in London during the war."

"So that must have been '43 or '44."

"Yes, it had to be. I could probably pin down the month."

"Is it worth it?" said Mary Gallagher.

"It was about nine o'clock at night, but of course still practically broad daylight. I had just come out of the Royal Automobile Club and was walking along Pall Mall and I saw this guy coming toward me. I recognized him immediately, but when he saw me he darted across the street. I was never terribly fond of him, but trying to duck me like that aroused my curiosity and I crossed the street after him and yelled at him. As soon as I called his name he stopped. 'You bloody fool,' he said. 'Don't you know when someone's trying to avoid you?' Then he laughed and I invited him back to the R.A.C. for a drink but he said he'd rather give me a drink in his rooms. His rooms were one room in a seedy old hotel in the neighborhood. He had some sherry and a half a bottle of whiskey and what was left of a bottle of gin. I remember saying there was enough to get us drunk if we mixed all three, and he shook his head. He had a very light Scotch and water and so did I. He made some crack about my being a major and I made some crack about his not being anything at all, judging by his clothes. Tweed jacket and gray flannel slacks. Naturally I guessed that he was in something or other, so I said the obvious thing, that he was in O.S.S. To my surprise he said he was. 'If I admit that I am,' he said, 'will you forget that you saw me? It's really important that you do.' So then it was my turn to laugh."

"I should think so," said Mary Gallagher.

"I told him that I was in O.S.S., in a different branch, but that I knew about the hotel where we were then sitting."

"Oh, what about the hotel?" said Mary Gallagher.

"It had been taken over by O.S.S."

"You never showed it to me when we were in London," said Mary Gallagher.

"I couldn't. It was bombed out, that same week."

"And Stimson was killed?" she said.

"No! Three or four very good men were, but not Stimson."

"Oh," she said.

"It was an interesting thing about O.S.S. people. It was never very hard for an American in O.S.S. to put two and two together and figure out that another guy was in the organization. But having made that discovery, you'd often find that you were up against a blank wall. You just didn't ask any more questions—unless you were specifically doing a job on the guy, which was quite another story. If they were running a security check on a guy, within the organization. But of course I wasn't doing that with Stimson. Our meeting was purely accidental. Like hell it was."

"What do you mean?"

"I simply mean that Stimson had been assigned to run a little check on me. The meeting was no more accidental than D-Day. It was planned deliberately."

"How do you know? Did he tell you?"

"He certainly did not. The way I found out was when I was given the job of running a check on someone else, and the whole technique was the same."

"Oh, then you're not sure he was spying on you?" said Mary Gallagher.

"Of course I'm sure."

"There are things you're not telling me," she said.

"That's right," he said.

"Why can't you tell me now, over twenty years later?"

"Because I have no right to," he said.

"All right. Go on with Stimson," she said.

"Well, now that I think of it, I can't. I have to stop right here."

"Because of security?"

"That's right," he said.

"Oh, how aggravating, Sherry."

"I'm sorry, but that's the way it is," he said.

"Why? Is he in the C.I.A.?"

"I have no idea. I have nothing to do with the C.I.A.," he said.

"I wonder."

"You don't have to wonder about that."

"You wouldn't tell me if you were," she said.

"Probably not."

"You realize, of course, that I'm going to be suspicious of everything you do. I think you *are* in the C.I.A."

"But you wouldn't say I was very active in it. Let's see now. I play golf three times a week with the same fellows. I'm busy in my garden. Go to Mass almost every Sunday. The grandchildren every other Sunday. Just trying to think of where I could squeeze in some spy work. We average one trip a month to New York, during which I could be spying from about half past nine in the morning till dinnertime. Of course I could also be having a rendezvous with Mavis Ware."

"I'd know *that* soon enough," said Mary Gallagher.

"Here, I go to the club once a month for the meeting of the board of governors. At least ostensibly. When you don't take me, I could easily be doing some undercover work. If it really comes down to it, you have many more opportunities than I have. How do I know you spend all that time at the supermarket and the hairdresser's? I'm here, on our vast three-acre estate, or out playing golf with three other retired senior citizens. But you could be anywhere."

"Now that you summarize our activities so thoroughly, we don't lead a very exciting life, do we?" said Mary Gallagher.

"Oh, I don't know. I was pretty pleased about my crocuses," he said.

"And your eagle on the sixth."

"Yes, my third shot would have been a hole-in-one on the second, the fourth, the eleventh, and the fourteenth. Sinking a hundred-and-eighty-yard approach. I forgot how long that famous shot of Sarazen's was at the Augusta National. I must look it up again. It may be in *The World Almanac.*"

"While you're looking it up, see if it tells how old Mavis Ware is," said Mary Gallagher.

He went to the bookshelves. "Mavis Ware. Ware, Mavis," he said. "God! She's sixty! Mavis Ware is sixty years old."

"I can believe it," said Mary Gallagher.

"That would make her about two years older than Stimson," he said. "I wonder where he is now."

"What does it say about Sarazen?"

"One minute," he said. "Just says he won it in 1935." He put the almanac back in its place. "I don't suppose there'd be any way of finding out what Stimson is doing now."

"Well, not tonight, anyway. So I think we can put that off till morning," she said. "Do you really care?"

"Oh, not terribly," he said.

"No. He sounds rather worthless," said Mary Gallagher.

(1966)

MEMORIAL FUND

Miss Ames came in and stood silently in front of the desk in an annoying way she had, waiting for him to speak.

"Yes, Miss Ames?" said Russell.

"There's a Mr. Jarwin outside to see you," she said.

"What about?" said Russell. "Who is he, and what does he want? You know how busy I am, Miss Ames."

"I do know how busy you are, Mr. Russell, but this man said he was a classmate of yours and wanted to see you about the Duke Brady Fund."

"Jarwin? . . . Oh, Lord, Jarwin," said Russell. "All right, I'll see him in five minutes."

Miss Ames went out, and Russell got up and took down his college yearbook from one of the crowded shelves. "J. Jarwin. Economics Club. Candidate for track in sophomore year. Played in band in junior and senior years." That was all, that was the recorded collegiate history of J. Jarwin. It was the opposite extreme from Russell's own and Duke Brady's lists of campus achievement, with their fashionable clubs, prom committees, athletic endeavors. Russell studied the picture of Jarwin, who had a thick pompadour and thick glasses and a high stiff collar, and he remembered the one time he had seen Jarwin away from college. That had been the summer vacation between junior and senior years. Russell had gone to visit some friends in the White Mountains, and in the intermission at the hotel dance Jarwin had come over to him: "Hello, Russell, do you remember me? I'm Jarwin. In your class."

"Oh, yes. How are you?"

"Fine. This is my band playing here. We're here all summer. How's Duke Brady?"

"Duke's fine. He's working as a lumberjack, keeping in shape for football." In September, back at college, Russell had kidded Duke Brady about running into his friend Jarwin, and the Duke hadn't had the faintest idea who Jarwin was. But there was one thing about Brady that Russell never quite liked: the Duke was by way of being a campus politician, and for the remainder of his days in college Brady had made a point of speaking to Jarwin. That was from September to April. Brady had quit college in April 1917, joined the Army, and matched his football and hockey reputation with a D.S.C. and a Croix de Guerre with a couple of palms. And now, in another war, the Duke was dead, killed in the crash of an Army transport plane.

Russell signalled to Miss Ames, and presently Jarwin bustled in. Russell rose and the two men shook hands. Jarwin's unfortunate pompadour was gone, and the glasses were perhaps a trifle thicker, but it was recognizably Jarwin, a curiously pushy little man whose pushiness had not got him anywhere in college. It was going to be just like that time in the White Mountains and the so-familiar mention of Duke Brady.

"You've got a nice office here," said Jarwin. "It's more like the kind of offices you see in England. I mean, the books all over the place and so on."

"Well, we're in the book business," said Russell.

"Yes, but not only the books. I mean the old furniture, the pictures. I almost expect you to serve tea."

"We do serve tea," said Russell. "We're not terribly high-powered, I suppose."

"Oh, don't get me wrong. I like it," said Jarwin.

Russell refrained from commenting that that was nice of him. "What are you doing these days?" he asked.

"I have my own business now. Jarwin Manufacturing. We make certain parts for guns, and that brings me around to the Fund, the Duke's Memorial Fund. I got your letter, the committee's letter, and I was wondering if you had the right idea, establishing a scholarship in his memory."

"Why, yes. I think it's a very good idea. We all thrashed it out pretty thoroughly and a scholarship seemed like the best idea."

"I don't," said Jarwin.

"No? That's interesting. Why not?"

"I'll tell you why not," said Jarwin. "First of all, from a purely business point of view, if you start a fund now you aren't going to know how to invest it to yield a uniform sum every year, therefore you don't know how much the scholarship will be worth from one year to another, and that isn't even taking into consideration inflation."

"How about war bonds?"

"Oh, don't think you have me there, Russell. I buy plenty of them for myself, but in this case I don't think it's a good idea. You certainly don't want to cash your war bonds, you want to hold on to them, so that means you wouldn't have what you might call a 'live' fund for some years to come, and in my opinion the memorial to the Duke ought to start right away. Have you thought of a marble shaft?"

"Naturally that came up."

"That's what I'm in favor of. Something permanent and something we can see in a few months' time. That's the kind of memorial the Duke ought to have. An inspiration, just as he was an inspiration to me."

"I see. Well, I think the committee have already made up their minds, Jarwin."

"Yes, probably have. That's why I came to see you, to see if I could get you to change their minds."

"I'm afraid not," said Russell.

"I didn't think you'd agree with me, but I have a counter-proposition. How much did you plan to put in the scholarship fund?"

"Three thousand dollars."

"Uh-huh. You call that enough for the memory of Duke Brady, with all the money there is in our class?"

"You sound as if you had some pretty big ideas," said Russell.

Jarwin smiled. "Not too big. You see, Russell, I was very fond of the Duke."

"He was my best friend," said Russell. "I, uh—"

"Go ahead, say it. You didn't know he knew me. Well, he didn't. He merely spoke to me, but he was an inspiration to me. I wanted to be like him, and if I couldn't be like him in college at least I could keep punching when I got out of college. I consider him to a great extent responsible for whatever success I've had in business."

"Is that so?"

"Yes, that's so, Russell, and that's why I want to make this proposition: you fellows on the committee can have your scholarship, but will you let me match the three thousand with another three thousand of my own so that you can build something permanent as a memorial to the Duke?"

Russell hesitated before answering, and then he spoke deliberately: "Jarwin, I think you ought to be reminded that I am only a member of the committee and not the whole committee, but I'll tell you now, quite frankly, that I'll take your proposition to the committee, but with the recommendation that they turn it down. You see, my dear fellow, I don't think you ought to be allowed to overwhelm us with your money. And I'll tell you something else, if there were to be any really large gifts to the fund, I think they ought to come from people who were close friends of the Duke's, not from someone that he didn't even know existed for three years. If it hadn't been for me, Duke Brady never would have known you existed."

"Do you think I don't know that?"

"Oh? How did you know it?"

"In senior year he started speaking to me and one day I asked him why, and he said you told him I considered him a friend of mine."

"He did?" said Russell.

"Oh, I guessed how it happened, Russell. That time in the White Mountains when I asked about him, you probably went back to college and you probably laughed about it and said you didn't know he was such a great friend of Jarwin's. That's true, isn't it? Isn't that about the size of it? It's all right, Russell, it was so long ago you wouldn't be hurting my feelings."

"To tell you the truth, it was," said Russell, ashamed.

"Yes, I was a sort of joke in college, but Duke Brady was nice to me, so here's a cheque, and you can do as you please with it." He took out a chequebook and wrote quickly while the two of them sat in silence. Jarwin tossed the cheque to Russell, and rose.

"And you know, Russell," said Jarwin. "If it had been you instead of Duke Brady, I think I'd have done the same thing. In a funny way you were good for me too. So long, Classmate."

(1972)

THE NOTHING MACHINE

Her dress and the modified beehive coiffure deceived no one about her age, and were not meant to. It was a comparatively simple matter to fix the important dates of her career and of her life: her class in college, so many years as a copywriter and copy chief, so many years with one agency as account executive, so many years as vice-president of one firm and then another. She did not claim to be forty or forty-five, but her record spoke for itself and her chic proclaimed her determination to quit only when she was ready and not one minute before. The only thing was—more and more she liked to have Monday and Tuesday and Wednesday evenings to herself, to whip up her own dinner, to read a while, to work if she felt like it, to watch what the competitive accounts were doing on television, to take a warm bath in a tub of scented water and go to bed at a time of her own choosing. All she had she had worked for, fought for, fought dirty for when she'd had to. She had gone through those years when they said terrible things about her, and she had known they were saying them; but now that was past, and she was up there where they had to respect her—or be respectful to her—and they gave her plaques now, and wanted her name on committees. "Oh, Judy's tough all right," they said. "But she had to be, to get where she did in this rat-race. There aren't many men around that started the same time she did."

Judith Huffacker waved a pink-gloved hand at the chairman of the board. He raised his hat and shook it in farewell, and then was hurried along by the passengers behind him. That was that, and she turned to the man at her side. "Where can I take you?"

"Well, I was going to suggest *I* take you to dinner. It's a little late, but some place like the Oak Room. How would that suit you?"

"No. No thanks. I've had a long day, but I'll drop you anywhere you say."

"Oh, come on. Have dinner with me. I don't want to go back to Detroit and admit I couldn't talk the famous Judith Huffacker into a dinner."

"Admit it to whom?"

"Any of the guys you know and I know."

"Like who, for instance?"

"Well—Jim Noble. Ed Furthman. Stanley Kitzmiller. You want me to name some more?"

"Production men. Don't you know any advertising men?"

"Sure, but I thought you'd be more interested in your impression on production men. You're aces with them."

"I'm glad to hear that."

"The ad men, of course, but that goes without saying."

"Not always, you may be sure. All right, let's go to the Oak Room."

When they were under way he said, "This your car?"

"Yes, are you impressed?"

"Naturally. I'm always impressed when people spend their own money when they don't have to. You could have had the use of one of our cars, couldn't you? Don't you rate that executive-car deal? I'm sure you do."

"Yes."

"And it takes a certain amount of guts to drive around in a foreign car when you're working with an American manufacturer."

"You put it correctly. I'm working with them, not for them. I've worked with a lot of them, don't forget, and if your company doesn't like my taste in cars, if that's going to make the difference, they can either get me fired or take their business elsewhere."

"Nobody'd fire you at this stage."

"They wouldn't call it that, but that's what it would be."

"Do you mind if I call you Judith?"

"No, I don't mind. What do I call you?"

"Van," he said. "At the plant they call me B.B., but my out-side friends call me Van."

"What is B.B. for?"

"Benjamin Brewster Vandermeer is the full handle. Now I can ask you, who was Huffacker?"

"He was my second husband."

"Oh, you were married twice? I didn't realize that. Are you divorced?"

"Twice. But Huffacker's dead. He died some time after we were divorced. I kept on using his name because I'd had three names in ten years and it was getting to be confusing."

"Have you any children?"

"I have a daughter, married and living in Omaha, Nebraska. I have two grandchildren. And I own a Mercedes-Benz."

"I don't want to sound oversensitive, but do you resent my asking you these questions?"

"Well, resent isn't the word exactly. Or maybe it is. I've spent so many years working with men, and with some success, working on equal terms. I don't like it when a man asks me the kind of questions he wouldn't ask another man. If you came to my house for a social visit it'd be different, but we've been together since nine o'clock this morning, talking some pretty technical stuff and all the give and take of a business conference. But as soon as we get alone together, you want to know about my sex life."

"You're absolutely right."

"Well, give up, because you're not going to find out."

"Oh, that isn't what I meant. When I said you were abso-lutely right I meant you were right to be annoyed. But you're kind of a legend, you know. You must be aware of that."

"Fully. I've read enough about myself to know that. And I've heard enough, too. The kind of stuff that *Fortune* can hint at but wouldn't dare come out and say it."

"Well, I can take the hint. Let's just be a couple of guys that haven't had anything to eat all day, and are hungry and irrita-ble. All right?"

"Fine."

"*I've* been married twice and *I* have two grandchildren. Now we're even, okay? I don't own a Mercedes-Benz, but I think they make a hell of an automobile. Now we've traded information just about fact for fact."

She wished she had not consented to have dinner with this man. All day he had been easy to work with because he had been brisk and efficient and bloodless. He had the right answers in his mind or readily available in his batch of papers, and it was not his job to relate his facts to the field of theory in which she functioned. At the airport he could have left her for a few minutes and in that brief time been lost in the crowd. She regretted that just that had not happened, so that she would now be on her way to her comfortable apartment and a warm, fragrant bath. She had had to change her mind about him too often: from a nothing-machine, with his quick mind and attaché case, to a lonesome out-of-towner, to one of the Detroit boys who gossiped about her, to a man who could express himself in sarcastic terms that compelled her respect. She very nearly told him she had decided to drop him at the Plaza, but the words she uttered were in a conciliatory tone: "You don't get to New York very often?"

"About once a month," he said. "Our department has a dinner at the University Club, usually on the second Monday. But I go back to Detroit the same night if I can."

"Oh, yes. I knew about those dinners. We have them, too, but I don't always have to go," she said.

"I suppose they do some good. For my part, they have a dubious value. I don't get home till around two o'clock in the morning and I like my sleep. But departmental dinners must be worth it or the company'd do away with them."

"They can be a bore, all right," she said.

"I don't need the inspirational presence of my fellow man," he said. "I can perform just as well over the telephone and the teletype, and those big martinis they serve at the University Club, they certainly do promote frank discussions. Here we are."

At the table he said, "They all seem to know you here, customers *and* waiters."

"I've been coming here a long time," she said.

"I'll tell you one thing. Whether you like it or not, you didn't get that reception because you were vice-president of an ad agency. That was for a good-looking woman. Shall we order?"

It was unexpectedly smart of him to have noticed the quality of the reception, but he was not making it easier for her to like him. He put his elbows on the table and clasped his hands and looked about the room. "All these people that I've never seen before and probably never will again. I don't suppose I'll see you again, either. At least not for a year."

"I guess not. You're originally from the Middle West, aren't you?"

"Hell, that's written all over me. Yes, I've lived in Wisconsin, Illinois, Indiana, Ohio, and Michigan. I was born Wisconsin. My father was a preacher, that's why we moved around so much. I graduated from Purdue and got a job near Indianapolis . . . Oh, here's somebody I don't want to see." He raised his water glass in front of his face, but he had been seen and recognized.

"Hyuh, there, Van. Do you remember me? Charley Canning?" The newcomer was in his middle fifties, dressed with expensive care by no tailor on this side of the Atlantic. He seemed sure of his welcome and had his hand out.

"Oh, hello there."

"*Hello* there? Have I changed that much, or have you got a lousy memory? Charley *Canning,* from Humphreysville. Or maybe I'm wrong. You *are* Benjamin Vandermeer?"

"Yes, and I lived in Humphreysville, but I can't seem to place you."

"Well, for Christ's sake, don't crack your brains trying. You know damn well who I am, but maybe you have your reasons for wishing I didn't remember you. Good day, sir." Canning stared angrily at Vandermeer and at Judith Huffacker, then went on his way.

"Why did you do that? He seemed all right, and he knew you were doing it deliberately."

He nodded. "I did it deliberately."

"But why? He doesn't know why you did it."

"No, and he wouldn't understand if I told him," he said. "I

haven't seen that fellow in thirty years. If I told *you* why I snubbed him you probably wouldn't understand either . . . I didn't order any wine. Are you used to having wine with your dinner?"

"Forget about the wine, and stop being evasive. I want to know why you disliked that man so. If it's not too personal."

"It isn't personal, in the sense of his doing something to me. Consciously, deliberately doing something to me." He looked at her quickly. "All right, I'll tell you.

"I went to live in Humphreysville, my first job after I graduated from Purdue. It's a little town about fifteen miles from Indianapolis, population about twelve-fourteen hundred, and I was assistant county engineer. A kind of a maid-of-all-work and utility outfielder. Highways. Water supply. Anything that was on a blueprint or you looked at through a transit. I liked it. I got twelve hundred a year, and that was twelve hundred more than a lot of my classmates were making. And I liked the town, the people. It was like going back home, to any of the other Middle Western towns I'd lived in. And like most Middle Western towns, especially Indiana, they were crazy about basketball, so when the high school coach had to quit, I took over the team. I'd played at Purdue and they knew that.

"Well, we had a pretty good season. Won sixteen and lost eight and came in second in the county league. And at the end of the season they had the usual banquet. My boys, and letter men from other years and a few leading citizens. Small. If we'd won the county league it would have been bigger, but they always had a team banquet regardless of how they came out. The basement of the Presbyterian church, which was used for a lot of community get-togethers because they had a kitchen and plenty of chairs et cetera. We had the high school principal give out the little miniature basketballs, silver. I still have mine at home. And it was a very nice sociable gathering. A lot of kidding among ourselves, replaying some of the games we lost, and recalling funny incidents that happened on our trips. And the whole thing broke up around nine-thirty, quarter of ten, because the boys had dates and the place where they hung out closed at eleven.

"But instead of that, eight of my boys and their dates all got into cars—not *their* cars. They didn't have cars, with one or two exceptions. There were cars waiting outside for them. And they all drove off to a roadhouse down near Indianapolis, where this fellow you just saw gave them another kind of a party. Got them all liquored up, and some of them had never taken a drink before, and when they got home that night some of them were sick, and the girls were crying, and the parents raised holy hell, and the whole town was in an uproar the next day. And that's why I don't like Canning."

"Was anybody hurt?"

"You mean drunken driving? No, nothing like that."

"What did you do?"

"How do you mean?"

"Well, about Canning?"

He shrugged his shoulders. "Nothing. Oh, I could have gone and had it out with him and most likely he would have ended up on the floor. That was what I felt like doing, I'll admit that. But if I didn't know my own boys better than that, that I'd been seeing every day and three-four nights a week for four months. And if they wanted to sneak off and go to a roadhouse with a fellow like Canning, maybe *I* didn't know *them* so well, either. No, I didn't do anything. But as soon as the first job came along, I left Humphreysville and I've never gone back since. A fellow like Canning, he probably got a big laugh out of seeing a bunch of kids get drunk. Canning was a rich guy. His father owned the hardware store and was agent for Deering and Delaval and companies like that. This fellow was a Dartmouth graduate, Phi Psi, I think he was. I wouldn't have accomplished anything by mopping up the floor with him, although I admit I was strongly tempted."

"Yes," she said.

He laughed. "Tonight, too. Here in the Plaza Hotel, New York City, I wanted to give him a punch in the nose. That would have been something, explaining that to the New York police. Thirty years later. You would have had to tell your friends you were out with a lunatic, all these people that know you."

"Yes, they'd have thought you were a lunatic. But I don't."

"Well, that's good. I'm glad to hear that."

They talked no more about Canning or Indiana or anything so remote as thirty years ago. He paid the bill and walked with her to her car and they shook hands. "Let me know if you're coming to Detroit," he said. "My wife and I'd be glad to have you stay with us."

"I'll do that, Van," she said. The lie was not as bad as some she had told. It was the most harmless lie imaginable. At home, comfortable at last in her lavender-scented bath, she thought of lies and of truth, and of a life she had not spent with a man who could be so unforgiving of a little thing that had happened thirty years ago. Humphreysville, Indiana. Good God!

(1962)

A PHASE OF LIFE

The radio was tuned in to an all-night recorded program, and the man at the good upright piano was playing the tunes that were being broadcast. He was not very original, but he knew all the tunes and the recordings, and he was having a pleasant time. He was wearing a striped pajama top which looked not only as though he had slept in it, but had lived in it for some days as well. His gray flannel slacks were wrinkled, spotted, and stained and were held up not with a belt but by being turned over all around at the waist, narrowing the circumference. On the rug in back of him, lined up, were a partly filled tall glass, a couple of bottles of beer, and a bottle of rye, far enough away from the vibration of the piano so they would not be spilled. He had the appearance of a man who had been affable and chunky and had lost considerable weight. His eyes were large and with the fixed brightness of a man who had had a permanent scare.

The woman on the davenport was reading a two-bit reprint of a detective story, and either she was re-reading it or it had been read by others many times before. Twice a minute she would chew the corners of her mouth, every four or five minutes she would draw up one leg and straighten out the other, and at irregular intervals she would move her hand across her breasts, inside the man's pajamas she was wearing.

The one o'clock news was announced and the woman said, "Turn it off, will you, Tom?"

He got up and turned it off. He took a cigarette from his hip pocket. "You know what the first money I get I'm gonna do with?" he asked.

She did not speak.

"Buy a car," he said. He straddled the piano bench, freshened his drink. "We coulda been up in the Catskills for the weekend, or that place in Pennsylvania."

"And tonight in one of those traffic jams. Labor Day night. Coming back to the city. And you could walk it faster than those people."

"But, Honey, we could stay till tomorrow," he said.

"I'd be in favor of that, but not you. Three nights away from the city is all you can take. You always think they're gonna close everything up and turn out all the lights if you don't get back."

"I like *Saratoga*, Honey," he said.

"Show me the difference between Broadway, Saratoga, and Broadway, New York. Peggy, Jack, Phil, Mack, Shirl, McGovern, Rapport, Little Dutchy, Stanley Walden. Even the cops aren't different. Aren't you comfortable here, Honey? If we were driving back from Saratoga tonight you'd be having a spit hemorrhage in the traffic."

"Fresh air, though," said Tom.

He kept straddling the piano bench, hitting a few treble chords with his left hand, holding his drink and his cigarette in his right hand. "Do you remember that one?" he said.

"Hmm?" She had gone back to her mystery novel.

"That was one of the numbers I used when you sent over the note. That was 'Whenever they cry about somebody else, the somebody else is me.' I was getting three leaves a week. The High Hat Box. Three hundred bucks for sittin' and drinkin'."

"Mm-hmm. And some kind of a due bill," she said.

"Uh-huh."

"And nevertheless in hock," she said.

"On the junk, though, Honey," he said.

"If you wouldn't of been taking that stuff it'd been something else."

"You're right," he said.

"Well? Don't say you aren't better off now, even without any three hundred dollars a week. At least you don't go around looking like some creep."

"Oh, I'm satisfied, Honey. I was just remarking, I used to get that three every Thursday. Remember that blue Tux?"

"Mm-hmm."

"I had two of them, and in addition I had to have two white ones. You know with the white ones, those flowers I wore in the button-hole, they were phonies. I forget what the hell they were made out of, but they fastened on with some kind of a button. They were made out of some kind of a wax preparation."

"I remember. You showed me," she said.

He put his drink on top of the upright and played a little. "Remember that one?"

"Hmm?"

He sang a little. " 'When will you apologize for being sorry?' I laid out two leaves for that. I liked it. Nobody else did."

"I did. It had a twist."

"The crazy one. Do you remember the cute crazy one? 'You mean to say you never saw a basketball game?' Where was it they liked that? Indianapolis."

"Yep," she said. She laid down the mystery novel, surrendering to the reminiscent mood. "I wore that blue sequin job. And of course the white beaded. Faust! Were they ever sore at me!"

"They loved you!" he said.

"I don't mean those characters from the cow barns. I mean the company manager and them."

He laughed. "Well, Honey, all you did was walk out on their show for some lousy society entertainer." He sneaked a glance at her. "I guess you been sorry ever since."

"Put that away for the night," she said, and picked up her mystery novel.

He played choruses of a half dozen tunes she liked, and was beginning to play another when the doorbell rang. They looked at each other.

"That wasn't downstairs. That was the *doorbell*," he whispered.

"Don't you think I know it?" she said. "Are you sure we're in the clear with the cops?"

"May my mother drop dead," he said.

"Well, go see who it is."

"Who the hell would it be tonight? Labor Day," he said.

"Go to the door and find out," she said. She got up and tip-toed down the short hall. He picked up the poker from the fireplace and held it behind his back, and went to the door.

"Who is it?" he called.

"Tom? It's Francesca."

"Who?" he said.

"Francesca. Is that Tom?"

He looked down the hall and Honey nodded. "Oh, okay, Francesca," he said. He stashed the poker and undid the chain lock and held the door open. In came Francesca, and her half-brother, Cyril, and a girl and a man whom Tom never had seen before.

"Is there someone else here?" said Francesca.

"No," said Tom.

"Honey's here, I hope," said Francesca.

"Oh, yeah," said Tom. "Come in, sit down." He nodded in greeting to Cyril.

"This is Maggie, a friend of ours," said Francesca, "and Sid, also a friend of ours."

"Glad to know you," said Tom. There was no shaking of hands. "These are friends of yours," he said, studying Francesca.

"Definitely. You have nothing to worry about," said Francesca. She sat down, and her half-brother lit her cigarette. She was in evening clothes, with a polo coat outside. The girl Maggie was in evening clothes under a raincoat. Both men were wearing patent-leather pumps and black trousers with gros-grain stripes down the sides, and Shetland jackets. Sid's jacket was too small for him and most likely came out of Cyril's wardrobe. Francesca and Sid looked about the same age—late thirties—and Cyril was a few years younger, and Maggie could not have been more than twenty-one.

"I know we should have called up. We drove in from the country. But we decided to take a chance." Francesca liked being haughty with Tom.

"That's all right. It's quiet tonight," said Tom.

"I was going to *ask* you if it was quiet tonight," said Francesca.

"Yeah, we were just sitting here listening to the radio. I was playing the piano," said Tom.

"Really? Have you anything in the Scotch line?" said Francesca.

"Sure," said Tom. He named two good brands.

They ordered various Scotch drinks, doubles all, and Tom told Francesca that Honey'd be right out. He opened Honey's door on the way to the kitchen and saw that she was almost dressed. "Did you hear all that?" he said.

"Yes," she said.

"What do you want?"

"Brandy, probly," she said.

He continued to the kitchen, and when he brought back the drinks Honey was sitting with the society group, very society herself with Francesca and Cyril, and breaking the ice for Maggie and Sid. Sid was holding Maggie's hand, but Tom broke it up by the way he handed those two their drinks.

"Oh, Von said to say hello," said Francesca.

"Really? What's with Von these days? We didn't see Von since early in the summer," said Honey.

"He was abroad for a while," said Francesca.

"He's thinking of getting married," said Cyril.

"God help her, whoever she is," said Honey.

Sid laughed heartily. "You're so right."

"Is that the Von we know?" said Maggie.

"Yes, but no last names here, Maggie," said Honey. "Except on checks." She laughed ladylike.

Maggie joined up with the spirit of the jest. "How do you know Von isn't marrying *me*?" she said.

"The gag still goes. If you're gonna marry Von, God help you. But my guess is you aren't," said Honey.

"I'm not, don't you worry," said Maggie.

"I'm not worried," said Honey.

"I oughta rise and defend my friend," said Sid. He was still laughing from his own comment.

"Have you *got* a friend?" said Honey.

"You're so right," said Sid, starting a new laugh.

"I understand you're moving," said Francesca.

"We were, but we had a little trouble. I'll speak to you about that, Frannie," said Honey.

"Anything I can do," said Francesca.

"Or me either," said Cyril.

"Well, it's the same thing, isn't it?" said Honey.

"Not entirely," said Cyril. "Frannie has the dough in this family."

"Ah, yes," said Francesca. "But you go to the office."

They all required more drinks and Tom renewed them. When he served the fresh ones the seatings had been changed. Honey and Francesca and Cyril were sitting on the davenport, and Maggie was sitting on the arm of Sid's chair. They sipped the new drinks and Francesca whispered to Honey and Honey nodded. "Will you excuse us?" she said, and she and Francesca and Cyril carried their drinks down the hallway. Tom went to the piano and played a chorus. He turned and asked Maggie and Sid if they wanted to hear anything.

"Not specially," said Maggie.

"No. Say, Old Boy, I understand you have some movies here," said Sid.

"Sure," said Tom. "Plenty. You ever been to Cuba?"

"*I* have. Have you, Maggie?"

"No. Why?"

"Well, then, let's go easy the first few, hah?" said Sid.

"Sit over here and I'll set everything up. I have to get the screen and the projection machine. By the way, if you ever want to buy any of these—"

"I'll let you know," said Sid.

Sid and Maggie moved to the davenport and crossed their legs while Tom set up the entertainment devices. "You want me to freshen your drinks before I start?" he said.

"That's a thought," said Sid.

Tom got the drinks and handed them over. "You know I have to turn out the lights, and some people prefer it if I keep the lights out between pictures. That's why I said did you want another drink now."

"Very damn considerate," said Sid. "When do we get to see the movies? Eh, Maggie?"

"I'm ready," she said.

The lights were turned off and the sound of the 16 mm. machine was something like the sound of locusts. The man and the girl on the davenport smoked their cigarettes and once in a while there was so much smoke that it made a shadow on the portable screen. Sid tried a few witty comments until Maggie told him, "Darling, don't speak."

In about fifteen minutes Tom spoke. "Do you want me to go ahead with the others?" he said.

"What about it, Kid? Can you take the others, or shall we look at those again, or what?" said Sid.

The girl whispered to him. He turned around. "Old Boy, have you got some place where we can go?"

"Sure," said Tom. "Room down the hall."

"Right," said Sid.

"I'll see if it's ready. I think it is, but I'll make sure."

He came back in a minute or so and stood in the lighted doorway of the hall and nodded. "Third door," he said.

"Thanks, Old Boy," said Sid. He put one of his ham-hands on Maggie's shoulder and they went to the third door.

Tom put the movie equipment away, and now that the lights were up he had nothing to do but wait.

The waiting never had been easy. As the years, then the months went on, it showed no sign of getting easier. The rye and beer did less and less for him, and the only time Honey got tough was if he played piano at moments exactly like this. He was not allowed to play piano, he *could* have a drink to pass the hour, but he could not leave the apartment because his clothes were in one room, and the little tin aspirin box that Honey did not know about was in another room. He was glad for that. He had fought that box for damn near a year, and lost not more than twice.

One of these days the thing to do was call up Francesca and get five palms out of her, just for the asking. Not spend it all on a Cadillac. A Buick, and wherever the horses were running at the time go there. What if Honey *did* get sore? What about giving up three leaves a week for her? And she'd always get along. What about tonight? Wasn't he ready to swing that poker for her? Where would Honey be if he let fly with that poker? Stepping over the body and on her way to Harrisburg, and leaving him to argue it out under the cold water with the Blues.

"What are *you* thinking about?"

It was Francesca.

"Me? I was just thinking," said Tom.

"Mm. A reverie," said Francesca. "What do I owe you?"

"Leave that up to you," said Tom.

"I don't mean Honey. I mean you," said Francesca.

"Oh," said Tom. "Including—"

"Including my friends," she said.

"Five thousand?" said Tom.

Francesca laughed. "Okay. Five thousand. Here's thirty, forty, forty-five on account. Forty-five from five thousand is five, four from nine leaves five. Forty-nine fifty-five. Tom, I never knew you had a sense of humor." She lowered her voice. "Tell Sid he owes you a hundred dollars. That'll make him scream."

"Sure."

"He has it, so make him pay," said Francesca. "He has something like two hundred dollars. Shall we wait for them, Cyril?"

"Oh, we have to," said Cyril.

"Here they are," said Francesca.

"Hundred dollars, Sid," said Tom.

"A what?" said Sid.

"Pay up or you'll never be asked again," said Francesca.

"A *hun*-dred *bucks*!" said Sid. "I haven't got that much."

"Pay up, Sid," said Francesca.

Maggie giggled. "I hope it was worth it," she said.

"Oh, by all means, but—am I giving the party?" said Sid.

"If you are you owe me plenty," said Francesca.

"I've some money," said Maggie.

"You know what that makes *you*, Sid," said Francesca. "Oh, Tom, I beg your pardon." She curtsied.

"Don't pay it then. Von never squawks," said Tom.

Sid took out his billfold and tossed Tom a hundred and

twenty dollars and another ten. "Well, let's get the hell out of here," he said.

They all said good night to Tom and he to them. He counted the money and was recounting it when Honey came in.

"We got any more beer in the icebox?" she said.

"Three or four," said Tom.

"I see one fifty, two twenties, and a lot of tens. It's all yours, sweetie. For not going away to the country." She sank down in a chair. "You had a funny expression on your face when I came in. What were you thinking of?"

"Francesca."

She laughed a little. "Well, anyway I don't have to be jealous of that bum. The beer, Tommy, the beer."

He went to get the beer gladly. From now on the waiting would not be so bad.

(1947)

PLEASURE

The taxi-drivers in front of the Coffee Pot said, "Hello, baby; hello, sweetheart; hi, kid; how you doin', baby; hey, what's your hurry, sweetheart?" She walked on. They kept it up until she turned her head slightly in their direction and called back at them, "Nuts!" She turned the corner, and her heels felt as though they were biting into the sidewalk, the way they always felt when she was angry. Every time she passed the Coffee Pot, every time she came near the taxi-drivers, she had her mind made up that she was not going to say a word to them. "I won't give them that satisfaction," she would say to herself. And every time she snapped back at them, it made her angry. Some evenings she would be on her way home in a good humor; tired, all right, but with a good day's work behind her and that much more money earned. Then she would come to the Coffee Pot, and the same thing would happen over again, and she would get home full of hatred and with her feet hurting again.

Down the block she walked until she came to a house with a broken iron fence in front of the basement, and went up the stone steps and inside. She hesitated at the door, found it unlocked, climbed three flights of stairs, and entered her room. She walked with her hand in front of her in the dark until she touched the bulb in the light fixture. She turned the switch once and the light went on and off, then she turned it again and this time the light stayed on. She pulled down the shade in the single window, and undressed and hung up her clothes. She drank a glass of water and then filled the washbasin and washed her stockings and hung them across the newspaper on top of the radiator. Then she opened the small package she had brought in with her, and laid a cinnamon bun on the table.

Five months since she had been really hungry. July, August, September, October, November. Almost five months, not quite, and there had been plenty to eat every day. At the cafeteria where she worked, first as dishwasher, but now as a clean-up girl, they provided two meals a day, and her pay was sixteen dollars a week. Now and then there was a dime for her. Her job as clean-up girl consisted of wiping off tables, seeing to it that the people had water to drink, keeping the chairs in their places. She wore a maid's uniform and cap, black with white collar and apron and black-and-white cap, and it looked all right. There was one mean-dispositioned old guy who often left a dime for her, and sometimes there would be people with kids whom she helped, and they would leave a dime. Never more than a dime, but a dime covered the "L" fare. When they first gave her the job of clean-up girl, she thought of herself as a sort of hostess, and finally one day she even said to the manager, "I guess I'm a sort of a hostess on this job."

"How do you mean?" he had said.

"Why, I make them comfortable. You know," she said. "Keep their glasses full, and see that they have napkins and stuff."

"Yeah?" he had said. "Well, don't get that idea. You're still gettin' dishwasher's scale, and any funny business and back you go." It was the first time she realized that the manager had sized her up. He had sized her up the same way the hack-drivers had sized her up. They just took one look at you, and they thought they knew all about you. She knew she didn't look altogether American. Why should she? Her mother was Polish, her father was Polish; so why should she look American?

She opened the bureau drawer and took out the candy box in which she always kept six or seven dollars. She figured that if a sneak thief came in her room while she was at work, he would open the bureau drawer first and take a look at the cheap rings and necklaces and say the hell with that, and then he would open the candy box and take the six or seven dollars and beat it. Now she saw that the money was still there. She put it back in the drawer and opened the door of the built-in closet. She took out two cheap suitcases, and then she lifted a loose board in the floor and saw that the little red-enameled box was where she had left it. She opened the box and counted the money: one hundred and twenty dollars. Every week she made herself put five bucks in the box. Five in the box, plus three she paid for the room, plus fifty cents a week for the "L," plus sixty cents a week cigarette money, plus fifty cents a week on the winter coat and another half a buck on the suit, and two bucks a week she sent her married sister—she wished she could account for the rest, but somehow she never could. She didn't really have to buy papers, because people were always leaving them in the cafeteria, and there were always enough to go around among the employees, but she kept on buying them because the man at the "L" station was blind. And she went to the movies a couple of times a week. "There ought to be two hundred and forty bucks there," she said, "instead of a hundred and twenty, if I'd of saved ten bucks a week." She closed the box, locked it, and put it back under the flooring. "But what the hell, a person has to have some pleasure," she said. And so saying, she lit a whole cigarette.

(1934)

PORTISTAN ON THE PORTIS

One night not so long ago I was having dinner with a friend of mine, Jimmy Shott, who used to be a good foot-in-the-door reporter until he accepted a lucrative position in the advertising game. Jimmy took me to an Italian place in the West Forties, and the idea was I would meet Damon Runyon. Well, Damon did not show, but just after Jimmy and I sat down in came two prize-fight managers. One of them was an older man, around fifty, who looked not unlike an uncle of mine. His name, and also the name of my uncle, is Mike. The other manager was Hymie, and he right away began talking fighters, and was very proud of one of his boys, who had won the decision in a preliminary to the Joe Louis exhibition in which Max Baer was the third man in the ring. At one time I covered a great many fights and I long ago learned that all you have to do to get along with fight managers is to nod and keep nodding and put on a slightly sleepy look and occasionally ask either a very dumb or a very smart question (and they are interchangeable). This went on while Jimmy and I ate the ravioli, and then Jimmy interrupted Hymie and asked him to give the wop waiter some double-talk, which isn't pig-Latin, which isn't *anything*. Hymie smiled, very pleased, and called the waiter. He dug his fork in a piece of veal and turned it over and over, and said to the waiter, "You portis on the portistan on the veal."

"Sir?" said the waiter, bowing.

"Portis. Portis on the portistan on the veal portis, and the stamportis," said Hymie, continuing to turn the veal over as though he had a sword with a red cape hanging from it, like a bull-fighter.

"I don't understn' sir," said the waiter.

"God damn it! I said the portis on the portistan on the *veal* portis and the veal—call the head waiter!"

The head waiter already was on his way, and Hymie repeated. The head waiter shooed the waiter away and said, "Once again will you repeat it please?" Then Jimmy burst out laughing and the head waiter caught on and laughed too, but not heartily. He didn't altogether get it, because Hymie, who is thirty-five years old, has the expression you think you see in the pictures of cops whose widows received yesterday the Departmental Medal of Honor. "Aah, what the hell," said Hymie.

As we were getting ready to go, Hymie asked us if we should like to go to Newark to see some fights, and we said we should. He would only be a little while finishing his dinner and we waited. While we sat there smoking and drinking coffee he and I discovered that we had been in Hollywood at the same time, and of course we knew a lot of people in common. He knew bigger people than I did, and two of his pals—*but* the best—were an actor and a crooner. Every morning the crooner would call him and say: "What do you hear from the mob, Hymie?" And Hymie would reply: "The mains are coming to town. The semi-mains just took over Kansas City." And the crooner would say: "What do you hear from Louie the Lug, Hymie?" And Hymie would say: "Louie the Lug? He's from the opposition. A wrong gee, Bing. A wrong gee. Strictly an opposition guy." And then: "We're gunna straighten him out, Bing. I sent for my iron-rod gun moll, and we're gunna straighten out Louie the Lug as soon as the mains get in town. The semi-mains just took over Kansas City." This kind of conversation would go on every day, the crooner talking movie gangster slang to Hymie and Hymie replying in kind.

Hymie finished his dinner and said good night to Mike, who was leaving, and then the three of us went out and got in Hymie's car, being joined by Tony, a friend of Hymie's. We drove like hell through traffic and down the elevated highway to the entrance to the tunnel. Hymie paid the toll, handing the

Port Authority cop a dollar, and as he got his change Hymie said, just above a whisper: "Wuddia hippum the mob?"

The cop paid no attention, and Hymie half turned around and said to me: "An opposition guy, John. We'll let the semi-mains take care of him. We'll get him straightened out." By that time we had reached the cop who takes the toll tickets.

"What d'ya hear from the mob?" said Hymie slowly.

The cop looked at him and then at the rest of us and said: "What mob?" but not liking it a bit.

Hymie gave the car the gas and we went down into the tunnel.

In New Jersey our troubles began the moment we left the Pulaski Skyway—the wrong way. We were in Newark, but not anywhere in Newark that we wanted to be. So every few blocks Hymie would stop and ask for directions. We were in a tough district, but that did not deter Hymie. After getting directions from boys hanging around poolrooms, from motormen and cops and women, Hymie would whisper to our informants: "Wuddia hippum the mob?"

He always got an answer. The young men who you could tell were mob timber would say they hadn't heard anything for a couple of days, or give some answer which showed they were aware that there was a mob. The motormen would just laugh and not say anything, afraid to say the wrong thing. The same with the cops, except that they did not laugh. They were simply afraid to say the wrong thing (our car was black and shiny and new). Once we encountered a wise kid who wanted to give us some repartee, and Hymie said: "Hey, *waaaaid* a minute, waid a *minute*, there, wise guy. A *wronggo*. An opposition guy. Maybe we better straighten 'im out."

"Hymie, we gotta get to them *fights*," said Tony.

"Yeah, but first we oughta spray this wise guy with hot lead, from our Thompson sub-machine-gun iron. This is a wise guy." But we drove on.

Hymie was in the corner for two boys or maybe three, all of them his brother's fighters, his brother also being a manager in that neck of the woods. Hymie is a good man in a corner, and I remember his boy won in one fight, another fight his boy was robbed, and I forget the other. We were sitting in the second or third row, and between rounds Hymie would talk to his boy, but just as he was climbing down from the ring he would call over to us: "Wuddia hippum the mob?" And we would point to the opposing fighter and yell out: "An opposition guy!"

"A wronggo," Hymie would say.

After the fights we went to the dressing-room while Hymie received. He also gave. He gave to the referee, who was on the take two ways. He slipped five bucks to one of the fight reporters (it is a pleasure to go out with someone like Hymie and find out which reporters, big or little, will accept cash gratuities). He picked Al Roth to beat Tony Canzoneri at the Garden (Canzoneri, of course, won). He spent a little time with the best of the boys he had seconded, trying, as he had done during the fight, to tell the boy that in short he would have no hands left if he persisted in punching Negroes in the head. After half an hour or so we left to continue our entertainment.

Our hosts were a handsome young man who was introduced only as Harry, and a man who looked like Warren Hymer, the movie actor, and was called Blubber. Harry told us that the week before he had organized the organ-grinders at two dollars a week per grinder. They took us to a very attractive bar and Harry called to the singer, Mabel or Melba, to come over and join us. "Sit with Hymie," said Harry. She sat next to Hymie, and he began right away:

"You uh portistan on the portis the joint?"

"Wha'?"

"Portistan. On the portis. Harry said you'd portis on the portistan the joint. That's what he told me."

"Liss-sunn," said Melba.

"Go on," said Harry. "Answer him yes or no."

"Well, if you say so," said Melba.

"I said so," said Harry.

"Well, then," said Melba.

"Oh, I don't want it that way," said Hymie. "Listen, you, Melba or whatever your name is, if you portistan the stan-portis—"

"I *said* I *would* didn't I?" she said.

"Okay, then I buy you a corsadge. You be my gun moll."

"Say, what is this?" said Melba.

"Sure. I buy you a corsadge and you put the shooting iron in it."

"Do I have to?" she asked Harry.

"What he says," said Harry.

"I tell you what I'll do for you," said Hymie. "I'll turn over my beer racket to you. I gave it to my sister but I'll take it back from her and give it to you if you'll be my gun moll. How'd you like to be my gun moll?"

"She's too dumb," said Harry. "She don't know what you're talking about. Let's eat. I want a steak. Who else wants a steak?"

The waiter came over (he didn't have to come very far) for our order, and Hymie said: "Listen, you donkey, Melba is going to be my gun moll so I want a steak, but I want a small portis with a portis on top, see? Then garnish it with a stan-portis and a portis medium—"

"Medium well done, sir?" said the waiter.

"Hey, I don't even think you're listening. Now get this, a small steak with a portis, but Melba wants a portistan portis on the ubbadate stanportis *steak*, with*out* the prawn portis. And a cup of tea, on account of Melba's going to be my gun moll, aren't you, Stupid?"

"Ha ha," she said.

"Oh, a wronggo," said Hymie.

"What's that, a wronggo?" said Harry.

"You hear him? Say, what are we, in the provinces or something? You don't know what wronggo is? Wait till the mains hear that. The mains and the semi-mains. They just took over Bushwick from the opposition and what they're gonna do, they're gonna take over this territory next week."

"No," said Blubber.

"He's nuts," said Harry. "Don't pay no attention to him when he's like this."

"That's what I thought," said Melba.

"*Not* you," said Harry. "You're his gun moll." At that Harry burst out laughing, the only time he laughed all night.

(1935)

THE PORTLY GENTLEMAN

Every evening before going to the theater he would eat a meal that for most men would have been dinner, but Don Tally called it a snack. Sometimes it would be a filet mignon covered with sauce Bearnaise, with a side order of hashed-in-cream potatoes; other times it would be four double lamb chops which he would pick up in his fingers and gnaw to the bone. When it was the lamb chops he would have a finger bowl brought to the table and his ablutions were a small theatrical performance even though he might be alone. His hands never forgot that they belonged to an actor—and that was the way it was; he did not consciously make a business of the elaborate dipping and drying of his hands. The hands did it themselves, with a separate instinct.

Whether he ate the filet or the lamb chops or the minute steak, and no matter what side dishes he consumed, his dessert was always the same: chocolate ice cream bathed in Kirsch, with half a dozen Maraschino cherries soaking in the bottom of the dish. Even at Palmedo's, which was not an expensive restaurant, the dessert cost him two-fifty. "Don't you think you could bring that down a little? Two-fifty for a chocolate sundae?" he once said to Palmedo.

"It will never be less," said Palmedo. "I would charge you more if I thought it would make you give them up."

"It might, but I doubt it," said Don Tally.

"I doubt it also. But I don't doubt that it will kill you. Even you, Don. My God, fellow, you will get the diabetes. I like to see a man eat, even those cream potatoes, my nice rich sauces. But seven times a week you cannot eat that mess."

"I can and do, Alfredo Palmedo. I only weigh two-ninety, and that's exactly ten pounds over a year ago. Do you know what I eat after the show?"

"Yes, a thick steak. Is good for you."

"What you don't understand, my devoted boniface, is how much energy I burn up in the theater. A man my size needs a lot of fuel to do two dances and a song eight times a week. The meat and potatoes keep me going, but the ice cream and Kirsch get me started. You wouldn't understand that."

"I understand that you eat that slop even when you are not in a show. That's what I understand."

"I know you love me, Alfredo. As soon as your hair gets completely white we can go steady."

"You, you, you! Some day I hit you, Don. I positively."

"If you do, I'll cry. And I'm a horrible sight when I cry."

"Aah, you make for me disgust," said Palmedo, and walked away. Whenever Palmedo was driven to the personal insult he would stay in the kitchen until Don Tally left for the theater, and on such occasions when Don Tally asked for the bill, the waiter would say, "No check. *Maison*. The boss says no check, Mr. Tally."

"I cannot insult a man and take his money," Alfredo once, and only once, explained.

"We ought to work out some kind of an arrangement," Don Tally said. "I'll let you call me a son of a bitch, and you can give me my dessert for—oh—sixty cents. How's that?"

"No good."

"A dollar?"

"No, no good. I know you, you force me to insult you again so I don't charge you again. Oh, no. I'm wise to you, Don Tally. No cigar but close."

"The expression is 'close, but no cigar,' my friend. I'll be glad to give you slang lessons."

"I will be glad to give you lessons. The difference between gourmet and gourmand."

"Watch it, pal. You're getting close to the insult. Very close. You better go elsewhere or you'll be insulting me into another free meal."

Don Tally nearly always worked. He could sing and dance, he could read lines in a way to please both director and author, he was cast as a jolly fat man or as a sinister fat man, he could play a little piano and tenor saxophone, and he was a member of the Society of American Magicians. He had been fat all his life; as a roly-poly kid in movie shorts; as a bit player in silent and talking pictures of college life at institutions called Haleton U and Calford U and Midwest State. In the days of stage presentations at the Balaban & Katz chain, when there would be a name band and a tap dancing team and a singer who was always known to the side-men as That Girl (no matter who she was, the musicians referred to her as That Girl), Don Tally would often be on the bill. It infuriated the dancing team when he got into their act, usually during their "challenge" dance, and accomplished the same steps that they worked so hard on. They got nowhere, because the producer of the stage show was well aware that the audiences got a big laugh out of seeing a fat slob do a nerve-roll and a cartwheel as well as the bone-thin hoofers whose act he was crabbing. All over the United States and Canada there were dancers and torch singers and roller skaters who hated Don Tally. The mention of his name was enough to provoke them to rude noises and vile epithets, and some of the performers would gladly have killed him. But they were afraid of him. If a hoofer lost his temper enough to attack him, Tally would swing his whole hefty arm, rather like a tennis-player doing a backhand volley, and send the hoofer sprawling and hurt. Tally would not use his fists: he saved his hands for the musical instruments, the card tricks, and the scene-stealing gestures in straight dramatic parts. Once in Detroit he was having trouble with a hoofer, a single whose split Tally had copied. Out loud, in front of Ted FioRito's band and the stage-hands, the hoofer called Tally an incestuous name. Tally walked slowly toward the hoofer, who wanted to fight and took a punch at Tally's face. The punch landed, but Tally kept moving forward until his belly was up against the hoofer's. Then, using his body as a battering-ram Tally pushed the hoofer until his back was to the naked brick wall. Tally had the man pinned against the wall and laughed at him and called him other unpleasant names, while the man tried to throw hooks at Tally's face. Then when he had insulted the man as grievously as he knew how, Tally raised his right foot and with the weight of his 300 pounds brought his heel down on the hoofer's instep. The hoofer was unable to finish out the week's booking. Threats of a lawsuit came to nothing; Tally had the entire stage crew and two dozen musicians as witnesses to testify that the fight had been started by the hoofer.

He always worked, although his salary varied from three hundred a week to a thousand, sometimes from one week to the next. He had to have money to eat, and he had to eat more than most men. The thousand-dollar jobs were, of course, short-lived and he was not always available for them. They were second-billing jobs at the two-reeler movie studios in Brooklyn and Harlem and Fort Lee. Stars like Ruth Etting and Lee Wiley would carry the pictures, but they needed a man like Don Tally to feed them lines. He was careful not to antagonize the real stars, and they helped him get work. But steady employment in a Broadway show or a stage-show policy movie house often made it impossible to take work in movie shorts, and his thousand-dollar jobs were rare. Still, he was able to consider himself a $50,000-a-year man, and all through the thirties and forties—his own and the century's—he ate and drank and spent money on the dolls, and if the dolls were not as high-class as the food and the booze, they were young and shapely and not too proud. A star, or a really ambitious young actress, would never be seen alone with him; he was good for some laughs in a party of four or more, but he offered nothing to the hard little girls on the way up or to the nervous women who wanted to stay on top. There were also some stories about him and his relations with women that could get a girl identified with his peculiarities, and he was not important enough to make that risk worthwhile. All the Broadway crowd knew that there were stories about him, but they did not know just what the stories were. You only had to look at him to surmise that there would be stories about him.

But in 1952 all that had gone before became subject to the amicable review that is called the second guess.

He was playing a comic butler in a second-rate musical comedy, pulling down $600 a week and beginning to wonder when the notice would go up that would announce the closing of the show. Business had fallen off badly after the benefit performances had run out, and the show was on two-fers. At such times Don Tally invariably relaxed. Other performers might begin to cut corners, to go less frequently to the expensive places, to drink a cheaper brand of booze; but Don Tally had never worried about any future, immediate or remote. Literally a holiday mood would come over him when a show was about to close; he was like a kid who liked school but welcomed vacation.

The week that the notice went up he was in all his usual haunts, and one night after the show he was with a doll and another couple in an East Side night club, laughing and scratching and making with the wisecracks. Two tables away from him sat Nigel Whaley, the English director who strangely had never before worked in New York or Hollywood. "Who is the rather portly gentleman?" said Whaley to his companion.

"That's a fellow named Don Tally," said Al Canton, the New York agent.

"Show biz, obviously, but what does he do?" said Whaley.

"A little of everything. Sings, dances, card tricks. Never very big. He's in a show that's just about to fold."

"Been noticing his hands," said Whaley. "What was her name, in the old silent films. Began with a zed. Za-Su Pitts! She was about your time, Al."

"How do you like that? My time. She was just as much your time."

"Mr. Tally's never been in films?"

"He started in pictures as a kid, sort of Our Gang comedies. But since then he's only been in some shorts, that I know of."

"An unattractive picture, Mr. Tally in shorts. In fact, an unattractive man, don't you think? But he might be useful. Could you have the studio gather up some of those shorts of his and run them for me in the next day or two?"

"Hell, they'd run *The Birth of a Nation* for you right now," said Canton.

"No need for that. I've seen it six times. Just see if they can get some prints of Mr. Tally's shorts."

Three days later Don Tally was introduced to Nigel Whaley by Al Canton, who then excused himself so that the director and the performer could talk private.

"I saw you were in town," said Tally. "On your way to the Coast, I gather."

"Yes, my first film in Hollywood, although I've done one or two for American companies at home. Tell me, Mr. Tally, where did you learn to use your hands? I caught your show last night, and it's quite extraordinary that you're still alive."

"Why so?"

"Well, if I were the Wayne girl, or What's-His-Name-Williams, I'd have had you poisoned months ago. You're really a very naughty man—but you know that, don't you?"

"Yeah, but they don't," said Don Tally. "They haven't been around long enough to know what goes on up there. She's an ex-band singer and he's a Hollywood re-ject. They don't know from nothin'."

"I'm sure of that," said Whaley. "You're closing Saturday week, if I'm not mistaken. Not to beat about the bush any further, there's a part for you in this film of mine."

"I knew you had something in mind, but I can't see what I'd be doing in your picture. I read the book when it came out, and I don't remember any part that I'd be right for."

"In the book there was nothing, you're quite correct. But we've been known to take liberties with novels and plays, and there *is* a part for you. The question is, could we work together? You and I. The part is a good one, Mr. Tally, but not an awfully big one, and I'd be very unhappy to find that you were holding up production because you wanted to do things your way and I preferred mine. You see, I do know about acting, Mr. Tally. I've done a little, and I have a theatrical background, at least three generations of it. So the question is, would you behave yourself? I put it to you this frankly, because I become very impatient once we start shooting, and on the set I'm king. A despot, and not a benevolent one."

"You wouldn't have to worry about me. If the money was

right, the guarantee and so forth. But I have to know this much from you. It isn't a comedy part, is it?"

"Most definitely not a comedy part."

"Then we're in business. I want to get away from comedy parts. Not entirely, but I'm fifty-two years of age, and I'm tired of doing pratfalls."

"Done and done. Have your agent see Mr. Lipson tomorrow and let them haggle over terms. I know you used to get a thousand a week in films, but I'm sure Mr. Lipson can do better than that now."

"You're bloody well right he can," said Don Tally.

Whaley looked at him. "By the way, Mr. Tally, you play an American. Please don't change your accent on my account."

"Righty-ho, governor."

"Frightful, perfectly frightful," said Whaley.

They got along splendidly thereafter, and when Whaley saw the performance he was getting out of Don Tally he was enthusiastically generous with his praise. "Just wait till you see Don Tally," he told interviewers before the premiere. "It's what you people call an Academy-award performance."

"Is it true that you've signed him to a personal contract?"

"No, it is not. But I intend to use him whenever I can."

"You really think he'll get the Academy award?"

"I didn't say that, did I? But they could do a great deal worse, and they often have."

Back once again in New York, wearing one of the town's largest double-breasted blazers with a set of gold buttons bearing the crest of one of the Stewarts (his mother was a Stewart), Don Tally was the unofficial, unpaid advance man for the new Nigel Whaley film. As premiere time approached, he was put back on salary to wangle publicity in the press and on the air. For two weeks he talked about Whaley's picture to the radio people and the lesser lights of metropolitan journalism—the foreign language reporters, the high school editors, the odd creatures from the neighborhood papers. The important reporters were being saved for Nigel Whaley and the stars of the picture, but Don Tally was delighted to get the build-up from the smallies. "I've been in every zeitung and on every fifty-watter from here to Hackensack," he told his agent, Miles Mosk. "I didn't know there were that many papers around."

"Well, you never know," said Miles Mosk. "I bet you could go in the El Morocco some night and like take a poll. See how many of them ever heard of Red Foley."

"You mean Grand Old Opry Red Foley?"

"Nashville, Tennessee," said Miles Mosk. "I bet you wouldn't find six people in Morocco that ever heard of Foley. But I just as soon have him as Sinatra."

"No you wouldn't," said Don Tally.

"Damn near. There's people drive a thousand miles— drive—a thousand miles one way to catch the Red Foley show. He sells a couple million records a month."

"Are you softening me up for a booking in East Garter Belt, South Dakota. If so, pal, you're wasting your time."

"What am I? A cluck? You're hot. But I'm just telling you, get all the publicity you can out of this. I don't care if it's Turkish or what it is. Get it. Those are the kind of people do the screaming at the premeer, not your white-tie-and-tails El Morocco set."

"Why do you think I've been letting them blow garlic in my kisser the last two weeks?"

"I thought you like garlic."

"When *I'm* eating it," said Don Tally. "Not second-hand from somebody else."

"You got those magazine notices I sent you," said Mosk. "From the *Newsweek* and the *Time?*"

"I know them by heart. I'm supposed to be a combination of Sydney Greenstreet and Peter Lorre, the *Time* one said. Not bad company, uh?"

"That's cockeyed, though. We're taking some ads in the trade publications and I'm not saying a word about Lorre or Greenstreet. We make like you passed them years ago."

"Yeah, but be sure you give Whaley all the credit."

"That's the whole ad, you thanking Nigel Whaley for the opportunity of working with him in his latest triumph, et cetera. You and Whaley. Thanks for the opportunity, but dignified. Not like some of them ads, sloppy from gratitude. You hear any more from him about his next picture? Who plays the Nazi colonel?"

"I asked him, and he said he thought Leo G. Carroll. He never even considered me."

"Why, the limey bastard, he as much as promised it to you."

"No, *you* promised it to me, only you never got around to letting Whaley in on your secret. Let's face it, pal, the closest you ever got to Nigel Whaley was the day I introduced you to him. He didn't seem to realize that you used to handle Fink's Mules."

"I never had nothing to do with that act. Nothing."

"Well, some of those acrobats and xylophone players I used to see in your office."

"You know what you sound like, Don? You sound like a client that was getting ready to go over to another agency. Am I anywhere near correct?"

"Not so near. You got me work when I wouldn't go out and hustle a buck myself. But you gotta remember this, Miles. Nigel Whaley saw me one night in a joint, the kind of a joint you don't frequent because you're such a slow man with a buck. Nigel Whaley wouldn't know you if he walked in here this minute. You got me booked into some of those night spots in Oyster Shell, New Jersey, and Duck Feathers, Long Island. I took the money—after you made your deduction. But you never got me the right dough for those five shows a day with B. & K. You always took their first offer."

"Don't tell me any more, Mr. Tally. I know the routine from here on. How I was afraid to go to bat for you because I had other acts I wanted to sell. Who's after you? M.C.A.?"

"Everybody is after me."

"Sure. Now they are. But five years ago, ten years ago, you were eating that chocolate ice cream with the Kirsch on it. From jobs M.C.A. got you, or I got you? Where was the Morris office when you got that kid in trouble in Pittsburgh? Mr. Don Tally, I got a nice home in Great Neck, a boy serving his internship at Mount Sinai Hospital, another boy studding law his second year at Columbia Law School. And I got annuities besides, to take care of Mrs. Mosk and I the rest of our natural lives. This I got from my ten percent of you and many's another talented artist I kept working steady. A person willing to work steady, I had the experience and the know-how and the numerous personal contacts whereby I pick up the long distance telephone and inside of three-four minutes I got a deal. Why do I take the first offer? Because the party at the other end of the line has this much respect for Miles Mosk that I'm gonna be in business next year or two years or three years, and if they don't treat me fair and square I remember that little fact when my client moves up the ladder of fame. I got the top dollar always, and I don't lose friends."

"What are we leading up to, Miles?"

"This we are leading up to. Namely, you going over to another agent will not deprive my eldest of a new stethoscope or my younger son of a legal volume. Mrs. Mosk will not be deprived either. If she wished to take in a show, I get her house seats, the hottest ticket in town, wearing her mutation mink I gave her for her birthday. No good table at your El Morocco. But they don't know Red Foley, either. Who could buy and sell seventy-five percent of your El Morocco people."

"So you're rich and you're in business for the fun of it, and you don't need me."

"Correction, please. Not rich. But comfortable. The other statements are correct. I never solicited a client and I never hung on to one that wished to sever the relationship. Here's ten dollars for my cup of coffee. And don't you call me—I'll call you. You should live so long."

"I'll send you the change of the ten-dollar bill," said Don Tally.

He had not anticipated such an early show-down with Miles Mosk, but it was as inevitable as other changes in his private and professional life. Miles Mosk had only fairly recently stopped wearing a wing collar to work, and he was more at home in the Hunting Room of the Astor than in Sardi's. He had never flown to Hollywood or anywhere else, although his religious orthodoxy was so nearly complete that he tried to avoid travel on Saturdays, and the airplane offered advantages in that respect. He was old-fashioned and the kind of cornball that probably enjoyed Red Foley even though he was not a client. Don Tally had been a Mosk client for nearly twenty years but had never laid eyes on Mrs. Mosk or the Mosk children. In the world that Don Tally was now entering, an agent like Miles Mosk was as out of place as a Franklin sedan. Don Tally had ordered a Bugatti, and was sorry it could not be delivered in time for the premiere.

He was dissuaded from wearing white tie and tails only by the information that Nigel Whaley, the male star, the producer of the film, and the British consul general would be wearing dinner jackets. Another problem which he need not have worried about was what lady to invite to accompany him to the opening. The amiable hookers whom he usually took out for an evening on the town were more or less automatically disqualified. He was informed a week before the opening that the publicity department had already decided that he was to escort Mrs. Townsend Bishop. He had never met Mollie Bishop, but he knew vaguely that she was a society broad who went to openings of everything—plays, movies, ballet, art exhibitions, fashion shows, the fall meetings at Belmont, the opera, and promisingly chic restaurants. She had money of her own and a substantial divorce settlement from Asa Bishop, the yachtsman and former racquets champion, who had retired to his farm on the Eastern Shore of Maryland to spend the third third of his life training Labradors in Chesapeake country. Mollie Bishop was no beauty and never had been, but she was able to spend $30,000 a year on clothes, and she was an authentic socialite whose name and wardrobe dressed up the occasions which attracted her presence. It was said of her that she had originated the expression, "fun party," although she denied having used it to describe the San Francisco opening of the United Nations.

Mollie was on the best of terms with the head men in various publicity departments. The quid pro quo arrangements were satisfactory to the press agents, who valued her name, and to her for the free tickets and a suitable escort. When it was suggested, timidly, that Don Tally was available to take her to the new Nigel Whaley film, she exclaimed: "But divine!

I saw the picture the other night at a private screening, and I love him with a *passion*!"

Accordingly Don Tally appeared at her Seventy-first Street duplex at seven on the dot, and they had a cup of soup and tidbits of steak together, just the two of them. He did not know that the bright smile was not for him alone, that it was Mollie's opening-night enthusiasm. "This'll be my second time for your picture, you know," she said.

"It is? When did you see it?"

"Sunday night at some friends of mine," said Mollie.

"You mean friends with a private projection room?"

"Yes, they show pictures almost every Sunday."

"Yeah, the only trouble with that is, you don't get the audience reaction in a projection room," said Don Tally.

"Oh, but you do. As much as you would in a small theater. It isn't just five or six people, and it isn't only the rich bastards. All the servants and the servants' families. They play to fifty people or probably more. They *call* it Loew's Locust Valley."

"Say, you're pretty hip," said Don Tally.

"Am I? Thanks. But what I wanted to say was, why haven't you been in movies before? I know I've seen you in musical comedy, on Broadway, but I can't understand why you haven't been in movies forever. Is it true that Nigel discovered you in Sardi's and had never seen you before?"

"Just about, yes. Do you know Nigel Whaley?"

"Oh, forever. I met Nigel—oh, dear. He wasn't still *at* Oxford, but very soon after. My ex-husband and I used to spend a lot of time in England, but he didn't care much for the theater and I adored it. Cons'quently, I had a lot of friends like Nigel. A grand gang, they were, and it was such fun knowing them before they became *globally* famous."

"Like Gertie Lawrence and Noel Coward?"

"Oh, sure. Gertie and I go back to *Charlot's Revue*. And Bea. And of course Noel was a dear, dear friend and I hope still is. I didn't see him last trip, he was so busy with television. I wish he wouldn't do television. Are you going to do television? Don't let them sign you up for that rot. You must be very careful what you do next, Mr. Tally. If I were you, I wouldn't work with anyone but Nigel, at least for a while."

"I'll settle for that, but I'm not in his next picture and he only does one or two a year, if that."

"Well, after tonight they'll all be knocking at your door. Just don't take the first thing that comes along. I've had so *many* friends that grabbed the first thing that came along after one big success. Especially be careful of those people in Hollywood. I'm sure they'll all want you to play this same part over and over again, and over and over and over."

"There aren't that many fat villains," said Don Tally.

"But look at Sydney Greenstreet. Good heavens."

"You really dig show business?"

"Oh, I dig. Yes, I dig," she said. "I'm getting the signal. The car is waiting for us, and we can't possibly be late."

"What signal?"

"The butler. Very unobtrusive but firm. Nigel is one of the few directors that doesn't think every butler has to be Arthur Treacher, by the way. Wasn't it *fahn* working with Nigel?"

In the reports of the premiere two of the society columnists had the same thought; that chic, soignée Mrs. Townsend ("Mollie") Bishop had stolen a march on Broadway and Hollywood by having as her escort the actor who scored the greatest personal triumph in the Nigel Whaley picture. The photo editors were especially grateful for pictures that had some novelty to them, and the pictures got a big play in all the papers. There were shots of Mollie Bishop and Don Tally getting out of her town car, and of them leaving the theater, and of them dancing together at the posh party at the St. Regis after the premiere.

With the late editions of the morning papers and the early editions of the afternoons scattered about his bedroom, Don Tally remembered that he had not asked Mollie Bishop for her phone number. But he remembered the address of her apartment, and he sent her twenty dollars' worth of flowers. In little more than an hour she telephoned him. "Thank you ever so much for the blooms," she said.

"I wanted to call you up, but I didn't know your number," he said.

"Why didn't you try looking in the book?" she said.

"I would of bet you'd have an unlisted number," he said.

"I have, but I'm in the book, too," she said. "Would you like *awfully* to come for dinner next Tuesday? Eight o'clock, black tie, and I think sixteen all told. Nigel is coming, and Sir George and Lady Repperton, and some strange friends of mine that I don't think you've met. You may not like them, but I can have your friends another time. Do say you can come."

"Try and stop me," he said.

The party was a dud, a mistake just short of catastrophe. Most of the men were there because their wives had wanted to see Don Tally close to or had been bullied into coming by Mollie Bishop. The women did not respond to Don Tally, and they seemed to have made a tacit agreement that if Mollie Bishop planned to sponsor the fat actor, she could expect no cooperation from them. At midnight the only guests remaining were Don Tally, Nigel Whaley, and a woman who was amorously inclined toward Whaley and making no effort to hide her impatience. "Nancy, you don't have to make the party any worse than it was," said Mollie Bishop.

"I'd have to try awfully hard," said Nancy.

"Oh, go on home," said Mollie Bishop. "Goodnight, Nigel. If you want to push this creature in front of a taxi, it's perfectly all right with me."

"Goodnight, Mollie dear. Goodnight, Tally. Don't s'pose I'll see you before I shove off for the homeland. Good luck to you."

"Thanks, Nigel," said Don Tally. "Thanks for everything."

"Notta tall, old boy," said Nigel Whaley.

When they were gone Don Tally looked at Mollie. "Well, I was a big fat bomb."

"You never know," said Mollie Bishop. "Sometimes a party like this turns out beautifully. If I'd kept it to ten. But Tuesday isn't a good night to have too many Wall Street types. They're all intent on business and they become simply deadwood."

"It wasn't only Wall Street. Nigel Whaley was here because

he thought he had to come. Not on account of me, but because of you."

"Yes, I'm afraid that's true. His nose may be a little out of joint because you got such good notices. I never saw that side of him before, but if I were you I wouldn't count on working for him again. Did anything happen while you were making the picture?"

"Yes. I got good. I guess I got too good."

"Yes, I guess you did. I imagine there are several other noses out of joint besides Nigel's. When a member of the supporting cast steals the notices from two quite big stars."

"Well, I had my big moment," said Don Tally.

"Do you think that's the way it's going to be?"

"Could be. I've seen it happen, so have you, you told me. But I was thinking, how would it be if you and I got married?"

"If you and I got married? To each other?" she said.

"That's right."

"But what on earth for?"

"Aren't you lonely?"

"Not that lonely," she said.

"Wait'll you hear my argument. The way you live now, you go around to all these shows, opening nights and so on, and every time you do you have to get somebody to go with you. Usually some fag that everybody knows is a fag. Well, one thing I'm not is a fag, I guarantee you."

"But what you are isn't necessarily what I want, is it?"

"Now wait a minute, hear me out. I'm a fat slob of an ex-vaudeville actor. In show business all my life. No education. No family connections good or bad. If you looked all over the United States you wouldn't find anybody that was wronger for you to marry. But that's my big pitch."

"Why? How?"

"Well, on the other hand, take you. You're a society dame with a zillion dollars and a lot of friends in society and show business that honestly don't give a God damn about you. I watched them tonight. You think they're your friends, and *they* think they're your friends. But they're not. And down deep you know it, kid. The guy you were married to, Bishop, he gave you a large bundle of dough because you were a nice girl that came from the same strata of society, but he couldn't stand the life you like. So now he's married to some dame that likes dogs as much as he does. I know. I asked around. Which leaves you where? Which leaves you all alone and rich, and you have to get movie press agents to find a fellow to take you out. Or else you get one of your fags. The way I see it, sex don't interest you. Just getting all gussied up and going to all these opening nights. I won't even make a guess how long it is since you went to bed with somebody. But that's all right. You don't want to. You don't have that problem. I do, but you don't. So therefore, if you married me, I'd come and live here and every night you wanted to go out, I'd be here instead of you having to comb the woods for somebody. The rest of the time I wouldn't be any trouble at all."

"It sounds like sheer heaven," she said.

"You're getting sarcastic but wait till I finish."

"Oh, there's more?" she said.

"Yeah. I only know you a week and I only saw you twice in that time, but I think I got you pretty well figured out. You're what they call an exhibitionist. You go to all these parties and spend all that dough on clothes because you want to attract attention. But you don't want guys making passes at you. You like to have your picture taken and see it in the papers, and all that business of women staring at you to look at your new evening gown. That's where you get your kicks. But if you wanted to get a real charge every time you went out, it'd be if you married me. Previous to this they look at you because you're a big society dame and spend a lot of money on clothes. But if you want to get them to really gawk at you, marry me. All those people, the society people and the hoi polloi that stand around at opening nights, when they see you and I together they'll think, oh, boy, look at those two sex monsters. That society broad with her cheap fat ham actor. They don't do that now, because you're always with some fag. But I got one of the worst reputations in show business. A decent woman, if there is any such thing, won't go out with me. I had that reputation since I was sixteen years old, and I wouldn't be surprised if I had it the rest of my life. All your society friends'd be trying to pump you and you'd just look wise and have the laugh on them. And meanwhile some of those dames would be making a pitch for me, just out of curiosity. So there's my argument. If you want to get a real charge out of life, you and I ought to veil up."

"Now can I take a deep breath?"

"Go right ahead," he said.

She tapped a cigarette so hard that it bent. He held up his lighter for her, but she shook her head. "As a matter of fact," she said. "A great deal of what you said is true. I wouldn't be so ready to admit it if I didn't know how true it was. You were rather rough on me, but no rougher than I've had to be myself. And it would be rather fun to lead you around like a centaur and catch the reactions of my friends. I've heard about your reputation, too. I don't see how you've kept out of prison. But why wouldn't it be much simpler if we omitted the marriage part?"

"The idea's no good if I have to go home at night," he said. "I have to live here twenty-four hours a day, seven days a week. Otherwise it'd be no different than what you have now."

"Yes, I'm afraid you're right," she said.

She was silent and remained silent so long that he wanted to speak, to say anything at all, but a soft sadness had come into her face that he wanted to respect, and did. In spite of the markings of the years about her eyes and under her chin, he could see how she had looked as a girl of twenty. She was breathing regularly if shallowly, and a couple of times she moistened her lips with her tongue. At last she spoke. "You see," she said. "I'm still in love with my husband." She turned to him beseechingly. "And I think you understand that."

"Yes, God damn it, I do," he said. He went to her and let her put her head on his shoulder. Very delicately he patted her coiffure.

(1966)

THE PRIVATE PEOPLE

The doorman, being a man in his late fifties, still gets a small charge out of uttering the name. "Good morning, Mr. Dorney," he will say, and if anyone happens to be nearby and asks the doorman if that was *the* Mr. Dorney, *Jack* Dorney, the doorman is very pleased.

"He must be—what? Sixty-three?" the other person may say.

"Sixty-three on the second day of last February," the doorman will say. "An Aquarius. You'll find that Fritz Kreisler and Havelock Ellis had the same birthday. The violin player and the, uh, the famous author. Also born the second of February. Will you be wanting a taxi, ma'am?"

Down the street goes Jack Dorney, headed toward Fifth Avenue. Seldom does anyone under thirty give him a second look; his image was, as it were, frozen by the makeup people in the movie studios so that it remained an indeterminate twenty-five to thirty-five until he was actually in his forties. His biggest pictures were made after he had ceased to be a juvenile and before the slightly protruding lower lip, the tentative frown, the almost vanished chinline, the free-growing eyebrows that now act as a disguise. Some people of a certain age will vaguely recognize his walk; he still walks like a dancer, briskly and rhythmically, as though he were going to be joined by Ruby Keeler at the corner of Seventy-ninth and Fifth.

But at Seventy-ninth and Fifth he is not going to be joined by anyone. He crosses Fifth to the west side of the Avenue and turns southward, and as he proceeds to Sixtieth he could be any carefully dressed man to most of the people who see him.

He wears crushable but never crushed English hats with narrow bands, dark blue or light gray topcoats, brown suede or black calf shoes, and regardless of the weather he carries an umbrella, tightly furled. At Sixtieth he has walked nearly a mile, and he hails a taxi to take him the rest of the way, even when it is only a few blocks. He has learned that between Sixtieth and Forty-second, from Sixth Avenue to Second, he risks chance encounters with old acquaintances, old friends, old girls, who want to borrow money or get drunk or grip his arm or reminisce. They are the ones who never fail to recognize him, who know that he made some good investments, who want to rewrite history so that a weekend in Palm Springs becomes a never-to-be-forgotten romance. Once there was a time when he could tell them he was stopping at the St. Regis, but now they all know he has settled in New York. They are bores, and even the genuinely pathetic ones can be mean. "Why, you stuck-up son of a bitch, you washed-up ham, don't give me that nice-to-see-you bit," one woman had screamed at him in front of the Pavillon. She wanted him to come to dinner with some of the old bunch and have their pictures taken for *Life*. She had this young photographer friend that . . .

At Sixtieth he takes a taxi to one of a few restaurants, one of his two clubs, places where people behave themselves. In these places he is known to all the staff, from busboy to manager or owner, and in most of them he knows their names. In the restaurants especially he goes back with a few of the waiters to the speakeasy days, when he would come to town from Hollywood and spend his money, as they used to say, like it was going out of style. With waiters he was always generous, not only at the end of an evening but in times of financial emergency; he gave them money for their children's tonsillectomies, for their schooling, and in several instances, for the burial expenses of the waiters themselves. One day he looked down from a box at Belmont and saw a waiter to whose funeral bills he had given a hundred dollars during a previous visit to New York; that night in his favorite speakeasy a waiter handed him an envelope containing a hundred dollars in fives and tens. "We understand you ran into Julio today," said the waiter.

"I didn't run into him. I just saw him," said Jack Dorney. "He looked pretty good for a dead man."

"Anyway, he asked us to give this back to you," said the waiter.

"If I remember correctly, it was you that took up the collection for Julio."

"I guess it was me," said the waiter.

"You know God damn well it was you," said Jack Dorney.

"You gonna say anything to the boss?" said the waiter.

"I might, and I might not," said Jack Dorney.

"It's worth my job, Mr. Dorney."

"Don't think I don't know that," said Jack Dorney. "You could have asked me for the money without playing me for a chump." He did not expose the waiter, but the next time Jack Dorney came to New York the waiter was working elsewhere. He never knew what happened to Julio.

One of Jack Dorney's clubs is traditionally theatrical and he goes there less frequently than to his other club, which has taken in perhaps a dozen actors in its history. He avoids the theatrical club for much the same reasons that he takes taxis at Sixtieth Street. There has always been some mystery about his getting into the society club, but enough of the right people made their move at the right time, and he got in ahead of some more obviously eligible candidates. He had gone to a rather second-rate prep school in New Jersey, and could claim relationship with no prestigious family, but he had been a 4-handicap golfer and sailed a succession of small boats, and in his Hollywood days had kept out of messes. Upon moving to New York he made himself agreeable to the men who like to play golf with celebrities who could come in with a 72, and they thought well enough of him to take him to lunch at the society club and eventually to ease him in to membership. It was a completely masculine operation: none of his sponsors knew his wife. But there were members of the club who had got in through their wives' connections, and they had not always turned out for the best. The men who supported his candidacy assumed that if he had stayed married to the same woman for twenty or thirty years or whatever it was, she must be all right.

He was a good fellow, so she was probably all right after all those years. He never said much about her, but somehow you got the impression that she kept busy with charity work or an interior decorating business that she was interested in. The Dorneys have no children—no son who might turn out to be an embarrassment when he was old enough to be put up for the club, no daughter who could create problems of getting her invited to the debutante dances. Jack was just a darn good fellow who had made a lot of money in the movie business and played awfully nice golf and was about as little actorish as he could possibly be, considering. In his quiet way he fitted in very nicely, and as a matter of fact it was something of a relief to go to the club and see at least one face that was not the same old run of Porcellian and Keys and Ivy kissers, one generation after another of the St. Grottlesex types. Not that Jack Dorney was strange-looking, or that he wore actorish clothes, but you could not help remembering that he was Jack Dorney the movie actor even if you didn't think much about it when you saw him in the bar or having lunch with one of the St. Grottlesex types.

After lunch he often goes to the midtown branch of his broker, to get there before the market closes. It is a pleasant place, a prolongation of the club atmosphere, and the men he sees there have long been accustomed to his presence. He is by way of being a specialist in a few stocks but he is a cautious trader and sometimes weeks go by without his giving the broker an order. Then he will make a little joke about giving the broker a commission so that he will continue to be welcome in the office, with its comfortable chairs and air conditioning. But the brokers have learned that there is nothing casual about the transactions, which usually take place in the last half hour before the closing of business and are nearly always profitable for Jack Dorney. He is said to have a feel for the market. This he denies. "The doorman at my apartment gives me my feel for the market," he says. "He's a nut on astrology, and every morning he tells me what kind of a day I'm going to have. That's my feel for the market." But he has also said that if he can make $100 a day, it comes to $30,000 a year, which is better than being a big operator and losing $5 a year. He has a horror of having to dip into capital.

After the market closes and he and his brokerage acquaintances have second-guessed the day's trading, he goes to a movie, to his dentist, to wherever and whatever will keep him engaged until five-thirty or six, and then he goes home.

The apartment is small, with an unstylish elegance that Celeste Dorney acquired in the Hollywood days. There is a Marie Laurencin in the foyer and a Raphael Soyer in the sitting-room, but not much of Jack Dorney's movie money was spent on pictures. The sitting-room is, as the decorators used to say, busy, with a profusion of jade, Meissen, cameo, Josiah Wedgwood, bell pulls, mirrors of all sizes, cloisonné, clusters of miniatures, porcelain snuff boxes, sterling ashtrays, a Lalique clock that stopped running in 1951, a crystal candelabrum with too-short candles, and a rather startling portrait-in-oils of Jack Dorney in the role of a Confederate captain that won him an Academy award. The baby grand piano is closed and on it rest a dozen silver-framed photographs of movie stars, directors, and producers. Against the wall is a portable bar, equipped with a sterling ice bucket and cocktail shaker, a few glasses, and a set of cut-glass bottles for Scotch, bourbon, rye, gin, vodka, and vermouth, each having a sterling label on a chain around the bottleneck.

"Oh, you're home," she says. He hangs his coat and hat in the foyer closet and goes to her and kisses her cheek.

"Back again, same day," he says.

"Well, who did you see?" she says. She tries to look at him, but her focus is pulled toward the bar.

"Who did I see? Well, I'll tell you who I did see, but he didn't see me. I was in a taxi. Hank Fonda."

"Oh, Hank. I wish we could get him and Jimmy Stewart to—do you remember what friends they used to be? And still are, I guess. But Hank's always in a play and did you read that Jimmy Stewart is supposed to be worth thirty million dollars? I can't believe it. Thirty million?"

"I saw that," he says. "Gin, or vodka?"

"Oh—vodka," she says, and from that he knows that she

has had a straight vodka while waiting for him to come home. She has a theory that the alcohol in vodka is odorless, therefore less detectable than gin.

"Well, Jimmy Stewart always knew what he was doing," he says, and mercifully gets to work on her cocktail.

"But think of anybody in our business with thirty million. Bing Crosby—but he's different. Oil, I guess."

"That's what it was. Oil. At least with Jimmy. With Bing it was oil, and orange juice, and God knows what all."

"Ronald Colman and Warner Baxter. They never made anything like that. Dick Barthelmess. Bill Powell. They were supposed to be the richest in the old days."

"Don't overlook Lew Cody in that setup," he says. "Hang a lip over that and see how it tastes."

"Don't say that, Jack. You know I don't like it. It's so vulgar."

"Well, I'm a vulgar man."

"No you're not, not any more," she says. She has the drink in her hand, and it will protect her from anything.

"You haven't tasted that," he says.

"I'm not in any hurry," she says. Nor is she, now that the glass is in her hand, less than a foot away from her lips. "You? Aren't you having anything?"

"No."

"Have something. Go on. Have something," she says.

"No thanks."

"I think it's awful of you to make me drink alone," she says.

"Hell, what difference does it make?"

"Well, then I'm just going ahead without you," she says, and finishes her drink in a sip and a gulp.

Every day they play this game. She has two more drinks, and at seven o'clock she is drunk, drunk for the night, ready for bed and four or five hours' sleep. He gets his dinner; heats the soup and unwraps the sandwich the maid has left in the icebox. He puts the dirty dishes in the kitchen sink and goes to his bedroom, where he has a TV and his personal junk and all the books he has read and plans to read.

He learned about reading from Celeste, fairly late in life and without preparation. In the early years of their marriage he would come home from the studio and say, "What do you *do* all day?"

"I'm not like you, I don't have to be doing something all the time. I can play tennis, and swim, if I feel like it. But I'd just as soon read."

"Read what?"

"Books, silly."

"What are you trying to do? Improve your mind?"

"It's too late for that. No, I've always liked to read."

"What? Love stories?"

"Sometimes. Sometimes not. I don't only read novels, you know. If there's something I think I'm going to like, I buy it. The people at the bookstore make suggestions, Dick and Marian. They have a pretty good idea of what I'll like."

Once in a while she would urge him to read a novel that she thought might have picture possibilities for him, but he would persuade her to tell him the plot without his having to read it. Then came the moment of his decision to quit acting in movies. "We have enough now," he said. "Nearly a million in tax-frees, and my studio pension. Let's get the hell out of here and start living. Let's go back to New York and be private people."

"I always have been private people," she said. "Nobody knows me if I'm not with you."

"Well, they damn soon won't know you when you're with me, because I'm washed up."

"Why do you say that?"

"Because it's true. If I enjoyed the work I'd be glad to play grandfathers, but at my age five o'clock in the morning comes too early. What's there in it for me? Smaller parts, lower billing, five o'clock calls and maybe a couple of hundred thousand more than we have now. No. We have enough, and my mind's made up, Celeste."

"You didn't happen to wonder whether I'd want to make a whole new start? The only friends I have are out here. Who will I know back there?"

"Who do you know here? Our friends are beginning to die off, can't get jobs."

"I have friends that you don't know about. Lots of them.

Not even in picture business. Some I've never even met their husbands, but they're friends of mine all the same."

"Then it ought to be easy to get to know the same kind of people in New York. There we'll be private people too."

"You'll never be private people—and I was never anything else," she said.

They sold their house on Belagio Drive at double the price they had paid for it. "I didn't even have to wait to make that extra hundred gees," he said. She said nothing. "Listen, there's no use of your sulking. I want to live in New York. You're not a Californian."

"Neither are most Californians," she said. "But most of them when they come here, they stay."

"That's because they have to. I don't have to," he said. "I'm washed up in pictures, and if we stayed here I'd rot. I don't even like the climate."

"I do like the climate and I hate New York. Too hot, too cold, too everything."

"You like the smog. You like driving on the freeways," he said.

"Oh, let's not talk about it any more. You want to move, so we're moving," she said.

He bought the apartment in the 79th Street cooperative that she chose. They shipped the things she wanted to the apartment and sold the rest to the purchaser of the Belagio Drive house. Once installed, he took her to the first-nights of plays and made an effort to provide a social life for her, but it was no go. The moment he left the apartment to have lunch with his golfing friends she would begin hitting the bottle, and servants lasted about a week.

"All right," he said one morning. "We've had it."

"We've had it?"

"We have had it," he said. "I'll cut it right down the middle. You take half, I'll take the other half. You go back to the coast and get a divorce. I'm staying here."

"Do you mean that?" she said.

"Of course I mean it," he said. "If you want to, you can leave today. I'll get you a plane reservation and you can be back in heaven tomorrow."

"Unfortunately I'm going to have to put it off for a while. You have some news for me. I have some for you. I'm going to have an operation."

"What kind of an operation?"

"A hysterectomy."

"When?"

"Monday," she said.

"When did you find out about this?"

"Yesterday."

"Well, I guess that changes things," he said.

"I hope so. I'm not going to be noble and all that. I need you to get me through this. When I'm all right again, I'll go to California and get the divorce, but I need you now, Jack. I'm scared."

"Is that why you've been hacking away at that bottle?" he said. "Why didn't you tell me?"

"That's not the reason I was drinking too much. Not at first. I got tight because I was miserable in New York. But then I went to see the doctor for a check-up, and he discovered something he didn't like. Yesterday he called up and told me to get ready to go to the hospital Saturday afternoon. I'm sorry, but that's the way it is. You have to see me through this."

"Of course I will," he said. "Is it Dr. Hawthorne?"

"Yes."

"Well, you have to admit one thing. You wouldn't be able to have Hawthorne if we were still living in California."

"I'll admit it," she said.

He took a room near hers in the hospital, and during the two weeks she was there he got through five books. "That's more books than I've read in five years," he said.

"Or maybe ten," she said.

"Or maybe ten. I must be getting old."

"We're neither of us any younger," she said.

"No, but I was surprised that I could concentrate that much," he said. "Ever since we've been in the hospital—at first I wondered what the hell I was going to do to kill time. Of course that book by James Thurber—I'd seen a lot of his drawings but I never read anything by him."

"He was a writer before he was a cartoonist," she said.

"I didn't like all the stories by Hemingway, but I liked some of them. Not much plot, but the dialog—did he ever write any plays?"

"Not that I know of," she said.

"Maugham. Of course I knew he wrote *Rain*."

"He didn't, though. He wrote a story that *Rain* was based on, but someone else wrote the play. I can never remember their names. Two people wrote the play."

"That's three books. The only one I couldn't finish was the one by Thomas Mann. What made you think I'd like that?"

"I wasn't sure you would, but I was trying you out. He wrote other things you might like. How did you like *The Great Gatsby*?"

"All right. I remember when it first came out, hearing people talk about it. Naturally I didn't read it then, but I heard about it. It's very dated. Prohibition and all that. And I'm positive the author was trying to be subtle, but I didn't get the hidden meaning, whatever it was. I met F. Scott Fitzgerald when he was on the Metro lot. Thalberg got him there, but he didn't last very long. If I'd known he was going to turn out to be so famous I'd have paid more attention to him, but all I remember was that he was a little guy with a Brooks Brothers shirt that asked me how much money I made. That's what he was doing that night, asking everybody how much money they were making. Kind of a gag with him."

"Yes, I guess he did that to get a rise out of people," she said.

"You know, if you hadn't had this operation I probably would have gone the rest of my life without reading a book. But I discovered something. I can actually sit down and if the first few pages hold my interest, I'll finish the book in two or three sittings. It's a handy thing to know. I may turn out to be a voracious reader, in my old age."

"Well, it can be a great satisfaction," she said.

The novelty of reading did not wear off, but from a novelty it changed to a fixed habit, so much so that in a few years there was always a book that he was reading. In his enthusiasm he sometimes discovered authors who were hardly obscure, and he made gaffes that exposed his unliterary past; but he was acquiring a personal taste, and above all he was busy in the mind. The good writers had uttered small and large truths and shocking lies that he had never heard of, but accepted and rejected in the process of forming his own taste. Zola would have been the man to write the great Hollywood novel; Faulkner should be writing a re-make of *The Birth of a Nation*; Rex Harrison ought to play Soames Forsyte. The pleasure of reading was conditioned by his three decades of life in the studios, but a transition was taking place and as reading for its own sake grew into a proclivity, he had only his past ignorance to remind him that he had not always been so fond of books.

He read a great deal more than any of the men he now saw, most of whom had quit reading when they were graduated from college. As a consequence and because he also played a good game of golf and could take a small boat through the treacherous waters of Plum Gut, he came to be regarded as something of a Renaissance man. The respect they showed him intensified his enjoyment of New York; no one in picture business had ever asked him to recommend a book. "If you don't mind my saying so, Jack—how did a guy like you ever put up with those dumbheads in Hollywood?" said one of his new friends.

"Oh, they weren't all that bad," he said.

Such tributes to his familiarity with books came from the men he saw but not from Celeste, who had been originally responsible for his interest and was now responsible for his maintaining it. Her recovery from surgery was satisfactory to the doctors, and she appeared to have adjusted herself to living in New York. But one afternoon, a few months after her return from the hospital, he came home and she was sitting at her desk with the telephone in her hand. She had a tumbler of gin or vodka on the blotter in front of her, and she was smoking a cigarette. She did not acknowledge his entrance. "Who else is there?" she said. She nodded and smiled. "Oh, what's she wearing? That same little white hat she always wears?" Again the nodding and smiling. "Put Betty on. I want to talk to Betty . . .

Hello, you old bitch. I hear some very interesting things about you and a very high-up person in Washington, D.C."

He went to his room and changed into lounging pajamas. A half hour later she was still talking on the telephone, but her coquettishness indicated that she was now talking to a man. "I have to hang up now," she said.

"That was a long one. Who were you talking to?"

"Who was I talking to? Betty Bond."

"You mean you've been on the phone to the coast all this time?" he said.

"Is there anything wrong with that?" she said.

"You weren't talking to Betty Bond just now," he said.

"Wasn't I? I guess I wasn't."

"No, you sure as hell weren't. I heard what you said," he said. "You like to talk dirty when you're stewed. Who was the guy?"

"I don't know. Some friend of Betty's. What difference does it make? Somebody talks dirty to me, I'll talk dirty to them."

"Oh, great. Just great," he said.

"Oh, great yourself. I'm going to bed."

"That's probably a good idea, and take the bottle with you," he said.

"Don' worry, kid. Don't you worry about that. I'll take the bottle with me you can be sure of that," she said.

When the monthly bill from the telephone company arrived he discovered that her calls to the coast would cost him more than eight hundred dollars. Three of the numbers he recognized; a fourth, a Crestview number, he did not know. "What's this Crestview number you called sixteen times in the last month?" he said. "And talked over three hundred dollars' worth?"

"A friend of Betty Bond's," she said.

"The one that talks dirty?" he said.

"He's good for some laughs," she said.

"I don't think he's that funny," he said. "I'm not laughing. I don't even know who this guy is, although I sure as hell have his phone number. I guess we're right back where we were before you had your operation. The same deal holds good. I'll cut it right down the middle, Celeste. You've had your operation, and you don't need me any more. So why don't you make your plans accordingly?"

"You mean get a divorce?"

"The same deal. For eight hundred dollars a month I'd like to get a few laughs, but I'd rather pick my own comic. You've obviously picked yours. By the way, does he call you eight hundred dollars' worth, or am I paying for it all?"

"Get me a reservation and I'll leave tomorrow," she said. "I'll stay with Betty for a while, till I find someplace."

"Rots of ruck," he said. "I'll get in touch with Henry Duskin and he'll find you some other lawyer. You can trust Henry."

He accompanied her to Idlewild the next afternoon. "I must say you're behaving like a perfect gentleman," she said.

"Never mind the sarcasm," he said. "Just be sure and get off that plane sober. I know Betty Bond, and you could wear out your welcome pretty quickly. She may like parties and all that, but she and Arthur aren't going to put up with—"

"Oh, don't start telling me about Betty and Arthur at this late date," she said. "Thanks for bringing me out here. I'll go see Henry Duskin tomorrow or the next day."

A week passed before he heard from her again, and then it was not from her but of her, through a telephone call by Henry Duskin, Jack's lawyer and friend. "She finally came to see me yesterday, after breaking two appointments," said Henry. "Jack, she's in pretty bad shape. I gave her the names of a couple of good lawyers, but she didn't even write them down. I offered to phone one from my office and she said there was no hurry. I'm a little afraid they may ask her to leave the Bel-Air."

"The Bel-Air? I thought she was staying at the Bonds'."

"She was, but she left there after two nights. I don't know whether it was by request, but I'm inclined to think it was. I got her in at the Bel-Air but I don't know how long they'll let her stay. They had to carry her out of the cocktail lounge the day before yesterday."

"Was she alone?"

"Then she was, but not later," said Henry Duskin. "Jack, I'm afraid this situation is a lot more serious than you led me to believe. I think you ought to get on a plane and come out here. You can stay at my house if you like, to avoid any publicity, but there was a line in one of the columns this morning that was unmistakably about Celeste and this Joe Albridge character. I'll read it to you. 'That former movie biggie's wife and her boy friend, initials J. A., don't care who knows it.'"

"Who is Albridge?"

"He's one of those guys you always see around Hollywood. In the old days they used to call them gigolos, but not any more. They call them 'ad execs' or just plain 'execs.' A lot of them came here after the war, looking for the soft touch."

"I'll be there sometime tomorrow," said Jack Dorney.

He was met at the airport by Henry Duskin, who had with him a stout man in a silk-like suit. "This is Morris Manville, does investigating for me," said Henry.

"My pleasure, Mr. Dorney," said Manville. "I go back a long way with you. To the time when you used to own that gray LaSalle. You wouldn't remember, but I let you talk me out of giving you a ticket."

"Morris was formerly in the Los Angeles Police Department."

"Till I broke my leg," said Manville.

"A hazardous occupation, motorcycle policeman," said Jack.

"Only I broke it playing touch football with some kids," said Manville.

"We can sit down and have a cup of coffee," said Henry. "Morris has another assignment."

The three men sat at an isolated table in the airport restaurant. "Proceed, Morris," said Henry.

"Will do," said Manville. He took out a notebook. "I have exact times and all that. License numbers, street addresses. All in here. But Henry says you'll just want the gist of it, so here goes. The lady I have down here as C. D., the fellow I refer to as J. A. They left the Bel-Air Hotel the day before yesterday shortly after luncheon and visited various private residences till around ha' past eight in the evening. Drove to the LaRue restaurant, only stayed there about ten minutes and then to an address on Pico where J. A. has an apartment. They were there steadily since, with the exception that J. A. left the apartment to have a prescription filled at the drug store in the Beverly-Wilshire Hotel. That was yesterday afternoon. During the night my relief man reported they had a visit from a doctor, and shortly after that a private ambulance took the woman C. D. to a private hospital out in the Valley, which she is still there. I or my assistant made no effort to ascertain what name she was registered under or any other information due to the fact that this particular private hospital is extremely uncooperative. The fact of the matter is, it's an expensive setup with a lousy reputation."

"Thank you, Morris. We won't keep you any longer," said Henry.

"You gave me an autograph for my daughter, Mr. Dorney. And now she has a kid starting to collect them."

"No autographs today, Morris," said Henry.

"No, course not. Discretion," said Manville. He shook hands and left.

"I really put him to work not so much for the information as some kind of protection," said Henry.

"Oh, I understand that, Henry," said Jack. "I'm glad you did."

"The question now is, do we go and get her? If *you* go, you'd better have me along, in case they want to be difficult. Then depending on what condition she's in, we ought to arrange to take her to a legitimate place I know in Altadena."

"She might be there a long time," said Jack.

"Do you know anything about the prescription, what that would be for?"

"Sleeping pills, I imagine. She could always call up Dr. White, used to be her doctor here."

"The combination of liquor and sleeping pills, I don't like that combination. Well, you sit tight for a few minutes and I'll call the place in Altadena. It's run by my brother-in-law's brother."

Henry Duskin had a black Cadillac limousine with a chauffeur, imposing enough in ordinary circumstances, but they were halted at the gate of the private hospital. A man in a uniform that closely resembled that of the Sheriff's Patrol stopped the car. "What name, sir?"

"I'm Henry Duskin, the attorney-at-law."

"Are you expected, Mr. Duskin?"

"I don't have an appointment, if that's what you mean. But I'm sure they'll recognize my name."

"Oh, I recognized your name all right. And the other gentleman? Can I have his name?"

"Come now, are you an American citizen?" said Henry.

"I certainly am."

"Then you ought to recognize this gentleman by sight."

"Oh—Jack Dorney? Uh-huh. I see. Well, just hold on a minute till I call the office," said the guard. "Routine regulations." He went to a lodge-sentry box, and they could guess that he was being asked a lot of questions on the telephone. His manner, when he returned, was that of a chastened man. "Go ahead, but stay in the car till you're told to get out," he said.

"By whom?" said Henry.

"By the proprietor, the head man," said the guard. "You aren't supposed to come here without an appointment. Go on."

The driveway was not long, but it was curved, and the entrance to the main house was invisible from the public road. The house was a ranch type, to which wings had been added. Some of the windows were covered with grillwork that would serve the same purpose as iron bars. At the entrance a deeply tanned man with a thin black moustache, wearing frontier pants and a stockman's jacket waited to greet them.

"I am Dr. Reznick. Would you gentlemen care to follow me to my private office please? This way, gentlemen, please. I was about to go for a ride on one of my palominos. We have several saddle horses for the use of our guests, and I myself am a keen horseman. Now, gentlemen, if you will kindly be seated, please." He pointed to a couple of carved Mexican chairs. "I am honored, of course, by the visit of two such distinguished gentlemen. Cigars, gentlemen? Cigarettes?"

"Dr. Reznick, we learned that Mrs. Dorney is a patient—"

"Please—guest. Guest."

"Guest. Patient. Inmate. The point is, she's here, and we've come to get her."

"So I assumed, of course," said Reznick. "Well, why not? She is free to leave. I sensed a certain aggressiveness in your attitude, Mr. Duskin, but I assure you none of our guests remain here against their will." He picked up a piece of paper that was lying on his desk. "As a lawyer, Mr. Duskin, you will find this document, which Mrs. Dorney signed, you will find this document carefully prepared."

"I was sure I would," said Henry.

"Guests enter my ranch voluntarily, stay as long as they like and only as long as they like. I am a doctor of medicine, but my services as a doctor are separate from my function as proprietor of this ranch. Look about you, gentlemen. Does this look like the office of a doctor? No. My clinic is elsewhere on the premises. But many of my guests come here and stay for weeks at a time without consulting me as a physician. They ride horseback, play tennis, swim in the pool, and relax. Listen to good music on occasion."

"Then this would be the last place a woman would come to if she had to have an abortion," said Henry.

"Under certain conditions, Mr. Duskin, we could perform an abortion. Or an appendectomy. Tonsillectomy. My clinic has all the necessary facilities. I myself am not a gynecologist, if that answers your question."

"Just what are you, Doctor?"

"What am I? I am an M.D. licensed to practice in the State of California, and the proprietor of a dude ranch. Unfortunately I am not also a graduate of law school, and am not equipped to bandy words with such a distinguished member of the bar as the renowned Henry Duskin."

"Oh, you're doing all right," said Henry.

"Yes. If my English were better. But only since 1935 I have been in this country."

"You speak better English than I do," said Jack Dorney.

"Ah, Mr. Dorney. I was wondering whether Mr. Duskin arranged to do all the talking, you were so silent. Utterly silent. A rare thing in your profession."

"Very rare," said Jack.

"Mrs. Dorney was not expecting you, but I can send for her. If you wish to take her away, I must urge you to see that she has rest. She was—exhausted when she came here. We could help her in a matter of weeks, or months, possibly. But Mr. Duskin obviously has preconceived notions of this institution, and I have no desire to convert Mr. Duskin. Your wife needs rest, Mr. Dorney, and then I think her physician would suggest psychiatric care. But I am not her physician, make that clear, Mr. Duskin. She has had no medication here except that which she brought with her, prescribed for her by Dr. White." He spoke into the desk inter-com. "Ask Mrs. Dorney to come to my office, please. I believe you will find her down at the swimming pool."

The three men made no conversational effort while waiting for Celeste to appear. She was not long. She was wearing a beach robe and wooden sandals, and when she saw Jack she said, "Oh, for Christ's sake."

"Your husband and Mr. Duskin have come to take you away," said Reznick.

"What if I don't want to go away?" said Celeste.

"Then you may stay, but under the circumstances I think you should go with them," said Reznick.

"What circumstances?" said Celeste.

"Henry's car is outside. We want to take you to a place we know about, run by his brother-in-law," said Jack.

"What kind of a place?" said Celeste. "I have nothing against this place."

"Be careful what you say now, Mr. Duskin," said Reznick.

"Thank you, Dr. Reznick. I'll be careful. Celeste, this place is a dump and Dr. Reznick is a phony. Please pack your bag and come with us. You know you can trust us, and you don't know the first thing about Dr. Reznick."

"Very careless talk for a lawyer," said Reznick.

"Get me in court, Dr. Reznick. I've found out enough about you in the last twenty-four hours to beat your brains out. Just get me in court. Are you coming, Celeste?"

"Oh—I guess so," she said. "I'll meet you at the car." She left.

"Do you wish to write me a cheque for Mrs. Dorney's bill?" said Reznick.

"Yes."

"The charge is $150 a day, or any part of a day. That will be $300 plus incidentals. I have the whole thing here. Ambulance, $85. Meals, $80. Beverages and Room Service, $28. Telephone, $22. Lending library, $2. That's $2 a week or any part of a week. Night maid service, $10. Under the contract I could charge you for a week, the minimum, but I'm only charging you for two days. That will be $527 plus tax. Five forty-three seventy-one. Make it out to J-R Ranch, Incorporated, please."

"Cheap at half the price," said Henry.

"Mr. Dorney will see how our bill compares with your brother-in-law's. Perhaps you may be putting your brother-in-law on the spot," said Reznick.

"Perhaps so," said Henry. "But my brother-in-law gets no customers from Mr. Joe Albridge. Mr. Joe Albridge never heard of my brother-in-law."

"Mr. Albridge happens to be a personal friend of mine, Mr. Famous Barrister Duskin," said Reznick.

"Yes, I find that very easy to believe," said Henry. "I don't doubt that for a minute."

"I know what you're hinting at, Duskin. I just wonder how you, a Jew, could believe in guilt by association."

"Dr. Reznick, long before anybody heard that phrase, guilt by association, there was an old saying, 'Birds of a feather flock together.'"

"Here's your cheque," said Jack, laying it on the desk.

"Thank you, sir," said Reznick. "I see that it's drawn on a New York bank. You have no assets in California, Mr. Dorney?"

"Don't answer that question," said Henry.

"The reason I asked it, Mr. Dorney, you may be called upon to testify in my suit against Mr. Duskin. In fact, you would be one of my important witnesses. But if you refused to come from New York State, the judge would attach your assets. That why I asked the question."

"Don't worry your pretty head about that, Dr. Reznick. If

you ever bring a suit against me, I guarantee you Mr. Dorney will be there. I can say that with such conviction because I know there will be no suit. Your lawyer will tell you that you must come into court with clean hands—and yours are filthy. Take care, Dr. Reznick, while you are making threats of lawsuits, take care that you do not put the same idea into the minds of other people. Come on, Jack, let's get out of this dump. It smells bad."

Celeste was waiting in the car, looking downcast, with her hands folded in her lap. Jack took the middle seat beside her and Henry sat on his right. "What is this place you want to take me to?" she said. "A head-shrinker?"

"He has a head-shrinker there," said Henry.

"Well, I probably could use one. But why go to all that expense? I know what's wrong with me. I know everything that's wrong with me, past, present and future. Take me to the head-shrinker if you like, but I'll tell you once and for all, I don't want to go. No psychiatrist is going to undo in a few months what it took me over fifty years to build up. And maybe I don't want to be changed."

"Where to, Mr. Duskin?" said the chauffeur.

"Let's head out the Valley and I'll tell you when to turn around," said Henry. He pressed the button that raised the glass partition behind the driver's seat.

"I know what I want," said Celeste. "Or what I don't want, is more like it. I don't want to be separated from my husband. If I *am* separated from you, Jack, I'll be dead in a year. Please take me back to New York with you."

"You can't say no to that, Jack," said Henry.

"No, I can't. I don't, either, as long as Celeste is sure she means what she says," said Jack.

"I mean it, all right," she said.

"I'm going to get in the front seat so you two can talk," said Henry. He told the chauffeur to stop the car, and changed his seat.

"If you'll take me back," said Celeste. "If you don't think I disgraced you."

"You mean with the Albridge guy?"

"Yes. It got in one of the columns," she said.

"I know that. Well, there were other times when I could have gotten in the columns. You know that."

"Yes, and there were other times when I could have gotten in the columns. Did you know that?"

"I wasn't in much of a position to say anything," he said.

"How much did you know?" she said.

"Well, I always thought you had a thing with George Ballow."

"It wasn't just a thing," she said. "Whenever you went off to Palm Springs and didn't take me, or any of those other trips you used to take, I'd ask George to come and stay with me. And he nearly always did. But after George died I wasn't so lucky. Some of the others weren't as nice as George. None of the others were as nice as George."

"Were there that many?"

"There were quite a few. Maybe even more than you had, because you'd have the same girl for a year at a time, and I always had different men."

"It's been quite a marriage," he said.

"Yes," she said. "Both of us doing these hateful things to each other—and to ourselves. I don't think you ever loved anyone else, and I know I didn't."

"If it was as bad as that I don't understand why you objected to leaving California?"

"Well, I don't object now. I can't wait to get out of here. Betty Bond put me out of her house, and they were getting ready to put me out of the hotel. The last few days I've been afraid to think. If you and Henry hadn't arrived today, I don't know what I'd have done, but it would have been pretty awful. I was just about ready to start on dope—all that was left. Liquor and sex weren't enough for me. What else was there? Sleeping pills, but I was afraid of them. An overdose, and I'd die. The strange thing is that I didn't want to die, to commit suicide. I may be self-destructive, but I also have a strong will to live. Maybe I just haven't reached the point of degradation where I have to commit suicide. When I had the operation, if you hadn't stood by me I might have committed suicide. Or if they hadn't gotten rid of the cancer. But you did stand by me, and they did get all the cancer, and my will to live came back full force. I don't know why it should be so strong in me, all things considered. I certainly wouldn't argue with anybody that said I was better off dead than alive. What am I? I've never done anything, I've never been anything. I contribute nothing, I have no talent. I haven't even produced an idiot child to prove that I can produce something. If I read about myself in a novel, I'd say, 'There is a woman we can all do without.' The only thing I can think of is that God must be keeping me alive till He gets around to me, and then—oh, boy! Will I be in for it!"

"God? You don't often mention God," he said.

"We're very close. I don't believe in Him, but we have frequent conversations. Dialogs. When you have no one else to talk to, the natural thing is to talk to God. Even if you don't believe in Him, it's so much better than talking to yourself. Even though you *are* talking to yourself. I hope you're not going to tell the man to drive to the nearest nut-house."

"You're not ready for the nut-house. Or if you are, so am I. I've had conversations with God too."

"You? But you've never had any religion at all. At least I was brought up a Catholic."

"You forget I went to a very strict school, run by very strict—Presbyterians, I think they were. Anyway, we had to say prayers. I heard about God. We had Bible readings and morning prayers, compulsory chapel six days a week. We didn't have to go to chapel on Saturday, but some boys went anyway. The athletes. They'd go and pray that they didn't get hurt in the football game, or drop the baton in the relay race. I was never one of those that prayed when I didn't have to, but I knew about God. I'd heard of Him, plenty."

"And you prayed the night before you got the Academy award. I remember that," she said. "My talking with God was different. Half the time I was arguing with Him."

"Did God ever win an argument with you?"

"No," she said.

"No, and I guess I never did either," he said.

"You won more arguments with me than God ever did," she said.

"If I did it was because I was paying the bills. I never won any argument with you that didn't have something to do with money. I was never able to change your mind about anything."

"You have now," she said.

"No I haven't," he said. "You're not going back to New York on account of anything I said. Face the facts. You're going back because you want to get away from California. You don't want to take the next step downward."

She was silent, and he went on. "You see, if you don't face the facts you're always going to want to come back. You mustn't in any way think that *I* won an argument with you. You must fully believe that *you* got fed up, *you* were disillusioned, *you* saw what was next for you. It's like the time you had an operation, only in this case you're the surgeon. I'm standing by you, as I did before, but you are performing the operation. If you're not fully convinced of this, you're always going to have some lingering doubt about New York, about California. You'll want to give California one more try. You mustn't have any mental reservations about that. You know it's just possible that you're attracted by the degradation, as you call it."

"It's more than possible," she said. "I am."

"Oh, then you see that?"

"Of course I see it. I'm not the first woman to be attracted to bad things."

"Well, there was Eve, in the Garden of Eden," he said.

"And you don't have to go back that far," she said. "I give you Betty Bond—"

"No thanks," he said.

"—who wants everything neat and tidy, meals on time and all that. But she loves evil, really loves it. If Arthur knew how she spends her afternoons, and where, and with whom!"

"Old stuff, about women like Betty," he said.

"Not old stuff to Arthur, though."

"Well, when he finds out, whenever that is, the newspapers

will have a field day, some lawyers will be buying some new Cadillacs, and the husbands of Betty's friends will look at their wives and wonder. I guess I'm lucky in that respect. You've told me all I need to know."

"I never thought you'd take it as well as you seem to. Why?"

"Fifteen or twenty years ago I wouldn't have," he said. "Ten years ago, five years ago. But that was before I gave up picture business. While I was still a big movie star, unquote, I couldn't afford to have the world know that you were two-timing me and getting away with it. I would have slapped you with a divorce suit and made you look pretty bad. But getting out of pictures changed my attitude. Getting out of pictures and living in New York. There nobody cares what we do, and I don't have to care how I look to the public. That's what's so nice about being private people. Out here, as long as I hung around, nobody would ever believe that I'd given up pictures. And it's true that as long as I stayed here, I was probably open to the first good offer. But moving to New York gave me a new kind of freedom and I don't want to live anywhere else. That may be why I'm more tolerant of what you've told me than I would have been otherwise. Tolerant sounds pompous—"

"I was going to say," she said.

"When what I really mean is that I'm enjoying life, in New York, and when you're enjoying life yourself, you're less inclined to be critical of other people."

"Can't you just be nice and say that even if I do behave like a tramp, I'm your wife?"

"All right, I'll say that," he said.

"I don't want to go back under false pretenses, on your side or mine. Being fed up with California isn't going to make me fall in love with New York, the way you have. The only thing I can promise you is that I'll stop nagging you about going back to California. That isn't much, but it's something. We're getting too old to demand perfection."

"And we probably wouldn't know it if we saw it," he said.

They returned to New York, and they are there now. He takes his walk to Sixtieth Street and puts in the time until evening. She is drunk at seven o'clock, and he is alone with the

TV and his reading until past midnight. He knows that when
he has turned out his light she waits a little while and goes to
the sitting-room and has some more to drink. Back in her bedroom she leaves the light on all night long. She cannot sleep
unless the light is on. Oh, it is not a very bright light.

(1966)

THE PUBLIC CAREER OF MR. SEYMOUR HARRISBURG

Seymour M. Harrisburg put away the breakfast dishes and took off his wife's apron and hung it in the kitchen closet. He frowned at the clock, the face of which was an imitation dinner plate, and the hands of which were a knife and fork. He tiptoed to the bedroom, put on his vest, coat and hat, and with one glance at the vast figure of his wife, he went to the door of the apartment. Opening the door he looked down and saw, lying on the floor, the half-clad body of Leatrice Devlin, the chorus girl who lived in the adjoining apartment. Thus began the public career of Seymour M. Harrisburg.

Miss Devlin was quite dead, a fact which Mr. Harrisburg determined by placing his hand above her heart. His hand roved so that no mistake was possible. The body was clad in a lacy negligee, and part of Miss Devlin's jaw had been torn away by a bullet or bullets, but she had not been disfigured beyond recognition.

Mr. Harrisburg, observing that there was some blood on his hand, wanted to run away, but it was five flights down to the street in the automatic elevator. Then his clear conscience gave him courage and he returned to his apartment and telephoned for the police. He readily agreed not to touch anything and not to leave, and sat down to smoke a cigarette. He became frightened when he thought of what was lying on the other side of the door, and in desperation he went to the bedroom and shook his wife.

"Get the hell out of here," said Mrs. Harrisburg.

"But, Ella," said Mr. Harrisburg. "The girl next door, the Devlin girl, she's been murdered."

"Get out of here, you little kike, and leave me sleep." Mrs. Harrisburg was a schicksa.

His repetition of the news finally convinced Mrs. Harrisburg, and she sat up and ordered him to fetch her bathrobe. He explained what he had come upon, and then, partly from his recollection of what he had seen, and partly from the complicated emotion which his wife's body aroused, he became ill. He was in the bathroom when the police arrived.

They questioned him at some length, frankly suspicious and openly skeptical until the officer in charge finally said: "Aw, puup, we can't get anything out of this mugg. He didn't do it anyhow." Then as an afterthought: "You sure you didn't hear anything like shots? Automobile back-firing. Nothing like that? Now think!"

"No, I swear honest to God, I didn't hear a thing."

Shortly after the officers completed the preliminary examination, the medical examiner arrived and announced that the Devlin woman had been dead at least four hours, placing her death at about 3 A.M.

Mr. Harrisburg was taken to the police station, and submitted to further questioning. He was permitted to telephone his place of employment, the accounting department of a cinema-producing corporation, to explain his absence. He was photographed by four casual young men from the press. At a late hour in the afternoon he was permitted to go home.

His wife, who also had been questioned by the police, had not missed the point of the early questions which had been put to Mr. Harrisburg. Obviously they had implied that there might have been a liaison between her husband and Miss Devlin. She looked at him again and again as he began to make dinner. To think that a hardboiled man like that cop could have believed for one minute that a woman like Devlin would have anything to do with Seymour. . . . But he had thought it. Mrs. Harrisburg wondered about Seymour. She recalled that before their marriage he was one of the freshest little heels she ever had known. Could it be possible that he had not changed? "Aah, nuts," she finally said aloud. Devlin wouldn't have let him get to first base. She ate the meal in silence, and after dinner she busied herself with a bottle of gin, as was her post-prandial custom.

Mr. Harrisburg, too, had noticed the trend of the official questions, and during the preparation of the meal he gave much speculative thought to the late Miss Devlin. He wondered what would have happened if he had tried to get somewhere with her. He had seen two or three of the men she had entertained in her apartment, and he felt that he did not have to take a back seat for any of them. He deeply regretted the passing of Miss Devlin before he had had an opportunity to get around to her.

At the office next morning Mr. Harrisburg realized that the power of the press has not been exaggerated. J. M. Slotkin himself, vice president in charge of sales, spoke to Mr. Harrisburg in the elevator. "Quite a thing you had at your place yesterday," said Mr. Slotkin.

"Yes, it sure was," said Mr. Harrisburg.

Later, after he had seated himself at his desk, Mr. Harrisburg was informed that he was wanted in the office of Mr. Adams, head of the accounting department.

"Quite a thing you had at your place yesterday," said Mr. Adams.

"Yes, it sure was," said Mr. Harrisburg. "Geez, I'll never forget it, reaching down and feeling her heart not beating. Her skin was like ice. Honest, you don't know what it is to touch a woman's skin and she's dead." At Mr. Adams' request Mr. Harrisburg described in detail all that had taken place the preceding day.

"Well, you sure got in all the papers this morning, I noticed," said Mr. Adams. "Pictures in every one of them." This was inaccurate, but certainly Mr. Harrisburg's picture had been in five papers.

"Yes," said Mr. Harrisburg, not knowing whether the company applauded this type of publicity.

"Well, I guess it's only a question of time before they get the man that did it. So any time you want time off to testify, why, only say the word. I guess they'll want you down at headquarters, eh? And you'll have to appear at the trial. I'll be only too glad to let you have the time off. Just so you keep me posted," said Mr. Adams with a smile.

Throughout the day Mr. Harrisburg could not help noticing how frequently the stenographers found it necessary to go to the pencil sharpener near his desk. They had read the papers, too, and they had not missed the hints in two of the smaller-sized journals that Mr. Harrisburg knew more than he had told the police. Hardly a moment passed when Mr. Harrisburg could not have looked up from his work and caught the eye of a young woman on himself. At lunch time Mr. Harrisburg was permitted and urged to speak of his experiences. The five men with whom he lunched almost daily were respectfully attentive and curious. Mr. Harrisburg, inspired, gave many details which he had not told the police.

The only unpleasant feature of the day was his meeting with Miss Reba Gold. Miss Gold and Mr. Harrisburg for months had been meeting after business hours in a dark speakeasy near the office, and they met this day. After the drinks had been served and the waiter had departed Mr. Harrisburg got up and moved to Miss Gold's side of the booth. He put his arm around her waist and took her chin in his hand and kissed her. She roughly moved away. "Take your hands off me," she said.

"Why, Reba, what's the matter?" said Mr. Harrisburg.

"What's the matter? You don't think I didn't get it what they said in the papers this morning. You and that Devitt or whatever her name is. Ain't I got eyes?"

"Geez, you don't mean to tell me you believe that stuff. You don't mean to tell me that?"

"I certainly do. The papers don't print stuff like that if it ain't true. You could sue them for liable if it wasn't true, and I don't hear you saying you're going to sue them."

"Aw, come on, don't be like that," said Mr. Harrisburg. He noticed that Miss Gold's heart was beating fast.

"Take your hands off me," she said. "I and you are all

washed up. It's bad enough you having a wife, without you should be mixed up with a chorus girl. What am I, a dummy, I should let you get away with that?"

"Aw, don't be like that," said Mr. Harrisburg. "Let's have a drink and then go to your place."

"Not me. Now cut it out and leave me go. I and you are all washed up, see?"

Miss Gold refused to be placated, and Mr. Harrisburg permitted her, after a short struggle, to depart. When she had gone he ordered another drink and sat alone with his thoughts of Miss Devlin, with whose memory he rapidly was falling in love.

The next day he purchased a new suit of clothes. He had been considering the purchase, but it now had become too important a matter for further postponement. What with being photographed and interviewed, and the likelihood of further appearances in the press, he felt he owed it to himself to look his best. He agreed with his wife that she likewise was entitled to sartorial protection against the cruelty of the camera, and he permitted her to draw two hundred dollars out of their joint savings account.

In the week that followed Mr. Harrisburg made several public or semi-public appearances at police headquarters and other official haunts. He was photographed each time, for the Devlin Mystery had few enough characters who could pose. The publicity increased Mr. Harrisburg's prestige at the office, Mr. Adams being especially kind and highly attentive each time Mr. Harrisburg returned to tell what line of questioning the authorities were pursuing. Miss Gold alone was not favorably impressed. She remained obdurate. But Mr. Harrisburg had found that Mr. Adams' secretary, who was blonde and a Gentile, was pleased to accompany Mr. Harrisburg to the speakeasy, and was not at all the upstage person she seemed to be in the office.

Then one day the police investigation began to have results. A Miss Curley, who had been one of the late Miss Devlin's intimates, admitted to the police that Miss Devlin had telephoned her the night of the murder. Miss Devlin had been annoyed by her former husband, one Scatelli, who had made threats against her life, according to Miss Curley. The night of the murder Miss Devlin had said over the telephone to Miss Curley: "Joe's around again, damn him, and he wants me to go back and I told him nuts. He's coming up tonight." Miss Curley explained that she had not spoken earlier in the case because Scatelli was a gangster and she was afraid of him. Scatelli was arrested in Bridgeport, Connecticut.

Mr. Harrisburg appeared before the Grand Jury, and it was after his appearance, when he was leaving the Grand Jury room with an assistant district attorney, that he first suspected that his news value had suffered as a result of Miss Curley's disclosures. For when he read the next day's newspapers he found only the barest mention of his name in one lone newspaper. Miss Curley, on the other hand, was all over the papers. Not only were there photographs of the young lady as she appeared after giving testimony, but the drama departments had resurrected several pictures which showed Miss Curley holding a piece of black velvet in front of her fair white form, and several others in which she was draped in feathers. Scatelli's rogues' gallery likenesses received some space.

The baseball season had become interesting, and Mr. Harrisburg could not help noticing that at luncheon the following day his colleagues' sole comment on the Devlin murder was that they saw where the police got that guy that did it. The remainder of the conversation was devoted to satirical remarks about the Brooklyns. In the afternoon, after hours, Mr. Harrisburg waited for Mr. Adams' secretary, but she left with Mr. Adams. Miss Gold walked past him without so much as a how-do-you-do, the little slut. Passed him up cold.

Mr. Harrisburg did not feel that this state of affairs could continue, and when the case came to trial he was smartly clad and nodded a friendly nod to the cameramen. Their faces were blank in response, but Mr. Harrisburg knew that they would come around at the proper time. However, when he gave his testimony the attorney for the defendant caused mild laughter with his tripping up Mr. Harrisburg. Mr. Harrisburg, describing the finding of the body, declared that Miss Devlin's chest was like marble, it was so cold; and that he had taken away his hand and found warm sticky blood on his fingers. The defense attorney suggested that Mr. Harrisburg was of more importance as a poet than as a witness, a suggestion with which the assistant district attorney secretly concurred. Getting down from the witness stand Mr. Harrisburg looked hesitantly at the photographers, but they did not ask him to remain.

Mr. Harrisburg's press the following morning did not total more than forty agate lines, and of pictures of him there were none. There was something wrong, surely, and he was lost in pondering this phenomenon when he was summoned to Mr. Adams' office.

"Now listen, Harrisburg," said Mr. Adams. "I think we've been pretty generous about time off, considering the depression and all that. So I just wanted to remind you, this murder case is all through as far as you're concerned, and the less we hear about it from now on, why, the better. We have to get some work done around here, and I understand the men are getting pretty tired of hearing you talk and talk and talk about this all the time. I've even had complaints from some of the stenographers, so a word to the wise."

Mr. Harrisburg was stunned. He stopped to talk to Mr. Adams' secretary, but all she had to say was: "I'm busy, Seymour. But I want to tell you this: You want to watch your step." She refused to meet him that afternoon, and by her tone she seemed to imply "any other afternoon." At luncheon Mr. Harrisburg was still so amazed that one of his colleagues said: "What's the matter, can't you talk about anything but that murder, Seymour? You ain't said a word."

Nor was there an improvement in the days that followed. Even one impertinent office boy told Mr. Harrisburg pointedly that he was glad Scatelli was going to get the chair, because he was sick of hearing about the case. Mr. Harrisburg began to feel that the whole office staff was against him, and this so upset him that he made a mistake which cost the company two thousand dollars. "I'm sorry, Harrisburg," said Mr. Adams. "I know it's tough to get another job in times like these, but you're just no good to us since that murder, so you'll have to go."

It was the next day, after he had passed the morning looking for another job, and the afternoon at a Broadway burlesque show, that Mr. Harrisburg came home and found a note tucked in his bankbook. The bankbook indicated that Mrs. Harrisburg had withdrawn all but ten dollars from their account, and the note told him that she had departed with a man whom she frequently entertained of an afternoon. "I should of done this four years ago," wrote Mrs. Harrisburg. Mr. Harrisburg went to the kitchen, and found that she had not even left him any gin.

(1935)

SPORTMANSHIP

Jerry straightened his tie and brushed the sleeves of his coat, and went down the stairway where it said "The Subway Arcade." The sign was misleading only to strangers to that neighborhood; there was no subway anywhere near, and it was no arcade.

It was early in the afternoon and there were not many people in the place. Jerry walked over to where a man with glasses, and a cigar in an imitation amber holder, was sitting quietly with a thin man, who also had a cigar.

"Hyuh, Frank," said Jerry.

"Hyuh," said the man with glasses.

"Well, how's every little thing?" said Jerry.

Frank looked around the place, a little too carefully and slowly. "Why," he said finally, "it looks like every little thing is fine. How about it, Tom? Would you say every little thing was O.K.?"

"Me?" said Tom. "Yes, I guess so. I guess every little thing is— No. No. I think I smell sumpn. Do you smell sumpn, Frank? I think I do."

"Aw, you guys. I get it," said Jerry. "Still sore. I don't blame you."

"Who? Me? Me sore?" said Frank. "Why, no. Would you say I was sore, Tom? This stranger here says I'm sore. Oh, no, stranger. That's my usual way of looking. Of course you wouldn't have no way of knowing that, being a stranger. It's funny, though, speaking of looks. You look the dead spit of a guy I used to know, to my sorrow. A rat by the name of Jerry.

Jerry—Jerry, uh, Daley. You remember that Jerry Daley rat I told you about one time? Remember him, Tom?"

"Oh, yes. Come to think of it," said Tom, "I recall now I did hear you speak of a heel by that name. I recall it now. I would of forgot all about the rat if you wouldn't of reminded me. What ever did happen to him? I heard he was drowned out City Island."

"Oh, no," said Frank. "They sent him to Riker's Island, the party I mean."

"All right. I get it. Still sore. Well, if that's the way you feel about it," said Jerry. He lit a cigarette and turned away. "I only come back to tell you, Frank, I wanted to tell you I'd be satisfied to work out the dough I owe you if you leave me have a job."

"Hmm," said Frank, taking the cigar out of his mouth. "Hear that, Tom? The stranger is looking for work. Wants a job."

"Well, waddia know about that? Wants a job. What doing, I wonder," said Tom.

"Yeah. What doing? Cashier?" said Frank.

"Aw, what the hell's the use trying to talk to you guys? I came here with the best intention, but if that's your attitude, *so long.*"

"Guess he's not satisfied with the salary you offered, Frank," said Tom.

Jerry was back on the stairway when Frank called him. "Wait a minute." Jerry returned. "What's your proposition?" said Frank. Tom looked surprised.

"Give me the job as house man. Twenty-five a week. Take out ten a week for what I owe you. I'll come here in the mornings and clean up, and practice up my game, and then when I get my eye back, I'll shoot for the house—"

"Using house money, of course," said Tom.

"Let him talk, Tom," said Frank.

"Using house money. What else? And the house and I split what I make." Jerry finished his proposition and his cigarette.

"How long id take you to get shooting good again?" said Frank.

"That's pretty hard to say. Two weeks at least," said Jerry.

Frank thought a minute while Tom watched him incredu-
lously. Then he said, "Well, I might take a chance on you,
Daley. Tell you what I'll do. You're on the nut. All right. Here's
my proposition: the next two weeks, you can sleep here and
I'll give you money to eat on, but no pay. You practice up, and
in two weeks I'll play you, say, a hundred points. If you're any
good, I'll give you thirty bucks cash and credit you with twenty
bucks against what you're in me for. Then you can use your
thirty to play with. That oughta be enough to start on, if
you're any good. I seen you go into many a game when you were
shooting on your nerve and come out the winner, so thirty
bucks oughta be plenty. *But* if you're no good at the end of two
weeks, then I'll have to leave you go. I'll charge up twenty
bucks against what you owe me, and you can go out in the
wide, wide world and look for adventure, the way you did
once before. Is that a deal?"

"Sure. What can I lose?" said Jerry.

"Sure, what can you lose? How long since you ate last?"

In two weeks Jerry had lost the tan color of his face, and his
hands were almost white again, but he looked healthier. Eating regularly was more important than the sun. The regulars
who had known Jerry before he stole the hundred and forty
dollars from Frank were glad to see him and made no cracks.
They may have figured Frank for a real sucker, some of them,
but some of the others said there were a lot of angles in a thing
like that; nobody knew the whole story in a thing of that kind,
and besides, Frank was no dope. It didn't look like it. Jerry
was brushing off the tables, putting the cues in their right
bins—the twenty-ounce cues into bins marked 20, the nine-
teen-ouncers in the 19 bins, and so on—and retipping cues,
and cleaning garboons and filling them with water, and dust-
ing everywhere. He caught on soon about the new regulars,
who wanted what table, and what they usually played. For
instance, every afternoon at three o'clock two guys in Tuxedos
would come in and play two fifty-point games, and the rest of
the afternoon, before they had to go and play in an orchestra,
they would play rotation. Well, you had to keep an eye on
them. They paid by the hour, of course, but if you didn't watch

them, they would use the ivory cue ball to break with in the games of rotation, instead of using the composition ball, which did not cost as much as the ivory ball and stood the hard usage better. The ivory ball cost Frank around twenty bucks, and you can't afford to have an ivory ball slammed around on the break in a game of rotation. Things like that, little things—that was where an experienced house man like Jerry could save Frank money.

Meanwhile he practiced up and his game came back to him, so that at the end of the two weeks he could even do massé shots almost to his own satisfaction. He hardly ever left except to go out to a place, a Coffee Pot on Fordham Road, for his meals. Frank gave him a "sayfitty" razor and a tube of no-brush-needed cream. He slept on the leather couch in front of the cigar counter.

He also observed that Frank was shooting just about the same kind of game he always shot—no better, and no worse. Jerry therefore was confident of beating Frank, and when the day came that ended the two weeks agreed upon, he reminded Frank of the date, and Frank said he would be in at noon the next day to play the hundred points.

Next day, Frank arrived a little after twelve. "I brought my own referee," said Frank. "Shake hands with Jerry Daley," he said, and did not add the name of the burly man, who might have been Italian, or even an octoroon. The man was dressed quietly, except for a fancy plaid cap. Frank addressed him as Doc, Jerry first thought, but then he realized that Frank, who was originally from Worcester, Massachusetts, was calling the man Dark.

Dark sat down on one of the high benches, and did not seem much interested in the game. He sat there smoking cigarettes, wetting them almost halfway down their length with his thick lips. He hardly looked at the game, and with two players like Frank and Jerry there wasn't much use for a referee. Jerry had Frank forty-four to twenty before Dark even looked up at the marker. "Geez," he said. "Forty-four to twenty. This kid's good, eh?"

"Oh, yeah," said Frank. "I told you one of us was gonna get a good beating."

"Maybe the both of you, huh?" said Dark, and showed that he could laugh. Then Jerry knew there was something wrong. He missed the next two times up, on purpose. "There they are, Frank," said Dark. Frank ran six or seven. "Got a mistake in the score, there," said Dark. He got up and took a twenty-two-ounce cue out of the bin, and reached up and slid the markers over so that the score was even.

"Hey," said Jerry. "What is it?"

"That's the right score, ain't it?" said Dark. "Frank just run twenty-four balls. I seen him, and I'm the referee. Neutral referee."

"What is it, Frank? The works or something?" said Jerry.

"He's the referee," said Frank. "Gotta abide by his decision in all matters. Specially the scoring. You have to abide by the referee, specially on matters of scoring. You know that."

"So it's the works," said Jerry. "O.K. I get it. Pick up the marbles." He laid down his cue. "What a sap I been. I thought this was on the up-and-up."

"I hereby declare this game is forfeited. Frank wins the match. Congratulate the winner, why don't you, kid?"

"This means I'm out, I guess, eh, Frank?" said Jerry.

"Well, you know our agreement," said Frank. "We gotta abide by the decision of the referee, and he says you forfeited, so I guess you don't work here any more."

"Congratulate the winner," said Dark. "Where's your sportmanship, huh? Where's your sportmanship?"

"Don't look like he has any," said Frank, very sadly. "Well, that's the way it goes."

"Maybe we better teach him a little sportmanship," said Dark.

"All right by me," said Frank. "One thing I thought about Mr. Daley, I thought he'd be a good loser, but it don't look that way. It don't look that way one bit so maybe you better teach him a little sportmanship. Only a little, though. Just give him a little bit of a lesson."

Jerry reached for the cue that he had laid on the table, but as he did, Dark brought his own cue down on Jerry's hands. "Shouldn't do that," said Dark. "You oughtn't to scream, either. Cops might hear you, and you don't want any cops. You don't want any part of the cops, wise guy."

"You broke me hands, you broke me hands!" Jerry screamed. The pain was awful, and he was crying.

"Keep them out of other people's pockets," said Frank. "Beat it."

(1934)

THE SUN-DODGERS

Back in the long nighttime of the Twenties and Thirties, when so many of the people I knew had jobs that made them sun-dodgers, Jack Pyne was known derisively as a mystery man. He was even called *the* mystery man, but it was not said in a way that would make you want to meet him or to inquire into the reason for calling him that. We all have our secrets, and Jack Pyne undoubtedly had his, but when he was referred to as a mystery man it was a term of contempt. In our set it was universally known that Jack Pyne made his living by peddling gossip to the Broadway columnists. They paid him no money, but Jack Pyne always had some chorus girls or bit players who paid him twenty-five dollars a week to get their names in the papers. The chatter writers would mention his clients in return for his acting as a spy or a messenger boy or procurer. You would be surprised to learn the names of some of the girls who once were clients of Jack Pyne. You might even be shocked and incredulous.

When business was good Jack Pyne sometimes had three or four clients, some of them paying him more than twenty-five dollars a week, and when business was exceptionally good Jack Pyne might have four individual clients, a second-rate night club, and a Broadway show. The night club seldom paid him any cash, but he was on the cuff there for meals and, within reason, free drinks for newspaper men. There were occasional periods when Jack Pyne probably had an income of close to two hundred dollars a week from the chorus girls and a hundred and fifty dollars a week as press agent for a musical comedy, in addition to the food and liquor he got free from the

264 THE NEW YORK STORIES

night clubs. It was in that way that he got the nickname of mystery man. "Who's Jack Pyne hustling for a buck now? The mystery man," someone once said. "Jack Pyne, the man of mystery."

We had favorite joints and favorite tables in the joints, and in the course of a single night, any night, we would move from a favorite table in one joint to a favorite table in one or two other joints, more or less according to a schedule. Jack Pyne always knew where we could be found at any hour between eleven P.M. and six o'clock in the morning. In our group there were, among the regulars, four or five newspaper men, a Broadway doctor, a Broadway attorney, one or two lyric-writers, a playwright, two or three press agents, a bookmaker, a detective from the Broadway Squad, sometimes a Catholic priest, a vaudeville actor turned sketch writer, a salesman for a meat packer, a minor poet, a real estate speculator, a radio announcer. At no time were all these men together at the same table, but they were the regulars of our group. There were other groups: the mobster group, the song-writing and music-publishing group, the gamblers, the minor hoods, and in the course of a night we might be visited briefly by members of the other groups, with the exception of the minor hoods. They kept to themselves because they did not want to go anywhere near a newspaper man; they did not want to be seen talking to a newspaper man. As a group, a class, they were the cruelest, stupidest, most evil men I have ever known, and I was afraid of them. I was not afraid of the big shots; they, with their new importance and power, generally behaved themselves in public, but the smallies, as we called the minor hoods, were unpredictable, reckless, and we knew the stories about them and their savagery. They were not all young men; some of them were in their forties and fifties, and I had a theory that the reason the older ones survived was that they had been out of circulation, in prison, and thus invulnerable to the high mortality rate among smallies. It was not only a theory I had; some of them had been in prison before Prohibition went into effect and came out to find that highjacking and gang warfare paid better than armed robbery and felonious assault, and not only paid better but were safer in that prosecution had become more difficult and the mobs retained clever attorneys. A man who had gone to prison for homicide in 1916 and was released in ten years would discover that in his absence an almost ideal situation had been created. If he could make a connection with an established mob he might easily make a living on a standby basis, with nothing to do but remain on call until the mob had some punishment to dole out. And if the punishment involved murdering a member of an opposition mob, the legal authorities often could not or would not make an arrest. The smallies were killing each other off in private mob warfare, and if you noticed that one of the familiar faces was missing from the smallies' table, you could usually guess why. But you had to guess, most of the time. I didn't know many of them by name, although I knew them by sight, and even when their bodies were found in Bushwick or in Dutchess County, the newspaper photographs did not identify them for me. One man with half his face shot away and curled up in the back of a sedan looks much the same as another man who died in the same circumstances. A man who had been soaked with gasoline as well as stabbed or shot might be the missing face from the smallies' table, but I could only guess.

When the tabloids came out with stories and pictures of a mobster's murder the regulars at our table postponed discussion of it, but we could not help looking at the smallies' table to see how they were taking it. Sometimes their table would be vacant, which usually meant that one or more of the smallies had been picked up by the police and the others were in hiding. The big shots were always at their own table, gabbing away as though nothing had happened, and probably from their point of view nothing had; the murder we were reading about had been ordered weeks before, and the actual killing was old hat to the big shots. This was New York, not Chicago, and it has never ceased to amaze me how few of the real big shots got killed. But of course there is the old saying that generals die in bed, too.

If we often stole glances at the smallies' table, they in turn spent a lot of time staring at us. Plainly they resented us and our presence; obviously they thought we did not belong in the same joints that they frequented—and in a way they were right, but we were sun-dodgers and had no place else to go. If they had had their way they could easily have got rid of us, and without working us over. I know I would not have gone to a joint after being warned off by a couple of those hoods. They had a neat trick of pushing a man to the sidewalk, laying his leg across the curbstone, and jumping on it. No guns, no knives, no acid. They had a hundred other tricks, too, to maim or cripple people, of either sex, who got in their way. But the big shots' visits to our table gave us a sort of *laissez-passer*, which, though it increased the smallies' resentment of our presence, protected us from abuse. I must qualify that statement a little bit: they would not have abused the detective from the Broadway Squad. *He* abused *them*, sometimes beat them up just to keep in practice. But he was a special case, a terrifying man with fist and boot, and not really one of our group. Two things were always, always said of Tommy Callaghan: he was a law unto himself, and he led a charmed life. He has been written about in articles and in fiction, and I think there was even a movie that was more or less based on his career. His attitude and policy were expressed very simply. "I hate hoods," he would say, and he made no distinction between the big shots and the smallies. One of the biggest of the big shots always had to tip his hat to Tommy Callaghan, no matter where they ran into each other; at the fights in the Garden, at the race track, or in a hotel lobby. But this is not a repetition of the legend of Tommy Callaghan. In this chronicle he plays a minor part, and having introduced him I will go on until I need him later in the story.

However, since I have been rambling along with digressions where I felt like making them, I want to put in a warning to those readers who may still retain an impression of those days and those people that may be charming, but has nothing to do with the truth. Broadway really was not populated by benevolent bookmakers who gave all their money to the Salvation Army, and bootleggers who were always looking around for a paraplegic newsboy who needed surgery, and crapshooters

who used their tees and miss-outs—crooked dice—in order to
finance a chapel. There is something about the words rogue
and rascal that brings a smile to the eyes of people who never
spent any time with rogues and rascals. And I have never been
able to accept the paradox of the prostitute who was faithful
to one man. The big shots and the smallies that I saw—and I
saw dozens of them—were unprincipled, sadistic, murderous
bullies; often sexually perverted, diseased, sometimes drug
addicts, and stingy. The women were just as bad, except when
they were worse. The picture of a band of jolly Robin Hoods
on Times Square is all wrong and not very romantic to those
who knew that perhaps the most spectacular gambler of them
all was nothing but a shylock—a usurer—and a fixer. And
now back to Jack Pyne.

The joint that usually was our last stop before going home
was a place called The Leisure Club, Fiftieth Street near Eighth
Avenue, on the second story. It had several things to recommend it: it stayed open until nine o'clock in the morning; it
was considered neutral territory by the important mob leaders;
the booze was basically good liquor that had been cut only
once; and it was not expensive. The Leisure offered no entertainment more elaborate than a colored piano player who also
sang dirty songs. His name was Teeth, the only thing he would
answer to. He played quite good piano, in spite of not having
eighty-eight notes to work with. It was a studio piano, and he
had to be inventive to do right by Youmans and Gershwin and
Kern on an abbreviated keyboard. The dirty songs were the
work of anonymous composers, and they were the same dirty
songs that could be heard in little joints all over town, or paro-
dies of songs by Cole Porter and Noel Coward. It was rather
high-class stuff for a joint like The Leisure, most of it too
subtle for the big shots and the smallies, but their girl friends
liked it.

The Leisure had not caught on with the Park Avenue-Junior
League-Squadron A crowd, probably because they would be
flocking to Harlem at just about the same hour that The Leisure was showing signs of action. In any event, The Leisure
was strictly a Broadway joint, not for post-debutantes or

squash players. It was for show people, newspaper men, various kinds of hustlers, and mobsters, in addition to the regulars whom I have already mentioned. Since for most of the customers it was the last place before going home, it was usually well filled, with no new male faces from night to night. There were, of course, new girls from the musical comedies and other night clubs, and women who had come in from out of town; but some of these girls and women soon became steady customers too.

At The Leisure our group gathered at a booth in the middle of a row of booths. When we were more than nine in number the waiters would put a table against the booth table as an extension, but that seldom was necessary. We hardly ever numbered fewer than five or more than nine and eight was the most comfortable; four on each side of the table and two at the open end. I describe the seating arrangements because I never saw anyone make room for Jack Pyne. If he joined our table, he had to sit at the open end. And I never heard anyone actually ask him to sit down.

He would come in, say a few words to the hatcheck girl, and head for our table. "Hello, there, you muggs," he would say.

Somebody would say, "Jack," and the others would nod—or not nod. There was one fellow, a newspaper reporter, who would be a bit more loquacious. "Why, hello there, Jack. We were just talking about you."

"Oh, yeah? What'd you say?"

"Just saying what a great fellow you were. We just got finished taking a vote."

"Come off it."

"On the level. We're raising a little purse to send you on a trip. Where would you rather go, Jack? Devil's Island? You speak French, don't you, Jack?"

"Lay off, lay off, you muggs."

There was no insult he would not take, whether it concerned his honesty, his morals, his manhood, his appearance, or his methods of earning a living. The newspaper reporter who suggested Devil's Island (and who had first called him a mystery man) would mention an extraordinary sexual perversion and suddenly say, "What's it like, Jack? I hear that's what you go for." Always, when they were making a fool of him, he would pretend to think they were kidding him, as though they would only kid a man they were fond of. But it was all insulting, often straight-factual, and finally not very funny. We all had a crack at insulting Jack Pyne, but he was so totally lacking in self-respect and so completely unable or unwilling to make any kind of retort that we finally did lay off, and he became a bore. I think we began to hate him then. He was a bore, and a terribly cheap individual, and because we had given up the mean sport of insulting him, he convinced himself that he was one of the boys.

We all read the same newspapers and heard the same gossip, and that went for Jack Pyne. He had the same information we had out of the newspapers, but now he had opinions as well. He was one of the boys, and he would hold forth on politics and sports and other topics of the day, and I've never known anyone who could be so consistently wrong about everything. We would sit in glassy-eyed silence while he told us what he thought was going to happen at City Hall or the Polo Grounds or the Garden. And why. If there were only four or five of us at the table we would fiddle with matchbooks, make rings on the table with our highball glasses, and neither look at Jack nor say a word to him. Then when he had said his say we would resume talking, but not about the topic Jack had just discussed. We would not agree with him, we would not contradict him; we would simply ignore all he had said. Almost literally we were giving him the freeze. When our group was larger, when there were so many of us that the waiter added the extra table, Jack Pyne was no problem. The larger group always meant that one of the Broadway columnists was present, and Jack Pyne knew better than to interrupt their monologs. The Broadway columnists were his gods, his heroes—and his bread and butter.

You may wonder why we put up with Jack Pyne. The answer is easy: in the beginning he had been a pathetic clown, and later there was no way to get rid of him. And I guess we were not very selective on the late shift. The meat salesman was no

Wilson Mizner, the radio announcer no Oliver Herford, the
Broadway doctor no James Abbott MacNeill Whistler. We did
not pretend to be the Algonquin Round Table, and there was
no test of wit that a man had to pass to be welcome in our
group. We were brought together by the circumstances of our
jobs and their unconventional hours, and the attraction of
convivial drinking. The married men among us never brought
their wives, and the rest of us rarely brought a girl. Our conversation would have bored women, and women would have
inhibited our conversation. From this distance I could not
repeat one of our conversations, not so much because the talk
was rough—although it was that—as because it was so immediately topical. It was lively, but evanescent, and the interrup-
tions by Jack Pyne only gave us a chance to get our breath.

Then one night—say around four o'clock in the morning—
the character of our meetings began to change. It was not
something we noticed at the time, but I know now that the
change began when one of the smallies came to our table and
said to Jack Pyne, "Hey, Pincus, I want to talk to you." Jack
got up and followed the gangster to an empty table. They
talked for five minutes or so, and Jack came back to our table
and the gangster returned to his group.

"Who's your friend, Jack?" said the newspaper reporter. "I
don't remember seeing him before. Don't want to see him
again, either."

"I went to school with him. We grew up together," said Jack
Pyne.

"He didn't look as if he went to school very long."

"No. I knew him in sixth grade. Seventh grade. Around
then," said Jack Pyne.

"He's been away?"

"I'll say he has. He was doing five to ten up the river. He
only got out about a month ago."

"What was the rap, Jack?"

"Why, I guess it was felonious assault. I didn't ask him, but
I remember hearing about it. I think he was up twice. I don't
know. I don't know for sure."

"He knew you. He made you the minute you came in tonight."

"Yeah. Yeah, I guess he did. I guess he was kind of expecting me."

"What has he, got some little broad he wants you to get her picture in the paper?"

"I didn't say that, did I?" said Jack Pyne.

"You didn't say anything, but that's a pretty good guess, isn't it? Your fame has spread far and wide, Jack. You're getting somewhere. Who's the broad? We'll find out, so don't be coy."

"Ella Haggerty. She's in the Carroll show."

"Mixed up with a hood like that? She does better than that, Jack."

"Not now she doesn't, and she better not. He's stuck on her."

"She doesn't need you to get her picture in the paper. I know Ella. You guys know Ella Haggerty."

Some of us did, and some of us didn't.

"I know her myself," said Jack Pyne. "She recommended me. She told Ernie to hire me, and Ernie said he went to school with me."

"Small world. What's Ernie's last name?"

"Black, he goes by. Ernie Black. It used to be Schwartz."

"Well, what the hell? Mine used to be Vanderbilt, but Buckley's easier to remember. I'll tell you something, Jack. Your friend Ernie, whether it's Black or Schwartz, he's got himself a very expensive lady friend."

"I know that."

"You know whose girl she was for a couple of years."

"I know."

"And where he had her living and all that? Those fur coats and diamonds."

"I been to her apartment. I know all that," said Jack Pyne.

"You know all that. Then what's she doing with some smallie like this Ernie Black? You don't go from J. Richard Hammersmith to some cheap hood just out of stir."

"She did."

"She did, but you better find out why, and you better get your money in advance. The way I see it, Jack, you've got nothing but trouble ahead of you. This coffee-and-cakes mobster, he hasn't got enough dough to keep her in bath salts. So he's going to have to get big all of a sudden, and how do you get big in his racket? You know as well as I do. From where he is, you start by killing somebody. That's the only way to make a fast big score. Homicide."

"I know, I know," said Jack Pyne.

"And even then you don't get rich, unless you happen to kill somebody very big. And if you kill somebody very big, you end up very dead. Jack, you ought to get out of this contract as quickly and as gracefully as you can."

"I can't," said Pyne. "I made a contract."

"Then leave town."

"Sure. Where would I go? My show closed Saturday and I got expenses."

"Well, if you don't want to take my advice, that's up to you," said Buckley.

"Who's the banker tonight?" said Jack Pyne.

"I am," I said.

Jack tossed me a five-dollar bill. "I had two drinks. Give me three bucks change."

I did so, and he left.

"You know," said Buckley. "I wouldn't be surprised if I accomplished something tonight. I think we finally got rid of the mystery man."

"Is that what you were doing?" I said.

"Sure. Everything I said was true, but Pyne hadn't looked at it that way. It just needed me to point out certain disadvantages."

Buckley was entirely correct. Days, then weeks, then years passed, and no more was seen of Jack Pyne. It was as though the sewer had swallowed him up. Our group, I have said, changed in character, and I may be putting too much emphasis on the effect Jack Pyne's disappearance produced. But there is no use denying the coincidence that the only time we were visited by one of the smallies, one of our number disappeared.

We didn't talk about the coincidence, but one of the smallies had invaded our territory despite the implied protection we enjoyed from the big shots.

Several months after Jack Pyne vanished a body was fished out of the East River. It was identified as Ernie Black, *né* Schwartz, and the mutilations indicated to police that Black had been tortured in gangster fashion. I advanced the theory that we might soon be welcoming Jack Pyne back to the fold, but I was wrong. Wherever he had gone, he liked it better than The Leisure, and not long after that The Leisure itself was raided and permanently closed. We had to find a new late spot, and in so doing we lost some of our group and recruited some newcomers. Then I changed jobs and got married and moved to Great Neck, and began leading a very different life from the one I had known.

That was more than thirty years ago. We have grandchildren now, and my wife and I last year bought a little house near Phoenix, Arizona. I have my retirement pay, a few securities, and an unsteady income from my writing. I occasionally sell a piece to a magazine and I have written two books, one of which did well as a paperback. Our two daughters are married and living in the East, and until about a month ago it looked as though we had it made. We liked Arizona; the climate suited us, we made new friends, we had no money worries, the future looked good. So did the past. Our new friends seemed to be entertained by my reminiscences of the old days, and now and then I could convert my reminiscences into an honest buck. For instance, I wrote a story about Ella Haggerty that I sold as fiction but was almost straight fact. Ella married a clarinet player in 1930 or '31 and shortly after that dropped out of sight. The piano player from The Leisure, the man known as Teeth, went to Paris, France, during the depression and became a great hit. He was married briefly to an English lady of title, and after World War II he was awarded the Medal of Resistance, which must have amused him as much as it did me. I had a letter from him in 1939. He was thinking of writing his memoirs even then, and he particularly called my attention to his new name—Les Dents. "It sounds like 'let's dance' if you pronounce it English style but I talk mostly French these days," he wrote. Only one of the former big shots is still alive. He is living, I believe, in Hot Springs, Arkansas. My friend Buckley, the newspaper reporter, was killed in the War. He and another correspondent, riding in a jeep in Italy, hit a land mine. His old paper established the Buckley Scholarship at a school of journalism, a memorial he would object to as he hated the very word journalism. My friends of the old days who have survived are in the minority, and Madge and I have our aches and pains as well as the obituary pages to remind us of the passage of time, but things were going all right until last month, when one afternoon Madge came to my workroom and said a man wanted to see me. "Who is he?" I said.

"I didn't ask him his name, but he wanted to make sure you had worked on the old New York *World*."

"Probably a touch," I said.

I went out to our tiny patio, and a man got up to greet me. He was wearing a white sombrero, the kind that costs about seventy-five dollars, and a gabardine coat and trousers that in the West they call a stockman's suit. "You don't remember me?"

"I'm afraid I don't," I said.

"Well, I shouldn't have expected you to. It's a long, long time," he said. Then, suddenly, he said: "Jack Pyne."

"Jack Pyne," I repeated. "*Jack Pyne?*"

"You think I was dead?"

"As a matter of fact I did," I said.

"Now you recognize me?"

"Yes, of course," I said. "Sit down. What can I get you to drink?"

"Not a thing," he said. "I just happened to hear in a round-about way that you were living out here, so I took it in my head to look you up. I bought your book. You must be coining money. I see it every place I go. Airports. Drug stores. You coulda cut me in." He smiled to show he was joking. "I reccanized Ella Haggerty, and I said to my wife, I said I introduced him to her."

"But you didn't," I said.

"I know I didn't, but it impressed the hell out of my missus. Like we took a trip over to Europe a couple of years ago, and did you ever hear of the famous entertainer, Les Dents? You know who that is?"

"Yes. Teeth, from the old Leisure Club."

"Oh, you knew that. Well, he remembered me right off. I was twenty pounds lighter then. Good old Teeth. He sat and talked with the wife and I for a couple hours, and all those French people and the international set, they couldn't figure out who we were."

"What are you doing now, Jack?"

"Well, I got a couple of things going for me. Different things. I got my money all invested in various enterprises. I only live about ten miles from here. You ought to come and take a look at my place. You have a car, don't you? Or I could send one for you."

"We have a car," I said. "But, Jack, what ever happened to you? You just disappeared into thin air."

"You mean way back? Oh, I just took it into my head one night, what was I wasting my time sitting around those night spots. So I sold my business—"

"What business?"

He shook his head somewhat pityingly. "Jack Pyne. I had one of the first if not *the* first really successful public relations concerns. You know, your memory ain't as good as it ought to be. I noticed a couple things in your book. Sure it was fiction, but you sure did take a lot of liberties. I mean, didn't you know Ella was my girl? I kept that dame for three years. She cost me a fortune. Maybe you were afraid I'd sue you for libel, but that's not the way I operate. I told my wife, I said this book was about an old girl friend of mine. That was before I read the book, and then she asked me which one was me and I said I guess you were afraid I'd sue you for libel. I wouldn't take an old friend into court. You ought to know me better than that."

"Well, I'll put you in my next book."

"No, don't do that. You don't have to make amends. But you and your wife come out and have dinner at my house and I'd like to straighten you out on those days. You remember Pete Buckley?"

"Sure."

"Always pestering me to meet Ella, but I said to him one night, I was glad to help him out any time he needed a send-in with one of those underworld characters. I knew them all. But it was one thing to tell my mob friends a guy was all right, and a very different story to introduce a thirty-five-dollar-a-week police reporter to my girl. I sent them a cheque when they had that memorial for Pete. Very sarcastic when he made his load, but a great newspaper man when he was sober. Great. No doubt about it." He stood up. "Old pal, I gotta see a couple executives downtown, but you and I are going to have a lot of fun together, cutting up the old touches. Right?"

We have not gone to his house, although we have heard it is one of the showplaces. But we see him a great deal. A great deal. He has found out where we are and he knows when we'll be home. It is a sad thing after so many years to have a house you love seem to turn into a night club table. Suddenly I miss Pete Buckley, too.

(1962)

THE TACKLE

Hugo Rainsford's name became prominent in the East, back in the Twenties, when he was so often referred to as the giant Harvard tackle, although he was actually only 6 feet 2 and his playing weight was never more than 220. But he looked big, and he was big against Yale and Princeton, especially in one Yale game in which he blocked a punt and scored a touchdown which won for Harvard; and in a Princeton game in which he tore the ball out of Eddie Gramatan's grasp and literally stole a touchdown from Princeton. You had to be strong and alert to do that. Hugo did not make Walter Camp's First All-America, because there was a tackle at Illinois and another at Wisconsin who were getting the benefit of Camp's fairly recent discovery that Western Conference football was superior to the brand played in the Big Three. Teams like Colby and Tufts were always trying to knock off Harvard, but the Big Ten schedules were really tough—and in addition to the conference teams there was always Notre Dame. Nevertheless Hugo Rainsford as a Second All-American tackle made a bigger and more lasting reputation than the men who played his position in the Western Conference. The eastern sportswriters had a way of forgetting about those Westerners and remembering anecdotes about Rainsford of Harvard, and he was called the giant tackle by reporters who had never seen him play. Moreover, he got a certain amount of publicity in the news columns, in which his football reputation was a secondary consideration. He was sued for breach of promise by a dancer in George White's Scandals (an action which was settled out of court); and he was arrested for punching a policeman outside a cabaret called the Pre Catelan on West 39th Street. Hugo's father, who was one of the Republican friends of Alfred E. Smith, managed to have the matter taken care of. Hugo was sent off to a ranch near Sheridan, Wyoming, where he fell in love with Gladys Tompkins, of Tompkins Iron & Steel (Pittsburgh, Sandusky, and Birmingham, Alabama). They were married that fall, in Sewickley, attended by 10 bridesmaids and 14 ushers, and to the music of Mike Markel. To the utter amazement of those who knew him—and thousands who did not—Hugo immediately settled down and vanished from the public prints. If you looked on the financial pages you would see his name and a one-column photograph of Hugo, wearing a starched collar and Spitalfields tie, and the briefest of announcements to the effect that H. B. Rainsford had been admitted to this partnership or elected to that directorate. He was, of course, the same Hugo Rainsford who by coincidence might be mentioned that same day in that same paper as the giant Harvard tackle, but he could not control the sportswriters' reminiscences. Once a year he would go to New Haven or to Boston for the Yale game, and he made his private contributions to the funds for the education of thick-calved high school boys from Brockton and Medford who might otherwise have turned up at Holy Cross. But he was not so impatient to learn the results of the Brown and Dartmouth games that he could not wait for the Sunday papers. Politeness to his friends rather than postgraduate enthusiasm of his own sustained Hugo's interest in football. Downtown in the daytime and at dinner parties in the evening, through the months of October and November, he was expected to comment as an expert, but all he really knew he got from George Trevor and Harry Cross, *The Sun* and the *Herald Tribune*. One afternoon on the fifth tee at Piping Rock a man in a suede windbreaker, playing in a foursome behind him, said, "Hugo Rainsford? What the hell are you doing here? Why aren't you at Princeton?"

"Oh, for Christ's sake lay off," said Hugo. The man was older, and Hugo did not know his name, but whoever he was he achieved the distinction of being the first football nut who irritated Hugo to the point of rudeness.

Gladys Rainsford stepped in. "Why don't you people go through?" she said. "I'm a terribly slow player."

The rebuffed suede windbreaker and his companions thanked her and hit their tee shots in silence. They tipped their caps to Gladys and left the tee.

"Well, you know what they're thinking," said Hugo.

"What?" said Gladys.

"They're sure you and I had a fight and that's why I'm so disagreeable."

"Do you know who he is? I think he's the father of that boy that plays for Yale. I'll think of his name in a minute."

"I suppose I ought to apologize to him later, but my heart won't be in it."

"Then don't say anything," she said.

"Oh, I'll tell him I took a nine on the fourth or something. No use antagonizing him unnecessarily. But suddenly I finally got fed up."

"Oh, I know. I'm on your side," she said. "Don't forget, they bore me too, and I don't even know anything about football."

"You know a damned sight more than most of them do. I only thank God I'm not Red Grange or Bronko Nagurski. I hate to think what they must have to put up with. Backfield men, and those western colleges. Oh, boy. I probably could have made the crew, but I didn't like rowing and I did like football. And with my marks I couldn't do both and hope to stay in college. Tough enough as it was."

"Well, Giant, the price of fame," she said.

"Now you cut that out," said Hugo.

"Go on, hit one out and show them how good you are," she said. "Anyway, the season'll be over in a week or two."

But the end of the season did not mean the inauguration of an annual moratorium on football talk. Since he had become—for a lineman—only a little less legendary than Tack Hardwick and Frank Hinkey, Jim Thorpe and Eddie Mahan, who played the end or the backfield, he had to accustom himself to surprise recognition, not so surprising to him as to the delighted individuals who were meeting him for the first time; and with the passing of the years they seemed to grow more astonished at his durability. It was hard to reconcile their points of view, held simultaneously, that he had been built of marble and iron, indestructibly, and that he was not only alive but playing golf, swimming, and engaged in the daily transactions of financial business. They seemed to believe he had accomplished prodigious feats of agility and strength while existing as a piece of statuary, heroic size. There were times when he wanted to remove his two front teeth, to pull up his pants and let them see a 10-inch scar, to show how vulnerable he had been to the taped fists and the pointed cleats of the gods who had played against him. But by the time he was in his thirties he had learned that the easiest way to handle a football nut was to let him do all the talking.

Hugo and Gladys had two daughters. "If you had a son would you want him to play football?" was a question that people felt compelled to ask him from time to time. His usual answer was that if the boy wanted to play, that would be all right. But on a trip to Bermuda, in the ship's bar, a woman who almost certainly had been a sociology major at her college asked him the same old question, and Hugo told her that he was bringing up his daughters to play football. "You're not serious," said the woman.

"Well, I should say I am," said Hugo. He thereupon got carried away with his fantasy and for the better part of an hour, as the Daiquiris came and went, Hugo described the weekends at his house in Locust Valley, the half-size football field on his place, the regulation goal posts, the tackling dummy, the eagerness with which his two Chapin School daughters were learning to place-kick, forward pass, and do the body-building calisthenics that he himself had learned at St. Bartholomew's and Harvard. "It's character building as well as body building," he told the woman. "Naturally I never expect them to really play football, but it's very good for them to learn to protect themselves. The give and take of life, you might say."

"You're not afraid they might hurt themselves?" said the woman.

"A few bruises," said Hugo. "Actually no more dangerous than if they went fox hunting, when you stop to think of it."

"I suppose so," said the woman. "And there's just the two of them."

"Oh, no. I wouldn't go to all that trouble just for my two. They have two teams. The girls from Miss Chapin's on one team, and the other team consists of girls from Spence and Green Vale and the Brearley. There're the Greens—they're the girls from Miss Chapin's—and the Blues, from the other schools."

"Is that so?" said the woman.

"It's really lots of fun," said Hugo. He looked at his watch. "Lord, I hate to break this up, but I've got to change. And so have you. My wife'll give me hell."

He had no further conversation with the woman, although she made some effort to get some more information. "I think you've made a conquest," said Gladys Rainsford. "That woman from Cleveland."

"Keep her away from me," said Hugo.

"Don't worry, I will," said Gladys.

It was about six months later that Gladys placed a clipping before him and said, "What the *hell* is this?"

The clipping was from a magazine published in Cleveland for local consumption. There was an old photograph of Hugo Rainsford in his football uniform, and a more recent picture of him in business clothes. "Where did this come from?" said Hugo.

"Lydia Williamson sent it to me. Read it," said Gladys.

The article was a reasonably accurate report of the conversation that had taken place in the bar of the Furness liner *Bermuda*, and was signed by Edith Trapnell McGaver. The title of the article was *Football for Girls*, and the subhead was "Ex-Harvard Star Tutors N.Y. Society Girls in Grid Tactics."

Hugo read the article with horrified fascination. Mrs. McGaver had had to use her imagination to depict the Rainsfords' Locust Valley football field, and she did so. She had expanded Hugo's remark as to the comparative safety of football and fox hunting, and had inserted a few observations of her own on the character-building aspects of contact sport. But in general the interview, as she called it, stuck to Hugo's statements.

"I never should have left you alone with her," said Gladys. "You're going to have a fine time living this down."

"Well—Cleveland," said Hugo. "Nobody around here'll see it."

"*You* hope," said Gladys.

But a Yale man in the Cleveland branch of a stock brokerage sent a dozen copies of the interview to New York friends, and in no time at all Hugo was being greeted as "Coach" Rainsford. Wherever he went—The Lunch Club, the Down Town Association, The Recess—some wisecracker had something to say about the article. They rang all the changes, from the evils of proselytizing young athletes to the fun Hugo must have in the girls' locker room. Inevitably, the Rainsfords' daughters saw the article. Marjorie, the firstborn, was tearful. "Daddy, how *could* you?" she said. The younger one, Mary, said, "Well, I guess there goes the Junior Assembly." So many of Hugo's and Gladys's contemporaries asked to be shown the football field at Locust Valley that Gladys had to warn them beforehand that it was a touchy subject. Hugo put an end to the use of the "coach" nickname by his friends. "Do you want me to swat you?" he would say. The word got around that Hugo *had* swatted an unidentified friend, and as no one wanted to be swatted by those ham hands, the joke got to be unfunny. "Hereafter, you'll know better than to get tight with strange women," said Gladys.

"She was strange, all right," said Hugo.

More or less indirectly the episode of the Cleveland interview caused his friends to avoid the whole topic of football. They stifled the impulse to make humorous mention of the interview, and having become overconscious of that restriction

they hesitated to speak of football in any connection. Except
for rare and casual references to the Yale game and Harvard's
prospects they finally had begun to relegate his football exertions
to his youth—and he was already in his thirties. The sports-
writers continued to celebrate his exploits; he was, after all, a
kind of brand name. It was practically a tradition among the
writers to compose at least one column a year in which the
Golden Age of Sport was recalled, and the basic cast of characters was always the same: Babe Ruth, Walter Hagen, Bill
Tilden, Tommy Hitchcock, Earl Sande, Jack Dempsey, and
Red Grange. (No matter how plainly the writers stated that
they were writing about the Twenties, they got angry letters
from fans of Bobby Jones, who forgot that Jones's Grand Slam
was in 1930, and from admirers of John L. Sullivan, who died
in 1918.) Hugo Rainsford was an added starter, but he was
legitimately of the glamorous decade, and his was a name that
broke the monotony of the traditional list. "I saw your name
in Grantland Rice's column the other day," somebody would
say.

"That's nothing," Hugo would say. "I saw Grantland Rice
at the National the other day." He was in his thirties, and he
was free.

He was not a very complicated man, and he was married to
a woman who did not search for complexities in him. They
lived, moreover, in a time when the headshrinker was a South
American Indian who had mastered the art of reducing the
size of a human skull, posthumously. Gladys Tompkins Rainsford was the well-educated granddaughter of an English immi-
grant who had established one of the great American fortunes.
Her father had gone to Princeton, taken a degree, and was easily persuaded to stay out of the way while Tompkins Iron &
Steel was operated by an efficient regency, headed by an uncle.
Tommy Tompkins sent his daughter to Foxcroft, and she chose
to go on to Bryn Mawr and then chose to resign in the summer
before her senior year, when she met Hugo Rainsford. Her
mother was a lumpy little woman who traveled to Palm Beach
and Bar Harbor by private car, was seldom without her para-
sol, and paid considerable sums in a hopeless effort to improve

her negligible skill at auction bridge. She said that champagne made her acid, but she drank it anyhow. Gladys loved her ineffectual father and from a distance could pity her vulgar, lonely mother; but her feeling for the positive young man with the football reputation and the hinted-at notoriety was never in doubt. He was to be hers on any terms that were necessary, and it happened that he wanted her too. They were very nearly asked to leave the dude ranch where they met, and all parties were greatly relieved when Gladys, on the last night of a pack trip, announced their engagement.

Through the early years of their marriage Gladys frequently observed Hugo's indifferent attitude toward football, which she put down to boredom. He had played it well, but since he could no longer play it, he had lost interest; he was the victim of bores who wanted to talk about something he had graduated from; he wanted to get away from football and make a career for himself in the financial district. But she was not convinced that she had come upon the true reason for his increasingly perfunctory attention to the devotees of the game and the game itself. After his first show of petulance on the Piping Rock golf course she commenced to wonder how important his antipathy to the game had become. His subsequent experience with the Cleveland interview revealed—or so Gladys believed—a sardonic and deep disgust with the game or some aspect of it.

It took patience, but she finally got the story, and like everything else about him, it was simple enough. "You're wrong about my not liking the game," he said. "I loved it, and I still do. If I had to do over again I wouldn't take back a minute of the playing, or the business of learning the plays, or getting hurt. I didn't like getting my teeth knocked out, but I honestly didn't feel that till the half was over. You don't, very much. You should have seen my leg when that son of a bitch jumped on me. The skin damn near came off with my stocking. But don't forget, I was dishing it out, not just taking it. A lot of fellows will tell you that they get the lump before the game starts, and they're all right after the first scrimmage. I don't think I ever did. The only thing I was afraid of was doing something

stupid, made to look silly by the opposing end, for instance.
And that happened more than once. But the physical part
didn't bother me, because I figured I was pretty strong and at
least an even match for most of the fellows on the opposing
teams. Also, generally speaking, a tackle is more out in the
open than the guards and the centers, and he's usually pretty
big, so he's easier to keep an eye on. That means he can't get
away with as much dirty stuff as some of the others, and I
never liked to play dirty. Oh, a little holding, maybe, but that
wasn't dirty. If you get away with it, fine. If not, 15 yards. And
if you got away with it too often the other team'd run a couple
of plays at you to keep you honest. That was how I lost my
front teeth. 'Let's get Rainsford,' they said. And they did.
Their end, their tackle, and their fullback hit me all at once.
Two straight plays. I must have been pretty groggy, but I can
remember that referee looking at me. O'Ryan, his name was,
and he was a dentist. Little fellow with a moustache, from
Tufts. I realized later that he was looking at me professionally.
My mouth. Oh, it was a lot of fun, and some of the guys I
know through football will be friends of mine for the rest of
my life.

"But not all.

"A name you never heard me mention was George Carr. I
only mention his name now because I have to. Otherwise you
wouldn't be able to understand how I feel about football. I
haven't mentioned George Carr's name since the year you and
I were married. He was a classmate of mine, both at St. Bartholomew's and Harvard. He came from Philadelphia. His
father was and probably still is a corporation lawyer, one of
those Philadelphia Club-Fish House-Rabbit Club types, and a
Harvard man himself. He was very anxious to have George
become a good football player, but George never quite made
it. He played in prep school, but at Harvard he didn't get his
freshman numerals, and in sophomore year he was dropped
from the squad before the first game. I suppose that was a
great disappointment to his old man, and George took it out
on all athletes, but particularly football players and most of
all, me. I didn't sweat over that. He bothered me about as

much as a gnat, a flea. Athletes were guys with strong backs and weak minds, and I was the prime example. Well, after we were married and I went to work downtown someone repeated a remark that George made. He told somebody that I'd do very well in Wall Street as long as I wore my sweater with the H on it. But that if I had to depend on my brains, I'd soon be like your father—sponging off Tompkins Iron & Steel.

"Now you know how I've always felt about your father. A very sweet man, who couldn't possibly duplicate what your grandfather'd done. In a way, your father was licked from the start. If he went out and made a pile of money on his own, people would still say he *hadn't* made it on his own. That he had fifty million to begin with. On the other hand, if he made a botch of it, he'd be blamed worse than a man that started with nothing. So your father did what he did and let your uncle take over, and I've never known a nicer man than your father. Therefore, when George Carr made that crack I called him up and told him I wanted to see him. He suggested having lunch, but I said I preferred to call on him at his apartment, which I did. Much to my surprise he had another fellow with him. His lawyer, he said, but if he was a lawyer he must have earned his way through law school by prizefighting, judging by his appearance. He looked plenty tough. His name was Sherman. I said I didn't think it was necessary to have Sherman hear what I had to say, but George insisted that it was. So I asked him if the cracks I heard were accurately quoted, and he said they were. He repeated them, and included what he'd said about your father. 'All right,' I said. 'I just wanted to make sure. Now do I take on Mr. Sherman first, or both of you two at a time?' Sherman said I'd better not start anything, and while he was still saying it I hit him. I went at him as hard as I ever hit anybody. He was used to getting punched, not to being tackled. I drove him against the wall, so he got it both ways. The impact of the tackle, and the impact of the wall. Then I did hit him with my fist and he went down, all the fight was out of him. Then I went to work on George, with my fists, and I said 'See how your brains get you out of this.' You know, I'd been used to that kind of mixing it. Sixty minutes a game, and this wasn't Marquis of

Queensberry rules. We wrecked some furniture, but I came through practically unscathed, and when I saw that the game was over for that day, I put on my hat and coat and went down to the Harvard Club and had a shower and a rubdown and a few drinks. Nothing ever came of it. Obviously George Carr wasn't going to go around town and tell people that I'd beaten up him and his bodyguard singlehanded. And I didn't tell anybody either."

"That must have been the first time you didn't show up for dinner," said Gladys.

"It was. I don't remember what excuse I gave, but you accepted it," said Hugo.

"But why did it turn you against football? I don't quite see that," said Gladys.

"I never did turn against football," he said. "But I wanted to get away from football, and people wouldn't let me. In other words, I didn't want George Carr to be right. You know I've never worn my sweaters."

"Oh, yes you have," said Gladys. "On the pack trip in Wyoming."

"Oh, did I? I guess I did," said Hugo.

"I *know* you did," said Gladys.

"Yes, it got quite cold at night, as I remember," said Hugo.

"Uh-huh," she said.

(1964)

THE WEAKLING

Robertson was a stranger to this club. He had played squash here many years ago, during his New York years in the financial district, and he thought he could find his way to the squash courts and the bar, but that was about all. "I am meeting Mr. J. L. Kemper," he said to the club attendant. "I'm Mr. Robertson."

The man looked at a small slip of paper. "Yes, Mr. Robertson. Mr. Kemper is expecting you. Will you go right upstairs and turn left? He's in the lounge."

"Thank you," said Robertson. He was far from sure that he would recognize Kemper, but Kemper seemed sure he would recognize Robertson.

It was early for the lunchtime rush and there were only a scattered few men in the lounge. Robertson stood in the doorway, and immediately a man got up and came toward him.

"Mr. Robertson? I'm Jack Kemper," said the man.

Robertson remembered him. He was changed greatly after nearly forty years, but the area above his mouth and below the hairline was still identifiable. He was of medium height or a trifle less, had put on weight, and had a good tailor. He was wearing the club tie, with its tiny embroidered insignia, and a white broadcloth shirt with a large gold collar-pin. He had a strong handshake.

"I'd have recognized you after all," said Robertson.

"I knew you right away. Shall we have a drink in here? The bar is going to be crowded in a few minutes, and these young fellows make a lot of noise. What would you like?"

"A very light Scotch on the rocks, if I may," said Robertson.

"Let's sit over here," said Kemper. They sat at a small table, with its inevitable kitchen matches and bowl of salted peanuts, and Kemper tapped the bell and gave the order. "It was very nice of you to come," said Kemper. "I had to be deliberately vague in my letter, for reasons that will become apparent."

Robertson smiled. "Well, you piqued my curiosity," he said. "A matter of some urgency, you said, but I couldn't imagine what."

"I'm sorry about that, but you'll see why," said Kemper.

"Where did we meet? I couldn't even remember that very well, although I knew you and I were contemporaries."

"I'm not sure where we met, but we went to a lot of the same parties and just for the hell of it I looked you up in one of the old newspaper files and discovered that you'd played squash in this club. In fact, you played me."

"Oh, did I? Who won?"

Kemper smiled. "I did. I creamed you. Actually, we had a pretty good team that year. We won our class. Do you still play?"

"Not squash, but I occasionally play tennis. Lawn *and* court. I just barely manage to get around, but I still keep at it."

"You look in fine shape," said Kemper. "I've become a golfer, which they say isn't much exercise but I don't know what the hell makes me so tired if it isn't exercise. That brings up the subject of my mysterious letter."

The waiter set down their drinks and when he was gone Kemper resumed. "Did you happen to see that George Mulvane died? You knew George, I'm sure."

"Yes, I did see that. I read the New York papers. At my club they get the airmail editions and I saw about George. I used to see him a fair amount in the old days, but when I went back to Chicago we lost touch."

"One does," said Kemper. He took a sip of his drink. "See if that's all right. Is it light enough?"

Robertson tasted his drink. "Fine, thanks," he said.

"Then you saw that George died on the golf course. At least that's where he had his attack. I didn't happen to be there, but I've always seen a lot of George. We were at school together, and during our college years we saw each other during the summers. I may have met you through George, I'm not sure."

"Possibly. I'd known him in college for three years. He was a class ahead of me."

"Yes, I know," said Kemper.

"And through him I met a lot of people in New York."

"I know that, too," said Kemper.

"Oh, do you?" said Robertson.

"One of them being Mae MacNeath."

"Yes, it was George that introduced me to Mae MacNeath," said Robertson.

"It was through George that *I* met Mae," said Kemper.

"Well, I daresay there were quite a few people that would have met her in any case, with or without George. She was extremely popular. Is she still alive?"

"Yes, she's alive. Living in a sort of nursing home out in New Jersey. Near Summit, it is."

"Oh, dear," said Robertson. "I don't imagine she likes that much. Not Mae. Do you ever see her?"

"Once or twice a year. George and I and Bob Webster more or less took turns going out to see her."

"That's damn nice of you. What is her condition?"

"Not very good, actually. Mentally or physically. She fell and broke her hip about five years ago, and it's very difficult for her to move around. Mentally—well, she has her good days and her bad days. Sometimes I've gone out to see her and the doctor that runs the place won't let me see her. Other times we've gone out there and she's been absolutely delightful."

"It's Mae you want to talk to me about, isn't it?" said Robertson.

"Yes," said Kemper. "Thanks for making it easier for me."

"All right," said Robertson.

"About ten years ago, I don't know if you heard about it, but Mae was arrested for some bad cheques. She was living then at a cheap hotel in the Forties. Oddly enough, a place I'd never heard of, but it was a regular hotel. None of us had seen Mae in recent years, but when she got in this jam she told her lawyer to get in touch with George Mulvane. Which he did, and

George went to her rescue. He made good on the cheques—seven or eight hundred dollars, it amounted to. And he got his own lawyers to persuade the people to drop the charges, including the district attorney's office. One smart little son of a bitch, probably a commie, wanted to crucify her and get his name in the paper because Mae was still in the Social Register. But he was talked out of it. Lawyers have their ways."

"Yes, they certainly have," said Robertson.

"Then George told me about it. He did everything through his lawyers, but he went to see Mae in her hotel and she was pitiful, in dreadful shape. Terrified of going to jail, and drinking like a fish. Here she was, you know, living a few blocks from all her old friends, but most of them didn't even know if she was alive. She had *some* money. An income of about three thousand a year, but almost half of that went to pay her room rent at the hotel, and she actually wasn't getting enough to eat. And of course food wasn't what she cared about. She stayed in her room most of the time, getting drunk and watching TV. When George went to see her the first time she was getting drunk with a Porto Rican, the elevator operator or bellboy or whatever he was."

"Oh, dear," said Robertson. "A familiar story, isn't it?"

"Yes, but not when it happens to someone you know," said Kemper. "Someone like Mae, at least."

"Oh, of course not," said Robertson. "I was only referring to the downward progress."

"Well, downward is downward. The details vary from one case to another, but it's always essentially the same story," said Kemper.

"I daresay," said Robertson.

"In any event, George felt he had to do something, and he talked to me about it and then Bob Webster, and we all agreed to contribute a certain amount to take care of Mae. We couldn't have her committed or certified incompetent, because none of us were related to her and we didn't want to do that anyway. George and I finally dug up a cousin of Mae's, a nice young woman that lived on Staten Island, who had never known Mae but agreed to act as next of kin. She signed her in at the nursing home, after being assured that we were taking all the financial responsibility. And so that's where Mae has been these past ten years. Freshen your drink?"

"No thanks," said Robertson.

"Unfortunately, George left no provision in his will to continue paying his share of Operation Mae, as we called it."

"Funny. May Day is what they use instead of S.O.S.," said Robertson. "May Day, May Day."

"We made a few jokes about that," said Kemper. "Very appropriate. But as I was saying, George didn't specify in his will that he wanted any money earmarked for Mae's upkeep. Quite understandably, as a matter of fact. Do you know Marjorie, George's wife?"

"I may have met her."

"Not exactly the type that throws her money around on philanthropies. And I always took for granted that George had never said anything about it to Marjorie. Knowing Marjorie, I would say that if he ever mentioned our little fund, she would threaten him with divorce. Marjorie wouldn't believe that George or anyone else would be that sentimental about an old girl friend. Even if she went and had a look at Mae in her present state. I don't think Mae's been to a dentist in at least fifteen years, and—well, her looks are gone, forever. You must be getting hungry. Shall we go in?"

"Not a bit. I'd rather hear what you have to tell me first," said Robertson. "Unless you're hungry."

"I can wait," said Kemper. "It won't take much longer."

"I can probably hasten things a bit. You want me to be the substitute for George in Operation Mae."

"Yes, I suppose that's fairly obvious," said Kemper.

"Why me?"

Kemper smiled. "Well, why any of us? Why George? Why me? Why Bob Webster?"

"And why not a half a dozen others that we could mention?" said Robertson.

"I suppose there were as many as that," said Kemper.

"You don't only suppose, do you?"

"If we counted every time Mae disappeared from a party

with some young man. Oh, I don't know. But I was given to understand that you and I and George and Bob Webster were the ones she liked best."

"Who told you that?"

"George did, and so did Mae. When George came to her rescue and told her that he and Bob and I were setting up this arrangement, she said, 'What about Al Robertson?' She seemed to think you belonged in the group. But if you feel otherwise, we can drop the whole matter. That's why I was so mysterious in my letter."

"What does it amount to, annually?"

"In money? Fifteen hundred a year, apiece. Since George died Webster and I've been making up the difference. If you want to look at it strictly from the money angle, George contributed for ten years. Not to mention what he put out in the beginning. But Mae isn't going to last ten years. A year would be more like it."

"Then I don't really see why I should come into it at all. That is, if you and Webster can do it without me."

"I guess we can. I know we can," said Kemper. "But if anything happens to me, I'm not sure Webster could assume the whole thing. There's quite a difference between fifteen hundred and forty-five hundred. If anything happened to Webster I might have a little difficulty making up his share and George's. On the other hand, if Bob and I were to kick off in the same year, you could handle the whole thing without a noticeable dent in your income."

"You seem pretty sure of that," said Robertson.

"Well, I read the papers, too, you know. Your granddaughter's coming-out party was supposed to've cost over a hundred thousand."

"It probably did, but I had nothing to do with that."

"I'm sure you didn't, but the girl's mother is your daughter," said Kemper. "Mr. Robertson, you're one of the four or five richest men in the Middle West. I read *Fortune*, too."

"Mr. Kemper, I haven't said I couldn't afford to make a contribution to this fund. What I've been trying to say, without actually saying it, is that I don't see why I should. It's at least forty years since I've seen or heard from Mae MacNeath. I never saw her after I went back to Chicago, although I've been to New York hundreds of times since then. I daresay I could have seen her, in that time, but I didn't much want to."

"Oh, well then I got a completely wrong impression."

"Yes, I'm afraid you did. To be perfectly candid about it, I never slept with Mae."

"Oh, then I did have the wrong impression. From what she told me, and the impression she always gave George, you were the love of her life."

"I wonder why she'd want you to believe that."

"Well, because you were Alvin Robertson, the tycoon. The only one of her old friends that made it big, as they say."

"Inheritance played a rather large part in that, as you no doubt know. The Robertson money was made by my grandfather. He was the one that got all those land leases from the government. My father and I had that to start with."

"Aren't you being a bit over-modest?" said Kemper.

"Not at all. I'm not inclined to be over-anything. Over-modest, or over-sentimental. My granddaughter speaks of me as a cold fish, and I'm not that either, but it's very disturbing to hear that Mae MacNeath has been giving the completely opposite impression."

"Well, she's certainly done that, I must say," said Kemper.

"It could be part of her—schizophrenia. They have a way of remembering things that never happened."

"No, apparently Mae had this thing about you long before she began cracking up."

Robertson was silent for a moment. "Mr. Kemper, you don't know the precise moment when she began cracking up. No one does. She may have started when she was fourteen."

"Yes, that's possible," said Kemper.

"Even earlier, in some cases. In any event, by the time she was eighteen, and began cutting up at those tea dances we used to go to at the Plaza and the Lorraine, she was well on the way to some kind of breakdown, and don't you agree?"

"She was never Alice-sit-by-the-fire, I admit that," said Kemper.

"You see, if I had never known Mae at all, and someone came to me for help—I have helped out in cases that were somewhat similar. But if I agreed to help Mae MacNeath now, you and Webster would be convinced that all she ever implied about me was true. How shall I say this without giving offense? Mae MacNeath, the crazy side of her, is attempting to blackmail me. Do you consider that an unfair statement?"

"Unfair, and inaccurate," said Kemper.

"I was afraid you would. But let me try again. When I was a young man and being invited to the coming-out parties, I could enjoy myself up to a certain point. I'll tell you what that point was. As long as they thought I was somebody named Al Robinson, I was allowed to have a good time. But you have no idea how many times a girl or her mother would get a certain look in her eye when she found out I was Alvin Robertson, *from Chicago*. 'From Chicago?' they'd say, and their whole manner would change. Some of the mothers would want to be sure, and they'd say, 'Oh, you must be Angus Robertson's grandson,' as though they knew the old boy. My grandfather never knew their kind of people, and my grandmother, who *wanted* to know them, could barely read and write. So that generation were never in society, even Chicago society. My father and mother were. They'd both been East to school and my mother's father was a bishop. An Episcopalian bishop, originally from Massachusetts. I grew up with no illusions about my own personal charm. My father had been all through it, and my bishop's-daughter mother saw to it that I was always on my guard. If you ever want to know where anyone stands socially and financially, ask a bishop's wife. My maternal grandmother had it all at her fingertips, and my mother had too. She never had to warn me in so many words about those Eastern girls and their mothers. I'd been warned since birth. Consequently, I learned to look out for that certain look when they found out my name was Robertson and I came from Chicago. And unfortunately, Mae MacNeath gave me that look. As long as she thought I was Al Robinson, down from New Haven, we had fun together. But she wanted to invite me to some party and I had to write out my name and address. 'Rob-ert-son?' she said. 'From Chicago?' Then it dawned on her. But it also dawned on me, Mr. Kemper. She stopped being fun, and I'm afraid she became a little too obvious. She tried to vamp me. Do you remember that expression?"

"Oh, yes. There was a song called 'The Vamp.'"

"And the original vamp came from Chicago. Theda Bara. I didn't happen to like Theda Bara, and I liked her even less when she called herself Mae MacNeath. A girl that had been fun, suddenly became rather nasty. In my opinion, that is. So I even stopped cutting in on her at dances. I didn't like the way she danced, if you know what I mean. It embarrassed me. Now I believe, Mr. Kemper, that as far back as that Mae convinced herself that there'd been something romantic between us. In actual fact, there never had been, you see. I liked Mae as long as she was fun, but when she began vamping me, I didn't like her at all. But you can see how she might build that up to a sort of frustration, so that as the years passed, I became something I never really was. Do you know that I never even kissed Mae?"

"Yes, I believe you," said Kemper. "I do now."

"I'm glad to hear that," said Robertson. "Do you think you could convince Webster of that fact?"

"Yes, I think I could."

"Good. In that case, I'll assume George Mulvane's share, but you must give me your word of honor that you never tell Mae. I won't have her think that I was such a weakling."

"I promise you, Mae will never know," said Kemper. "We can order lunch here, you know, and have another drink before we go upstairs."

"Let's do that, shall we?" said Robertson. He sat back in his chair and looked around the room. "This is a rather nice place. I think I might join. There's old Tom Conville. I think I'll go over and say hello to him, if you'll excuse me. Only be a minute."

(1966)

WE'RE FRIENDS AGAIN

I know of no quiet quite like that of a men's club at about half past nine on a summer Sunday evening. The stillness is a denial of the meaning and purpose of a club, and as you go from empty room to empty room and hear nothing but the ticking of clocks and your own heel taps on the rugless floor, you think of the membership present and past; the charming, dull, distinguished, vulgar, jolly, bibulous men who have selected this place and its company as a refuge from all other places and all other company. For that is what a club is, and to be alone in it is wrong. And at half past nine on a summer Sunday evening you are quite likely to be alone. The old men who live there have retired for the night, sure that if they die before morning they will be discovered by a chambermaid, and that if they survive this night they will have another day in which their loneliness will be broken by the lunch crowd, the cocktail crowd, and the presence of a few men in the dining-room in the evening. But on a summer Sunday evening the old men are better off in their rooms, with their personal possessions, their framed photographs and trophies of accomplishment and favorite books. The lounge, the library, the billiard and card rooms have a deathly emptiness on summer Sunday evenings, and the old men need no additional reminder of emptiness or death.

It is always dark in my club at half past nine in the evening, and darker than ever on Sunday in summer, when only the fewest possible lights are left burning. If you go to the bar the bartender slowly folds his newspaper, which he has been reading by the light from the back-bar, takes off his glasses, says

"Good evening," and unconsciously looks up at the clock to
see how much longer he must stay. Downstairs another club
servant is sitting at the telephone switchboard. There is the
spitting buzz of an incoming call and he says, " 'Devening, St.
James Club? . . . No sir, he isn't . . . No sir, no message for you
. . . Mr. Crankshaw went to bed about an hour ago. Orders
not to disturb him, sir . . . You're welcome. Goodnight." The
switchboard buzzes, the loudest, the only noise in the club,
until the man pulls out the plug and the weight pulls the cord
back into place, and then it is quiet again.

I had been a member of the St. James for about ten years,
but I could not recall ever having been there on a Sunday until
this night a year or so ago. I was summoned on the golf course
by an urgent message to call the New York operator, which I
did immediately. "Jim, I'm sorry to louse up your golf, but can
you get a train in to New York? I don't advise driving. The
traffic is terrible."

"There's a train that will get me to Penn Station about eight-
thirty," I said. "But what's this all about?"

The man I was speaking to was Charles Ellis, one of my best
friends.

"Charley? What's it all *about*?" I repeated.

"Nancy died this afternoon. She had a stroke after lunch."

"Oh, no. Charley, I can't tell you—"

"I know, and thanks. Are you still a member at the St.
James?"

"Yes, why?"

"Will you meet me there? I'll tell you why when I see you."

"Of course. What time will you get there?"

"As soon after eight-thirty as I can."

For a little while the stillness of the club was a relief from
the noise and unpleasantness of the train, which was filled
with men and women and children who had presumably been
enjoying themselves under the Long Island sun but were now
beginning to suffer from it, and if not from the damage to
their skin, from the debilitating effects of too much picnic
food and canned beer. At Jamaica there was an angry scramble as we changed trains, and all the way from Jamaica to

Penn Station five men fought over some fishing tackle on the car platform while three young men with thick thatches and blue jeans tormented two pansies in imitation Italian silk suits.

The bartender gave me some cold cuts and bread and cheese and made me some instant coffee. "How late do you work, Fred?" I said.

"Sundays I'm off at ten," he said, looking at the clock for the fifth or sixth time. "Don't seem worth the while, does it?"

"I'm expecting a friend, he's not a member."

"Then if I was you I'd make sure Roland knows about it. He's just as liable to fall asleep. You know, asleep at the switchboard? You heard the old saying, asleep at the switch. That fellow can go to sleep with his eyes open."

"I've already spoken to him," I said. I wandered about in the lounge and the library, not to be out of earshot when Charley Ellis arrived. As all the clocks in the club struck ten Fred came to me, dressed for the street, and said: "Can I get you anything before I go?"

"Can you let me have a bottle of Scotch?"

"I can do that, and a bowl of ice. You want soda, Mr. Malloy?"

"Just the Scotch and the ice, thanks."

"About the only place you can drink it is in your room, if you want water with it. I have to close up the bar."

"It's all right if we sit here, isn't it?"

"Jesus, if you *want* to," said Fred.

At that moment Charles Ellis arrived, escorted by Roland.

"Oh, it's Mr. Ellis," said Fred. "Remember me? Fred, from the Racquet Club?"

"Yes, hello, Fred. Is this where you are now?"

"Six and a half years," said Fred.

"Thanks very much, Fred," I said. "Goodnight."

"I'll bring you the bottle," said Fred.

"I don't want a drink, if that's what you mean," said Charles Ellis. "Unless *you've* fallen off the wagon."

"Then never mind, thanks, Fred. Goodnight."

Fred left, and I switched on some lights in the lounge.

"You saddled with that bore?" said Charley.

"I don't see much of him," I said.

"I'm sorry I'm so late. I got here as soon as I could. I called this number but it didn't answer."

"That's all right. I guess Roland had the buzzer turned off."

"Hell of an imposition, taking you away from golf and so forth. How is Kay?"

"Very distressed, naturally. She said to give you her love."

"I almost asked her to come in with you."

"She almost came," I said. "But she has her grandchildren coming tomorrow."

He was silent, obviously wondering where to begin.

"Take your time," I said.

He looked up at me and smiled. "Thanks." He reached over and patted my knee. "Thanks for everything, Jim."

"Well, what the hell?"

"First, why did I want to see you here? Because I didn't want to ask you to come to the apartment, and I didn't want to go to the Racquet Club."

"I figured something like that."

"How did it happen, and all that? Nancy and I were spending the weekend at her uncle's. We went out to dinner last night, and when we came home she said she had a headache, so I gave her some aspirin. This morning she still had the headache and I asked her if she wanted me to send for a doctor, but she didn't. She said she hadn't slept very well, and I probably should have called the doctor, but I didn't. Then there were four guests for lunch and I didn't have a chance to speak to her. In fact the last thing I said to her was before lunch, I told her that if she didn't feel better after lunch, she should make her excuses and lie down. And that's what she did. She excused herself, shook her head to me not to follow her, and about twenty minutes later the maid came and told us she was dead. Found her lying on the bathroom floor. I can't believe it. I can't be devoid of feeling, but I just can't believe it."

"Did the doctor give you anything?"

"You mean sedative? Tranquilizers? No, I haven't needed anything. I guess I must be in some sort of shock."

"Where are the children?"

"Well, of course Mike is in Germany, still in the Army. And I finally located Janey about an hour ago, at a house in Surrey where she's spending the weekend. She's been abroad all summer. She's flying home tomorrow and Mike has applied for leave. The Army or the Red Cross or somebody will fly him home in time for the funeral." He paused.

"Wednesday morning at eleven o'clock. Church of the Epiphany, on York Avenue. I decided Wednesday so that Mike could be here, in case there's any hitch." He looked about him. "You couldn't ask for a gloomier place than this, could you?"

"No, it's certainly appropriate."

"Well, what do I do now, Jim? You've been through it."

"Yes, I've been through it. The answer is, you're going to be so damn busy with details the next few weeks that you won't have too much time to know what hit you. You're going to find out how really nice people can be. Maybe you haven't thought about that lately, but you're going to find out. You're also going to find out that some people are shits. Real shits. I'll give you the two worst. The old friend that won't make any effort at all except maybe to send you a telegram, if that. You'll be shocked by that, so you ought to be prepared for it. I mean very close friends, guys and women you grew up with that just won't come near you. Then there's the second type, just as bad. He'll write you a letter in a week or two, and it'll be all about himself. How sad *he* is, how well he knew Nancy, how much he appreciated her, and rather strongly implying that *you* didn't know her true worth as well as he did. You'll read one of those letters and reread it, and if you do what I did, you'll throw it in the wastebasket. But the next time you see the son of a bitch, he'll say, 'Hey, Ellis, I wrote you a letter. Didn't you ever get it?' So be prepared for those two. But against them, the nice people. The *kind* people, Charley, sometimes where you'd least expect it. A guy that I thought was about as cold a fish as there is in the world, he turned out to have more real heart than almost anybody. In my book he can never do another wrong thing. The third group I haven't mentioned. The lushes. But they're obvious and you can either put up with them or brush them off. The only advice I can give you—keep busy. Don't take any more time off from your work than you absolutely have to."

"And when will it really hit me?"

"I don't know when, but I know how. Suddenly, and for no apparent reason. When your guard is down. You'll be in the subway, or walking along the street, not any favorite street full of memories, but any anonymous street. Or in a cab. And the whole God damn thing will come down on you and you'll be weeping before you know it. That's where nobody can help you, because it's unpredictable and you'll be alone. It'll only happen when you're relaxed and defenseless. But you're not relaxed, really. It's just that you're weak, *been* weakened without realizing what it's taken out of you. Emotional exhaustion, I guess it is. Then there are two other things, but I won't talk about them now. They may not happen to you, and I've told you enough."

"Thanks, Jim."

"Charley, you know what let's do? Let's go for a walk. We won't run into anybody."

"Yes. Nothing against your club, but I think I've had it here."

So the two of us went for a not too brisk walk, down Fifth Avenue, up Fifth Avenue, and to the door of Charley's apartment house. The doorman saluted him and said: "Sorry fur yur trouble, Mr. Ellis. A foine lovely woman, none foiner."

I happened, and only happened, to be looking at Charley as the doorman spoke. He nodded at the doorman but did not speak. I took his arm and led him to the elevator. "Mr. Ellis's apartment," I said, and frowned the elevator man into silence. He understood.

We got off at Charley's floor, the only apartment on that floor, and he went to the livingroom and sat down and wept without covering his face. I stayed in the foyer. Five minutes passed and then he said: "Okay, Jim. I'm okay now. What can I give you? Ginger ale? Coke? Glass of milk?"

"A ginger ale."

"It hit me sooner than we expected," he said. "Do you know what it was? Or what I think it was? It was the doorman saying nice things, and he didn't really know her at all. He's only been here a few weeks. He doesn't know either of us very well. Why don't you stay here tonight, instead of going back to that God damn dreary place?"

"I will if you'll go to bed. And don't worry, you'll sleep."

"Will I?"

"Yes, you'll sleep tonight. Twenty blocks to a mile, we walked damn near four miles, I make it. Take a lukewarm tub and hit the sack. I'll read for a while and I'll be in Mike's room. Goodnight, Charley."

"Goodnight, Jim. Thanks again."

One afternoon in 1937 I was having breakfast in my apartment in East Fifty-fifth Street. I had worked the night before until dawn, as was my custom, and I was smoking my third cigarette and starting on my second quart of coffee when the house phone rang. Charley Ellis was in the vestibule. I let him in and he shook his head at me in my pajamas, unshaven, and with the coffee and newspapers beside my chair. "La Vie de Bohème," he said.

"That's right," I said. "Come on out, Mimi, and stop that damn coughing."

Charley looked at me with genuine alarm. "You haven't got a dame here, have you? I'm sorry if—"

"No dame."

"I don't want to interrupt anything."

"I wouldn't have let you in," I said. "But I've just been reading about you, so maybe I would have. Curiosity. Who is Nancy Preswell?"

"Oh, you saw that, did you? Well, she's the wife of a guy named Jack Preswell."

"All right, who is *Jack* Preswell?" I said. "Besides being the husband of a girl named Nancy Preswell."

"Well, you've met him. With me. Do you remember a guy that we went to the ball game with a couple of years ago?"

"I do indeed. I remember everything about him but his name. A very handsome guy, a little on the short side. Boyish-looking. And now I know who she is because I've seen them together, but I never could remember his name. Not that it mattered. He didn't remember me at all, but she's quite a beauty. Not *quite* a beauty. She *is* a beauty. And you're the home-wrecker."

"According to Maury Paul I am, if you believe what he writes."

"He's often right, you know," I said. "He had me in his column one time with a woman I'd never met, but I met her a year or so later and he turned out to be a very good prophet. So it's only your word against his."

"I didn't come here to be insulted," he said, taking a chair.

"Well, what did you come here for? I haven't seen or heard from you in God knows how long." It always took a little while for Charley Ellis to get started on personal matters, and if I didn't talk a lot or kid him, he would sometimes go away without saying what he had intended to say. "Now I understand *why*, of course, but I gather Mrs. Preswell hasn't even gone to Reno yet."

"If you'll lay off this heavy-handed joshing, I guess you'd call it, I'd like to talk seriously for a minute."

"All right. Have a cup of coffee, or do you want a drink? If you want a drink, you know where it is."

"I don't want anything but your respectful attention and maybe some sound advice. What I really want is someone to talk to, to talk things out with."

Charley Ellis was about thirty-three years old then, and not a young thirty-three. He had stayed single because he had been in love with his first cousin, a lovely girl who was the wife of Junior Williamson, Ethridge B. Williamson, Junior; he had wanted to write, and instead had gone to work for his father's firm, Willetts & Ellis. His father knew about the second frustration, but I was now more convinced than ever that I was the only person to whom Charley had confided both.

"You may be right, you know," he said. "I probably am the home-wrecker. At least a good case could be made out against me. Nancy and Jack never have got along very well, and made no secret of the fact. But I guess I'm the first one that shall we say took advantage of the situation. They had a couple of trial separations but they always went back together until I happened to come into the picture during the last one."

"But you're not blaming yourself or anything like that, I hope."

"Not one bit. That's a form of boasting, or so it always seemed to me."

"And to me, too. That's why I'm glad you're not doing the *mea culpa* act."

"Oh, hell no. I didn't create the situation," he said.

"Do you know who did?"

"Yes, I do," said Charley. "Franklin D. Roosevelt, your great pal."

"Yeah. The inventor of bubonic plague and the common cold, and now the louser-up of the Preswell marriage. You've been spending too much time at Willetts & Ellis. You ought to come up for air."

"You were bound to say something like that, but it happens to be a fact. Preswell was one of the bright young boys that went to Washington five years ago, and that didn't sit too well with Nancy or her family. Then two years ago Preswell himself saw the light and got out, but he'd made a lot of enemies while he was defending Roosevelt, and he came back to New York hating everybody. He said to me one time, 'They call me a traitor to my class, like the Glamor Boy himself, but my class has been a traitor to me.' He used to go around telling everybody that they ought to be grateful to him, that he and Roosevelt were holding the line for the American system. But then when he quit, he was just as violent against Roosevelt as anybody, but nobody would listen. He'd been so God damn arrogant when he was *with* Roosevelt, said a lot of personal things, so nobody cared whose side he was on. And of course he began to take it out on Nancy."

"What does this gentleman do for a living?"

"He *was* with Carson, Cass & Devereux, but they don't want him back. That's just the point. Nobody wants him."

"Was he a good lawyer?"

"Well, *Harvard Law Review*, assistant editor, I think. I don't really know how good a lawyer he was. With a firm like Carson, Cass, you don't get any of the big stuff till you've been there quite a while. He has nothing to worry about financially. His father left him very well fixed and Nancy has money of her own. Her father was, or *is*, Alexander McMinnies, Delaware Zinc."

"Oh, that old crook."

"Why do you say that? You don't know whether he's a crook or a philanthropist."

"He could be both, but even if he is your girl's father, Charley, you know damn well what he is. I'll bet the boys at Carson, Cass have sat up many a night trying to keep him out of prison."

"And succeeded, in spite of Roosevelt and Homer S. Cummings."

"Those things take time," I said.

"Get your facts right. Mr. McMinnies won in the Supreme Court. Unless you were looking forward to the day when Franklin D. decides to abolish the courts and all the rest of that stuff. Which is coming, I have very little doubt."

"You don't really think that, but you have proved beyond a doubt that Roosevelt loused up Preswell's marriage. Aren't you grateful?"

"You're a tricky bastard."

"It's so easy with you guys. You have a monomania about Roosevelt."

"Monophobia."

"No, wise guy. Monophobia means fear of being alone. So much for you and your four years at the Porcellian."

"I could correct you on that four years, but I hate to spoil your good time."

"All right, we're even," I said. "What's on your mind, Charley?"

"Yes, we can't even have a casual conversation without getting into politics," he said. "Can we forget about politics?"

"Sure, I like to rib you, but what's on your mind? Nancy Preswell, obviously."

He was smoking a cigarette, and rubbing the ashes from the glowing end into the ash tray as they formed, turning the cigarette in his fingers. And not looking at *me*. "Jim, I read a short story of yours a few months ago. Nancy read it, too. She liked it, and she said she'd like to meet you. It was that story about two people at a skiing place."

"Oh, yes. 'Telemark.'"

"That's the one," he said. "They agree to get married even though they weren't in love. Was that based on your own experience—if you don't mind my asking?"

"No. I was in love when I got married, we both were. But it didn't last. No, that story was invention on my part. Well, not all invention. What is? When I was in Florida two years ago I saw this couple always together and always talking so earnestly, so seriously, and I began to wonder what they were talking about. So I thought about them, forgot them, and remembered them again and changed the locale to a skiing place, and that was the story."

"Nancy liked the story, but she didn't agree with you. You seemed to imply that they *should* have gotten married."

"Yes, I believe that, and they did."

"That's what Nancy didn't agree with. She said they were both willing to face the fact that they weren't in love, but where they were dishonest was in thinking they could make a go of it without being in love."

"I didn't imply that they'd make a go of it," I said. "But it seemed to me they had a chance. Which is as much as any two people have."

"I didn't get that, and neither did Nancy. We both thought you were practically saying that this was as good a start as two people could have."

"So far, so good, but that's *all* I implied."

"Do you think they *really* had a chance? Nancy says no. That marriage hasn't any chance without love, and not too much of a chance with it."

"Well, what do you think? How do you feel about it?"

"I wasn't ready for that question."

"I know damn well you weren't, Charley, and that's what's

eating you. It may also be what's eating Nancy. Does she know you were in love with Polly Williamson?"

"Never. You're the only one that knows that. But here I am, thirty-three, Jim. Why can't I get rid of something that never *was* anything?"

"Go to Polly and tell her that you've always been in love with her, and can't be in love with anyone else."

"I'm afraid to," he said, and smiled. "Maybe I'm afraid she'll say she feels the same way, and divorce Junior."

"Well, that's not true. She doesn't feel the same way, or you'd have found out before this. But if you admit to yourself that you're afraid, then I think you don't really love Polly as much as you think you do, or like to think you do. I was in love with Polly for one afternoon, and I told her so. I meant it, every word of it. But every now and then I see her with Williamson and I thank God she had some sense. A girl with less sense might conceivably have divorced Williamson and married me, and how long would that have lasted? Polly is Williamson's wife, prick though he may be. And if she wants Williamson, she certainly doesn't want me, and probably not you. Has Polly ever stepped out on her own?"

"I think she did, with a guy from Boston. An older guy. I don't think you'd even know his name. A widower, about forty-five. Not a playboy type at all. Very serious-minded. Just right for Polly. You know, Polly has her limitations when it comes to a sense of humor, the lighter side. She was born here, but her father and mother both came from Boston and she's always been more of a Boston type than New York. Flowers and music and the children. But she does her own work in the garden, and she often goes to concerts by herself. What I'm saying is, no *chi-chi*. She's a good athlete, but there again it isn't what you might call public sport. The contest is always between her and the game itself, and the things she's best at are games like golf or trap-shooting. Skiing. Figure-skating. Polly damn near doesn't need anyone else to enjoy herself. And God knows she never needed me." He paused. "Did you ever hear her play the piano?"

"No."

"She's good. You know, Chopin. Rachmaninoff. Tschaikovsky."

"Charley, I just discovered something about you," I said.

"What?"

"*You're* a Bostonian."

"Maybe."

"The admiring way you talk about Polly, and of course you're a first cousin. Isn't it practically a tradition in Boston that you fall in love with your first cousin?"

"It's been known to happen, but I assure you, it had nothing to do with my falling in love with Polly."

"Do you mind if I take issue with you on that point? I have a theory that it had a *lot* to do with your falling in love with Polly, and that your present love affair, with Nancy, is your New York side."

He laughed. "Oh, God. How facile, and how stupid . . . I take back stupid, but you're wrong."

"Why am I wrong? You haven't given the theory any thought. And I have, while listening to you. You'd better give it some thought, and decide whether you want to be a New Yorker or a Bostonian."

"Or you might be wrong and I won't have to make the choice."

"Yes, but don't reject my theory out of hand. You're a loner. You wanted to be a writer. You're conventional, as witness working in the family firm against your will, but doing very well I understand. And you were talking about yourself as much as you were about Polly."

"Not at all. I was a great team-sport guy. Football in school, and rowing in college."

"Rowing. The obvious joke. Did you ever meet that Saltonstall fellow that rowed Number 5?"

"I know the joke, and it was never very funny to us. A Yale joke. Or more likely Princeton." He seemed to ignore me for a moment. He sat staring at his outstretched foot, his elbow on the arm of his chair, his cheek resting on the two first fingers of his left hand while the other two fingers were curled under the palm. "And yet, you may have a point," he said, judicially. "You just may have a point. Dr. Jekyll and Mr. Hyde. Larry Lowell and Jimmy Walker. Waldo Emerson and Walter Winchell. This conversation may be the turning point of my whole life, and I'll owe it all to you, you analytical son of a bitch."

"That's the thanks I get. Watery compliments."

He rose. "Gotta go," he said.

"How come you're uptown at this hour?"

"I took the afternoon off," he said. "I have a perfectly legitimate reason for being uptown, but I know your nasty mind. Will you be in town next week? How about dinner Tuesday?"

"Tuesday, no. Wednesday, yes."

"All right, Wednesday. Shall we pick you up here? I'd like Nancy to see the squalor you live in."

"Others have found it to have a certain Old World charm," I said. "All right, Mimi. You can come out now."

"Listen, don't have any Mimi here Wednesday, will you, please?"

"That's why I said Wednesday instead of Tuesday."

"Degrading. And not even very instructive," he said.

"Not if you don't want to learn."

My apartment was actually a comfortable, fairly expensively furnished two rooms and bath, which was cleaned daily by a colored woman who worked full-time elsewhere in the building. But Charley Ellis's first remark when he arrived with Nancy Preswell was: "Why, look, he's had the place all spruced up. Is all this new?"

"All goes back to Sloane's in the morning," I said. "How do you do, Mrs. Preswell?"

"Wait a minute. You haven't been introduced," said Charley. "You could have put me in a hell of a spot. What if this hadn't been Mrs. Preswell?" He was in high good humor, determined to make this a pleasant evening.

"I often wish I weren't," she said, without bitterness, but as her first words to me they were an indication that she knew Charley confided in me. "By the way, how do you do?"

"I've often seen you. Well, pretty often," I said.

"And always pretty," said Charley.

I looked at him and then at her: "You've done wonders with

this guy. I hardly recognize the old clod." My remark pleased her, and she smiled affectionately at Charley. "Gallantry, yet," I said.

"It was always there," said Charley. "It just took the right person to bring it out."

"I like your apartment, Mr. Malloy. Is this where you do all your writing?"

"Most of it. Practically all of it."

"Oh, you type your stories?" she said, looking at my type-writer. "But don't you write them in longhand first?"

"No. I don't even write letters in longhand."

"Love letters?"

"I type them," I said.

"And mimeographs them," said Charley. "Shall we have a free drink here, saving me two and a quarter?"

"The market closed firm, but have you ever noticed that Charley hates to part with a buck?"

"No, that's not fair," said Nancy Preswell.

"Or true. What's the name of that friend of yours, that writes the Broadway stories?"

"Mark Hellinger?"

"Hellinger. Right. I thought he was going to have a stroke that night when I paid a check at '21.'"

"I very nearly had one myself."

"No, now that isn't fair," said Nancy Preswell.

"I'm softening him up for later," I said.

We had some drinks and conversation, during which Nancy slowly walked around, looking at my bookshelves and pictures. "I gather you don't like anything very modern," she said.

"Not in this room. Some abstract paintings in the bathroom."

"May I see your bedroom?"

"Believe me, that's the best offer he's had today," said Charley.

"A four-poster," she said.

"Early Wanamaker," I said. "*Circa* 1930."

"All you need is a rag rug and a cat curled up on it. I like it. That's not your father, is it?"

"My grandfather. Practically everything in this room is a copy of stuff I remember from when I was a kid. I depended entirely on their taste."

"But you bought it all yourself, so it's your taste, too," said Nancy Preswell. "Very interesting, and very revealing, considering what some of the critics say about your writings."

"What does it reveal to you?" I said.

"That basically you're very conventional."

"I could have told you that," I said.

"Yes, but I probably wouldn't have believed you if I hadn't seen your apartment."

"I think I ought to tell you, though. I went through an all-modernistic phase when I lived in the Village."

"Why are you for Roosevelt?" she said.

"No! Not tonight, please," said Charley.

"You shouldn't be, you know," she persisted.

"Shall we not argue about it? I'm for him, and you're not, and that's where we'd be if we argued till tomorrow morning," I said.

"Except that I think I could convince you. You don't know my husband, do you? I know you've met him, but you've never talked with him about Roosevelt."

"When was *he* most convincing?" I said. "When he was with him, or against him?"

"He was never in the least convincing when he was for him. And he's not very convincing now. But as a writer you should be able to disregard a lot of things he says and go beneath the surface. Then you'd see what a man like Roosevelt can do to an idealist. And my husband *was* an idealist."

"Don't look at me. I'm not saying a word," said Charley.

"I do look at you, for corroboration. Jack *was* an idealist. You may not have liked him, but you have to admit that."

"Yes, he was," said Charley.

"And so were you. But Jack did something about it. You played it safe."

"Jim is wondering why I'm not taking this big. The reason is we've had it out before," said Charley.

"Many times," said Nancy Preswell. "And probably will again."

"But not tonight, shall we?" said Charley Ellis.

"I hate Mr. Roosevelt," she said. "And I can't stand it when a writer that I think is good is *for* him. I'm one of those people that think he ought to be assassinated, and I just hope somebody else does it, not my poor, drunken, disillusioned husband."

"Is he liable to, your husband?" I said.

"I don't suppose there's any real danger of it. But it's what he thinks of day and night. I don't want you to think I love my husband. I haven't for years. But Jack Preswell was an idealist, and Roosevelt turned him into a fanatic."

"He might have been a fanatical idealist."

"*He was!* Four years ago, that's what he was. But there's nothing left now but the fanaticism. Don't you see that, Mr. Malloy? Mr. Roosevelt took away his ideals."

"How are you on ideals, Mrs. Preswell?"

"If that's supposed to be a crusher, it isn't . . . I have a few, but they're not in any danger from—that awful man. Now I've said enough, and you probably don't want to have dinner with us."

"Yes, I would. You're a very attractive girl."

"As long as I don't say what I think? That's insulting, and now I'm not sure *I* want to have dinner with *you*."

There was a silence, broken by Charley: "Well, what shall we do? Toss a coin? Heads we dine together, tails we separate."

"I'll agree to an armistice if Mr. Malloy will."

"All right," I said. "Let's go. Maybe if we have a change of scenery . . ."

"I promise I'll be just as stupid as you want me to be," said Nancy Preswell.

There was not another word about politics all evening, and at eleven o'clock we took a taxi to a theatre where I was to meet an actress friend of mine, Julianna Moore, the female heavy in an English mystery play. Julie was about thirty, a girl who had been prematurely starred after one early success, and had never again found the right play. Her father was a history professor at Yale, and Julie was a well-educated girl whom I had first known in our Greenwich Village days. We had been lovers then, briefly, but now she was a friend of my ex-wife's and the mistress of a scenic designer.

Nancy Preswell began with compliments to Julie, ticking off six plays in which Julie had appeared.

"You must go to the theatre all the time, to have seen some of those sad little turkeys," said Julie.

"I go a lot," said Nancy.

"Did you ever do any acting?"

"*Did* I? 'Shall I speak ill of him that is my husband? / Ah, poor my lord, what tongue shall smooth thy name . . .'"

"'When I, thy three-hours wife, have mangled it?' Where and when did you do Juliet?" said Julie.

"At Foxcroft."

"I'll bet you were a very pretty Juliet," said Julie.

"Thank you. If I was, that says it all. I was cured."

"Well, I was the kind of ham that never was cured, if you don't mind a very small joke . . . I always thought it would have been fun to go to Foxcroft. All that riding and drilling."

"Where *did* you go?"

"A Sacred Heart school in Noroton, Connecticut, then two years at Vassar."

"Where did you go to school, Charley," I said.

"I don't know. Where did you?" he said.

"Oh, a Sacred Heart school in Noroton, Connecticut. Then two years at Foxcroft," I said.

"Too tarribly fonny, jost too tarribly fonny," said Julie.

"That's her Mickey Rooney imitation. Now do Lionel Barrymore," I said.

"Too tarribly fonny, jost too tarribly fonny," said Julie.

"Isn't she good?" I said. "Now do Katharine Hepburn."

"Who?" said Julie.

"She's run out of imitations," I said.

We went to "21," the 18 Club, LaRue, and El Morocco. We all had had a lot to drink, and Julie, who had played two performances that day, had soon caught up with the rest of us by drinking double Scotches. "Now the big question is, the all-important question—*is*," said Julie.

"What is the big question, Julie dear?" said Nancy.

"Ah, you like me, don't you? I like you, too," said Julie. "I like Charley, too. And I used to like Jim, didn't I, Jim?"

"Used to, but not any more."

"Correct. Jim is a rat. Aren't you, Jim?"

"Of course he's a rat," said Nancy. "He's a Franklin D. Roosevelt rat."

"I'm a Franklin D. Roosevelt rat. You be careful what you say," said Julie.

"The hell with that. What was the big question?" said Charley.

"*My* big question?" said Julie.

"Yes," said Charley.

"I didn't know I had one. Oh, yes. The big *question. Is.* Do we go to Harlem and I can't go on tomorrow night and I give my understudy a break. *Or. Or.* Do I go home to my trundle bed—and you stay out of it, Jim. You're a rat. I mean stay out of my trundle. Nevermore, quoth the raven. Well, what did my understudy ever do for me? So I guess we better go home. Right?"

"Yeah. I haven't got an understudy," said Charley. He signaled for the check.

"Jim, why are you such a rat? If you weren't such a rat. But that's what you are, a rat," said Julie.

"Pretend I'm not a rat."

"How can I pretend a thing like that? I'm the most promising thirty-year-old ingénue there is, but I can't pretend you're not a rat. Because that's what you are. Your ex-wife is my best friend, so what else are you but a rat? Isn't that logical, Jim? Do you remember Bank Street? That was before you were a rat."

"No, I was a rat then, Julie."

"No. No, you weren't. If you were a rat then, you wouldn't be one now. That's logical."

"But he's not a bad rat," said Nancy.

"Oh, there you're wrong. If he was a good little rat I'd take him home with me. But I don't want a rat in my house."

"Then you come to my house," I said.

"All right," said Julie. "That solves everything. I don't know *why* I didn't think of that before. Remember Bank Street, Jim?"

"Sure."

She stood up. "*Good*night, Nancy. *Good*night, Charley." On her feet she became dignified, the star. She held her mink so that it showed her to best advantage and to the captains who said, "Goodnight, Miss Moore," she nodded and smiled. In the taxi she was ready to be kissed. "Ah, Jim, what a Christ-awful life, isn't it? You won't tell Ken, will you?"

"No. I won't tell anybody."

"Just don't tell Ken. I don't want him to think I care that much. He's giving me a bad time. Kiss me, Jim. Tell me I'm nicer than Nancy."

"You're much nicer than Nancy. Or anybody else."

She smiled. "You're a rat, Jim, but you're a nice old rat. It's all right if I call you a rat, isn't it? Who the hell is she to say you aren't a bad rat? She's not in our game, is she?"

"No."

"We don't have to let her in our game. But *he* does, the poor son of a bitch."

When she saw my bedroom she said: "Good Lord, Jim, I feel pregnant already. That's where Grandpa and Grandma begat. Isn't it? I hope *we* don't beget."

I was still asleep when she left, and on my desk there was a note from her:

Dear Rat:
You didn't use to snore on Bank Street. Am going home to finish my sleep. It is eight-fifteen and you seem good for many more hours. I had a lovely time and have the hangover to prove it. Want to be home in case K. calls as he said he would. In any case we are better off than Nancy and Charles. Are they headed for trouble!!!
                                                                              Love,
                                                                                 J.

P.S.: The well-appointed bachelor's apartment has a supply of extra toothbrushes. My mouth tastes like the inside of the motorman's glove. Ugh!!!
                                                                                 J.

The motorman's glove. Passé collegiate slang of the previous decade, when the word whereupon was stuck into every sentence and uzza-mattera-fact and wet-smack and swell caught on and held on. I read Julie's note a couple of times, and "the motorman's glove" brought to mind two lines from *Don Juan* that had seemed strangely out of character for Byron:

> Let us have wine and women, mirth and laughter,
> Sermons and soda-water the day after.

The mirth and laughter, the wine and women were not out of character, but there was something very vulgar about Byron's taking soda-water for a hangover as I took Eno's fruit salts. An aristocrat, more than a century dead, and a man I disliked as cordially as if he were still alive. But he had said it all, more than a hundred years ago. I made a note to buy a copy of *Don Juan* and send it, with that passage marked, to Julie. At that moment, though, I was trying to figure out what she meant by Nancy and Charley, headed for trouble. There was trouble already, and more to come.

I waited until four o'clock and then telephoned Julie. "It's the rat," I said. "How are you feeling?"

"I'll live. I'll be able to go on tonight. Actually, I'm feeling much better than I have any right to, considering the amount I drank. I went home and took a bath and fiddled around till Ken called—"

"He called, did he?"

"Yes. There isn't going to be anything in the columns about you and me, is there?"

"My guess is a qualified no. If we went out again tonight there would be, but—"

"But we're not going out again tonight," she said. "I don't have to tell you that last night was a lapse."

"You don't have to, but you did," I said.

"Now don't get huffy," she said. "It wouldn't have happened with anyone else, and it wouldn't have happened with you if it hadn't been for the old days on Bank Street."

"I know that, Julie, and I'm not even calling you for another date. I want to know what you meant by—I have your note here—Nancy and Charley headed for trouble. Was something said? Did something happen that I missed?"

"Oh, God, I have to think. It seems to me I wrote that ages ago. And it was only this morning. Is it important? I could call you back?"

"Not important."

"*I* know. I know what it was. Is Nancy's husband a man named Jack Preswell?"

"Yes."

"Well, he was at Morocco last night. Standing at the bar all alone and just staring at us. Staring, staring, staring. I used to know him when I was a prom-trotter, back in the paleolithic age."

"How did you happen to see him and we didn't?"

"Because I was facing that way and you weren't," she said. "Maybe I should have said something. Maybe I did."

"No, you didn't."

"I don't think I did. No, I guess I didn't, because now I remember thinking that I wasn't positively sure it was he. But when you and I left I caught a glimpse of him, and it was. If anybody was tighter than we were, he was. His eyes were just barely open, and he was holding himself up by the elbows. I'll bet he didn't last another ten minutes."

"Well, just about," I said.

"What do you mean?"

"Have you seen the early editions of the afternoon papers?"

"No. I don't get the afternoon papers here."

"Preswell was hit by a taxi at 54th and Lexington. Fractured his skull and died before the ambulance got there. According to the cops he just missed being hit by a north-bound cab, and then walked in front of a southbound. Four or five witnesses said the hack driver was not at fault, which is another way of saying Preswell was blind drunk."

"Well, I guess I could almost swear to that, but I'm glad I don't have to. I won't, will I?"

"Not a chance. He wasn't with us, and none of us ever spoke to him. The *Times* and the *Trib* will print the bare facts and people can draw their own conclusions. The *News* and the *Mirror* will play it up tonight, but it's only a one-day story. However, there is one tabloid angle. If the *Mirror* or the *News* finds out that Nancy was in Morocco with Charley—well, they could do something with that."

"And would you and I get in the papers?"

"Well, if I were the city editor of the *News* or the *Mirror*, and a prominent actress and an obscure author—"

"Oh, Lord. And I told Ken I went straight home from the theatre. Jim, you know a lot of those press people . . ."

"Julie, if they find out, your picture's going to be in the tabloids. I couldn't prevent that."

"And they *are* going to find out, aren't they?"

"The only straight answer is yes. You spoke to a lot of people as we were leaving. Waiter captains. People at the tables. If you can think of a story to tell Ken, I'll back you up. But maybe the best thing is to tell him the truth, up to a certain point."

"He'll supply the rest, after that certain point. He knows about Bank Street."

"That was eight years ago. Can't you have an evening out with an old friend?"

"Would you believe that line?"

"No," I said. "But I have a very suspicious nature."

"You're a blind man trusting a boy scout compared to Ken. He didn't believe me when I told him I went straight home from the theatre. But in the absence of proof—now he's got his proof."

"Well, then have a date with me tonight. Make the son of a bitch good and jealous."

"I'm almost tempted. When will we know about the *News* and the *Mirror*?"

"Oh, around nine o'clock tonight."

"You'll see them when they come out, before I can. If they mention me, will you stop for me at the theatre? That isn't much of an offer, Jim, but for old times' sake?"

"And if you're not mentioned, you have a date with Ken?"

"Yes," she said.

"All right. You understand, of course, this is something I wouldn't do for just anybody, take second best."

"I understand exactly why you're doing it, and so do you," she said.

"I detect the sound of *double entendre.*"

"Well, that's how I meant it. You're being nice, but you also know that nice little rats get a piece of candy. And don't make the obvious remark about piece of what. Seriously, Jim, I can count on you, can't I?"

"I would say that you are one of the few that can always count on me, Julie. For whatever that's worth."

"Right now, a great deal."

"Well, I wish you luck, even though I'll be the loser in the deal."

"You didn't lose anything last night. And I may have lost a husband. He was talking that way today."

"Do you want to marry him?"

"Yes, I do. Very much. Too much. So much that all he ever sees is my phony indifference. Too smart for my own good, I am. Jim, ought I to call Nancy Preswell, or write her a note?"

"A note would be better, I think."

"Yes, I do, too."

"I've been calling Charley all afternoon, and nobody knows where he is. But he'll be around when he wants to see me."

"It's a hateful thing for me to say, but in a way he's stuck, isn't he?"

"He wants to be."

"He's still stuck," said Julie.

At about eleven-twenty I was standing with the backstage doorman, who was saying goodnight to the actors and actresses as they left the theatre. "Miss Moore's always one of the last to leave," he said. "We us'ally break about five to eleven, but tonight she's later than us'al. I told her you was here. I told her myself."

"That's all right," I said.

"She dresses with Miss Van, one flight up. I'll just go tell her you're here."

"No. No thanks. Don't hurry her," I said.

"She's us'ally one of the last out, but I don't know what's keeping her tonight."

"Making herself look pretty," I said.

"She's a good little actress. You know, they had to change the curtain calls so she could take a bow by herself."

There were footsteps on the winding iron stairway, the cautious, high-heeled footsteps of all actresses descending all backstage stairways, but these were made by Julie. She did not make any sign of recognition of me but took my arm. "Goodnight, Mike," she said.

"Goodnight, Miss Moore. See you tomorrow. Have a good time," said the doorman.

"Let's go where we won't see anybody. Have you got the papers? I don't mind being seen with you, Jim, but I don't want to be seen crying. As soon as Mike said 'Mr. Malloy,' I knew. Tomorrow the press agent will thank me for the publicity break. Irony."

I took her to a small bar in the New Yorker Hotel, and she read the *News* and the *Mirror*. The *Mirror* had quite a vicious little story by a man named Walter Herbert, describing the gay foursome and the solitary man at the bar of El Morocco, and leaving the unmistakable inference that Jack Preswell had stumbled out into the night and thrown himself in front of a taxi. The *News*, in a story that had two by-lines, flatly said that Preswell had gone to the night club in an attempt to effect a reconciliation with his wife, who was constantly in the company of Charles Ellis, multi-millionaire stockbroker and former Harvard oarsman, and onetime close friend of the dead man. The *Mirror* ran a one-column cut of Julie, an old photograph from the White Studios; the *News* had a more recent picture of her in the décolleté costume she wore in the play. There was a wedding picture of Preswell and Nancy in the *News*, which also came up with a manly picture of Charley Ellis in shorts, shirt, and socks, holding an oar. There was no picture of me, and in both papers the textual mention of Julie and me was almost identical: Julie was the beautiful young actress, I was the sensational young novelist.

"Were we as gay as they say we were? I guess we were," said Julie.

"The implication is, that's what happens to society people when they mix with people like you and me."

"Exactly. They only got what they deserved. By the way, what did they get, besides a little notoriety? I'm beginning to feel sorry for Preswell. I lose a possible husband, but it must hurt to be hit by a taxi, even if you do die right away."

"You're taking it very well," I said.

"I thought Ken might show up, if only to demand an explanation. He loves to demand explanations. Have you talked to Ellis?"

"No. I'd like to know if there's anything in that *News* story, about Preswell and the reconciliation. I doubt it, and nobody will sue, but either the *News* has a very good rewrite man or they may have something. If it's something dreamed up by the rewrite man he ought to get a bonus, because he's taken a not very good story and dramatized the whole scene at Morocco."

"Thank goodness for one thing. They left my father and mother out of it," she said. "Poor Daddy. He groans. He comes to see me in all my plays, and then takes me to one side and asks if it's absolutely necessary to wear such low-cut dresses, or do I always *have* to be unfaithful to my husband? He told Thornton Wilder I'd have been just right for the girl in *Our Town*. Can you imagine how I'd have had to hunch over to play a fourteen-year-old?"

We were silent for a moment and then suddenly she said: "Oh, the hell with it. Let's go to '21'?"

"I'll take you to '21,' but no night clubs."

"I want to go to El Morocco and the Stork Club."

"No, you can't do it."

"I'm not in mourning."

"I used to be a press agent, Julie. If you want to thumb your nose at Ken, okay. But if you go to El Morocco tonight, you're asking for the worst kind of publicity. Capitalizing on those stories in the *News* and *Mirror*. You're better than that."

"Oh, the hell I am."

"Well, you used to be."

"The hell with what I used to be. I was a star, too, but now I'm just a sexy walk-on. And a quick lay, for somebody that calls me up after eight years. Why *did* you take me out last night?"

"Because you're a lady, and so is Nancy."

"Oh, it was Nancy you were trying to impress? I wish I'd known *that*."

"I have no desire to impress Nancy. I merely thought you'd get along with her and she with you."

"Why? Because she did Juliet at Foxcroft?"

"Oh, balls, Julie."

"Would you say that to Nancy?"

"If she annoyed me as much as you do, yes, I would. If you'll shut up for a minute, I'll tell you something. I don't like Nancy. I think she's a bitch. But I like Charley."

"Why do you like Charley? He's not your type. As soon as you make a little money you want to join the Racquet Club and all the rest of that crap. That apartment, for God's sake! And those guns. You're not Ernest Hemingway. Would you know how to fire a gun?"

"If I had one right now I'd show you."

"When did you get to be such pals with Charley Ellis?"

"I was hoping you'd get around to that. I knew him before I knew you, before I ever wrote anything. As to the armament, the shotguns belonged to my old man, including one that he gave me when I was fourteen. I do admit I bought the rifle four years ago. As to the apartment—well, you liked it last night. If you want to feel guilty about it, go ahead. But you said yourself it was a damned sight more comfortable than that studio couch on Bank Street. What do you want to do? Do you want to go to '21' and have something to eat, or shall I take you home?" I looked at my watch.

"It isn't too late to get another girl, is it?"

"That's exactly what I was thinking."

"Some girl from one of the night clubs?"

"Yes."

"I thought they only went out with musicians and gangsters."

"That's what you thought, and you go on thinking it. Do you want to go to '21'?"

"How late can you get one of those girls?"

"Two-thirty, if I'm lucky."

"You mean if you call up now and make the date?"

"Yes."

"You're a big liar, Jim. They have a two o'clock show that lasts an hour, so you can call this girl any time between now and two o'clock, and you won't meet her till after three. I know the whole routine. A boy in our play is married to one of them."

"The girl I had in mind isn't a show girl and she isn't in the line. She does a specialty."

She put her chin in her hand and her elbow on the table, in mock close attention. "*Tell* me about her specialty, Jim. Is it something I should learn? Or does one have to be double-jointed?"

"You want to go to '21'?"

"I'm dying to go to '21'," she said.

"Well, why didn't you say so?"

"Because you're such a grump, and I had to get a lot of things out of my system."

We used each other for a couple of weeks in a synthetic romance that served well in place of the real thing; and we were conscientious about maintaining the rules and customs of the genuine. We saw only each other and formed habits: the same taxi driver from the theatre, the same tables in restaurants, exchanges of small presents and courtesies; and we spoke of the wonder of our second chance at love. It was easy to love Julie. After the first few days and nights she seemed to have put aside her disappointment as easily as I was overcoming my chronic loneliness. We slept at my apartment nearly every night, and when she stayed at hers we would talk on the telephone until there was nothing more to say. We worried about each other: I, when the closing notice was put up at her theatre, and she when a story of mine was rejected. A couple of weeks became a couple of months and our romance was duly noted in the gossip columns: we were sizzling, we were hunting a preacher. "Would you ever go back to the Church?" she said, when it was printed that we were going to marry.

"I doubt it. Would you?"

"If Daddy wanted me to get married in the Church, I would."

"We've never talked about this."

"You mean about marriage?"

"*Or* the Church. Do you want to talk about marriage?"

"Yes, I have a few things I want to say. I love you, Jim, and you love me. But we ought to wait a long time before we do anything about getting married. If I'm married in the Church I'm going to stick to it."

"You wouldn't have with Ken."

"No, but he never was a Catholic. If I married you, in the Church, I'd want a nuptial Mass and you'd have to go to confession and the works. With a Protestant—Ken—I couldn't have had a nuptial Mass and I'd have been half-hearted about the whole thing. But marrying you would be like going back to the Church automatically. I consider you a Catholic."

"Do you consider yourself a Catholic?"

"Yes. I never go to Mass, and I haven't made my Easter duty since I was nineteen, but it's got me. I'm a Catholic."

"It's gone from me, Julie. The priests have ruined it for me."

"They've almost ruined it for me, but not quite. I don't listen to the priests. I can't tell that in confession, but that's why I stay away. Well, one of the reasons. I don't believe that going to bed with you is a sin."

"The priests do."

"Let them. They'll never be told unless I marry a Catholic and go to confession. That's why I say we ought to wait a long time. I'm thinking of myself. If I marry a Catholic, I'll be a Catholic. If I don't I'll be whatever I am. A non-practicing member of the faithful. I'll never be anything else."

"Well, neither will I. But I'm a heretic on too many counts, and the priests aren't going to accept me on my terms. It wouldn't be the Church if they did. It would be a new organization called the Malloyists."

"I'll be a Malloyist until we get married."

"There's one thing, Julie. If you get pregnant, what?"

"If I get pregnant, I'll ask you to marry me. I've had two abortions, but the father wasn't a Catholic. It was Ken. I paid for the abortions myself and never told him I was pregnant. I didn't want to have a baby. I wanted to be a star. But if I ever get pregnant by you, I'll tell you, and I hope you'll marry me."

"I will."

"However, I've been very, very careful except for that first night."

I have never been sure what that conversation did to us. I have often thought that we were all right so long as we felt a future together without getting down to plans, without putting conditional restrictions on ourselves, without specifying matters of time or event. It is also quite possible that the affection and passion that we identified as love was affection and passion and tenderness, but whatever sweetness we could add to the relationship, we could not add love, which is never superimposed. In any event, Julie stayed away one night and did not answer her telephone, and the next day I was having my coffee and she let herself in.

"Hello," I said.

"I'm sorry, Jim."

"I suppose you came to get your things," I said. I took a sip of coffee and lit a cigarette.

"Not only to get my things."

"You know, the awful thing is, you look so God damn—oh, nuts." She was wearing a blue linen dress that was as plain as a Chinese sheath, but there was more underneath that dress than Chinese girls have, and I was never to have it again. Someone else had been having it only hours ago.

"All right," I said. "Get your things."

"Aren't you going to let me say thank-you for what we had?"

"Yes, and I thank you, Julie. But I can't be nice about last night and all this morning." I took another sip of coffee and another drag on my cigarette, and she put her hand to her face and walked swiftly out of the room. I waited a while, then got up and went to the bedroom. She was lying face down on my unmade bed and she was crying.

"You'll wrinkle your dress," I said.

"The hell with my dress," she said, and slowly turned and sat up. "Jim." She held out her arms.

"Oh, no," I said.

"I couldn't help it. He came to the theatre."

"Oh, hell, I don't want to hear about that."

"I promised him I wouldn't see you again, but I had to come here."

"No you didn't, Julie. I could have sent you your things. It would have been much better if you'd just sent me a telegram."

"Put your arms around me."

"Oh, now that isn't like you. What the hell do you think I am? I've had about two hours' sleep. I'm on the ragged edge, but you don't have to do that to me."

She stood up and slipped her dress over her head, and took off her underclothes. "Can I make up for last night?" she said. "I'll never see you again. Will you put your arms around me now?"

"I wish I could say no, but I wanted you the minute I saw you."

"I know. That's why you wouldn't look at me, isn't it?"

"Yes."

She was smiling, and she could well afford to, with the pride she had in her breasts. "How do you want to remember me? I'll be whatever you want."

"What is this, a performance?"

"Of course. A farewell performance. Command, too. You don't want me as a virgin, do you?"

"No."

"No, that would take too much imagination on *your* part. But I could be one if that's what you want. But you don't. You'd much rather remember me as a slut, wouldn't you?"

"Not a slut, Julie. But not a virgin. Virgins aren't very expert."

"You'd rather remember me as an expert. A whore. Then you'll be able to forget me and you won't have to forgive me. All right."

She knew things I had never told her and there was no love in the love-making, but when she was dressed again and had her bag packed she stood in the bedroom doorway. "Jim?"

"What?"

"I'm not like that," she said. "Don't remember me that way, please?"

"I hope I don't remember you at all."

"I love him. I'm going to marry him."

"You do that, Julie."

"Haven't you got one nice thing to say before I go?"

I thought of some cruel things and I must have smiled at the thought of them, because she began to smile too. But I shook my head and she shrugged her shoulders and turned and left. The hall door closed and I looked at it, and then I saw that the key was being pushed under it. Twenty-three crowded years later I still remember the angle of that key as it lay on the dark-green carpet. My passion was spent, but I was not calm of mind; by accident the key was pointed toward me, and I thought of the swords at a court-martial. I was being resentenced to the old frenetic loneliness that none of us would admit to, but that governed our habits and our lives.

In that state of mind I made a block rejection of a thousand men and women whom I did not want to see, and reduced my friendships to the five or ten, the three or five, and finally the only person I felt like talking to. And that was how I got back in the lives of Charley Ellis and Nancy McMinnies Preswell Ellis.

They had been married about a month, and I was not sure they would be back from their wedding trip, but I got Charley at his office and he said he had started work again that week. He would stop in and have a drink on his way home.

"Gosh, the last time I was in this apartment—" he said, and it was not necessary to go on.

"You ended up getting married, and I damn near did myself."

"To Julia Murphy?"

"Close. Julianna Moore. In fact, your coming here rounds out a circle, for me. She ditched me today."

"Are you low on account of it?"

"Yes, so tell me about you and Nancy. I saw the announcement of your wedding, in the papers."

"That's all there was. We didn't send out any others."

"You lose a lot of loot that way," I said.

"I know, but there were other considerations. We wanted people to forget us in a hurry, so Nancy's mother sent short announcements to the *Tribune* and the *Sun*. You can imagine we'd had our fill of the newspapers when Preswell was killed."

"I don't have to imagine. It was the start of my romance, the one that just ended." I told him what had happened, a recital which I managed to keep down to about fifteen minutes. I lied a little at the end: "So this morning she called me up and said she'd gone back to her friend Mr. Kenneth Kenworthy."

"Well, you might say our last meeting here did end in two marriages," said Charley.

"If he marries her. He's been married three times and if she marries him she's going to have to support herself. He has big alimony to pay. I hope they do get married. Selfishly. I don't want any more synthetic romances. They're just as wearing as the real thing, and as Sam Hoffenstein says, what do you get yet?"

"Everything, if it turns out all right. You remember Nancy and her theory that nobody should get married without love, the real thing? That story of yours we talked about—'Telemark'?"

"Yes."

"Well, to be blunt about it, I really forced Nancy to marry me. All that notoriety—I put it to her that if she didn't marry me, I'd look like a shitheel. So on that basis—"

"Oh, come on."

"It's true. That's why she took the chance. But what was true then isn't true now. I want you to be the twenty-fifth to know. We're having a child."

"She never had any by Preswell?"

"No, and she wanted one, but his chemistry was all wrong. We expect ours in March or April."

"Congratulations."

"Thank you. Needless to say, I'm an altogether different person."

"You mean you have morning sickness?"

"I mean just the opposite. I'm practically on the wagon, for one thing, and for the first time in my life I'm thinking about someone besides myself. Get married, Malloy, and have a baby right away."

"I *like* to think about myself," I said.

"That's bullshit, and it's a pose. All this crazy life you lead, I think you're about the lonesomest son of a bitch I know."

I bowed my head and wept. "You shouldn't have said that," I said. "I wish you'd go."

"I'm sorry, Jim. I'll go. But why don't you drop in after dinner if you feel like it?"

"Thanks," I said, and he left.

He had taken me completely unawares. His new happiness and my new misery and all that the day had taken out of me made me susceptible of even the slightest touch of pity or kindness. I stopped bawling after two minutes, and then I began again, but during the second attack I succumbed to brain fag and fell asleep. I slept about three hours and was awakened by the telephone.

"This is Nancy Ellis. I hope you're coming up, we're expecting you. I'll bet you haven't had your dinner. Tell me the truth?"

"As a matter of fact, I was asleep."

"Well, how about some lamb chops? Do you like them black on the outside and pink on the inside? And have you any pet aversions in the vegetable line?"

"Brussels sprouts. But do you mean to say you haven't had your dinner?"

"We've had ours, but I can cook. Half an hour?"

It was a pleasant suburban evening in a triplex apartment in East Seventy-first Street, with one of the most beautiful women in New York cooking my supper and serving it; and it was apparent from their avoidance of all intimate topics that they had decided how they would treat me. At ten-thirty Nancy went to bed, at eleven Charley went in to see how she was, and at eleven-thirty I said goodnight. I went home and slept for ten hours. Had it not been for Nancy and Charley Ellis I would have gone on a ten-day drunk. But during those ten days I met a fine girl, and in December of that year we were married and we stayed married for sixteen years, until she died. As the Irish would say, she died on me, and it was the only unkind thing she ever did to anyone.

The way things tie up, one with another, is likely to go unnoticed unless a lawyer or a writer calls our attention to it. And sometimes both the writer and the lawyer have some difficulty in holding things together. But if they are men of purpose they can manage, and fortunately for writers they are not governed by rules of evidence or the whims of the court. The whim of the reader is all that need concern a writer, and even that should not concern him unduly; Byron, Scott, Milton and Shakespeare, who have been quoted in this chronicle, are past caring what use I make of their words, and at the appointed time I shall join them and the other millions of writers who have said their little say and then become forever silent—and in the public domain. I shall join them with all due respect, but at the first sign of a patronizing manner I shall say: "My dear sir, when you were drinking it up at the Mermaid Tavern, did you ever have the potman bring a telephone to your table?"

I belonged to the era of the telephone at the tavern table, and the thirty-foot extension cord that enabled the tycoon to talk and walk, and to buy and sell and connive and seduce at long distances. It is an era already gone, and I may live to see the new one, in which extrasensory perception combines with transistors, enabling the tycoon to dispense with the old-fashioned cord and *think* his way into new power and new beds. I may see the new era, but I won't belong to it. The writer of those days to come will be able to tune in on the voice of Lincoln at Gettysburg and hear the clanking of pewter mugs at the Mermaid, but he will never know the feeling of accomplishment that comes with the successful changing of a typewriter ribbon. A writer belongs to his time, and mine is past. In the days or years that remain to me, I shall entertain myself in contemplation of my time and be fascinated by the way things tie up, one with another.

I was in Boston for the tryout of a play I had written, and Charley Ellis's father had sent me a guest card to his club. "The old man said to tell you to keep your ears open and be sure and bring back any risqué stories you hear."

"At the Somerset Club?"

"The best. Where those old boys get them, I don't know, but that's where they tell them."

I used the introduction only once, when I went for a walk to get away from my play and everyone concerned with it. I stood at the window and looked out at the Beacon Street traffic, read a newspaper, and wandered to a small room to write a note to Mr. Ellis. There was only one other man in the room, and he looked up and half nodded as I came in, then resumed his letter-writing. A few minutes later there was a small angry spatter and I saw that a book of matches had exploded in the man's hand. "*Son* of a *bitch!*" he said.

His left hand was burned and he stared at it with loathing.

"Put some butter on it," I said.

"What?"

"I said, put some butter on it."

"I've heard of tea, but never butter."

"You can put butter on right away, but you have to wait for the water to boil before you have tea."

"What's it supposed to do?"

"Never mind that now. Just put it on. I've used it. It works."

He got up and disappeared. He came back in about ten minutes. "You know, it feels much better. I'd never heard of butter, but the man in the kitchen had."

"It's probably an old Irish remedy," I said.

"Are you Irish?"

"Yes. With the name Malloy I couldn't be anything else."

"Howdia do. My name is Hackley. Thanks very much. I wonder what it does, butter?"

"It does something for the skin. I guess it's the same principle as any of the greasy things."

"Of course. And it's cooling. It's such a stupid accident. I thought I closed the cover, but I guess I didn't." He hesitated. "Are you stopping here?"

"No, staying at the Ritz, but I have a guest card from Mr. Ellis in New York."

"Oh, of course. Where did you know *him*?"

"His son is a friend of mine."

"You're a friend of Charley's? I see. He's had another child, I believe. A daughter, this time."

"Yes. They wanted a daughter. I'm one of the godfathers of the boy."

"Oh, then you know him very well."

"Very," I said.

"I see. At Harvard?"

"No, after college. Around New York."

"Oh, yes. Yes," he said. Then: "Oh, *I* know who you are. You're the playwright. Why, I saw your play night before last."

"That wasn't a very good night to see it," I said.

"Oh, I didn't think it was so bad. Was I right in thinking that one fellow had trouble remembering his lines? The bartender?"

"Indeed you were."

"But aside from that, I enjoyed the play. Had a few good chuckles. That what-was-she, a chorus girl? They do talk that way, don't they? It's just that, uh, when you hear them saying those things in front of an audience. Especially a Boston audience. You know how we are. Or do you? We look about to see how the others are taking it. Tell me, Mr. Malloy, which do you prefer? Writing books, or writing for the stage?"

"At the moment, books."

"Well, of course with an actor who doesn't remember lines. A friend of mine in New York knows you. She sent me two of your books. I think one was your first and the other was your second."

"Oh? Who was that?"

"Polly Williamson is her name."

So here he was, the serious-minded widower who had been Polly Williamson's only lover. "That was damn nice of Polly. She's a swell girl."

"You *like* Polly. So do I. Never see her, but she's a darn nice girl and I hear from her now and again. Very musical, and I like music. Occasionally she'll send me a book she thinks I ought to read. I don't always like what she likes, and she knows I won't, but she does it to stimulate me, you know."

I had an almost ungovernable temptation to say something coarse. Worse than coarse. Intimate and anatomical and in the realm of stimulation, about Polly in bed. Naturally he misread my hesitation. "However," he said. "I enjoyed your first book very much. The second, not quite as much. So you're James J. Malloy?"

"No, I'm not James J. Malloy. I'm James Malloy, but my middle initial isn't J."

"I beg your pardon. I've always thought it was James J."

"People do. Every Irishman has to be James J. or John J."

"No. There was John L. Sullivan," said Hackley.

"Oh, but he came from Boston."

"Indeed he did. But then there was James J. Wadsworth. I know he wasn't Irish."

"No, but he was sort of a friend of Al Smith's."

"*Was he really?* I didn't know that. Was—he—really? Could you by any chance be thinking of his father, James W. Wadsworth?"

"I am. Of course I am. The senator, James W. Wadsworth."

"Perfectly natural mistake," said Hackley. "Well, I have to be on my way, but it's been nice to've had this chat with you. And thank you for the first-aid. I'll remember butter next time I set myself on fire."

On the evening of the next day I was standing in the lobby of the theatre, chatting with the press agent of the show and vainly hoping to overhear some comment that would tell me in ten magic words how to make the play a success. It was the second intermission. A hand lightly touched my elbow and I turned and saw Polly Williamson. "Do you remember me?" she said.

"Of course I remember you. I told you once I'd never forget you." Then I saw, standing with but behind her, Mr. Hackley, and I was sorry I was quite so demonstrative. "Hello, Mr. Hackley. How's the hand?"

He held it up. "Still have it, thanks to you."

"Just so you can applaud long and loud."

"The bartender fellow is better tonight, don't you think?"

"Much better," I said. "I'm glad you can sit through it a second time."

"He has no choice," said Polly Williamson.

"I hadn't, either," said Hackley. "I'll have you know this lady came all the way from New York just to see your play."

"You did, Polly?"

"Well, yes. But I don't know that I ought to tell you why."

"Why did you?" I said.

"Well, I read excerpts from some of the reviews, and I was afraid it wouldn't reach New York."

"We've tightened it up a little since opening night. I think the plan is now to take it to Philadelphia. But it was awfully nice of you to come."

"I wouldn't have missed it. I'm one of your greatest fans, and I like to tell people I knew you when."

"Well, I like to tell people I know you."

"I suppose you're terribly busy after the show," said Hackley.

"Not so busy that I couldn't have a drink with Polly and you, if that's what you had in mind."

They waited for me in the Ritz Bar. Two tweedy women were sitting with them, but they got up and left before I reached the table. "I didn't mean to drive your friends away," I said.

"They're afraid of you. Frightened to death," said Hackley.

"They're pretty frightening themselves," I said, angrily.

"They are, but before you say any more I must warn you, one of them is *my* cousin *and* Charley Ellis's cousin," said Polly Williamson.

"They thought your play was frightful," said Hackley.

"Which should assure its successes," said Polly. "Maisie, my cousin, goes to every play that comes to Boston and she hasn't liked anything since I don't know when."

"*The Jest*, with Lionel and Jack Barrymore, I think was the last thing she really liked. And not so much the play as Jack Barrymore."

"I don't think she'd *really* like John Barrymore," I said.

"Oh, but you're wrong. She met him, and she does," said Hackley. It seemed to me during the hour or more that we sat there that he exerted a power over Polly that was effortless on his part and unresisted by her. He never allowed himself to stay out of the conversation, and Polly never finished a conversational paragraph that he chose to interrupt. I was now sure that their affair was still active, in Boston. She had occasion to remark that he never went to New York, which led me to believe that the affair was conducted entirely on his home ground, on his terms, and at as well as for his pleasure. I learned that he lived somewhere in the neighborhood—two or three minutes' walk from the hotel; and that she always stayed with an aunt who lived on the other side of the Public Garden. Since they had not the slightest reason to suspect that I knew any more about them than they had told me, they unconsciously showed the whole pattern of their affair. It was a complete reversal of the usual procedure, in which the Boston man goes to New York to be naughty. Polly went to Boston under the most respectable auspices and with the most innocent excuses—and as though she were returning home to sin. (I did not pass that judgment on her.) Williamson was an ebullient, arrogant boor; Hackley was a Bostonian, who shared her love of music, painting, and flowers; and whatever they did in bed, it was almost certainly totally different from whatever she did with Williamson, which was not hard to guess at. I do know that in the dimly lighted bar of the hotel she seemed more genuinely at home and at ease than in her own house or at the New York parties where I would see her, with the odd difference that in Boston she was willingly under the domination of a somewhat epicene aesthete, while in New York she quietly but, over the years, noticeably resisted Williamson's habit of taking control of people's lives. After fifteen years of marriage to Williamson she was regarded in New York as a separate and individual woman, who owed less and less to her position as the wife of a spectacular millionaire. But none of that was discernible to me in her relations with Hackley. She did what he wanted to do, and in so doing she completed the picture of her that Charley Ellis had given me. In that picture, her man was missing. But now I saw that Hackley, not the absent Williamson, was her man.

It was hardly a new idea, that the lover was more husband than the husband; but I had never seen a case in which geography, or a city's way of life, had been so influential. Polly not only returned to Hackley; she returned to Boston and the way of life that suited her best and that Hackley represented. There was even something appropriately austere about her going back to New York and Williamson. Since divorce was undesirable, with Williamson, the multi-millionaire, she was making-do. The whole thing delighted me. It is always a pleasure to discover that someone you like and have underestimated on the side of simplicity turns out to be intricate and therefore worthy of your original interest. (Intricacy in someone you never liked is, of course, just another reason for disliking him.)

"I have to go upstairs now and start working on the third act," I said.

"Oh, I hope we didn't keep you," said Hackley.

"You did, and I'm very glad you did. The director and the manager have had an hour to disagree with each other. Now I'll go in and no matter what I say, one of them will be on my side and the other will be left out in the cold. That's why I prefer writing books, Mr. Hackley . . . Polly, it's been very nice to've seen you again. Spread the good word when you go back. Tell everybody it's a great play."

"Not great, but it's good," said Polly. "When will you be back in New York?"

"Leaving tomorrow afternoon."

"So am I. Maybe I'll see you on the train."

There was a situation in my play that plainly needed something to justify a long continuing affair, something other than an arbitrary statement of love. In the elevator it came to me: it was Polly's compromise. In continuing her affair with Hackley, Polly—and the woman in my play—would be able to make a bad marriage appear to be a good one. The character in the play was a movie actress, and if Polly saw the play again she never would recognize herself. The director, the manager, and I agreed that we would leave the play as-is in Boston, and open with the new material in Philadelphia. Only three members of the cast were affected by the new material, and they were quick studies. One of them was Julianna Moore.

I had said to my wife: "Would you object if I had Julie read for the part?"

"No. You know what I'd object to," she said.

"Well, it won't happen. There won't be any flare-up. Kenworthy is doing the sets, and they seem to be making a go of it."

There was no flare-up. Julie worked hard and well and got good notices in Boston, and I got used to having her around. I suppose that if she had come to my room in the middle of the night, my good intentions would have vanished. But we had discussed that. "If people that have slept together can never again work together," she said, "then the theatre might as well fold up. They'd never be able to cast a play on Broadway. And as to Hollywood . . ."

"Well, if you get too attractive, I'll send for my wife," I said.

"You won't have to. Ken will be there most of the time," she said. "Anyway, Jim, give me credit for some intelligence. I know you thought this all out and talked it over with your wife. Well, I talked it over with Ken, too. He hates you, but he respects you."

"Then we're in business," I said, and that was really all there was to it. I made most of my comments to the actors through the director, and Julie was not the kind of woman or actress who would use acquaintance with the author to gain that little edge.

Polly Williamson was at the Back Bay station and we got a table for two in the diner. "Do you think Mr. Willkie has a chance?" she said.

"I think he did have, but not now. Roosevelt was so sure he was a shoo-in that he wasn't going to campaign, and that was when Willkie had his chance. But luckily I was able to persuade the President to make some speeches."

"You did?"

"Not really," I said. "But I did have a talk with Tim Cochran in August, and I told him that Roosevelt was losing the election. I was very emphatic. And then one of the polls came out and showed I was right."

"Are you a New Dealer? I suppose you are."

"All the way."

"Did you ever know Jack Preswell? I know you know Nancy, Nancy Ellis, but did you know her first husband?"

"I once went to a baseball game with him, that's all."

"That's a tragic story. You know how he was killed and all that, I'm sure, but the real tragedy happened several years before. Jack was a brilliant student in Law School and something of an idealist. He had a job with Carson, Cass & Devereux, but he quit it to get into the New Deal. I probably shouldn't be saying this . . ."

"You can say anything to me."

"Well, I *want* to. Nancy is married to my cousin and I know you and he are very good friends, but all is far from well there, you know."

"No, I didn't know. I haven't seen them lately."

"Nancy and her father hounded Jack Preswell. They were very contemptuous of his ideals, and when he went to Washington Nancy wouldn't go with him. She said it would be a repudiation of everything she believed in and her father believed in and everything Jack's *family* believed in. As a woman I think Nancy was just looking for an excuse. Nancy is *so* beautiful and has been told so *so* many times that she'd much rather be admired for her brains. Consequently she can be very intolerant of other people's ideas, and she made Jack's life a hell. Not that Jack was any rose. I didn't agree with him, but he had a perfect right to count on Nancy's support, and he never got it. Not even when he got out of the New Deal. She should have stuck by him, at least publicly."

"Yes, as it turned out, Preswell became as anti-New Deal as she was, or Old Man McMinnies. I knew a little about this, Polly."

"Well, did I tell it fairly? I don't think you could have known much of it, because she was at her worst in front of his friends. She's a very destructive girl, and now she's up to the same old tricks with Charley. You don't know *that*, do you?"

"No."

"She's gotten Charley into America First. You knew that?"

"No, I didn't."

"Yes. And even my husband, as conservative as he is, and his father, they've stayed out of it. What's the use of isolationism now, when we're practically in it already? I agree with you,

I think Roosevelt's going to win, although I just can't vote for him. But he'll get in and then it's only a question of another *Lusitania*, and we'll be in it too. So I don't see the practical value of America First. We ought to be getting stronger and stronger and the main reason I won't vote for Mr. Roosevelt is that he's such a hypocrite. He won't come out and honestly say that we're headed toward war."

"A little thing about neutrality and the head of the United States government."

"Oh, come. Do you think Hitler and Mussolini are hoping for a last-minute change of heart? Roosevelt should be uniting the country instead of playing politics. This nonsense about helping the democracies is sheer hypocrisy. There is no France, there's only England."

"You're very fiery, Polly."

"Yes. We have two English children staying with us. Their father was drowned coming back from Dunkerque. Nancy has Charley convinced that their presence in our house is a violation of neutrality. She said it wouldn't be fashionable to have two German children. When have I ever given a darn about fashion? That really burned me up."

I became crafty. "How do they feel about this in Boston? What does Mr. Hackley think?"

"Ham? The disappointment of his life was being turned down by the American Field Service. He'd have been wonderful, too. Speaks French, German, and Italian, and has motored through all of Europe. He'd make a wonderful spy."

"They'd soon catch on to him."

"Why?"

"If he burnt his hand, he'd say 'Son of a bitch,' and they'd know right away he was an American."

"Oh, yes." She smiled. "He told me about that. He's nice, don't you think?"

She was so nearly convincingly matter-of-fact. "Yes. He and I'd never be friends, but of his type I like him. Solid Boston."

"I don't know," she said. "Charley's almost that, and you and he have been friends quite a long time. Poor Charley. I don't know what I hope. Oh, I do. I want him to be happy with Nancy. I just hate to see what I used to like in him being poisoned and ruined by that girl."

"And you think it is?"

"The Charley Ellis I used to know would have two English children staying with him, and he'd probably be in the Field Service, if not actually in the British army."

"Well, my wife and I haven't taken any English children, and I'm not in the Field Service, so I can't speak. However, I'm in agreement with you in theory about the war. And in sentiment."

"Look up Charley after your play opens. Talk to him."

"Do you think I'd get anywhere in opposition to Nancy?"

"Well, you can have a try at it," she said.

I did have a try at it, after my play opened to restrained enthusiasm and several severe critical notices. Charley and I had lunch one Saturday and very nearly his opening remark was: "I hear you caught up with Polly and her bosom companion?"

I was shocked by the unmistakable intent of the phrase. "Yes, in Boston," I said.

"Where else? He never leaves there. She nips up there every few weeks and comes home full of sweetness and light, fooling absolutely no one. Except herself. Thank God I didn't go to Oxford."

"Why?"

"Well, you saw Hackley. He went to Oxford—after Harvard, of course."

"You sound as if you had a beef against Harvard, too."

"There are plenty of things I don't like about it, beginning with der Fuehrer, the one in the White House," he said. "Polly fill you up with sweetness and light, and tell you how distressed she was over Nancy and me?"

"No, we had my play to talk about," I said.

"Well, she's been sounding off. She's imported a couple of English kids and gives money to all the British causes. She'd have done better to have a kid by Hackley, but maybe they don't *do* that."

"What the hell's the matter with you, Charley? If I or anyone else had said these things about Polly a few years ago,
you'd have been at their throat."

"That was before she began saying things about Nancy,
things that were absolutely untrue, and for no reason except
that Nancy has never gone in for all that phony Thoreau stuff.
Nature-lover stuff. You know, I think Polly has had us all
fooled from 'way back. You fell for it, and so did I, but I
wouldn't be surprised if she'd been screwing Hackley all her
life. One of those children that Junior thinks is his, *could* very
well be Hackley's. The boy."

"Well, I wouldn't know anything about that. I've never seen
their children. But what turned you against Polly? Not the
possibility of her having had a child by Hackley."

"I've already told you. She's one of those outdoor-girl types
that simply can't tolerate a pretty woman. And she's subtle, I'll
give her that. She puts on this act of long-suffering faithful
wife, while Junior goes on the make, and of course meanwhile
Polly is getting hers in Boston."

"But you say not getting away with it."

"She got away with it for a long time, but people aren't that
stupid. Even Junior Williamson isn't that stupid. He told
Nancy that he's known about it for years, but as long as she
didn't interfere with his life, he might as well stay married to
her. Considering the nice stories Polly spread about Preswell
and Nancy, I think Nancy showed considerable restraint in
not making any cracks about Hackley and Polly's son. Nancy
has her faults, but she wouldn't hurt an innocent kid."

The revised portraits of Junior Williamson, tolerating his
wife's infidelity for years, and of Nancy Ellis, withholding gossip to protect a blameless child, were hard to get accustomed
to. I did not try very hard. I was so astonished to see what a
chump Nancy had made of my old friend, and so aggrieved by
its effect on him, that I cut short our meeting and went home.
Three or four months later the war news was briefly interrupted to make room for the announcement that Mrs. Ethridge Williamson, Jr., had established residence in Reno,
Nevada. "A good day's work, Nancy," I said aloud. Much less

surprising, a few months later, was the news item that Mrs. Smithfield Williamson, former wife of Ethridge Williamson, Jr., millionaire sportsman and financier, had married Hamilton Hackley, prominent Boston art and music patron, in Beverly, Massachusetts. The inevitable third marriage did not take place until the summer of 1942, when Lieutenant Commander Williamson, USNR, married Ensign Cecilia G. Reifsnyder, of the Women Accepted for Volunteer Emergency Service, in Washington, D.C. It seemed appropriate that the best man was Lieutenant Charles Ellis, USNR. The bride's only attendant was her sister, Miss Belinda Reifsnyder, of Catasauqua, Pennsylvania. I gave that six months, and it lasted twice that long.

My war record adds up to a big, fat nothing, but for a time I was a member of an Inverness-and-poniard organization, our elaborate nickname for cloak-and-dagger. In Washington I moved about from "Q" Building to the Brewery to South Agriculture and houses that were only street addresses. One day in 1943 I was on my way out of "Q" after an infuriatingly frustrating meeting with an advertising-man-turned-spy, a namedropper who often got his names a little bit wrong. In the corridor a man fell in step with me and addressed me by my code nickname, which was Doc. "Do I know you?" I said.

"The name is Ham," said Hackley.

"We can't be too careful," I said.

"Well, we can't, as a matter of fact, but you can relax. I called you Doc, didn't I?" He smiled and I noticed that he needed dental work on the lower incisors. He had grown a rather thick moustache, and he had let his hair go untrimmed. "Come have dinner with Polly and me."

"I can think of nothing I'd rather do," I said.

"Irritating bastard, isn't he?" he said, tossing his head backward to indicate the office I had just left.

"The worst. The cheap, pompous worst," I said.

"One wonders, one wonders," said Hackley.

We got a taxi and went to a house in Georgetown. "Not ours," said Hackley. "A short-term loan from some friends."

Polly was a trifle thick through the middle and she had the beginnings of a double chin, but her eyes were clear and smiling and she was fitting into the description of happy matron.

"You're not at all surprised to see me," I said.

"No. I knew you were in the organization. Charley told me you'd turn up one of these days."

"Charley Who?"

"Heavens, have you forgotten all your old friends? Charley Ellis. Your friend and my cousin."

"I thought he was at CINCPAC."

"He's back and forth," she said. She put her hand on her husband's arm. "I wish this man got back as often. Would you like to see Charley? He's not far from here."

"Yes, but not just now. Later. I gather you're living in Boston?"

"Yes. My son is at Noble's and my daughter is still home with me. How is your lovely wife? I hear nothing but the most wonderful things about her. Aren't we lucky? Really, aren't we?"

"We are that," I said. Hackley had not said a word. He smoked incessantly, his hand was continually raising or lowering his cigarette in a slow movement that reminded me of the royal wave. I remembered the first time I had seen him and Polly together, when he would tack on his own thought to everything she said. "Are you still with us?" I said.

"Oh, very much so," he said.

"Can you tell Jim what you've been doing?"

"Well, now that's very indiscreet, Polly. Naturally he infers that I've told you, and he could report me for that. And should," said Hackley. "However, I think he can be trusted. He and I dislike the same man, and that's a great bond."

"And we like the same woman," I said.

"Thank you," said Polly.

"I've been in occupied territory," said Hackley. "Hence the hirsute adornment, the neglected teeth. I can't get my teeth fixed because I'm going back, and the Gestapo would take one look at the inside of my mouth and ask me where I'd happened to run across an American dentist. Hard question to answer.

So I've been sitting here literally sucking on a hollow tooth. Yes, I'm still with you."

"I wish I were with *you*—not very much, but a little."

"You almost were, but you failed the first requirement. I had to have someone that speaks nearly perfect French, and you took Spanish."

"I'm highly complimented that you thought of me at all. I wish I did speak French."

"Yes, the other stuff you could have learned, as I had to. But without the French it was no go. French French. Not New Orleans or New Hampshire."

"Do you go in by parachute—excuse me, I shouldn't ask that."

"You wouldn't have got an answer," said Hackley. He rose. "I wonder if you two would excuse me for about an hour? I'd like to have a bath and five minutes' shut-eye."

As soon as he left us Polly ceased to be the happy matron. "He's exhausted. I wish they wouldn't send him back. He's over fifty, you know. I wish they'd take me, but do you know why they won't? The most complicated reasoning. The French would think I was a German agent, planted in France to spy on the Resistance. And the Germans would know I was English or American, because I don't speak German. But imagine the French thinking I was a German. My coloring, of course, and I *am* getting a bit dumpy."

"Where are your English children?"

"One died of leukemia, and their mother asked to have the other sent back, which was done. John Winant helped there. The child *is* better off with her mother, and the mother is too, I'm sure."

"Ham wants to go back, of course," I said.

"I wonder if he really does. Every time he goes back, his chances—and the Germans are desperate since we invaded Italy. It's young men's work, but a man of Ham's age attracts less attention. Young men are getting scarcer in France. Oh, I'm worried and I can't pretend I'm not. I can to Ham, but that's because I have to. But you saw how exhausted he is, and he's had—"

"Don't tell me. You were going to tell me how long he's been home. Don't. I don't want to have that kind of information."

"Oh, I understand. There's so little I want to talk about that I'm permitted to. Well, Charley Ellis is a safe subject. Shall I ask him to come over after dinner?"

"First, brief me on Charley and Nancy. I haven't seen him for at least a year."

"Nancy is living in New York, or you could be very sure I'd never see Charley. I didn't want to ever again. It was Nancy that stirred up the trouble between Junior and me, and I'm very grateful to her now but I wasn't then. Junior'd had lady friends, one after another, for years and years, and if he'd been a different sort of man it would have been humiliating. But as Charley pointed out to me, oh, twenty years ago, there are only about half a dozen Junior Williamsons in this country, and they make their own rules. So, in order to survive, I made mine, too. I really led a double life, the one as Mrs. Ethridge Williamson, Junior, and the other, obviously, as Ham's mistress. You knew that, didn't you?"

"Well, yes."

"I didn't take anything away from Junior that he wanted. Or withhold anything. And several times over the years I did stop seeing Ham, when Junior would be going through one of his periods of domesticity. I was always taken in by that, and Junior can be an attractive man. To women. He has no men friends, do you realize that? He always has some toady, or somebody that he has to see a lot of because of business or one of his pet projects. But he has no real men friends. Women of all ages, shapes, and sizes and, I wouldn't be surprised, colors. He married that Wave, and the next thing I heard was she caught him in bed with her sister. Why not? One meant as much to him as the other, and I'm told they were both pretty. That would be enough for Junior. A stroke of luck, actually. He's paying off the one he married. A million, I hear. And she's not going to say anything about her sister. What will those girls do with a million dollars? And think how much more they would have asked for if they'd ever been to the house on

Long Island. But I understand he never took her there. That's what he considers home, you know. Christmas trees, and all the servants' children singing carols, and the parents lining up for their Christmas cheques. But the Wave was never invited. Oh, well, he's now an aide to an admiral, which should make life interesting."

"Having your commanding officer toady to you?"

"That, yes. But being able to pretend that you're just an ordinary commander, or maybe he's a captain now, but taking orders and so on. An admiral that would have him for an aide is the kind that's feathering his nest for the future, so I don't imagine Junior has any really unpleasant chores."

"Neither has the admiral. He's chair-borne at Pearl."

"Yes, Charley implied as much. I've talked too much about Junior, and you want to know about Charley and Nancy. Well, Nancy stirred up the trouble. I never would have denied that I was seeing Ham, if Junior'd asked me, but that isn't what he asked me. He asked me if Ham were the father of our son, and I felt so sick at my stomach that I went right upstairs and packed a bag and took the next train to Boston, not saying a single word. When I got to my aunt's house, Junior was already there. He'd flown in his own plane. He said, 'I asked you a question, and I want an answer. *Entitled* to an answer.' So I said, 'The answer to the question is no, and I never want to say another word to you.' Nor have I. If he was entitled to ask the question, which I don't concede, he was entitled to my answer. He got it, and all communication between us since then has been through the lawyers."

"What about Nancy, though?"

"Oh, bold as brass, she told people that she thought my son's father was Ham. Which shows how well she doesn't know old Mr. Williamson. The boy looks exactly like his grandfather, even walks like him. But she also didn't know that Mr. Williamson is devoted to the boy, wouldn't speak to Junior for over a year, and worst of all, from Mr. Williamson's point of view, I have my son twelve months of the year and at school in Boston, so his grandfather has to come to Boston to see him. I refuse to take him to Long Island. And Mr. Williamson says I'm perfectly right, after Junior's nasty doubts. Doubts? Accusations."

"But you and Charley made it up," I said.

"Yes and no. Oh, we're friends again, but it'll never be what it used to be. Shall I tell you about it? You may be able to write it in a story sometime."

"Tell me about it."

"Charley was getting ready to ship out, his first trip to the Pacific, and he wrote me a letter. I won't show it to you. It's too long and too—private. But the gist of it was that if anything happened to him, he didn't want me to remember him unkindly. Then he proceeded to tell me some things that he'd said about me, that I hadn't heard, and believe me, Jim, if I'd ever heard them I'd have remembered him *very* unkindly. He put it all down, though, and then said, 'I do not believe there is a word of truth in any of these things.' Then he went on to say that our friendship had meant so much to him and so forth."

"It does, too, Polly," I said.

"Oh, James Malloy, you're dissembling. You know what he really said, don't you?"

"You're dissembling, too. I know what he used to feel."

"*I* never did. I always thought he was being extra kind to an awkward younger cousin," she said. "And he never liked Junior. Well, since you've guessed, or always knew, you strange Irishman, I'll tell you the rest. I wrote to him and told him our friendship was just where it had always been, and that I admired him for being so candid. That I was hurt by the things he had said, but that his first loyalty was to Nancy. That I never wanted to see Nancy again, and that therefore I probably would never see him. But since we lived such different lives, in different cities, I probably wouldn't see him anyway, in war or peace."

"But you did see him."

"Yes. We're friends again. I've seen him here in Washington. We have tea together now and then. To some extent it's a repetition of my trips to Boston to see Ham. Needless to say, with one great difference. I never have been attracted to Charley that way. But I'm his double life, and the piquancy, such as it is, comes from the fact that Nancy doesn't know we see each other. Two middle-aged cousins, more and more like the people that come to my aunt's house in Louisburg Square."

"Do you remember the time we came down from Boston?"

"Had dinner on the train. Of course."

"You said then, and I quote, that all was far from well between Nancy and Charley."

She nodded. "It straightened itself out. It wasn't any third party or anything of that kind. It was Nancy reshaping Charley to her own ways, and Charley putting up a fight. But she has succeeded. She won. Except for one thing that she could never understand."

"Which is?"

"That Charley and I like to have tea together. If she found out, and tried to stop it, that's the one way she'd lose Charley. So she mustn't find out. You see, Jim, I don't want Charley, as a lover or as a husband. I have my husband and he was my lover, too. As far as I'm concerned, Charley is first, last and always a cousin. A dear one, that I hope to be having tea with when we're in our seventies. But that's all. And that's really what Charley wants, too, but God pity Nancy if she tries to deprive him of that."

For a little while neither of us spoke, and then she said something that showed her astuteness. "I'll give you his number, but let's not see him tonight. He doesn't like to be discussed, and if he came over tonight he'd know he had been."

"You're right," I said. "Polly, why did you divorce Williamson?"

"You're not satisfied with the reason I gave you?"

"It would be a good enough reason for some women, but not for you."

She looked at me and said nothing, but she was disturbed. She fingered her circle of pearls, picked up her drink and put it down without taking a sip.

"Never mind," I said. "I withdraw the question."

"No. No, don't. You gave me confidence one day when I needed it. The second time I ever saw you. I'll tell you."

"Not if it's an ordeal," I said.

"It's finding the words," she said. "The day Junior asked me point-blank if he was the father of my son, I had just learned that I was pregnant again. By him, of course. One of his periods of domesticity. So I had an abortion, something I'd sworn I'd never do, and I've never been pregnant since. I had to have a hysterectomy, and Ham and I did want a child. You see, I couldn't answer your question without telling you the rest of it."

After the war my wife and I saw the Ellises punctiliously twice every winter; they would take us to dinner and the theatre, we would take them. Dinner was always in a restaurant, where conversation makes itself, and in the theatre it was not necessary. Charley and I, on our own, lunched together every Saturday at his club or mine, with intervals of four months during the warm weather and time out for vacations in Florida or the Caribbean. Every five years on Charley's birthday they had a dance in the ballroom of one of the hotels, and I usually had a party to mark the occasion of a new book or play. We had other friends, and so had the Ellises, and the two couples had these semi-annual evenings together only because not to do so would have been to call pointed attention to the fact that the only friendship was that of Charley and me. Our wives, for example, after an early exchange of lunches never had lunch together again; and if circumstances put me alone with Nancy, I had nothing to say. In the years of our acquaintance she had swung from America First to Adlai Stevenson, while I was swinging the other way. She used the word valid to describe everything but an Easter bonnet, another favorite word of hers was denigrate, and still another was challenge. When my wife died Nancy wrote me a note in which she "questioned the validity of it all" and told me to "face the challenge." When I married again she said I had made the only valid decision by "facing up to the challenge of a new life." I had ceased to be one of the authors she admired, and in my old place she had

put Kafka, Kierkegaard, Rilke, and Camus. I sent her a copy
of Kilmer to make her velar collection complete, but she did
not think it was comical or cute.

Charley and I had arrived at a political rapprochement: he
conceded that some of the New Deal had turned out well, I
admitted that Roosevelt had been something less than a god.
Consequently our conversations at lunch were literally what
the doctor ordered for men of our age. To match my Pennsylvania reminiscences he provided anecdotes about the rich, but
to him they were not the rich. They were his friends and enemies, neighbors and relatives, and it was a good thing to hear
about them as such. Charley Ellis had observed well and he
remembered, and partly because he was polite, partly because
he had abandoned the thought of writing as a career, he gave
me the kind of information I liked to hear.

We seldom mentioned Nancy and even less frequently, Polly.
If he continued to have tea with her, he did not say so. But one
day in the late Forties we were having lunch at his club and he
bowed to a carefully dressed man who limped on a cane and
wore a patch over his left eye. He was about sixty years old.
"One of your boys," said Charley.

"You mean Irish?"

"Oh, no. I meant O.S.S."

"He must have been good. The Médaille Militaire. That's
one they don't hand out for traveling on the French Line."

"A friend of Ham Hackley's. He told me how Hackley died."

All I knew was that Hackley had never come back from France
after my evening with him in Washington. "How did he?" I said.

"The Germans caught him with a wad of plastic and a fuse
wire in his pocket. He knew what he was in for, so he took one
of those pills."

"An 'L' pill," I said.

"Whatever it is that takes about a half a minute. You didn't
know that about Ham?"

"I honestly didn't."

"That guy, the one I just spoke to, was in the same operation. He blew up whatever they were supposed to blow up, but
he stayed too close and lost his eye and smashed up his leg.

You wouldn't think there was that much guts there, would you? He knew he couldn't get very far, but he set off the damn plastic and hit the dirt." Charley laughed. "Do you know what he told us? He said, 'I huddled up and put my hands over my crotch, so I lost an eye. But I saved everything else.' We got him talking at a club dinner this winter."

"I wish I'd been here."

"Not this club. This was at the annual dinner of my club at Harvard. He was a classmate of Ham's. I don't usually go back, but I did this year."

"Did you see Polly?"

"Yes, I went and had tea with her. Very pleasant. Her boy gets out of Harvard this year. Daughter's married."

"We got an announcement. What does Polly do with her time?"

"Oh, why, I don't know. She always has plenty of things to do in Boston. A girl like Polly, with all her interests, she'd keep herself very busy. I must say she's putting on a little weight."

"What would she be now?"

"How old? Polly is forty-one, I think."

"Still young. Young enough to marry again."

"I doubt if she will," said Charley. "I doubt it very much. Boston isn't like New York, you know. In New York a woman hates to go to a party without a man, but in Boston a woman like Polly goes to a party by herself and goes home by herself and thinks nothing of it."

"Nevertheless she ought to have a husband. She's got a good thirty years ahead of her. She ought to marry if only for companionship."

"Companionship? Companionship is as hard to find as love. More so. Love can sneak up on you, but when you're looking for companionship you shop around."

"Maybe that's what Polly's doing, having a look at the field."

"Maybe. There's one hell of a lot of money that goes with her, and she's not going to marry a fortune-hunter. Oh, I guess Polly can take care of herself."

"Just out of curiosity, how *much* money is there?"

"How much money? Well, when Polly's father died, old Mr. Smithfield, he left five million to Harvard, and another million to a couple of New York hospitals, and a hundred thousand here and a hundred thousand there. I happen to know that he believed in tithes. All his life he gave a tenth of his income to charity. So if he followed that principle in his will, he was worth around seventy million gross. I don't know the taxes on that much money, but after taxes it all went to Polly. In addition, Ham Hackley left her all his money, which was nothing like Cousin Simon Smithfield's, but a tidy sum nonetheless. I also know that when Polly divorced Junior Williamson, old Mr. Williamson changed his will to make sure that the grandchildren would each get one-third, the same as Junior. That was quite a blow to Junior. So all in all, Polly's in a very enviable position, financially."

"Good God," I said. "It embarrasses me."

"Why you?"

"Don't you remember that day I told her I loved her?"

"Oh, yes. Well, she took that as a compliment, not as a business proposition. She's never forgotten it, either."

"Well, I hope Polly holds on to her good sense. When I was a movie press agent I made a great discovery that would have been very valuable to a fortune-hunter. And in fact a few of them had discovered it for themselves. Big stars, beautiful and rich, would come to New York and half the time they had no one to take them out. They depended on guys in the publicity department. I never would have had to work for a living."

"How long could you have stood that?"

"Oh, a year, probably. Long enough to get tired of a Rolls and charge accounts at the bespoke tailors. Then I suppose I'd have read a book and wished I'd written it. I knew a fellow that married a movie star and did all that, and he wasn't just a gigolo. He'd taught English at Yale. He took this doll for God knows how much, then she gave him the bounce and now he's living in Mexico. He's had a succession of fifteen-year-old wives. Once every two or three years he comes to New York for a week. He subsists entirely on steak and whiskey. One meal a day, a steak, and all the whiskey he can drink. He's had a stroke and he knows he's going to die. I could have been that. In fact, I don't like to think how close I came."

"I don't see you as Gauguin."

"Listen, Gauguin wasn't unhappy. He was doing what he wanted to do. I don't see myself as Gauguin either. What I don't like to think of is how close I came to being my friend that married the movie actress. That I could have been."

"No, you were never really close. You were no closer than I was to marrying Polly. You thought about it, just as I did about marrying Polly. But I wasn't meant to marry Polly, and you weren't meant to steal money from a movie actress and go on the beach in Mexico."

"Go on the beach? Why did you say that?"

"It slipped. I knew the fellow you're talking about. Henry Root?"

"Yes."

"Before he taught at Yale he had the great distinction of teaching me at Groton. You know why he *stopped* teaching at Yale? Bad cheques. Not just bouncing cheques. Forgeries. There was one for a thousand dollars signed Ethridge B. Williamson, Junior. That did it. He had Junior's signature to copy from, but that wasn't the way Junior signed his cheques. He always signed E. B. Williamson J R, so his cheques wouldn't be confused with his father's, which had Ethridge written out. Henry was a charming, facile bum, and a crook. You may have been a bum, but you were never a crook. Were you?"

"No, I guess I wasn't. I never cheated in an exam, and the only money I ever stole was from my mother's pocketbook. And got caught, every time. My mother always knew how much was in her purse."

"Now let me ask you something else. Do you think Henry Root would ever have been a friend of Polly's? As good a friend, say, as you are?"

"Well—I'd say no."

"And you'd be right. When she was Polly Smithfield he'd always give her a rush at the dances, and it was an understood thing that Junior and I would always cut in. I don't think we have to worry about Polly and fortune-hunters, or you about how close you came to being Henry Root. I don't even worry about how close that damn story of yours came to keeping Nancy from marrying me."

"Oh, that story. 'Christiana.' No. 'Telemark.' That was it, 'Telemark.'"

"You don't even remember your own titles, but that was the one."

"I may not remember the title, but the point of the story was that two people could take a chance on marriage without love."

"Yes, and Nancy was so convinced that you were wrong that she had it on her mind. You damn near ruined my life, Malloy."

"No I didn't."

"No, you didn't. My life was decided for me by Preswell, when he walked in front of that taxi."

I knew this man so well, and with his permission, but I had never heard him make such an outright declaration of love for his wife, and on my way home I realized that until then I had not known him at all. It was not a discovery to cause me dismay. What did he know about me? What, really, can any of us know about any of us, and why must we make such a thing of loneliness when it is the final condition of us all? And where would love be without it?

(1960)

THE WOMEN OF
MADISON AVENUE

Mrs. Dabner walked boldly if not bravely up Madison Avenue, thinking of how she would look to someone in a bus. How often, when she came to New York, she would be in a Madison Avenue bus and see a woman like herself—nice-looking, well-dressed, late-thirtyish, early-fortyish—and wonder what the woman was doing, where she was bound, what she was thinking. "I'll bet I know a lot of people you know," she would say to that woman. "I'll bet we could sit down together and inside of five minutes—why, we might even be related."

There were always so many attractive women on Madison Avenue after lunch. They would come in pairs from the restaurants in the upper Fifties and the Sixties, say a few words of farewell at the Madison Avenue corner, and go their separate ways, the one on her way to the hairdresser or to finish her shopping, the other deciding to walk home. So many of them were so attractive, and Ethel Dabner liked to look at them from her seat in the bus. But today she was walking, and inside one of those buses, looking at her, possibly thinking how attractive *she* was, might be the one woman in New York who had good reason to hate her. Ethel Dabner did not like people to hate her, and if she could ever sit down and have a sensible talk with Laura Howell she could make Laura realize that she really had no reason to hate her. But how long since anyone had been able to sit down and have a sensible talk with Laura Howell?

Ethel Dabner turned her head to look at a crowded bus, but what was the use of looking for a woman she had never seen?

At Sixty-fourth Street she left Madison Avenue and was glad to leave it, with its crowded buses and all those women, one of whom could have been Laura Howell. She let herself in the ground-floor apartment and was relieved, though not surprised, to find that she was alone. Half past three, he had said, and that was half an hour away, but sometimes he was early and invariably he was punctual. "I may even be a little late today," he had said. "I don't know how long this meeting'll last, but if I'm still in there at ha' past three I'll get word to you."

"You'll get word to me? How will you get word to me? You can't tell your secretary to call me and say you'll be late."

"No, but . . ."

"But what?"

"Well, I was thinking," he said. "I can tell Miss Bowen to call this number and have her say that Mr. Howell would be late for his appointment with Mr. Jenkins."

"Who's Mr. Jenkins?"

"There is no Mr. Jenkins, but you're Mr. Jenkins's secretary. Do you see? You'll answer, and Miss Bowen will think you're Mr. Jenkins's secretary."

" 'Tisn't worth the bother. You just get here when you can."

"Well, just so you understand I may be a little late."

"Honey, I understand. All you have to do is tell me you'll be a little late."

He was so careful, so elaborate, so—as he put it—ready for any and all contingencies. The simple thing, to meet her in her hotel, was too simple for him. "I could run into sixty-five thousand people in your hotel," he had said. "I could just be *seen* there, without knowing who saw me." And so there was this apartment, rented by his bachelor son who was now in the army. "I told Robbie I'd keep it for him while he was away, for when he got leave."

"Who do you think you're kidding? Doesn't he know you want it for yourself?"

"If he wants to guess, but he's on my side."

"One of these days we'll be there and the door'll fly open and there'll be your son and a half dozen of his G.I. buddies."

"No. He'll have a little problem of getting the key. I took care of *that* contingency."

"How many people do you know in New York?"

"Half the girls I went to school with and a lot of their husbands. First *and* second husbands, if it comes to that."

"All right. You're in town for a visit. Couldn't you be calling on someone on East Sixty-fourth Street? Someone they don't know?"

"I guess I could. I guess so."

It was a strange apartment for such goings-on. From the beginning she had felt as though they had invaded the dormitory rooms of a sophisticated undergraduate. There were a few college souvenirs: an initiation paddle marked D.K.E., some group photographs, some pewter mugs and silver trophies; but the pictures on the walls were esoteric moderns, the statuettes unidentifiable forms in ebony and aluminum, and hanging above the fireplace a small collection of Polynesian stringed instruments. In the bathroom there was an explicit drawing of a nude, that seemed to have been cut rather than drawn, the lines were so sharp, and the nakedness of the woman offended Ethel Dabner. It was a *map* of a woman, without mystery, without charm, without warmth or even sensuality, and she hated the drawing and the German who had made it, so much so that she based her dislike of her lover's son on the fact that he would own such a picture.

She hung her street clothes in Robbie's closet, in among the plastic-covered civilian suits and the treed shoes. She put on his kimono and went to the kitchen and filled a bucket with ice cubes from the nearly empty refrigerator. Burt would want a Scotch and soda when he arrived, and now she had nothing to do but wait.

If he had been his usual punctual self he would be here now; it was half past three. But in spite of having been forewarned, she was annoyed to find that at three-thirty-two he had not arrived. He was two minutes late, and she had had to fish in her purse for glasses in order to read the time on her wristwatch. Her watch, her rings, her bracelet, her necklace lay on the coffee table, and she thought of taking them to the bathroom and leaving them on the glass shelf, where they would be all together in one place when she was ready to put them on again. But she had no desire to go back to the bathroom; she had a desire *not* to go back to the bathroom and that nasty drawing.

Every little sound she made was distinct in the silence of the apartment, but in a little while the outside street noise began to break up into individual sounds, notably the sounds of the buses starting and stopping. There were the other sounds, too, but her ear kept going back to the special sounds of the buses, and she thought of the women on the buses, looking out at the women who walked, the attractive, well-dressed women who had decided to walk home after a pleasant, happy lunch with a woman friend. What would she be thinking about, the attractive woman who was walking home? How nice it was to have Jane Jones for a friend? How well Jane looked? She would walk up Madison Avenue, this woman, with a little smile on her face because she was thinking of her friend Jane Jones, and that was one of the things that would make her attractive, that smile of appreciation for her friend. People in the buses would look out at her and think what an attractive woman she was, a woman other women could trust.

Fourteen minutes to four, and the telephone rang. "Hello," she said, then, remembering: "Mr. Jenkins's office."

There was a loud laugh at the other end. "It's me," he said. "I just broke up the meeting. I told those bastards we had to wind it up by quarter to four, so I'll be right there, honey."

"Well, you just hurry, d'you hear?" she said.

"Listen, I'm just as eager as you are," he said.

"I didn't mean that," she said. "I'm just tired of sitting here all by myself in this apartment."

"Shouldn't take me but twenty minutes," he said.

"All right," she said, and hung up.

So sure of himself, so sure of her, whichever it was she hated it. She hated what he took for granted, then she wanted and needed him, was as eager as he was. And now she found that a

decision had been made for her; he had not made it, she had
not made it, but it was there and only needed to be acted upon.
She got all dressed again and satisfied herself that anyone seeing her from the bus would consider her very attractive and
nice. She took the nasty picture down from the bathroom wall
and put it face down on the floor and stamped on it. She next
put the apartment key on the coffee table near the ice bucket,
and for the last time she left the apartment.

In the bus she got a seat next to the window and at Sixtieth
or maybe it was Sixty-first Street an attractive, nice-looking
woman walking up Madison happened to look in the window
and catch her eye. Ethel Dabner smiled and bowed, and the
nice-looking woman smiled back.

(1962)

YOUR FAH NEEFAH NEEFACE

This woman, when she was about nineteen or twenty, had a stunt that she and her brother would play, usually in a railroad station or on a train or in a hotel lobby. I saw them work the stunt under the clock at the Biltmore in the days when that meeting-place was a C-shaped arrangement of benches, and I remember it so well because it was the first time I ever saw the stunt and the first time I ever saw her or her brother. It was more than thirty years ago.

She was sitting there, quite erect, her legs crossed, smoking a cigarette and obviously, like everyone else, waiting to meet someone. She was wearing a beret sort of hat that matched her suit, and it was easy to tell by the way she smoked her cigarette that she had handled many of them in her short life. I remember thinking that I would like to hear her talk; she was so self-possessed and good-humored in her study of the young men and young women who were keeping dates at the clock. The drag she took on her cigarette was a long one; the smoke kept coming from her nostrils long after you thought it was all gone. She was terribly pretty, with a straight little nose and lively light blue eyes.

Presently a young man came up the stairs in no great hurry. He was wearing a black topcoat with a velvet collar and carrying a derby hat. He was tall, but not outstandingly so, and he had tightly curled blond hair—a 150-pound crew type, he was. He reached the meeting-place, scanned the faces of the people who were seated there, and then turned away to face the stairs.

He watched the men and women coming up the stairs, but after a minute or so he turned his head and looked back at the girl, frowned as though puzzled, then again faced the incoming people. He did that several times, and I began to think that this was a young man on a blind date who had not been given a full or accurate description of his girl. She meanwhile was paying no attention to him.

Finally he went directly to the girl, and in a firm voice that everyone under the clock could hear he said, "Are you by any chance Sallie Brown?"

"I am, but what's it to you?" she said.

"Do you know who I am?" he said.

"No."

"You don't recognize me at all?"

"Never saw you in my whole life."

"Yes you did, Sallie. Look carefully," he said.

"I'm sorry, but I'm quite positive I've never seen you before."

"Asbury Park. Think a minute."

"I've been to Asbury Park, but so've a lot of people. Why should I remember you?"

"Sallie. It's Jack. I'm *Jack*."

"Jack? Jack Who? . . . No! My brother! You—you're Jack? Oh, darling, darling!" She stood up and looked at the people near her and said to them, rather helplessly, "This is my brother. My *brother*. I haven't seen him since—oh, darling. Oh, this is so wonderful." She put her arms around him and kissed him. "Oh, where have you *been*? Where have they been keeping you? Are you all right?"

"I'm all right. What about you?"

"Oh, let's go somewhere. We have so much to talk about." She smiled at all the other young men and women, then took her brother's arm and they went down the stairs and out, leaving all of us with the happy experience to think about and to tell and re-tell. The girl I was meeting arrived ten or fifteen minutes after Sallie and Jack Brown departed, and when we were in the taxi on our way to a cocktail party I related what I had seen. The girl waited until I finished the story and then said, "Was this Sallie Brown blond? About my height? And was her brother a blond too, with curly hair cut short?"

"Exactly," I said. "Do you know them?"

"Sure. The only part of the story that's true is that they are brother and sister. The rest is an act. Her name is Sallie Collins and his name is Johnny Collins. They're from Chicago. They're very good."

"Good? I'll say they're good. They fooled me and everybody else."

"They always do. People cry, and sometimes they clap as if they were at the theater. Sallie and Johnny Collins, from Chicago. Did you ever hear of the Spitbacks?"

"No. Spitbacks?"

"It's a sort of a club in Chicago. You have to be kicked out of school to be a Spitback, and Johnny's been kicked out of at least two."

"And what about her?"

"She's eligible. She was two years behind me at Farmington."

"What was she kicked out for?"

"Oh, I don't know. Smoking, I think. She wasn't there very long. Now she's going to school in Greenwich, I think. Johnny's a runner downtown."

"What other tricks do they do?"

"Whatever comes into their heads, but they're famous for the long-lost-brother-and-sister one. They have it down pat. Did she look at the other people as much as to say, 'I can't believe it, it's like a dream'?"

"Yes."

"They can't do it as much as they used to. All their friends know about it and they've told so many people. Of course it annoys some people."

"What other *kind* of thing do they do?"

"Oh—I don't know. Nothing mean. Not practical jokes, if that's what you're thinking of."

"I'd like to meet her sometime. And him. They seem like fun," I said.

I never did meet Johnny. He was drowned somewhere in

northern Michigan a year or so after I was a member of their
audience at the Biltmore, and when I finally met Sallie she was
married and living in New Canaan; about thirty years old,
still very pretty; but instinctively I refrained from immediately
recalling to her the once famous long-lost-brother stunt. I do
not mean to say that she seemed to be mourning Johnny after
ten years. But fun was not a word that came quickly to mind
when I was introduced to her. If I had never seen her before or
known about her stunts I would have said that *her* idea of
fun would be the winning of the Connecticut State Women's
Golf Championship. Women who like golf and play it well
do seem to move more deliberately than, for instance, women
who play good tennis, and my guess that golf was her game
was hardly brilliant, since I knew that her husband was a
4-handicap player.

"Where are you staying?" she said, at dinner.

"At the Randalls'."

"Oh, do you sail?"

"No, Tom and I grew up together in Pennsylvania."

"Well, you're going to have a lot of time to yourself this
weekend, aren't you? Tom and Rebecca will be at Rye, won't
they?"

"I don't mind," I said. "I brought along some work, and
Rebecca's the kind of hostess that leaves you to your own
devices."

"Work? What kind of work?"

"Textiles."

"Well, that must be a very profitable business these days,
isn't it? Isn't the Army ordering millions of uniforms?"

"I don't know."

"You're not in that kind of textiles?"

"Yes, I am. But I'm not allowed to answer any questions
about the Army."

"I would like to be a spy."

"You'd make a good one," I said.

"Do you think so? What makes you think I would?"

"Because the first time I ever saw you . . ." I then had been in her company for more than an hour, and felt better about recalling the incident at the Biltmore.

"How nice of you to remember that," she said, and smiled. "I wonder why you did?"

"Well, you were very pretty. Still are. But the whole performance was so expert. Professional. You could probably be a very good spy."

"No. That was all Johnny. All those things we used to do, Johnny thought them up. He was the brains of the team. I was the foil. Like the girl in tights that magicians always have. Anybody could have done it with Johnny master-minding . . . Would you like to come here for lunch Sunday? I happen to know that Rebecca's without a cook, so you're going to have to go to the club, otherwise. Unless of course you have another invitation."

I said I would love to come to lunch Sunday, and she thereupon engaged in conversation with the gentleman on her left. I was surprised to find on Sunday that she and I were lunching alone. We had cold soup, then were served crab flakes and some vegetables, and when the maid was gone Sallie took a piece of paper from the pocket of her blouse. "This is the clock at the Biltmore that day. This is where I was sitting. Here is where you were sitting. If I'm not mistaken, you were wearing a gray suit and you sat with your overcoat folded over your lap. You needed a haircut."

"By God, you're absolutely right."

"You had a watch on a chain, and you kept taking it out of your pocket, and putting it back."

"I don't remember that, but probably. The girl I was meeting was pretty late. Incidentally, went to Farmington with you. Laura Pratt."

"Oh, goodness. Laura. If she'd been on time you never would have seen the long-lost-brother-and-sister act. She hated me at Farmington, but I see her once in a while now. She lives in Litchfield, as I suppose you know. But have I convinced you that I remembered you as well as you remembered me?"

"It's the greatest compliment I ever had in my life."

"No. You were good-looking and still are, but what I chiefly remembered was that I was hoping you'd try to pick me up. Then I was just a little bit annoyed that you didn't try. God, that was forever ago, wasn't it?"

"Just about," I said. "How come you didn't say anything at dinner the other night?"

"I'm not sure. Selfish, I guess. That was *my* evening. I wanted you to do all the remembering, and I guess I wanted to hear you talk about Johnny."

"He drowned," I said. "In Michigan."

"Yes, but I didn't tell you that. How did you know?"

"I saw it in the paper at the time."

"Rebecca told me you were getting a divorce. Does that upset you? Not her telling me, but breaking up with your wife."

"It isn't the pleasantest experience in the world," I said.

"I suppose not. It never is. I was married before I married my present husband, you know."

"No, I didn't know."

"It lasted a year. He was Johnny's best friend, but other than that we had nothing in common. Not that a married couple have to have too much in common, but they ought to have something else besides loving the same person, in this case my brother. Hugh, my first husband, was what Johnny used to call one of his stooges, just like me. But somehow it isn't very attractive for a *man* to be another man's stooge. It's all right for a sister to be a stooge, but not another man, and almost the minute Johnny died I suddenly realized that without Johnny, Hugh was nothing. As a threesome we had a lot of fun together, really a lot of fun. And with Hugh I could have sex. I don't think there was any of that in my feeling for Johnny, although there may have been. If there was, I certainly managed to keep it under control and never even thought about it. I didn't know much about those things, but once or twice I vaguely suspected that if either of us had any of that feeling for Johnny, it was Hugh. But I'm sure he didn't know it either."

"So you divorced Hugh and married Tatnall."

"Divorced Hugh and married Bill Tatnall. All because you were afraid to pick me up and ditch Laura Pratt."

"But I could have become one of Johnny's stooges, too," I said. "I probably would have."

"No. Johnny's stooges all had to be people he'd known all his life, like me or Hugh, or Jim Danzig."

"Who is Jim Danzig?"

"Jim Danzig was the boy in the canoe with Johnny when it overturned. I don't like to talk about poor Jim. He blamed himself for the accident and he's become a hopeless alcoholic, at thirty-two, mind you."

"Why did he blame himself? Did he have any reason to?"

"Well—he was in the canoe, and they were both a little tight. It was at night and they'd been to a party at the Danzigs' cabin and decided to row across the lake to our cabin, instead of driving eight or nine miles. A mile across the lake, eight and a half miles by car. One of those crazy ideas you get when you're tight. Johnny would have been home in fifteen minutes by car, but they started out in the canoe, heading for the lights on our landing. I guess there was some kind of horseplay and the canoe overturned, and Jim couldn't find Johnny. He kept calling him but he didn't get any answer, and he couldn't right the canoe, although Jim was almost as good a boatman as Johnny—when sober. But they'd had an awful lot to drink, and it was pitch dark. No moon. And finally Jim floated and swam ashore and then for a while was lost in the woods. It was after Labor Day and most of the cabins were boarded up for the winter, and Jim in his bare feet, all cut and bleeding by the time he got to the Danzigs' cabin, and a little out of his head in addition to all he'd had to drink. I think they had to dynamite to recover Johnny's body. I wasn't there and I'm glad I wasn't. From the reports it must have been pretty horrible, and even now I'd rather not think about it."

"Then don't," I said.

"No, let's change the subject," she said.

"All right. Then you married Tatnall."

"Married Bill Tatnall a year and a half after Hugh and I were divorced. Two children. Betty, and Johnny, ages six and four. You haven't mentioned any children. Did you have any?"

"No."

"Children hold so many marriages together," she said.

"Yours?"

"Of course mine. I wouldn't have said that otherwise, would I? How often do you see the Randalls?"

"Oh, maybe once or twice a year."

"Did they know you were coming here for lunch?"

"No," I said. "They left very early this morning, before I was up."

"That explains it, why you don't know about Bill and me. Well, when you tell them you were here today, don't be surprised if they give you that tut-tut look. Naughty-naughty. Bill and I raise a lot of eyebrows hereabouts. Next year it'll be some other couple, but at the moment it's Bill and I."

"Who's the transgressor? You, or your husband?"

"It's the marriage, more so than Bill or I individually. In a community like this, or maybe any suburban or small-town community, they don't seem to mind adultery if they can blame one person or the other. The husband or the wife has to be the guilty party, but not both."

"I don't agree with you," I said. "I think that when a marriage is in trouble people take sides, one side or the other, and they mind a great deal."

"Yes, they want the marriage to break up and they want to be able to blame one or the other. But when the marriage doesn't break up, when people can't fix the blame on one person, they're deprived of their scandal. They feel cheated out of something, and they're outraged, horrified, that people like Bill and I go on living together. They really hate me for putting up with Bill's chasing, and they hate Bill for letting me get away with whatever I get away with. Bill and I ought to be in the divorce courts, fighting like cats and dogs. Custody fights, fights about alimony."

"But you and your husband have what is commonly called an arrangement?" I said.

"It would seem that way, although actually we haven't. At least not a spoken one. You see, we don't even care that much about each other. He just goes his way, and I go mine."

"You mean to say you never had a discussion about it? The first time he found out you were unfaithful to him, or he was unfaithful to you? You didn't have any discussion at all?"

"Why is that so incredible?" she said. "Let's have our coffee out on the porch."

I followed her out to the flagstone terrace and its iron-and-glass furniture. She poured the coffee and resumed speaking. "I guessed that Bill had another girl. It wasn't hard to guess. He left me severely alone. Then I guessed he had another, and since I hadn't made a fuss about the first one I certainly wasn't going to make a fuss about the second. Or the third."

"Then I gather you began to have gentlemen friends of your own."

"I did. And I guess Bill thought I'd been so nice about his peccadillos that he decided to be just as nice about mine."

"But without any discussion. You simply tacitly agreed not to live together as man and wife?"

"You're trying to make me say what you want me to say, that somehow we did have a discussion, a quarrel, a fight ending in an arrangement. Well, I won't say it."

"Then there's something a lot deeper that I guess I'd better not go into."

"I won't deny that, not for a minute."

"Was it sexual incompatibility?"

"You can call it that. But that isn't as deep as you seem to think it was. A lot of men and women, husbands and wives, are sexually incompatible. This was deeper, and worse. Worse because Bill is a yellow coward. He never dared come out and say what he was thinking."

"Which was?"

"He got angry with me one time and said that my brother Johnny'd been a sinister influence. That's as much as he'd actually say. That Johnny'd been a sinister influence. He didn't dare accuse me—and Johnny—of what he really meant. Why didn't he dare? Because he didn't want to admit that his wife had been guilty of incest. It wasn't really so much that incest was bad as that it had happened to his own wife. Someone,

one of Bill's lady friends, had planted that little idea in his thick skull, and he believed it. Now he fully believes it, but I don't care."

"A question that naturally comes to my mind," I said, "is why are you telling me all this?"

"Because you saw us together without knowing us. You saw Johnny and me doing the long-lost-brother act. How did we seem to you?"

"I thought you were genuine. I fell for it."

"But then Laura Pratt told you it was an act. What did you think then?"

"I thought you were charming. Fun."

"That's what I hoped you thought. That's what we thought we were, Johnny and I. We thought we were absolutely charming—and fun. Maybe we weren't charming, but we were fun. And that's all we were. And now people have ruined that for us. For me, at least. Johnny never knew people thought he had a sinister influence over me. Or me over him, for that matter. But aren't people darling? Aren't they lovely? They've managed to ruin all the fun Johnny and I had together all those years. Just think, I was married twice and had two children before I began to grow up. I didn't really start to grow up till my own husband made me realize what people had been thinking, and saying, about Johnny and me. If that's growing up, you can have it."

"Not everybody thought that about you and Johnny."

"It's enough that anybody did. And it's foolish to think that only one or two thought it," she said. "We did so many things for fun, Johnny and I. Harmless jokes that hurt nobody and that we thought were uproariously funny. Some of them I don't ever think of any more because of the interpretation people put on them . . . We had one that was the opposite of the long-lost-brother. The newlyweds. Did you ever hear of our newly-weds?"

"No," I said.

"It came about by accident. We were driving East and had to spend the night in some little town in Pennsylvania. The car broke down and we went to the local hotel and when we went to register the clerk just took it for granted that we were husband and wife. Johnny caught on right away and he whispered to the clerk, loud enough for me to hear, that we were newlyweds but that I was shy and wanted separate rooms. So we got our separate rooms, and you should have seen the hotel people stare at us that night in the dining room and the next morning at breakfast. We laughed for a whole day about that and then we used to do the same trick every time we had to drive anywhere overnight. Didn't hurt anybody."

"What else did you do?"

"Oh, lots of things. And not only tricks. We both adored Fred and Adele Astaire, and we copied their dancing. Not as good, of course, but everybody always guessed who we were imitating. We won a couple of prizes at parties. Johnny was really quite good. 'I lahv, yourfah, neeface. Your fah, neefah, neeface.'" She suddenly began to cry and I sat still.

That was twenty years ago. I don't believe that anything that happened to her since then made much difference to Sallie, but even if it did, that's the way I remember her and always will.

(1962)

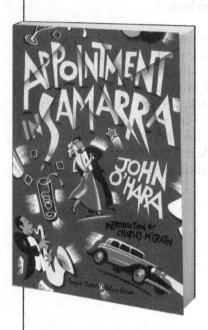

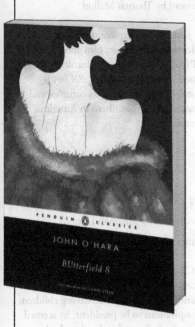

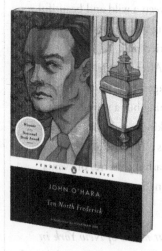